THE YEAR'S BEST
DARK FANTASY & HORROR
VOLUME TWO

THE YEAR'S BEST
DARK FANTASY & HORROR:
VOLUME TWO

EDITED BY
PAULA GURAN

Other Anthologies Edited by Paula Guran

Published 2021 by Pyr®

Cover image © Shutterstock
Cover design by Jennifer Do
Cover design © Start Science Fiction

Inquiries should be addressed to

Start Science Fiction
221 River Street, 9th Floor
Hoboken, New Jersey 07030
PHONE: 212-431-5455
WWW.PYRSF.COM

10 9 8 7 6 5 4 3 2 1

ISBN 978-1-64506-032-1 (paperback)
ISBN 978-1-64506-033-8 (ebook)

Printed in the United States of America

To Elora:
May you never know true darkness.

CONTENTS

INTRODUCTION:
STRANGER DAYS

PAULA GURAN

> *Horror is everywhere. It's in fairy tales and the evening headlines, it's in street corner gossip, and the incontrovertible facts of history. It's in playground ditties* (Ring-a-ring o' roses *is a sweet little plague song) . . . it's on the altar bleeding for our sins . . .*
>
> —CLIVE BARKER, *A-Z OF HORROR*

It has been, as I write this, almost exactly one year since the World Health Organization declared a global pandemic and the United States entered a lockdown. It has also been almost exactly one year since I began the introduction ("Strange Days") to the previous volume of this series with this:

> *These are unsettling times. The world changed forever as I compiled this anthology, and we don't yet know what it has changed into. . . . Why, some must be asking, would anyone want to read dark fantasy or horror while a pandemic rages, the economy (and who knows what else) topples, and people are dying and suffering?*

INTRODUCTION

Did I answer the question? If you weren't perspicacious enough to read last year's anthology (*tsk!*) you can still buy the book and find out. Or read that introduction on my website (paulaguran.com).

I'm not the only one to have had similar thoughts. A recent study's title—"Pandemic Practice: Horror Fans and Morbidly Curious Individuals Are More Psychologically Resilient During the COVID-19 Pandemic"—sums up its results and answer to the question. The researchers found that "horror fiction may not lead you to find ways to enjoy life during a pandemic, it might help you learn how to deal with the fear and anxiety that stems from something like a pandemic."[*]

This may be true, and it ties into the traditional view of horror: we enjoy it because it gives us a type of closure—the bad stuff, the monsters, the evil is destroyed or at least controlled. Order or some semblance of it is restored.

Restoring order, however, is not always the aim of modern dark fiction. As Gina Wisker writes in her 2004 essay, "Demisting the Mirror: contemporary British women's horror," "Horror explores the fissures that open in our everyday lives and destabilizes our complacency about norms and rules . . ." It also has a "politicized role as exposer of social and cultural deceits and discomforts . . ."

Horror can comfort and give us a feeling of control but is also challenges and discomforts, even in these challenging and uncomfortable times.

Horror, I'm sure someone has noted, is nothing if not paradoxical.

Before we go too much further, it's probably best to mention (as I do almost annually) that I'm not offering a definition of dark fantasy. Or horror for that matter. You can read last year's introduction on that point or, more directly, the very first introduction to this series from *The Year's Best Horror and Dark Fantasy: 2010*—"What The Hell Do You Mean By 'Dark Fantasy And Horror?'"—also republished on the aforementioned website.

---

[*] Scrivner, C., Johnson, J. A., Kjeldgaard-Christiansen, J., & Clasen, M. (2021). Pandemic practice: Horror fans and morbidly curious individuals are more psychologically resilient during the COVID-19 pandemic. Personality and individual differences, 168, 110397. https://doi.org/10.1016/j.paid.2020.110397

And, of course, a reminder that although this is *Volume Two*, it is really *Volume Twelve* as the series started in 2010 (covering stories first published in 2009). The title change is due to a publisher change (from Prime Books to Pyr Books).

Back to less practical matters . . .

During the last year, the horrific daily intruded on the mundane. But that's the thing about horror—and dark fantasy, weird fiction, or what have you—it is rooted not only in the fantastic of nightmares and the imagination but in everyday real life.

But, given the circumstances, has my/our perception of what horror changed in the last year?

I don't have an answer, of course. Maybe after time has passed there will eventually be one. But in the very short-term retrospective—after reading hundreds of stories, selecting thirty, and offering another two hundred as "recommended," I have some random observations.

- It wasn't until after I started assembling this volume that I realized how often homes, houses, and other domiciles played important roles in many of the selected stories. None of them are traditional "haunted house" tales, but the concept of "home" popped up more often than I had initially realized. Considering most of us have been home more than usual lately, this is . . . interesting.

- I often choose stories set in the future and I did so again this year—about half a dozen times. But in some cases, the futures involved seem so close, so logical, that I'm not sure they can really be considered science fiction. In a few cases, there is more of the supernatural involved in the future than science.

- Along those lines, although the stories are not all science fictional, three stories involve the human genetic code and three climate change. Again, because the stories are all wildly different, I didn't realize this until final compilation.

- My purview for these volumes is expansive. I've never concentrated on "horror" per se, never really sought stories guaranteed to scare and certainly not those that merely shock. My schtick tends toward tales that disturb, unsettle, disrupt, discomfort, intrude, etc. That's not changed, but I wonder if there was an overall trend this last year toward, well, just "dark" as opposed to "horror." Or maybe it is just that there is a wider range of publications now featuring "dark" but not necessarily "horror" fiction.

- Along those lines, if you look at the sources of selected and recommended works—which you should and then seek them out—you'll find a wide variety of publications. Many of them are not places one would expect to find horror or dark fantasy, yet there it is. Is darkness creeping deeper into literature or do I just find it because I am looking?

- In the last few years, genre fiction has (finally) become more diverse and more publishing opportunities have become available for writers who are not white, do not have an exclusively Western perspective, are not heterosexual, and who are not cisgender male. Consequently, the cultural milieu and characters portrayed have broadened. This positive trend has continued in the last year and, as always, is reflected in my selections. Have I chosen more of it? I don't know, but I feel I have a great deal more to choose from.

- I didn't realize until after biographies were assembled that about twenty of the thirty stories included are by writers who identify as women. I don't think this the first time the contents have had a female majority, but I think that is the largest margin.

- An aspect of both the preceding point and what Wisker refers to as "politicized," are the couple of blatantly feminist stories and several others with more subtle messages of that type. Again, nothing new for me or this series, but maybe (or maybe not) notable.

- Far too early for this one, but I warned you this was random. Dystopic and other science fiction often supposes governmental upheaval—although I don't think anyone ever imagined a president of the United States denying he was defeated in a free, fair, and secure election and then urging a mob to attack Congress—but after the January 6, 2021 assault on the Capitol by Trump-supporting insurrectionists, one can't but wonder if this will play into dark fiction now.

- Stories directly inspired by the pandemic did not, of course, start being published until later in 2020. That said, we (suitably) start volume two with a COVID-19-based tale by Victor LaValle who was commissioned (along with twenty-eight others) by the *New York Times* to "write new short stories inspired by the moment." They were "inspired by Giovanni Boccaccio's 'The Decameron,' written as the plague ravaged Florence" in the fourteenth century.

And that's probably an excellent note on which to end the introducing and start with the reading.

Paula Guran
National Respect Your Cat Day 2021

RECOGNITION

VICTOR LAVALLE

Not easy to find a good apartment in New York City, so imagine finding a good building. No, this isn't a story about me buying a building. I'm talking about the people, of course. I found a good apartment, and a great building, in Washington Heights. Six-story tenement on the corner of 180th and Fort Washington Avenue; a one-bedroom apartment, which was plenty for me. Moved in December 2019. You might already see where this is going. The virus hit, and within four months half the building had emptied out. Some of my neighbors fled to second homes or to stay with their parents outside the city; others, the older ones, the poorer ones, disappeared into the hospital twelve blocks away. I'd moved into a crowded building and suddenly I lived in an empty house.

And then I met Mirta.

"Do you believe in past lives?"

We were in the lobby, waiting for the elevator. This was right after the lockdown started. She asked, but I didn't say anything. Which isn't the same as saying I didn't respond. I gave my tight little smile while looking down at my feet. I'm not rude, just fantastically shy. That condition doesn't go away, not even during a pandemic. I'm a Black woman, and people act surprised when they discover some of us can be awkward, too.

"There's no one else here," Mirta continued. "So I must be talking to you."

Her tone managed to be both direct and, somehow, still playful. As the elevator arrived, I looked toward her, and that's when I saw her shoes. Black-and-white pointed oxfords; the white portion had been painted to look like piano keys. Despite the lockdown, Mirta had taken the trouble to slip on a pair of shoes that nice. I was returning from the supermarket wearing my raggedy old slides.

I pulled the elevator door open and finally looked at her face.

"There she is," Mirta said, the way you might compliment a shy bird for settling on your finger.

Mirta might've been twenty years older than me. I turned forty the same month I moved into the building. My mom and dad called to sing "Happy Birthday" from Pittsburgh. Despite the news, they didn't ask me to come home. And I didn't make the request. When we're together, they ask questions about my life, my plans, that turn me into a grouchy teenager again. My father ordered me a bunch of basics though; he had them shipped. It's how he has always loved me—by making sure I'm well supplied.

"I tried to get toilet paper," Mirta said in the elevator. "But these people are panicking, so I couldn't find any. They think a clean butt is going to save them from the virus?"

Mirta watched me; the elevator reached the fourth floor. She stepped out and held the door open.

"You don't laugh at my jokes, and you won't even tell me your name?"

Now I smiled because it had turned into a game.

"A challenge then," she said. "I will see you again." She pointed down the hall. "I am in Number 41."

She let the elevator door go, and I rode up to the sixth floor, unpacked the things I'd bought. At that time I still thought it would all be over by April. It's laughable now. I went into the bathroom. One of the things my dad sent me was thirty-two rolls of toilet paper. I slipped back down to the fourth floor and left three rolls in front of Mirta's door.

* * *

A month later, I was used to logging in to my "remote office," the grid of screens—all our little heads—looked like the open office we once worked in; I probably spoke with my co-workers about as much now as I did then. When the doorbell rang, I leapt at the chance to get away from my laptop. *Maybe it's Mirta.* I slipped on a pair of buckled loafers; they were raggedy, too, but better than the slippers I wore the last time she saw me.

But it wasn't her.

It was the super, Andrés. Nearly sixty, born in Puerto Rico, he had a tattoo of a leopard crawling up his neck.

"Still here," he said, sounding pleasant behind his blue mask.

"Nowhere else to go."

He nodded and snorted, a mix between a laugh and a cough. "The city says I got to check every apartment now. Every day."

He carried a bag that rattled like a sack of metal snakes. When I looked, he pulled it open: silver spray-paint cans. "I don't get a answer, and I got to use this."

Andrés stepped to the side. Down the hall; Apartment 66. The green door had been defaced with a giant silver "V." So fresh, the letter still dripped.

"'V.' For 'virus'?"

Andrés's eyebrows rose and fell.

"Vacant," he said.

"That's a nicer way to put it, I guess." We stood quietly, him in the hall and me in the apartment. I realized I hadn't put on my mask when I answered, and I covered my mouth when I spoke.

"The city is making you do this?" I asked.

"In some neighborhoods," Andrés said. "Bronx, Queens, Harlem. And us. Hot spots." He took out one of the cans and shook it. The ball bearing clicked and clacked inside. "I'll knock tomorrow," he said. "If you don't answer, I got the keys."

I watched him go.

"How many people are left?" I called out. "In the building?"

He'd already reached the stairs, started down. If he answered, I didn't hear it. I walked onto the landing. There were six apartments on my floor. Five doors had been decorated with the letter "V." No one here but me.

You'd think I would run right down to Mirta's place, but I couldn't afford to lose my job. The landlord hadn't said a word about rent forgiveness. I went back to the computer until end of day. I felt such relief when Number 41 hadn't been painted. I knocked until Mirta opened. She wore her mask, just like me now, but I could tell she was smiling. She looked from my face to my feet.

"Those shoes have seen better days," she said, and laughed so joyfully that I hardly even felt embarrassed.

Mirta and I made trips to the supermarket together; two trips to the store each week. We walked side by side, arm's length apart, and when we crossed paths with others, we marched single file. Mirta talked the whole time, whether I was next to her or behind her. I know some people criticize chatty folks, but her chatter fell upon me like a nourishing rain.

She came to New York from Cuba, with a short stay in Key West, Florida., in between. She'd lived in Manhattan, from the bottom to the top, over the span of forty years. She played piano and idolized Peruchín; had performed with Chucho Valdés. And now she gave lessons to children in her apartment for $35 an hour. Or at least she had done that, until the virus made it unsafe to have them over. I miss them, she said, every time we talked, as four weeks became six, and six became twelve. She wondered if she'd ever see her students and their parents again.

I offered to help set up remote piano lessons. I'd use my job's account to set up free chat sessions for her. But this was three months in and Mirta had lost her playful ways. She said: "The screens give the illusion that we're all still connected. But it's not true. The ones who could leave, left. The rest of us? We were abandoned."

She stepped off the elevator.

"Why pretend?"

She scared me. I can see that now. But I told myself I'd become busier. As if I'd transformed.

But I fled from her. We were all living on the ledge of despair, so when she said it—"We were abandoned. Why pretend?"—it was as if she spoke from down in that pit. A place I found myself slipping into often enough already. So I went to the store by myself, and I held my breath when the elevator passed the fourth floor.

Meanwhile, Andrés continued to work. I didn't see him. He knocked on the door each morning, and I knocked from the other side. But I saw evidence of his work. Three apartments on the first floor marked with a "V" one week. Next time I went to the store the other three were painted.

Four on the second floor.

Five on the third.

One afternoon I heard him kicking at a door on the fourth floor. Shouting a name I hardly recognized through the muzzle that was his mask. I left my place and walked down. Andrés looked shrunken at the door of Number 41. He kicked at it desperately.

"Mirta!" he shouted again.

He turned with surprise when I appeared. His eyes were red. The fingers of his right hand were entirely silver now; it looked permanent. I wondered if he'd ever be able to wash off the spray paint. But how could he, if the job was never done?

"I left my keys," he said. "I gotta get them."

"I'll stay," I said.

He sprinted down the stairs. I stood by the door, didn't bother knocking. If that kicking didn't wake her, what could I do?

"Is he gone?"

I almost collapsed.

"Mirta! Were you messing with him?"

"No," she said through the door. "But I wasn't waiting on him. I was waiting around for you."

I sat so my head was at about the same level as her voice. I heard her labored breathing through the door. "It's been a while," she finally said.

I rested the side of my head against the cool door. "I'm sorry."

She sniffed. "Even women like us are scared of women like us."

I lowered my mask, as if it were getting in the way of what I truly needed to say. But I still couldn't find the words.

"Do you believe in past lives?" she said.

"That's the first thing you ever asked me."

"When I saw you by the elevator, I knew we met before. Recognition. Like seeing a member of my family."

The elevator arrived. Andrés stepped out. I raised my mask and got to my feet. He unlocked the door.

"Be careful," I said. "She's right there."

But when he pushed the door open, the hall sat empty.

Andrés found her in bed. Dead. He came out carrying a bag, my name written on it. Her black-and-white oxfords were inside. A note in the left shoe. *Give them back when you see me again.*

I have to slip on an extra pair of socks to make them fit, but I wear them everywhere I go.

ODETTE

ZEN CHO

Odette's time for hope was short.

Early that morning, the first morning of the rest of her life, she'd gone out of her house to the end of the garden. The air was as pure as the breath that first animated the clay of Adam's flesh. She looked out over the island and saw no limitations.

But then she saw him—Uncle Andrew, in his polo shirt and khaki shorts, coming out for his daily morning walk. He pretended not to see her as he opened the gate and passed her by, but he knew she was there.

Odette realized her life had not changed after all. She would have to live with Uncle Andrew for the rest of her life.

He had only died the day before.

Uncle Andrew had insisted on being discharged from hospital.

"If it is my time, I will die with dignity," he said. He spoke slowly, pausing between words to struggle for breath. "A Christian shouldn't be scared of death."

It wasn't Odette's place to disagree. Uncle Andrew's friends from church stepped in for her.

"Andrew, God helps those who help themselves," said Auntie

Gladys. "You are still so young. Don't you think it's too soon? Let the doctors treat you."

"God can wait for a while," said Auntie Poh Eng. "He knows how much we all need you!"

All this was no less than what Uncle Andrew expected, but he was inflexible. "The doctors have had their chance. They poke me here, there, everywhere also, they still don't know how to cure me. God is calling me back to Him. I'm not so foolish as to put my faith in humans over God."

Auntie Poh Eng took Uncle Andrew's hand. Her eyes were full of tears.

"God has been good to let us have you for so long," she said.

Auntie Poh Eng was Odette's favorite of their church friends. Her only flaw was an unfailing affection for Uncle Andrew. But this was a flaw shared by all Uncle Andrew's friends. It was not Odette's place to complain.

Her place was by Uncle Andrew's side, except when she was in the laundry room, or the kitchen, or in the dining room polishing the heirloom silver. Just because Uncle Andrew was about to die didn't mean he was about to let standards slip. They had a cleaner who came in every day to go over the house, but the clothes Uncle Andrew wore and the food he ate had to come fresh from Odette's hands. As for the various antiques and other treasures Uncle Andrew had accumulated over the years, they could not of course be entrusted to a cleaner who only earned RM600 a month.

Uncle Andrew had collected enough that looking to the upkeep of his possessions, cooking for him, keeping him in clean clothes and nursing him was too much for one person. Odette suggested that perhaps the cleaner could cook and do the laundry:

"Then I can put hundred per cent into looking after you and the house, Uncle."

"You should already be putting in hundred percent," said Uncle Andrew. "Who is paying for you to live? Not like you have so much to do. When Beatrice was alive she did all this and more. She didn't even have a degree, not like you. She never complained. You young people are spoilt. Given too much."

"Auntie Letchumi is a better cook than me. Maybe you'll feel like eating more, Uncle. It'll be good for your health."

"Instead of learning to cook better, you want to pay someone else to do it," said Uncle Andrew. "You're useless! If not for my money I don't know what you'd do—end up lying in the street like a tramp. I don't eat all this Indian food."

"If you don't want her to cook for you, what if we ask her to do the laundry? It will give me more time."

"What else are you doing with your life? Do you have a job? Do you have a husband? All you have to do is take care of your uncle who has done so much for you. Even that you don't want to do. I sacrifice for you and still you are so selfish."

Odette was of the unfortunate mold which does not grow less sensitive with time and use. She fell silent. Crying irritated Uncle Andrew to a fury. He took it as an unjustifiable assertion of self.

"After I die your life will be very easy," said Uncle Andrew. "My time left here is short. But you can't even wait until God takes me." He coughed.

"I'm sorry, Uncle," said Odette.

"There's no use saying sorry," said Uncle Andrew. "You shouldn't be so selfish in the first place. If your hand causes you to sin, cut it off."

He banged the bedside table, but though Odette jumped she wasn't really scared. Five years ago the force of the blow would have rocked the table back and forth on its legs. Now Uncle Andrew was so weak it barely rattled the glass of water Odette had brought him. She watched the surface of the water tremble and go still and hid a smile.

Uncle Andrew only spoke this way when they were alone. His friends did not see this side of him.

The friends watched Odette bring in meals, give Uncle Andrew his medicine, serve him hot drinks, fluff his pillow. They didn't see her change his bedsheets every day, bathe and dress him, do the laundry, eat only in the brief intervals granted her between chores—standing at the kitchen counter, stuffing the food into her mouth, dry-eyed.

Auntie Poh Eng told her:

"You are taking Jesus' life as your model. Life is hard now, but God will reward you in the end."

Odette only shook her head. "I don't need His reward, Auntie."

After all, Uncle Andrew had always been so kind to her. He was known for his kindness. A pillar of the church, counsellor to his friends, benign dispenser of advice to their children.

It was all the more impressive in one who had done so well for himself. Look at that beautiful house he lives in, said his friends, in the foothills overlooking the sea. The only tragedy in Uncle Andrew's life was that he had no children of his own. But then, he had Odette.

To Odette his kindness had been wearyingly comprehensive. It had covered sending her to university and insisting that she stay in his home for the duration of her course. He never asked for rent—she wouldn't have been able to pay it. In return for accommodation she did the household chores.

She hadn't minded staying at home for university. It had meant living with Uncle Andrew, but she was used to that. The house was almost enough to make up for it.

It was the mansion of a nineteenth-century Peranakan merchant. Uncle Andrew liked to give out, and seemed to half-believe, that it had been in the family for generations, but he had bought it when he was in his forties from the businessman's great-grandson.

"Fella said he's an artist." Uncle Andrew snorted. "Cannot even hold onto the house his father gave him."

Whatever he had been, the great-grandson had had an eye for beauty. Upon Uncle Andrew's arrival the house was exquisitely preserved. No incongruity had been permitted in it, no disruption to its elegant lines.

Uncle Andrew had improved the plumbing and installed air conditioners in every room. He filled the house with big ugly imitations of Western masterpieces, ludicrous photos of himself and Auntie Beatrice, and imposing jade sculptures he bought on trips to China ("I haggled them down to RM500 from RM3,000. These Chinamen will skin you if you don't watch out"). He replaced the Victorian tile flooring with marble and brought in white leather sofas and glass coffee tables.

But the bones of the house shone through these embellishments.

Odette loved the graceful, shuttered windows, the intricate latticed vents, the pillars topped with carvings of cranes and fruit. The very gutters were wonderful because they fit so well with the building: they had that perfection that comes from being impeccably appropriate. The beauty and intricacy of the house was such that it could sustain even the incongruity of Uncle Andrew's additions and turn them into something marvelous.

The house was the only thing Odette loved. It was worth staying for.

She'd made the mistake of trying to leave once. Right after she graduated from university Auntie Beatrice died. It was sudden—cardiac arrest, the doctors said.

Odette understood that her aunt had finally given up.

She had not known Auntie Beatrice well, though they had lived under the same roof for many years. Auntie Beatrice had compacted herself so efficiently she seemed to take up no space in the world. Two days after her death Odette found herself struggling to remember what her aunt's face looked like.

Odette had started applying for jobs with a sense of foreboding.

When she was offered a teaching job, she was nonplussed. She had not really expected to get a job. But here it was, her ticket to another life. She would be teaching at a tuition center in Singapore—would be able to pay rent, feed herself, and live without reference to Uncle Andrew.

But there was the house. If Odette took the job, she would have to leave it. She would not see it again. Uncle Andrew had made it clear when she started university that she was not getting a degree so that she could enter the workforce.

"God has been generous," he said. "As long as I live, nobody else in the family will need to work."

Odette struggled with her decision for days. A week after she'd received the offer, she woke up suddenly in the middle of the night.

Uncle Andrew's bedroom was air-conditioned, but Odette wasn't allowed to turn on the air conditioner in hers—the expense of it. The windows were open and outside the cicadas were shrieking insistently. The mosquito coil burning under her bed scented the air. Moonlight shone through the air vents high in the walls. Seeing the inky tracery of the shadows cast on the floor, Odette felt a shock of love.

In Singapore it would be an ugly little flat she lived in—bare of flourishes, with grilles on the windows and white fluorescent lighting. She would sit on a cheap sofa from IKEA and watch TV. She would have surrendered the glories of carved ivory and old rosewood armoires in favor of that cold idol, freedom.

Odette went back to sleep with her mind made up.

The next morning Uncle Andrew was waiting for Odette when she came back from the wet market with the groceries. A letter was on the table in front of him.

"All the money I spent on you, and you go and do this?" said Uncle Andrew. "I treat you like my own daughter. Fed you since you were small. Paid for you to go to uni. Someone like you, you think you would have this kind of lifestyle if I didn't pay for you?"

Odette's voice came out strangely calm. "I thought if I get a job, I can be less of a burden on you, Uncle."

"So clever to make excuses now, hah?" said Uncle Andrew. His face had gone dark red. He slammed the table. The letter fluttered. "Don't try to lie to me. You want to run off! Sick of listening to your uncle, is it?"

A prickling sensation spread up Odette's nose and behind her eyes. "I'm sorry I didn't tell you. I forgot."

"You think I'm stupid?" roared Uncle Andrew. "Useless! Idiot! If you're so rushed to get out of this house, get out! Go pack your things and get out! If you don't even know how to be grateful, why should I spend any more money on you? Go lah! Go!"

Odette was sobbing. "Uncle, I just wanted to contribute. I'm ashamed to keep taking your money. I'm an adult already."

"You think I'm the kind of person who won't support their own niece?" said Uncle Andrew. "My friends will be very surprised to hear that. You ask the church people, my staff. Everybody will say Andrew Teoh isn't afraid to spend money on his family. You know better than all these people, is it?"

Odette shook her head. "I was going to reject the offer, Uncle."

"Nice story," said Uncle Andrew. "What for you go and apply then?"

The house gave her the right thing to say.

"I wanted to try," said Odette. "But when they offered, I knew I couldn't accept. I don't want to leave this house."

Uncle Andrew stared at her. The color in his face faded to pink.

"Hmph," he said. He crumpled the letter and threw it at her. It hit Odette on the shoulder and fell to the floor.

"I don't want to see that again," said Uncle Andrew. "Go put the food in the fridge."

After this, a merciful blankness descended on Odette. She felt nothing and could even laugh at a couple of Uncle Andrew's jokes at dinner.

The next morning at church, Uncle Andrew sent Odette to the car a couple of times—first for a packet of tissues, then for a copy of a magazine he'd promised Auntie Gladys. When Odette came back with the Reader's Digest, Auntie Gladys said:

"So guai your niece, Andrew. If my daughter was so helpful I'll be very happy."

"Beatrice and I did our best to bring her up," Uncle Andrew said. "But what's the most we can do, a childless couple like us?"

"You've done better than so many parents. Odette is lucky to have you all to look after her."

Uncle Andrew inclined his head. "As long as I'm alive, she'll always have a home."

They turned their eyes on Odette—Auntie Gladys's face distant and tender with thoughts of her daughter in America, Uncle Andrew looking just past Odette's ear. She smiled as expected.

When she got home she shut the door to her room and crawled into bed. Her body was sour with hatred. Her eyes burnt with tears.

The house absorbed them—weathered her storm—until she lay boneless on her bed and saw love shine through the vents, as it had done the night she decided to stay.

Odette had been young when her parents died. She didn't miss them as people—more as symbols of a warmth locked in the past, rendered forever inaccessible by their deaths.

Her mother's family were numerous but lived in Indonesia. Though only a cousin of her father, Uncle Andrew staked his claim before any of her other relatives arrived on the scene. God had been good to them, he said, and he and Beatrice had never intended to waste their good fortune on themselves. Beatrice would enjoy having someone to fuss over. She regretted the fact that they had no children. Uncle Andrew made out that his wife had been the prime mover behind their offer to adopt Odette.

Even then Odette had found this hard to believe. Auntie Beatrice was the quietest woman she had ever met. She never looked up. She spoke in a whisper. It was hard to imagine her daring to want anything.

Uncle Andrew, on the other hand, impressed Odette with unfavorable force. She was still at an age where she only understood snatches of what grown-ups said to her. She watched his face instead of listening to his words, and what she saw worried her.

Two weeks after her parents' death, she was dozing in the back seat of his car as it wound up the hill towards his home.

She always remembered her first sight of the house. Auntie Beatrice had bored her and Uncle Andrew frightened her, but she knew the house to be a friend the moment she laid eyes on it.

How blue it had looked against the green velvet backdrop of the forest—the intense blue of the sea in paintings of summer days. The red tiles on its roof reflected the last of the setting sun; the lanterns hung under the eaves cast a golden glow over the deepening twilight. As she passed through its double doors her skin prickled with the shivery, delightful excitement of being on holiday.

She was given a teak bed with white linen sheets and a headboard carved with peacocks. She slept soundly for the first time since her parents had died.

The house had been made to be loved, but what lived in it was not a real family.

Odette was the only person who knew what the house wanted. Uncle Andrew brooded over his possessions, indulged in tantrums, and tended his public persona as though it was a bonsai. Auntie Beatrice floated through the rooms, never denting a cushion or ruffling a rug.

But Odette divined the house's secrets. Nooks under staircases and crannies between sofas and walls, the perfect size for an eight-year-old to daydream in. Columns of light that moved around the house, picking whatever room suited their fancy. Wistful silences lying in wait in the concrete-floored courtyard, open to the sky.

She watched birds build their nests in the eaves and spiders construct webs in forgotten corners. She knew the moods of the house as well as she knew Uncle Andrew's.

This made her life easier, as Uncle Andrew's moods made her life harder. The house comforted her when Uncle Andrew tore up her homework, upbraided her for her stupidity and ugliness, told her she should have died when her parents did, that he never should have taken her in.

It was not so bad living with Uncle Andrew. Other children got beaten. Other children had nothing to eat. Uncle Andrew usually aimed to miss. He gave her food and clothing and even gifts at birthdays and Christmases. She didn't know how to articulate what was wrong until she heard a stranger's offhand remark.

"I always forget how beautiful your house is, Andrew," said one of his friends. "It's made for peace."

Odette looked past the friend at Uncle Andrew's smiling face. Uncle Andrew did not know or want peace, in a house made for peace. He desecrated it by living there. She had not hated him before that moment.

She didn't cry when Uncle Andrew told her she would have to find somewhere else to live.

"I looked after you long enough already," he said. "People your age are married, have their own house, children! I've done my part. If by now you haven't found a husband, you can only blame yourself."

Uncle Andrew was moving to Singapore.

"I have a lot of friends there, and I know the pastor of my new church," he told Auntie Poh Eng and the rest. "As a Christian in Malaysia, you never know . . . In Singapore the lifestyle is more convenient. An old man like me, I cannot be driving myself around forever. This Odette never learnt, she's too scared to go on the roads. In Singapore at least you can rely on public transport, not like here."

Odette had not been allowed to learn to drive. She was thirty-one and she had never had a job.

"Odette will like it," said Auntie Poh Eng, smiling at her. "Singapore is nice for young people. More fun, yes?"

"Ah, Odette won't be coming with me," said Uncle Andrew. "So boring for her to live with an old man. She's going to find her own place. These young people want to be independent. You give them your sweat and blood and at the end of the day, they go off and do what they want."

"That's the way of life," said Auntie Gladys. "But what are you going to do with the house, Andrew? Are you keeping it? It's been in your family for so long."

Uncle Andrew shook his head. "Selling. My grandfather would be upset, but things have changed since his day. A big old house, you must spend so much for upkeep. I'm not earning anymore. I don't want to worry about it in my old age. There's a developer who's very interested. Not many heritage buildings around that are so well-preserved. He wants to turn it into a hotel. The Mat Salleh like all this kind of thing."

Most of the friends nodded, but Auntie Poh Eng looked at Uncle Andrew as if for the first time her belief in him had wavered.

"You're selling to a developer?" she said. "To make it into a hotel?" But she remembered herself almost at once. "Of course most people cannot afford such a beautiful house. Maybe it's nice for them to have the chance to stay here also, even if it's for one or two nights only."

"I haven't answered the developer yet. I'm hoping to find someone who wants to live here," said Uncle Andrew smoothly. "It's very sad to have a home turned into something commercialized. Next best thing would be if the government buys it. Make it into a museum for everybody to visit."

Auntie Poh Eng beamed, her belief in Uncle Andrew restored.

"That would be perfect," she said.

It wasn't Odette's idea. She was standing in the kitchen wiping her hands when she saw a strand of hair on the countertop.

Hair in his food was the greatest sin anyone could commit against Uncle Andrew. Odette picked up the strand of hair and put it in the bin.

The idea was given to her.

Odette already knew Uncle Andrew's birth date. It was easy to find out the time. He kept his birth certificate in the second drawer of the desk in his study, along with his passport and IC.

It was easy, too, to get strands of his hair. She peeled them off his pillows and dug them out of the drain in the shower. She was unflinching in her preparations. She gathered fingernail clippings and even saved a scab he'd picked at absently and discarded on one of the ugly coffee tables.

She'd never done magic before, but she knew how it was done. You went into all that was too close, too sticky, the things human beings didn't share with one another—that was what the hair and fingernails were for. You did it with strong love or strong hatred.

She poured malice into Uncle Andrew, a patient poison that impregnated the food he ate and released fumes into the air he breathed. And it worked. He sickened. His breath grew short and he could no longer enjoy his meals. He became thin and weak and his body was racked with pain.

The doctors said it was cancer, but Odette knew what was killing him. Sometimes she was even a little afraid of the house.

The manner in which Uncle Andrew chose to depart this life was appropriately Victorian. It was a still hot afternoon and Odette was refilling his glass of water when he opened his eyes and said:

"Jesus is calling me."

Odette paused with the glass in her hand, unsure of how to respond.

"Do you want a drink, Uncle?" she ventured.

"Sit down, girl," snapped Uncle Andrew. "People are dying, and you still want to do housework. Remember, Mary, not Martha, was praised by the Lord."

Odette sat down. Uncle Andrew was still speaking, more to himself than to her.

"I'm still young. If not for this cancer, I could have been useful to my fellow men for many years. But His will be done. In Heaven," he added contemplatively, "I will see Beatrice again."

It wasn't clear whether the prospect gave him any pleasure.

Odette felt called upon to fill the gap left by the absence of his friends.

"Don't talk like that, Uncle," she said. "There's still hope. The doctor said—"

17

"Doctors! What do doctors know?" said Uncle Andrew. "Of course there's still hope. What is better than the hope of the Kingdom of Heaven? I have nothing to reproach myself with."

His wandering eyes settled on her with some of their former keenness.

"Nothing," he repeated. "Will you be able to give the account of yourself to Him that I will be able to give? Look into your conscience. Ask yourself."

Odette stayed silent, but she could not help a quick intake of breath then. She was so close.

"Hah," said Uncle Andrew triumphantly. "You see! Look to yourself! Look to yourself before it's too late!"

He didn't die then—only later, after his shouting had sent him into a coughing fit and Odette had given him water and been snarled at for spilling some on him. Finding fault with her put him in such a good mood that he went to sleep with little trouble after that. The next morning Odette found him cold in his bed.

When Uncle Andrew had realized he was dying he'd willed the house to the church. Odette would get a legacy—an annuity of RM8,000 a year.

"More than a lot of people earn by their own hard work," said Uncle Andrew. "You are lucky."

Odette agreed with Uncle Andrew that this was generous. She resented him no more for this than for anything else, though the bulk of his wealth would go to a successful nephew in Canada who hadn't visited in years.

"Jit Beng has children," said Uncle Andrew.

Jit Beng had an Ivy League degree and a big job in a multinational company. Uncle Andrew yearned over Jit Beng with a stifled affection he had never shown his wife or Odette.

Odette didn't care about the money. It was the house she wanted, and it was easy enough to alter the will. She was the one who had filled out the blanks while Uncle Andrew dictated. She'd bought the will-making kit for him from a bookshop. Uncle Andrew didn't believe in lawyers.

Nobody questioned the result. Everyone except Uncle Andrew had thought Odette should get the house. The church got the RM8,000 a year, a generous donation from a faithful servant of the Lord.

Even Jit Beng got something. Odette willed him a kamcheng, part of a Nyonyaware set that had mostly been destroyed when Uncle Andrew had thrown the pieces at her for going to a friend's house after school. She swathed the kamcheng in layers of bubble wrap and posted it to Jit Beng herself.

After the funeral she came home and lay on the chaise longue in the front hall, gazing up at the gorgeous wooden screens that blocked the heat of the sun.

She would have the coffee tables removed. The gigantic TV, that would go. Maybe she could sell it. She'd already put most of the sculptures and paintings away when Uncle Andrew got too ill to come downstairs to see them, but there were a couple she liked and that she would keep.

She would clear away the clutter, give the house space. Let it breathe.

Her eyes were shut, but if she opened them she would see the light shining through her skin, like moonlight through the filigreed vents. For the first time in her life she gave herself up to happiness.

Uncle Andrew walked his usual route. Down the driveway, up the slope to the top of the hill, then back down again to the back gate, where he let himself in.

Odette had been standing by the pillars at the entrance, waiting for him. Her hand curled around a pillar, drawing strength from the house. Perhaps she hadn't really seen him, she told herself. He wouldn't come back. She had just imagined it.

She knew this was a lie. It was not a surprise to see him return. When he lifted the latch on the gate, the sunlight shone through his arm.

If he had been alive she would have felt the movement of air on her skin as he walked past her. He didn't so much as glance at her, though he knew she was there. Temper held him, its weight crumpling his forehead, pulling his mouth taut.

He would be silent for days, pointedly ignoring her in his pique. His anger would fill the house like dark oily smoke. The stench would get into everything.

Life would be the same as it had always been.

Odette saw that the house needed Uncle Andrew more than it loved her. It needed him as much, perhaps, as she did. It would never let either of them go.

The harsh glare of the sun hurt her eyes. It was too hot to be outside. She let go of the pillar and saw that a splinter had driven itself into her palm.

She turned and went into the house. The shade enveloped her, cool as the air in a crypt. The doors swung shut, closing her in.

DAS GESICHT

DALE BAILEY

A fly alights on the table grooms itself, is gone.

Even now, after all these years, it is all the old man can do not to recoil. Even now, he remembers the flies. Even now, he dreams of them.

He looks at the woman across from him. She is young, impossibly so. His experience of aging—and he is now irrefutably old, born at the rag end of a long-dead century—is that he lives on unchanged while everything around him grows progressively younger.

His infirmities give this notion the lie. He looks at the world through a film of cataracts. Constipation binds his guts. But inwardly, he feels the same as he'd felt five decades ago.

Inwardly, he is terrified.

Udo Heldt's words have lodged inside his head like fishhooks. *Peel back the surface of the world and it's all butchery, isn't it? Everything. Butchery and filth and corruption.*

What will this young woman—this Eleanor Farrell—make of the sentiment, he wonders. For it's Udo Heldt who brought her here.

She's come to ask about *Das Gesicht.*

She's come to ask about *The Face.*

* * *

He'd nearly turned her away.

He'd spent more than fifty years trying to unlive it, disremember it, undream it from his dreams, and if he had not been entirely successful, neither had he wholly failed. He was eighty- eight years old. He'd spent the first third of his life chasing down his aspirations. He'd spent the rest of it running away from them. He'd renounced the calling that had summoned him across an ocean, to the broken shelf of a continent not his own. He'd forsaken the lush boulevards of Los Angeles for the grimy streets of Brooklyn. He'd abandoned the woman he'd loved.

No.

He did not want to think of Udo Heldt. He did not want to think of *Das Gesicht*.

"The film is lost," he'd told her when she called. "It was never released. Why should it interest you?"

"It may not have been released, but it was screened. I've tracked down nearly a dozen oblique allusions to it," she said. "Three or four diaries, a handful of letters in private collections. No one wanted to talk about what actually happened at the screening—but no one seemed to be able to forget it, either."

"Please, Miss—"

"Farrell," she said. "Look, Mr. King. It's of historical interest, if nothing else. Lon Chaney was said to be there. James Whale. A handful of others. Pola Negri. Tod Browning. They were universally revolted by it. Chaney called it vile, Tod Browning blasphemous."

"It was a long time ago. No one wants to hear those old stories."

"I promise you. I'm not doing some *Hollywood Babylon* hack job," she'd told him.

"You are chasing ghosts," he'd said.

"Even ghosts should have their say." And then, to his undoing: "You should give her a voice. After all, you loved her, didn't you?"

She didn't say her name. She didn't have to.

There had not been a day in nearly sixty years that the old man had not thought of her. Not one. Not since the day in 1919 (had it really been so long ago?) when he'd strolled into a Berlin cinema on a whim. Not since he'd seen her in *Küss Mich*, a movie of little distinction, in a role of even less. The next day, he'd returned to the theater with Heldt. And when the lights went down, the director, too, through the cam ra's eye, saw not the woman on the screen—not Catrin Ammermann, as she was then billed—but the woman she was striving to become.

By the time she took the role of the young wife in *Der Verdammte Schlüssel* almost a year later, Heldt had dubbed her Catrin Amour. But it was the man operating the camera—it was Heinrich König, it was the old man—who'd made her a star.

Now, in his dim, second-floor walk-up, with traffic whispering outside the curtained windows and dust sifting down on the tables and the antimacassars and the framed black-and-white photos that throng every surface—now that Eleanor Farrell has flown across the country to speak with him—now that her little cassette recorder is unwinding its reel, patient as the hours—now that Catrin Amour is dead and beyond hurt—now, he can say it. And why shouldn't he? All her life she had been no one and she had wanted desperately to be someone. All the great ones are alike in that way, he tells Miss Farrell: they are forever chrysalids on the verge of a magnificent transformation. That is the secret of his profession. You do not shoot the woman in front of the camera. You shoot the woman she wishes to become.

"Alchemy, Udo called it," he says.

"What was he like?"

How is he to answer that, the old man wonders. He remembers Heldt as a small, sinewy man, with a shock of dark hair and fervid, black eyes. He remembers his near-crippling limp, the legacy of an Allied round at Passchendaele. "I'm lucky to have a leg at all," Heldt had once told him. "The fucking surgeon was a butcher. He should have cut the fucking thing off and handed me a crutch."

The cinema was his crutch.

Only on the set did Udo Heldt know anything akin to joy—and even there, his fury infused every frame the old man had shot on his behalf. *Der Verdammte Schüssel*, his first film, ends with the gory decapitation of Bluebeard's young wife, betrayed by the bloody key.

"Did you serve in the war?" Miss Farrell asks.

The old man nods. He'd been wounded in the first days of fighting, at Liège. Unlike Heldt, he'd been spared the endless horror that followed: the gas, the artillery, the grenades, and, most of all, the vast wasteland of barbed wire and landmines between the rat-infested trenches, where Lewis guns spat out death at five hundred rounds a minute, and flyblown corpses bloomed like roses.

Dulce et decorum est pro patria mori.

Heinrich König had survived intact.

The war had scooped out Udo Heldt's soul.

The old man falls into silent rumination.

Miss Farrell gets up to look at the photos. They stand by the dozen on bookshelves and end tables: flappers and vamps and innocents alike, icons of the silent era: Mary Pickford, Norma Talmadge, Theda Bara. So many others. The old man wonders if Miss Farrell sees herself among them. She is not a beautiful woman; she is pale and freckled, with a sharp nose and green, inquisitive eyes. But in the right hands—in *his* hands—the camera could be coaxed to love her.

Such is the alchemy of the aperture, the paradox of the eye.

Heldt was already musing aloud about these issues when he wrote *Die Wölfe*. They had storyboarded the film together. The old man can remember it almost shot by shot even now, though little footage survives beyond the scene that juxtaposes the hunter's death against his wife's garden party, crosscutting his face, twisted in horror as he is torn apart by wolves, with those of the revelers, garish with laughter, and effectively dissolving the line between agony and exhilaration.

No one but Heldt could have conceived that sequence. No one but the old man could have shot it.

Miss Farrell runs her finger across the top of one picture frame. Lifts another one to her face.

"Clara Bow," the old man says.

He can lay his hand upon any one of the photos, even in the dark.

"This is you beside her?"

"Yes."

He studies her studying him, measuring him against the amiable rogue in the photo, with his unhandsome, equine face. He is no longer so tall. His jacket hangs upon him. His age-yellowed collar sags at the neck. His tie is too narrow.

It has been years since he's entertained a caller.

"You came to Hollywood in '21," Miss Farrell says, placing the picture back on the shelf, angling it into something proximate its original position. He will have to adjust it when she is gone.

"Yes," he told her as she takes her seat across from him. "Sol Wurtzel at Fox had seen *Die Wölfe*. We came together, the three of us. Udo would have it no other way."

They'd crossed on the *Hansa*, an unhappy time. The old man, Heinrich, had been in love with Catrin Amour, of course. He'd been in love with her from the moment he walked into that Berlin cinema. But she had eyes only for Heldt. Somewhere along the way he'd become *ihr Liebhaber*, her lover, her Svengali. Catrin believed that he'd made her a star, little understanding that he could not have done it on his own. He needed the camera eye. The camera needed the man behind it.

They were alone upon the deep when everything went wrong.

Catrin Amour came pounding at Heinrich's stateroom door well after midnight, in some cold, de d hour when the ship rolling gently through the swells lulled the soul into a sleep like death. Waking, he'd thought there'd been a disaster—a boiler that had blown out the hull, an iceberg collision, the *Titanic* torn asunder as the frigid deep engulfed her. It had been a disaster, of course, but a purely personal one that would cleave not the ship, but their little trio, along fault lines none of them had before acknowledged.

Catrin was incoherent, sobbing. There had been an altercation. She could tell him nothing—she would tell him nothing—beyond that solitary admission, and he could have read that much in the bruise blossoming upon her cheek. He found her some ice, put her to bed, and spent the rest of the night pacing the tiny stateroom, torn between fury and fear.

Catrin awoke toward dawn. Ignoring his protests, she let herself out into the corridor. She had to see Heldt. She had to apologize. She had to make things right.

Heinrich thought it had ended there.

But late that afternoon, Heldt found him alone on the foredeck, leaning against the railing and staring out over the heaving, black water. The sky smoldered. The wind coming in across the waves whipped their hair. The air smelled of brine.

They stood there for a long time, the old man at a loss for words.

Finally, Heldt said, "Something happened to me in the war. I never told you about it. This was in the summer of '17, when the advance had ground to a halt. We spent most of our time hunkered down in the trenches, smoking and playing cards, while the boys behind us lobbed shells at the enemy lines. It was a gloomy day, and the night that followed was black as sin, moonless, with lowering clouds and gusts of icy rain. You couldn't see much beyond three or four feet.

"It was after midnight when we went over the top. It was chaos, Heinrich. You could hear the intermittent boom of the sixty-pounders and the chunk of the Lewis guns chopping rounds into the mud. Tracers slashed green streaks through the darkness. When a shell dropped, the sky would light up a smoky crimson, revealing the hellish doomscape around you: men screaming and dying, their bodies dancing grotesquely in the blizzard of .303s. And everywhere the stench of gas and gunpowder and the miasma of rotting corpses that had not yet been recovered—that might never be recovered.

"And then I heard the whistle of a descending shell. The night exploded around me. I squeezed shut my eyes, I took a breath—

"—and I was staring up into the flawless blue vault of a bright morning sky. I hurt—everything hurt, Heinrich—but I was whole. I'd survived. The explosion had driven me back into a deep pit in the wasteland. The stench of the place was unbearable. I haven't the words to describe it.

"A constant, low hum filled the air. It was the buzz of flies, Heinrich. Thousands of them. Dense, whirling clouds of them, their bodies glistening black and green when they came to rest upon me. I still hear that loathsome insect drone. I will see the sheen of their eyes until the day I die. I'd fallen into a pit of corpses, and the flies had come to feed."

The old man cannot bring himself to share the details that followed.

Eleanor Farrell is already looking at him in dismay. Yet he can't help recalling Heldt's description of the flies gathering around his eyes, of the flies clogging his nostrils and worming their way between his lips.

The rest, though—

"I lurched up," Heldt had told him. "Waving my arms to keep them away, I staggered toward the rim of the pit. I began to climb, clawing my way through mud and snarls of barbed wire and decomposing bodies."

He'd been almost to the top when the hand had closed around his ankle. Slipping to his knees, Heldt found himself staring down into the countenance of a wounded Tommy. Half his face had been shot away, revealing a complex ligature of muscle and tendon, with here and there a white grin of bone. His eyeball lay exposed within its shattered orbit. Flies massed everywhere upon this broken visage. They sipped at the wells of his nostrils and devoured the raw flesh that strung his jaw. They squirmed into the crevice beneath his eyeball to glut themselves upon his brain. "Kill me," the Tommy whispered. Heldt reached for the blade sheathed at his belt. It was the only thing to do. It would be a mercy. And then he had a nightmare vision of his companions in the trenches—men who'd eaten and gambled and battled alongside him—*Dreckfressers* like himself, mud gluttons conscripted into a war they'd never chosen to fight, gunned down by British machine guns. He turned away.

"*Lassen sie schlemmen*," he said. Let them feast.

He kicked loose the Tommy's hand and clambered up out of the pit. He'd made it safely back to the German line by nightfall.

The *Hansa* plowed on through the murky water.

"Why did you tell me this?" Heinrich had asked at last.

Heldt stared out at the sea. "That is when I learned the true nature of all things. Peel back the surface of the world, and it's all butchery, isn't it? Everything. Butchery and filth and corruption." And then Heldt met his gaze. "There is nothing I will not do, Heinrich. Nothing."

Miss Farrell's little recorder winds the tape tight, and snaps off. She digs a fresh cassette out of her bag and gets the machine running again.

"What happened in Hollywood " she asks. The old man snorts.

"Hollywood was Udo Heldt's undoing," he says. "In the end, Hollywood undid us all. *Der Verdammte Schlüssel* and *Die Wölfe* were widely admired. But they were not the kind of films Sol Wurtzel could make at Fox. He'd thought Heldt could be tamed, that his enormous talents could be channeled into more conventional pictures. But Heldt could not be tamed. He was a great filmmaker, but what made him great was that he had an unflinching vision. Strip him of that vision, and put him to work making romantic comedies—"

The old man laughs.

Not that Heldt would make romantic comedies—or any other movie Wurtzel sent him.

They reached a stalemate: Heldt made no films at all.

Catrin and Heinrich, meanwhile, both found work quickly enough. Catrin's star never reached the heights it had risen to in Germany, but she was well-known and well-paid; in the days of silent film, language and accent were no barrier to stardom. Soon she and Heldt were living in the Hollywood Hills—unmarried, igniting the kind of small scandal that kept her safely in the public eye. And Heinrich's skills were much in demand. His work was never less than professional, often excellent. He worked with most of the stars of the era—

—here Eleanor Farrell glances around at the photos once again—

—and the ones he didn't work with he met. But *Der Verdammte Schlüssel* and *Die Wölfe* nagged him. With Heldt, he had been great. He wanted to be great again.

By this time, the wounds inflicted on the *Hansa* had healed—imperfectly, true, but well enough that Catrin, Heldt, and Heinrich spent many long evenings together, hashing over the latest Hollywood gossip. Catrin contrived not to mention the occasional bruises that shadowed her face, and Heinrich contrived not to notice them. Udo drank, and late at night, when Catrin had retreated upstairs to bed, he talked film.

He had seen everything. He saw every picture that came out of Europe. He screened all of *der Blödsinn*, the drivel—his word—produced in Hollywood. A withering critic, he scorned even the best films, reserving the occasional kind word for Heinrich's work on otherwise worthless pictures, and for Murnau and Wiene and some few other

Germans in their darker modes. "But even they flinch when they come hard up against the truth," Heldt would say. Heinrich did not ask what he meant by truth. He remembered all too well their conversation aboard the *Hansa*. He would not forget the horror of the Tommy's fate. He knew that he'd been obscurely threatened. *Butchery, filth*, and *corruption*—these words lingered in his mind.

But Heldt had still more to say on film in the abstract. Commercial pictures, with their neat plots and their happy endings, were a perversion of the cinema, he argued. The image may tell a story. It may coax and manipulate. It may deceive. But it must not lie. It may be a fiction, but inside the fiction there must be truth. "The biggest lie cinema tells," he said, "is embedded in the very medium itself, is it not—the paradox of the moving image, which is still, and the still image, which moves."

So it went, Heldt's talk of pictures and paradoxes—so it might have gone on forever, the old man supposes, but for what happened on Monday, October 13, 1924. The date is scored into the old man's memory. It was the night Udo Heldt destroyed Catrin Amour's film career; it was the night *Das Gesicht* was born.

Catrin would never speak of what had happened. All the old man knew was that a hammering at his door once again woke him deep in the blackest hour of the morning. Swimming up out of the depths was very much like waking that night on the *Hansa*—a sense of confusion resolving into the certainty of disaster: icebergs, torpedoes, exploded boilers, something beautiful shattered and devoured by the deep, a world consumed by a war that would not end.

It was Catrin, of course. Heinrich's forebodings as he pulled on his dressing gown proved correct. Heldt had carved open her cheek. A doctor was summoned. The police were not—Catrin wouldn't permit it. It was clear to all of them that her career in pictures was over.

For a few weeks, they all waited for something to happen. Nothing happened. Heldt showed up neither in anger nor remorse. The picture Catrin was about to start shooting was quietly recast. The few rumors in the press were swiftly extinguished. The studios kept the gossip columns on a pretty short leash in those days. Catrin Amour, it became known, had tired of acting. She had chosen a life of seclusion. She might well go back to Germany.

In the meantime, her slashed cheek healed into a puckered scar. The doctor had done his work as well as he could. So had Heldt. Catrin stayed on with Heinrich. He and Catrin were companions, nothing more. They never shared a bedroom. This was Catrin's decision, not Heinrich's.

"I loved her very much," the old man tells Miss Farrell. Miss Farrell says nothing. What is there to say?

The reels of her tape recorder continue to turn, eating time. The old man clears his throat. "Then I ran into Heldt again.

I was eating lunch at the counter of the Musso & Frank Grill, when he slid onto the stool next to me—"

"Why don't you move on down the counter?" Heinrich had said. Heldt didn't bother responding. "I want you to shoot a picture for me, Heinrich," he said—though by this time the old man had started calling himself Henry King.

"I asked you to move on down the counter."

"Just think about it," Heldt said, and then he moved on down the counter, and out the door onto the street.

The hell he would think about it, Heinrich told himself.

Yet he thought about little else. He thought about *Der Verdammte Schlüssel* and he thought about *Die Wölfe* and he thought about the trivial picture he was working on now, and the feather- weight of a director, who barely knew which end of the camera to point at his actors. Heinrich might as well have been directing the picture himself. He supposed he was.

He mentioned the encounter at the Musso & Frank Grill to Catrin, who took little interest in the business these days—or anything else, for that matter. They rarely talked, and when they did talk, they said nothing of consequence. Heinrich had once told her he didn't even see the scar when he looked at her. She replied that she saw nothing else. But when he said that he'd run into Heldt, a light came into her eyes that he hadn't seen for months. He realized that she was still in love with him.

Which is how, a few nights later, they wound up at Heldt's house—

though, of course, it was really Catrin's house, too. That night Heinrich learned that she didn't seem to resent anything Heldt did or wanted from her. It was her money that had paid for it, just as it was her money that Heldt had been subsisting on during their time apart. But Catrin didn't resent it. It turned out that she'd even consent to go back in front of the camera for him. And it turned out that Heinrich would consent to stand behind it.

But what was the project Heldt had in mind?

He wanted to work inside the paradox, he said, where the still picture and the moving one meet. And then he went on to describe the film he had in mind. *Das Gesicht*, Heldt called it. *The Face*. It sounded like the most static—and least interesting—picture Heinrich could imagine. It would, nonetheless, be the most difficult challenge Catrin would ever confront as an actress. She would need to do the impossible. She would need to remain utterly still—utterly—for an hour and more.

And Catrin was not alone.

"Technically, it was the most difficult challenge I ever faced, as well," the old man tells Eleanor Farrell. "Together, the three of us would make a great film—or we would fail. We made a great film, Miss Farrell. Thank God, it does not survive."

"You will want to know how it was done, of course. Does it matter? Would you understand if I explained it? Alchemy, Heldt called it. But *Das Gesicht*—there is alchemy, and there is alchemy."

The old man shakes his head.

"Did something happen on the set of *Das Gesicht*?" the young woman asks.

"Nothing unexpected, Miss Farrell. I was present for the entire shoot—a single day, but a trying one. The finished film looked like a single take, but such a long take was, of course, impossible. It is impossible even now. Like all films, *Das Gesicht* was an illusion. Like all films, it was constructed in the editing room."

"What happened at the screening, Mr. King?"

The old man sighs. He doesn't answer for a long time.

* * *

"I wondered even then who would be interested in such a film," he says when he finally resumes. "Technicians like myself, perhaps, who would want to know how we had pulled off the illusion of the long take. And there would be interest among Hollywood's aristocracy, who would wonder if Heldt's new film—privately financed and shot in a rented studio—could possibly live up to the achievements of *Der Verdammte Schlüssel* and *Die Wölfe*. But as for a real audience? The film had none. There would be no release. It was art for art's sake, I suppose: an expression of a single man's private obsession. He insisted that it would be his finest film."

"And Catrin Amour?"

"She never spoke to me of it. She loved him, of course, as I loved her, perhaps to a greater and in a different degree. She loved him enough to surrender up her ruination for his art. As far as I could tell, she did so without ill will or regret. I never asked her why. Any such inquiry seemed to me somehow obscene. So we shot the film and retreated to the editing room, painstakingly matching up and splicing shots. The details"—the old man shrugs—"they will have little interest to you. You wish to know of the screening. You wish to know of the film itself. You wish to hear about *Das Gesicht*."

Eleanor Farrell does not respond.

She lets the silence spin out, trusting, he supposes, that he will come to it in his time. And he will. Having come this far, what can he do but unburden himself? And so, slowly—haltingly—he begins to speak.

Between the three of them—Heinrich, Catrin Amour, and Udo Heldt—they put together a select guest list: James Whale and Tod Browning and Lon Chaney were there, as Miss Farrell had said. But there were others, Barbara La Marr, Sol Wurtzel, Louise Brooks, and Nita Naldi. The great cinematographers of the day, G. W. Bitzer and John Arnold. Others. Perhaps twenty- five people, no more. The old man cannot recall them all, not after all these years. Heldt's greatest regret was that the German directors he respected—Murnau, Wiene, Lang—would not be present—though he told Heinrich that he hoped to take the film to Germany, as well.

And so they gathered in a small screening room on the Fox lot.

Heinrich was there, of course. And Catrin Amour came, too. Udo Heldt escorted her in just as the lights were going down, her face artfully veiled to reveal the unmarked arc of one high cheekbone—and to hide the scar that Udo had slashed into her face on the other side. The men murmured, standing to greet her. She merely nodded and let Udo lead her to her seat in the gathering dark.

The room fell silent but for the whir of the projector as it cast out its light upon the screen. The title came up, white on black—

—*Das Gesicht*—

—and dissolved into darkness. Then the screen brightened to reveal an image of a woman's face—Catrin Amour's unmarred face—in medium-close profile and to the right of center, so that it commanded the screen without overwhelming it. She was beautiful, the old man says. Not even the tiniest imperfection was visible, not even a pore. There was an audible intake of breath at this vision: Catrin Amour, her lips relaxed into an enigmatic half smile, her hair falling in dark waves around her shoulders. Everything about the image was utterly still. If you saw it as the audience saw it, if you saw it here before you, the old man says, nodding at the pictures that surround them—if you saw it before you now, you would mistake it for a still photo—until the woman blinked. And when the woman on-screen *did* blink—when Catrin Amour blinked at last—someone laughed in the darkness, mirthlessly, a release of tension, nothing more.

And still the image held.

What at first was confusing—was this a moving picture at all?— became gradually mesmerizing, because the image both fulfilled and defied every expectation. It lived entirely in the paradox of the moving image.

If you have ever spent a long time living with a child, the old man says to Eleanor Farrell, you may have had the experience of looking at a photo from many months in the past and feeling a moment of shock, an instant of cognitive dissonance, for the child before you is palpably different from the child in the photo—yet the change has happened so gradually, right before your eyes, day by day, that you barely notice it until confronted with her image from another era.

This was the experience of watching *Das Gesicht*. The image appeared never to move. You only occasionally awakened to realize that the angle of vision had changed: you were no longer looking at Catrin Amour in pure profile but from a subtly different perspective, as though the camera was tracking slowly, impossibly slowly, in an arc around her. It was a still picture. And then you realized that the still picture had been a moving one all along—and thus the paradox was exposed. Catrin Amour blinked, and you awoke from your trance to realize that she was no longer as she had been.

The film ran an hour. That's how long it took to describe that arc around Catrin Amour's face, how long it took the viewer to progress from perfection into imperfection, from the unscarred face to the horrifically mutilated one: Udo Heldt's not very subtle metaphor for his vision of the world as he had shared it on the Hansa: *Peel back the surface of the world, Heinrich, and it's all butchery, isn't it?*

In the moment the scar was fully revealed, you could feel the mood of the audience shift: This was the masterpiece of the man who had made *Der Verdammte Schlüssel* and *Die Wölfe*?

The old man pauses again. He is a long time gathering his thoughts.

This time Miss Farrell risks a question. "That was it?"

The old man recognizes the implication in her voice. She too has been duped. She has traveled all the way across the country for this revelation? This was *Das Gesicht*? The old man is briefly tempted to answer her in the affirmative.

But he has come too far to stop now.

"No, Miss Farrell," he says. "There is more." He doesn't wait to hear the follow-up question. He plunges on. "Chaney was right. It was a vile picture. It was a blasphemous one." He takes a long breath. "What you must understand, Miss Farrell, is that I was there—I was there on the set of the film. I was there in the editing room for weeks. With my hands I shaped the illusion of the unbroken take. With my hands I created the trickery. I had seen every frame of that footage, including the many, many feet we left on the cutting-room floor, a hundred times or more. And what I saw next, I did not see on the set. What I saw next, I never filmed."

What the old man had seen next—what they had all seen next—was nothing more, and nothing less, than a fly emerge from Catrin Amour's left nostril. An optical illusion, a speck of dust on the print, a flaw in the film, Heinrich thought. And then the camera, a camera he had been operating, moved in for a tight shot—a shot he had never taken. And in this new shot, a second fly emerged from Catrin's nostril. It took flight and landed on the scar Udo Heldt had carved into her cheek. A third fly followed.

Another. And then another.

She might have been a mannequin, the woman on the screen was so still. Then her mouth bulged grotesquely, as though she were going to vomit, and flies boiled forth from within her. She spewed them out in handfuls, in clots, in seething mouthfuls; she spewed them out by the hundreds. They massed on her neck and chin, launching themselves intermittently into the cloud that swirled around her. And still they came, streaming out of her mouth and nostrils in swarms. And Catrin Amour—the Catrin Amour on the screen—remained utterly unmoved.

Flies began one by one to land on the camera lens, blurring the image of *das Gesicht*—of the face—into a spume of bodies, engorged with putrescence. They probed the air for the carrion stench of food. Heinrich flinched from the scrutiny of the enormous compound eyes—from the filth and corruption that lay exposed before him, the sordid truth inside the lie. At last, the loathsome creatures obscured the image of *das Gesicht*'s defiled beauty altogether. Catrin Amour was gone. The screen writhed with insectile turmoil an instant longer—

—and then it went abruptly black.

For a heartbeat, silence reigned.

Catrin Amour began to scream. Someone fumbled on the lights, plunging the room into chaos. Some few of the audience— Lon Chaney among them—sat in stunned horror. Most reeled blindly toward the doors. In the back row, someone retched. Heinrich stumbled in Catrin's direction, shoving people aside.

Udo Heldt was already there, tearing away Catrin's veil.

Heinrich lurched to a halt, snatching at the back of a seat to support himself.

He could no longer see Catrin's face.

He could no longer see anything but scar.

DAS GESICHT

Eleanor Farrell says nothing.

The daylight behind the curtains has faded, draping shadows over the photographs surrounding them: still images that move now only in the old man's imagination, that speak only in his memory.

The old man wonders if she believes him. He wonders if he cares.

"Saying it was true," the young woman says at last. "How could it have happened?"

"I don't know," Heinrich König says. "I know only the things I have seen, Miss Farrell. Whether they are true things—" He shrugs. "The camera also lies."

She pauses, clearly unsatisfied with this response, but what is he to say? There is mystery in the world.

"What happened next?"

"You know the rest. I destroyed the print. I destroyed the negative. I destroyed everything. I did it that night. And when I was finished, I drove east. I was done with pictures."

"And Catrin?"

"I left her to him, to my shame. I did not return to Los Angeles for her funeral after the suicide."

"Yet you loved her."

"I loved Catrin Ammermann. I loved the woman she was striving to become. I loved the dream of Catrin Amour. But after *Das Gesicht*, I could not see her any longer. I could see only the scar she made in the world."

"And Udo Heldt?"

"He died in a car accident three years later, Miss Farrell. You know this. The fact is readily available."

"I don't know how you feel about it."

"Do my feelings matter?" he asks, and when she does not answer, he says, "I did not grieve Udo Heldt. I am glad his movies—our movies— are gone from the world. I repent the finest work I ever did. I repudiate it. I disavow *Der Verdammte Schlüssel* and I disavow *Die Wölfe*. If I had been able to destroy them, too, I would have. I take comfort that only fragments survive."

"But—"

The old man reaches out and touches a button on her recorder. The reels grind to a halt. Into the silence that follows, he says, "You are still young, Miss Farrell. Forget *Das Gesicht*. Find a hap-pier illusion and hope that it is true."

And then, slowly, the old man stands—a difficult process but, he reflects, not one that he would willingly surrender. He supposes that he will soon have no choice in the matter.

He straightens his tie and glances at Miss Farrell. He wants to give her the foolish advice that old men call wisdom, but he has already indulged himself sufficiently in that respect: perhaps she will forget *Das Gesicht* and perhaps she will not. He hopes so— for in unburdening himself, he understands, he has burdened her. And he has given Udo Heldt's picture new life. He would give her something else, if he could. Perhaps he will not have to adjust the angle of Clara Bow's photograph, after all.

She hesitates for a moment when he extends it to her. "Mr. King, I couldn't—"

"Please, Miss Farrell. Let me grant you a brighter memory for your visit than the one I have already given you."

She gazes at the photo. "It's inscribed."

"Yes. I was new to America when that picture was made. She was kind to me."

"Okay, then." The young woman tucks the photo into her bag. She smiles—she is more beautiful than he had thought—and thanks him. And that is enough. He sees her out and then he is alone in the dark apartment.

He sits quietly, listening to the traffic outside, and looking at the photos that surround him—mementos of a life he'd surrendered more than five decades ago. He'd led several other lives in the interim, but it is that first one—the life he'd shared with Udo Heldt and Catrin Amour— that matters.

After a time, he eats sparingly—a can of soup, nothing more— and then he sees himself to bed.

Sleep is a long time coming. He keeps thinking of the films he made with Udo Heldt. He keeps thinking of *Das Gesicht*.

He disavows it. He disavows them all. He lays very still.

In the darkness above him, a fly cuts circles in the air.

THE SYCAMORE AND THE SYBIL

ALIX E. HARROW

Before I was a sycamore I was a woman, and before I was a woman I was a girl, and before I was a girl I was a wet seed wild in the hot-pulp belly of my mother. I remember it: a pulsing blackness, veins unfurling in the dark like roots spreading through the hidden places of the earth. You remember things different, once you're a tree.

Of course that's about all trees can do: stand there and remember. We can't run or spit or sing; we can't fuck or dance or get good and drunk on a full moon; we can't hold our mother's hands or stroke the cheek of a fevered child. We're towers without any doors or windows; we are prisons and prisoners both, impregnable and alone.

But they can't hurt us any-damn-more, at least not without working up a sweat, and that's not nothing.

(If you're wondering why a woman would trade her limbs and her beating heart for a little slice of safety, well—maybe you're young. Maybe the world has changed. Maybe you're dumb as a moss-eaten stump.)

It's the same bargain we've been making for centuries, one way or another: give up your life in order to keep living. Give him your saltwater skin; give him your voice; give him your thousand stories. Give up your body and live forever rooted to the bank of the Big Sandy, dreaming and watching. Do what you can to stay alive. That's just how it is.

But sometimes I think, in the slow tree-sap way I think now: *It shouldn't be.*

It was early fall the first time she came running through my woods.

September is one of my better months: my leaves go all gold-speckled and copper-kissed, and my bark shines white as a knuckle-bone. I arrange my fallen leaves like a skirt around my roots, a graceful arc of rust and red, and when the sun slants just right even the squirrels have to stop their gossiping to admire me.

But she hardly noticed me. She kept her eyes on the ground, foot-steps pounding. You don't have time to admire the view when there's a wolf snapping at your heels.

Oh, not a *real* wolf—there hasn't been a real wolf in Crow County since I was a girl with legs instead of limbs and the state paid three dollars a pelt for them, and anyway those poor creatures never hunted women except in fairytales.

This was one of those two-legged wolves who wore a coat and a tie, who waxed their hair smooth as brass and smiled too damn much. He was a handsome wolf, nicely-dressed and clean, but so was mine. They'll eat you just the same, in the end.

The girl was a looker, too—sugar-maple hair curling around a white face, legs like pale birch branches beneath her skirt—but it didn't really matter. Wolves don't hunt deer for their looks.

"Wait," he called, voice honey-soft and pleading. "Please."

It was the please that did it, that thin coat of politeness like paint over a rotten fence-post. The girl stopped, so close to me now I could smell the clammy uncertainty rising off her skin and turned back to face him.

"Kat, my love, don't run from me. Never run from me." His face was fetchingly flushed, a single waxen curl hanging against his cheek.

"I didn't—I'm not sure—" She was backing towards my trunk, leaning away from him.

He stepped closer. "Not sure of what? My love for you?" He reached for her hands, trapped them limp and white in his grip. "How could you doubt it? I've loved you since the moment I saw you."

The owl that lived in my hollow branch gave a small cough of disgust. *Ain't the first time he's said that*, she muttered. Owls tend to overhear a lot of this kind of thing, given their habit of swooping silently through the night and perching in haylofts and trees, and in general they hold low opinions of romance, sex, and menfolk. Minnie, who was almost twenty and had seen more human night-doings that most owls, was bitter as twice-brewed coffee.

The wolf reached a hand to cup the girl's face, his eyes shining with earnestness. "Tell me you feel the same way."

She hesitated. I felt the tremor of it through the earth, the way her weight shifted back and away. "I—" But then he was kissing her and her hands were still trapped in his like a pair of fresh-killed rabbits and her back was pressed against the coolness of my trunk.

Once when I was still a sapling, a hunter staked a steel trap among my green roots and a fox found it two days later. I'd felt every panicked heartbeat, tasted every hot-penny drop of its blood. The girl wasn't scrabbling or whining, but her pulse beat the same desperate rhythm against my bark. Trapped.

Maybe you're thinking: *No, she isn't.* Maybe you're wondering why she hasn't tried to run or scream or put her hand to his chest and say, "No thank you, sir," because after all he's a gentleman-wolf in a button-down shirt, not some slavering beast. But I could feel the hunger of him, the way he pressed her against my trunk hard enough for my bark to carve patterns in her flesh. She wouldn't have gotten far.

There was one other thing she could have done, of course, but I guess she didn't know the words.

My Great-aunt Daphne taught them to me when I was young: old, secret words, the ones you say when the wolf is at your throat and there's nowhere left to run and you don't know any witching strong enough to strike out at him, so you strike inward, instead.

You say the words and you are no longer a woman. You are a slim little maple, leaves damp-pink in the spring, or a juniper with powder-blue berries, or a sycamore rising tall and round on the banks of the Big Sandy. You are fleshless and voiceless and alone, and so you are finally safe.

I could have told them to her. I could have written the words in the shadow-pattern of my leaves against the sky, or whispered them in a puff of pollen, or pressed them into her skin.

But I didn't. Because speaking them would have stolen her beating heart and her pale-birch legs and her maple-red curls, because she would never have seen her Great-aunt Daphne again or her Mama or her baby brother with his dandelion-fluff hair. Because her only friends would be chickadees and moles and the grumpy barred owl who lived in her dead branch, and her heartwood would turn dark and hard as a coal-seam.

Because I was no longer sure it was a price worth paying.

I didn't see her again until January. January is a sleeping, blind month, when my sap runs deep and slow in the center of me and my leaves rot around my ankles. The woods turn stark and bony-fingered, and only the hollies and hemlocks still gleam green through the grayness. Mostly people stay away.

But not her. She came slowly this time, unpursued. The bright red of her hair was swirled beneath a winter cap and muddy snow speckled her skirts. I was glad to see her—being a tree is lonely business, even with Minnie around—until I saw the way her hand was tucked between the buttons of her shapeless coat, cupping her belly.

Oh, hell. Now that I was listening for it I could hear it thumping away in the middle of her, that dove-wing echo of her own pulse. A green seed growing in the dark.

The girl watched the river hiss below her, frost-eaten at the edges and slate-gray in the center. Her expression had a dangerous sort of idleness in it, as if she were wondering what might happen if she stepped off the bank and into the Big Sandy, but didn't much care. It wasn't a desperate expression, because the chase was already over and she'd been caught and eaten and swallowed whole. It was how Red Riding Hood might've looked as she curled in the darkness of the wolf's belly.

I could still have given her the words. I could have offered her a kinder death than the suffocating ice of the river. But—

It's not fair, goddammit.

It wasn't fair that we were always the ones who had to lose, to change, to become-something-else. To give ourselves up. It wasn't fair that all we had in our defense were these few, desperate magics that hurt no one but ourselves.

I think it used to be different. I think we used to know more. Sometimes when I sink down into the deep-down sleep of trees I can almost remember the wild times in the land-before, when we painted ourselves in madder and clay and danced around solstice bonfires, when every witch had a familiar loping or slinking or winging beside her, when we flew through the night on strips of alder and ironwood. I remember when our magic turned outward rather than inward and the wolves stayed in the shadows, fearful of our flames and the words bright and sharp as knives on our tongues.

(You remember things different, once you're a tree.)

But then we forgot, or were made to forget. Something happened—a plague, I think, something cruel that swept across the world in a cold tide of suffering—and fear made the wolves brave. They came for us, and then there were no more midnight bonfires. Burning was for books, then, and for witches.

(I can remember the taste of smoke, the hiss and snap of burning flesh. Sometimes I think I can see her face, my great-great-great-something-thing-or-other tied back-to-back with the rest of her coven, looking up out of the deepness of time with red-cedar eyes and a sad smile. Sometimes I even think the smile is for me, somehow—as if she'd been suspended in this last second before her burning, waiting for her daughter's daughter's daughter to remember her—but it's probably just the lonely dream of a sycamore who used to be a woman).

All we have left to us now are weak, domestic magics—"the natural womanly arts," my school-teachers called them. We charm peonies into blooming early; we convince the wash-water to stay hot and the bread to bake evenly; some of us can soothe a colicky baby or deliver a breech birth safely, but I don't know how much of that is magic and how much is just know-how, or if there's any real difference between the two.

A few pitiful scraps of the old spells have survived, whispered from mother to daughter and aunt to niece, but they aren't what they used to be. They can't be. If women went around turning men into pigs or conversing with thunderstorms or calling winged demons up from Hell—

well, they'd be staked and burned and their precious words would be nothing but ash and bone. Scattered, forgotten, buried.

The girl was still looking down at the river, half-mesmerized, but her hand was no longer hidden in her coat. She was twisting and worrying at her finger, as if something chafed there. It gleamed gold in the weak winter light.

Huh. It was Minnie, watching from her hole. *He's caught her good and proper, now.*

My wolf hadn't ever intended to marry me. He was the oldest son of a judge, the kind of boy who'd never had to chop his own wood or wash his own clothes, and I was nobody. Just a stringy-haired, under-sized girl with pox scars pitting my cheeks and black-stained fingers from gathering walnuts in the woods. But he'd seen me and he'd wanted me, and he'd been raised to think wanting something was the same as deserving it. So he'd chased me down the Big Sandy one day at dusk, a wolf in white linen, and his jaws had closed around my throat and I'd said the words because there was nothing else to do.

Would it have been better if he'd wooed and wed me, instead? If I'd had to wake up every morning with that golden collar wrapped around my finger, smelling the stink of him on my skin, facing an endless line of the same mornings like a mirror reflecting itself forever?

Minnie was right; that girl was caught good and proper. And all women's witching could offer her was a slower, safer death.

To hell with women's witching. I'd let her drown herself before I'd help her build her own lonely prison of wood and sap.

But she didn't drown herself. She pressed both hands to her middle, right over the thrumming green seed in her belly, and turned away from the Big Sandy. She left the woods with her head bowed, mourning.

Minnie's wingtip brushed the soft punk of my wood inside her hole. *Oh, Sylvie, hon, ain't nothing you can do. It's just the way it is.*

I went to sleep for a while after that. I'd been doing that more and more often over the years—letting my woman-self curl down deep in the heartwood, unseeing, protecting her from the endless turning of seasons and the things she can't fix and the words she doesn't know. But this time—maybe it was the mournful tilt of the girl's head, the weariness of her footsteps over my root-tips—I didn't intend to wake up again. I was finished with watching and longing, with loneliness and rage and the-way-things-were.

I slept deep and remembered deeper.

I remembered way back down the centuries until the line of my mothers and their mothers fractured into a thousand branching roots. Until I found her: the woman with the red-cedar eyes and the sad smile.

I could see the bloody glow of flames along her cheekbones, the blurred outlines of women burning beside her. The heat lifted their hair from their faces, as if they were floating in river-water rather than flames. A blackbird circled high above her, calling a mournful song down to his mistress.

I flinched away from their suffering and all the nothing-I-could-do-about-it, but I was held fast by those red-cedar eyes.

It's not so bad, really.

She didn't speak the words: she thought them, and the memory of their thinking echoed down to me through all the births and deaths between us.

My own thoughts were scattered and half-sleeping, but I managed something along the lines of *the hell it's not.*

Her smile twisted, wry and weary, so like my Aunt Daphne I felt my branches shiver way back in the here-and-now.

At least I saved my daughters from the flames, and I have my sisters beside me.

Jealousy wormed in my heartwood, like a woodlouse burrowing. Even my dying would be lonely.

And at least all my words won't burn with me.

She smiled again, and this time it wasn't sad or wry. It was fierce, shining white through the rising red of the flames around her. The black-bird trilled in triumph.

Some of them I gave to my daughters, and some of them I will give to you, Sylvia.

The memory of my own name was like an axe blade against my trunk, biting deep. I'd left my name behind me when I sunk down into my sleeping, forgotten it along with every other human thing (fresh-pressed cider on my tongue, laughter, a hand held fast in mine). How had she known it?

I knew you before your mother's mother was born. The witch's thoughts were faint now, sundered by smoke and pain. *Before they burned me, they called me the Sybil of Saxony.*

In the final seconds before the flames stole her voice, the witch shouted the words to the smoke-eaten stars.

And oh, they were good words. Words of change and transformation and reckonings long-overdue, vengeance passed like a coal from mother to daughter to niece. Powerful words, burning so bright I could feel the heat of them even through the greasy weight of centuries.

They were the words I'd needed when I was young and still-breathing, when the wolf was nipping at my heels. Now it was too late—I was lipless and voiceless and the wolf had already won. If I had eyes, I would have wept at the waste.

Then the witch's hair caught fire and the words became screams became nothing at all.

I wanted to save her somehow, to help her—I wasn't a woman anymore but I still remembered what we owed one another—but I couldn't. Because her death had already happened, because I was just a sycamore, not a sybil, and the only words I knew were the slow secrets trees whisper to one another through the turning seasons.

But when you can't do what you want, you do what you can. I lingered in the depths of my own memory and gave her the tree-words for rainwater trickling through the earth, the delicate lace of frost on my bark, the feather-touch of the first snow.

I watched her face ease and her eyes close. And then the Sybil of Saxony was gone and I was alone in the deep-dark with nothing but the words she had given me. The words that had come too late to save me.

It took a long time drifting in that lonely dark before it occurred to me, with a feeling like the first leaf unfurling after a long winter, that the words weren't meant for me at all.

It took me a while to wake up.

I slept through the green froth of spring, the flowering of the tulip poplars and the hesitant greening of the fiddlehead ferns. I swam upward through the years, following the memory of my true-name and the thin hope that I wasn't too late.

The pennywort and laurel were in full bloom by the time I came back to my sycamore-self. Minnie was waiting for me, watching me with her gas-lamp eyes full of worry.

'*Bout time*, she snapped, and winged off to kill something furred and small. I thought of the sybil and her blackbird and wondered idly if familiars had really been Satanic spirits the way the preachers said, or if they'd just been pleasant company.

I wished I could follow Minnie out of the woods, smell the sunset on her feathers and her claws on my true flesh—but all I could do was wait.

It was past the summer solstice, when my crown turns deep emerald and the sun soaks into me like honey wine, before she came again.

I'd been just about to give up waiting—figuring she'd settled into her cozy cage and decided to survive, like so many of us do—but seventy-odd years as a tree will teach you patience.

She came slowly down the bank, and she wasn't alone: her wolf was at her side. She was swaying, flat-footed, as round and ripe as a peach; he was sweating through his suit. They held hands, and I could see the red mark where the ring cut too tightly into her puffy fingers.

He pulled her beneath the thick summer-shade of my canopy. He leaned close, pressing himself against the hard roundness of her belly, hands moving over her body. It should have looked like tenderness or at least lust, but it looked more like a man rubbing down his prize horse, delighting in his ownership.

"William, I don't feel well. Please." He ignored her. She looked up at my tangled leaves, reeling and desperate and almost-resigned—and saw something that made her eyes spark and catch like twin matches.

She shoved the wolf away from her. I could tell from the open hole of his mouth that she'd never touched him like that before, never turned her silent no into a physical thing.

He ran his tongue over his teeth as if testing their sharpness, then smiled wide and false. "Kat! Is that how a married woman should behave?" It was her chance to laugh and take it back, to turn defiance back into deference, to kiss him and make it better.

But I saw her eyes flick backwards to my trunk, to the place she'd been trapped and taken nine months before, and then to the riverbank where she hadn't drowned herself. I could see them reflected in the paleness of her eyes: the choices she'd had taken from her, the choices she'd made. The choices she could still make.

Her chin lifted. "No. It isn't." The fine muscles of her throat were drawn tight. "But maybe I don't want to be a married woman anymore."

I watched the change come over him: the languid ease left his limbs, the tolerant patience evaporated like dew. "What are you saying, Kat?" There was a lowness to his voice now, almost a growl.

"I'm saying—I'm saying I don't want this. Me and the baby are leaving. We'll go to the city, I'll find work—we'll be fine, the two of us—here." Her voice trembled on the last word. Her hands shook as she wrested the ring from her finger and held it out to him.

Minnie made a high, worried croon.

The wolf didn't move. He just stared at her, panting a little, sweat pearling on his forehead. The charming smile slid like hot wax from his face, leaving something bare-toothed and animal behind it. Something strangely afraid, like a lean winter-wolf watching his prey escape.

He took a single step towards her and the whole shape of his body was a promise of pain. His hands curled into fists, his lips peeled away from his teeth—and I knew when he reached her he would make her take those brave, doomed words back into herself, make her choke on them—he would take this last and bravest choice from her, too—

Except he never reached her. Because I had already given her the words.

I had sung them in my sap, written them on the sky in the patterns of my leaves, woven them atop the earth with knotted roots. I had carved them into my own white bark.

The girl wasn't a witch, but she'd gone long enough without power to recognize it when it danced naked in front of her.

She spoke the words, and oh, how sweet they sounded.

They cost her, I could see that, burning her deep inside wherever we keep our souls. But this time the hurt didn't stay locked-up inside her, turning her organs to tree-knots and her skin to wood-grain; this time it soared outward, wildfire-hungry, and found a worthier mark.

There was a long, wrenching moment when the world seemed to shudder with the force of his changing, and the sound of a scream or a howl lit the forest, but then it was over and there were no more words left to speak.

Instead of a man there was only an ugly little tree rooted on the riverbank where he'd stood: a stunted chokecherry, its bark black and its leaves curled with blight.

My laugh was a summer breeze rustling through my leaves.

The girl stared at the chokecherry tree with her arms wrapped tight around her belly and her chest heaving. She didn't scream, or weep. Instead she knelt and scrabbled in the dirt at its feet. She dropped something small and golden into the hole and buried it. Her eyes when she stood were a bright, molten amber. Wolf-like.

And now she would leave, and I would stay behind on the riverbank, waiting and watching from my lonely prison until I hollowed from the inside out, until finally I keeled over into the Big Sandy and nobody was left to remember my name.

It would have to be enough.

(It wasn't enough. I wanted more—the softness of skin, the taste of witchspeak on my tongue, the whole world mine for the walking— but at least I had the memory of her wolfish eyes. At least my words wouldn't die with me.)

But the girl didn't leave. She turned back to me, a queer half-smile on her face and her maple-hair curling around her cheeks. She stepped close, raising her pale fingers to trace the letters that had appeared on my hard flesh. Her mouth moved, soundless, as if she were remembering the heat of the words on her tongue.

It was only then that I wondered what else those words might do. If they could turn a heart to wood, could they turn heartwood back to flesh?

Oh, oh, please.

"Thank you," the girl whispered. And then she said the words a second time.

And this time they were mine. They burrowed into me like hacksaws or drill-bits, hot metal. They burned but it was a drunken, delicious blazing, like the first blush of a sunburn in summer.

Somewhere in the deep heart of me, in a place that had almost but not quite turned to rot and sawdust over the years, something woke up. It thudded back to life, clumsy and faint but alive, and I thought: *oh, it's like this*. It's like one hand reaching for another, words whispered from witch to woman, sybil to sycamore, down through time in a long unbending line, despite the snapping of wolves and the crackling of flames. It's like each woman doing what she can until one day, somehow, it is enough.

The words cost her, I could tell, but she was young and brave and she had the strength of that second life hammering away below her ribs. She leaned her forehead against me for a few minutes, eyes closed, shivering a little. My newfound pulse thudded against her skin.

She straightened, rolling her shoulders back, and patted my shuddering bark.

Then she left. She strode from the woods with her spine straight and her fingers bare, with all her choices laid out before her like the rich fruit of some endless orchard, a new myth in the making. She did not look behind her.

In September I went walking out after her.

It took me a while to finish up all my changing, see—trees are slower than women. I spent the whole summer turning my sap to green-scented blood, my leaves to silver hair, my wood-grain to muscle and bone. It was a second birthing, but I remembered my first one well enough to know how it was supposed to go.

Minnie was patient with me. She perched in a tolerant willow across the bank and offered a steady stream of *oh honey*'s and *shit, girl*'s .

Don't stop now, hon, she told me. And I didn't.

When I walked out of the woods and into the bright September dawn, tall and old and naked as a jaybird, she swooped after me and perched on my shoulder.

THE STONEMASON

DANNY RHODES

What are these fantastic monsters doing in the cloisters
before the eyes of the brothers as they read?
           —BERNARD OF CLAIRVAUX (CIRCA 1130 CE)

When he found a moment for a hurried lunch, he carried his satchel through the cathedral grounds to his favorite spot in the walled garden, a little bench there. He liked to observe the visitors as they appeared through the stone archway and crossed the garden, following the path towards the Queningate. Such ordinary things soothed him.

It was one of those bright winter days, the light sharp and exacting, the keen air piercing to the nose, but there was a gentle touch of warmth in the sunlight, a soft caress on his forehead and cheekbones.

He rested his satchel on his lap, opened it and took out his foil wrapped sandwiches. He felt the soft texture of the bread between his fingers, lifted the sandwich to his mouth and took a bite. He savored the rich, oily taste of the cheese, stared upwards at the blue sky, stared into the blue, through and beyond the blue. He ate his sandwiches like that, present in one place but drifting towards another, thinking, the best he could, of nothing, and trying not to think of what happened to him in the Dark Entry.

It was so, incredibly hard.

Birdsong. On the outer edge of his hearing. He focused on it. A blackbird.

Da-de-dilly-da-dot.

De-dilly-da-dot-dot.

The song lasted for a time, settled his inner being, aided his escape from the demands that had been heaped upon him, the demands he'd heaped upon himself, but inevitably the blackbird's song became the chirp-chirp of starlings and then, abruptly, the chip of his pitcher on the stone, the chip-chip of his pitcher, repetitive, deliberate, busy. Always busy. Became chattering, the chattering of tiny voices, then just one voice, a disturbing presence, something that had been bothering him since that evening in the Dark Entry. Something intrusive. Something that refused to let him be.

He startled himself awake. His sandwich lay half-eaten on his lap. A robin appeared beneath the bench, picked up a crumb and zipped away. He sighed. The long days on the project, the intricate precision of the work, were doing things to his nerves. He was flattered to have been given the task, but he'd not truly understood the gravity of it, not foreseen the extended hours, the lost weekends, the stress it would cause at home. He'd not realized how Lucy would be less than under-standing, less than appreciative of the extra income, somehow unable, or unwilling, to connect one with the other.

It wasn't working out with Lucy. They had become separate, con-nected only by their joint responsibility for Ava. For a while work had been a welcome respite, but it hadn't lasted. The feeling of escape had become tainted by the daily anxiety of returning to an emotionally cold house, a tense atmosphere, mounting resentment on both sides.

And then everything shifted.

First there had been the incident in the Dark Entry. It happened one evening after work. He'd locked up his studio and made his way through the Dark Entry in the direction of the Green Court. He surely hadn't imagined the unnatural presence that revealed itself, the disturbed thing at his shoulder, somehow both pressing against and recoiling from him in the same instant, hadn't imagined the profound feeling of dread that had overcome him, a feeling that seemed to emanate from the very shadows themselves. Nor had he imagined the smell that infiltrated his nostrils, not just damp, not just decay. If malignity had an odor, that is what he had smelt.

He spoke about it. Of course he did. The others, those that knew, smiled impishly as they told him the tale of the servant who had been walled up in the Dark Entry, the suffering she'd endured, the things she'd cried out about the father of her unborn child, the curses she'd made before she fell silent, until she was just a story, someone who may or may not have been, something that had happened or never happened.

Two days later, whilst he was still reeling from the experience, still trying to make sense of it, came the discovery of the raised gland on Ava's neck.

He remembered the cold, indefatigable terror of the moment, the ill-advised internet searches that followed, the alarm bells ringing louder and louder. He recalled Ava's eyes looking up at his, the fear he felt as he looked back at her. Him trying to hide his fear. To not let it out.

"How do you feel?" he asked, again and again.

"Fine," she said.

"You don't feel tired? You don't feel unwell?"

"No, silly," she said. And smiled. Enough to melt his heart.

The car parks. The waiting. The doctors and nurses. The stark, sterile corridors. The immeasurable contrast between the hospital buildings and his place of work. The tests. The impenetrable numbers. The opaque unknowing mixed with the stark clarity of the process. The long dark hours. The lying awake. The pondering. The searching. The burrowing deep, deep, deep into the soul. The silent, hypocritical prayers. To anybody and anything that might answer.

The promises he'd made.

That he knew he couldn't keep.

And all the while, Lucy more distant, further and further removed, unrecognizable from the person he had once thought he loved.

And all the while that smell infiltrating his nostrils, so that he caught it here and there unexpectedly. Something threatening. Something hostile. Something taking pleasure in his torment. Something that wanted to deny others what had been denied of itself.

Meanwhile, the job forever pressing.

"Take your time," they said. "There's no rush."

"Let us know," they said.

"Someone else can do it," they said.

"No," he said. "No, they can't do it. No. No. No."

So here he was, wrestling with the work, fighting to meet a deadline that had been stretched as far as it could possibly be stretched. The scaffolding was due to come down. The sculpture would be the last thing to go up and then the scaffolding would come down. So the sculpture had to be ready.

The robin made one more trip and then didn't reappear. He walked back through the gardens and the herbarium. A cluster of half-bored schoolchildren were gathered in the Great cloisters, a guide talking to them about the origins of the cathedral stone. Their blue and white uniforms. Their bags of many colors. He met eyes with a young girl. Her dark hair. Her perfect skin. He thought of Ava, not yet at school, and felt the dread of a moment yet to pass. What if she never went to school, wore a uniform, the little white socks and black shoes?

He ducked indoors, made his way through the choir and down the stone steps into the crypt. The smell of damp. The mustiness. More noticeable to him now. He passed the smudged black shape on one of the columns there. Always fun to watch the tourists encounter it for the first time. The ghost of a clergyman according to the story. Hardly imaginative. But only a story, one he would have dismissed under normal circumstances, one he *had* dismissed. Except now he found himself stopping at the column and studying it.

And wondering.

Tall and shrouded it loomed over him. For the first time, he saw something darker in its form, malevolent intent, and for a second, no more than a second, he felt an uncomfortable tremor in the base of his spine.

Something had loosened his grip on things. Since that singular, almost imperceptible moment in the Dark Entry he'd started imagining the stories of tormented monks and tortured servants to be real, so that every moment he spent alone in the vaults of the cathedral, in the silent gardens and surrounds, filled him with anxiety. And sadness. As if he was akin to the many ghosts about the estate and capable of experiencing their suffering. He told himself nothing had changed, that he didn't believe in any of it, but he felt as though he believed in all of it. Perhaps this was what it meant to be haunted. Not so much a fear of what one had witnessed, more the fear of what one *might* witness, so that living became ominous expectancy and a person strung out.

He worked in a place that held death at its core. It was present in everything. Once it had been a comfort to him, made him feel time was not linear but circular instead, so that everything was part of what had come before and what was yet to be. Now though, with Ava on his mind, such thoughts terrified him, as though there would be no escaping the agony of losing her, just an endless spiral of recurring despair.

He reached his studio, pushed open the door and flicked on the light. There were mouse droppings on the floor. He brushed them away. The sculpture was as he'd left it. Of course it was. He circled it, trying to comprehend it. He was meant to be following the drawing but the thing coming out of the stone was nothing like the drawing. He didn't understand how it had come to be so. But here it was, a monstrosity unfolding before him. It was meant to be a human face, and it was, two eyes, a nose, a mouth, but he hadn't intended it to look this way, so hostile, so twisted, so angry with the world. He imagined the face a century from now, high on the north-west tower, eaten by wind and rain. He imagined a future stonemason scratching his head, trying somehow to reconcile the drawing with the horrific thing it had become. It was meant to be male but this thing he'd created was discernibly female.

Still, he set himself to work, trying to save it, chipping away, chip-chip chipping, shaving, sculpting, as was his craft, his vocation. He worked beyond his hours, focused wholly on the task. Then he downed tools and set about tidying up for the night. He stepped back, eyed it from a distance. It was no better. If anything it was angrier. He lifted the dust sheet to cover it, moved to the door and turned out the light. The sudden dark reached out toward him as he pulled the door shut. He felt its chill fingers on his collar.

He walked down the Long Passage, avoiding the Dark Entry, experiencing the now familiar reluctance to go home, the gathering dread. He wanted to see Ava before her bedtime but he did not want to see Lucy. He wondered when that had changed.

He drifted to the pub instead, ordered a pint and took himself to a quiet corner where he could see what was coming at him. He supped his pint and sketched in his little notebook, not thinking, just affecting something on the page, shaping how he imagined the sculpture was meant to look, recalling what he had seen in the shape of it before he covered it with the sheet.

And how the two were not the same.

It was in the anguished nature of the eyes, the overextended mouth. It was in those things.

The pub door opened. For a moment he felt the darkness enter the place and the menace of its presence. A couple walked in. They sat across from him. They laughed about something. A shared secret. He thought about Lucy, their lack of laughter. He thought about the future. It stretched before him, barren and featureless. But first there was Ava to consider, another round of tests. She was all that mattered. She really was.

He finished his pint and left. Deep winter. Mist in the air. Everything shrouded and ambiguous. The darkness thick and heavy, threatening in a way he'd forgotten it could be threatening.

The alleyway leading to his gate was the worst part. It reminded him of the Dark Entry. He felt something behind him, something on the path. He smelled something, a smell like wet stone, or he thought he did. The job was seeping into his being.

When he reached the house it was quiet. He closed the door silently behind and him sat in the kitchen for a time, watching the mist through the window.

He and Lucy were renting a place that backed on to the city cemetery. So there was that too, a constant reminder of mortality. Sometimes he walked amongst the stones, and lately, only lately, he'd found himself singling out the delicately decorated shrines of newly buried children.

He couldn't imagine. He truly couldn't imagine.

The cemetery contained further oddities, foxes, owls, other creatures of the night. He heard them in the dark hours. He'd come home a few weeks back to find the scattered, bloodied remnants of some poor creature on his lawn. He'd feared it was Ava's rabbit, but it wasn't. Clearing the carcass away with a shovel he'd turned to look at the house to find Ava staring at him out of the conservatory window. He'd raced inside, ushered her away.

None of Ava's test results led in a specific direction. They meandered from specialist to specialist, Ava showing no signs of being ill, but the gland remaining pronounced, as if her body knew something nobody else knew. And deep down inside a particular dread wouldn't leave him, that it was only a matter of time before the symptoms of something serious presented themselves.

In bed beside Lucy, a presence filled the space between them. Something cold. He stared over her shoulder at the bedroom window, the gap in the curtains, the prowling darkness beyond. He watched it as it watched him. He woke three times in the night to the sound of Ava coughing. Each time, he rose and stood in the moonlit room gazing down at his daughter, filled by a surge of love so powerful it almost overwhelmed him.

He told himself it was just a cough.

Just a cough.

Into the vaults then. Another day on the job. Into the dark recesses, the underbelly of the cathedral beyond the trail and traipse of visitors, feeling the darkness seeping into his soul, a burrowing cold in his body and his mind, his mental state affected, darkly damaged.

The Long Passage seemed longer, unfamiliar to him. He heard a noise, a door closing, and turned his head, expecting to see someone behind him, one of the clergy, a member of facilities, an archivist, a guide. There was nobody. Just the hollow echo of his footsteps. But still he felt it, the presence of something, an otherness. He reached the studio door and took out his keys. The metallic jangle was amplified in the passage. He pushed the key into the lock. As he did, he heard a sound beyond the door, a startled movement he thought, something alarmed by his arrival. Interrupted.

He hesitated.

He looked back over his shoulder and down the Long Passage, unusually eager for company. But there was no one. Only him. As he pushed the door open something dropped to the floor in his studio. He heard the sharp sound of one of his tools striking the stone tiles, bouncing and clattering to a standstill. There was a terrible moment when he was met by an impenetrable slab of darkness. He reached for the light switch and could not find it, felt himself stricken, horrifyingly exposed, with the emptiness of the Long Passage behind him and the smothering blackness of his studio ahead. His fingers located the switch and in the nanosecond before the light flooded the room, he saw something, or he thought he did, a pair of tormented eyes peering back at him. And then the light filled the space and all was ordinary.

Or almost ordinary.

One of his pointing trowels was lying on the stone floor. Perhaps he'd left it precariously placed on his bench. The rush of air had dislodged it. The eyes were just a reflection of the light from the corridor on a surface. Of course they were.

And a dead mouse. Wet fur. Tiny teeth laced with blood. Its eye looked up at him, through him, beyond him, into a vast emptiness.

He pulled the cover off the sculpture. The grotesque stared back at him. Its expression had changed. It seemed to be smirking. He carried the dead mouse to the bin. He must tell facilities about them, about how they were everywhere.

He worked through the morning under the bare light. Now and then, between the chip-chip of his pitcher, he heard the sound of staff walking along the Long Passage, and voices, mumbled and indecipherable. Nobody came to see how he was getting on. Nobody at all.

Lunch in the garden. His respite. A golden carpet of leaves on the four-square lawn, the steps slippery with fallen leaves and matter, precarious, dangerous, a devil to navigate. A person could fall, bang their head on the stone. The unsettling silence of the garden on this day. Nobody came through the stone archway. Nobody walked across the garden, following the path. The air was thick with moisture that clung to him, a heavy, cloying fog that seemed a sentient being, capable, almost, of life.

He consumed his sandwiches, rose to his feet and walked, tentatively, back in the direction of his studio, the mist thickening, rolling and rippling all around him. The path at his feet. The border of the path at the very edge of his vision. The manicured lawn swallowed by mist. The hulking, monolithic cathedral nothing but a dull and shapeless shadow, monstrous and massive, reducing him to insignificant nothingness. As he turned down the little path by the yew tree the cathedral rose up before him, doubling and trebling in its vastness.

Over there was the Dark Entry. He couldn't see it. He could only sense it. Only feel the thing that was confined within it. But it had touched him. It had singled him out and cursed him. Cursed him, his wife and his daughter. He was certain of it. Or *she* had.

He hurried, dangerously, back inside. He stopped in the choir. The stalls were empty. He stood amongst them, listening. Something above him. Something high up. A movement there. Something watching him. Something concealing itself. Something that wanted to inflict pain upon him. He studied the balcony. There was nothing to see, except perhaps the light and shadow fluctuating there, creating soft shapes that ebbed and billowed, neither there or not there, real or unreal. He turned away, pushed open the door to the Long Passage, made his way back to his studio.

Later, much later, he draped the dust sheet over the sculpture, moved to the door. He turned to look at the sculpture one more time. A single draped sheet in the middle of the studio. A shapeless ghost. He closed the door and walked down the Long Passage. He told himself he couldn't hear the sheet dragging along the floor, that if he returned to the studio now he would not find the sheet in a crumpled heap on the stone tiles, that the sculpture was not living, that it could not live, that it was only made of stone.

He turned into the cobbled streets, the mist thick in the darkness, the Christmas lights subdued and softened, people hunkered close to each other, or into themselves, shoulders pulled tight, collars high, hands buried in pockets. Music from a bar somewhere. Muffled and muted. He thought about Christmas drawing forever closer, and that led him, rapidly, to thoughts of Ava. He felt a chill in his bones and a desperate longing for a past domestic contentedness that he could barely recall.

He spent the night drifting in and out of nightmares.

Arguments with Lucy.

Ava's cough.

The timeless thing in the Dark Entry. He felt its loitering presence in the heavy darkness of the room and the heavier darkness of sleep. He felt *her* presence.

He woke with a start, sat up, sucked in a lungful of air. He stared about the room, orientating himself, securing himself. He got out of bed and went to the bathroom. He stood over the toilet for a time. But he didn't need the toilet. It was all in his head. He wandered back along the landing and poked his head into Ava's room. It was dark inside. He couldn't see anything. He considered creeping up to her bed, making sure she was okay, but he chose not to. The last thing they needed now was for him to wake her.

He returned to his own bed, rested his head on the pillow and turned to face Lucy's back, stared at the curve of her shoulder and her skin that looked like stone. He reached out across the space between them to touch her and then drew his hand away. He lay in bed listening to the sound of Lucy breathing, a sound like a breeze gusting through a stone archway, and listening to the sounds of the night. He drifted towards sleep, was awakened by squealing and screaming. A fox at the rabbit? He leapt out of bed, raced across the landing and down the stairs. He reached the back door, opened it, stared out on to the lawn, felt the chill air on his nakedness.

The sound transformed, became the sound of Ava screaming from within the house. He ran back up the stairs and into Ava's room. He flicked on the light. Ava's bed was empty. Her bedroom window was open. He ran to the window and looked down upon the moonlit gardens.

He thought he saw something underneath the neighbor's cherry tree, something skulking away with something struggling in its arms. Something with a stretched mouth and anguish ridden eyes. Something like a woman but not a woman. Something unimaginable.

He ran back downstairs and out onto the lawn. He peered over the fence. The thing was gone. There was just the smell, the lingering odor, something festering. He thought of the Dark Entry. Surely not. He turned, raced back upstairs. Frantic. Breathless. Hot despite the chill. Ava stood in the bathroom doorway, bleary eyed.

"What's happening?" she asked.

He picked her up, pulled her close to him.

"Nothing," he said. "Nothing at all."

He carried Ava to her room, lay her in bed, tucked her in with her favorite teddy. He waited for her to drift off. He felt the side of her neck with the ends of his fingers, pressed his fingertips against the hardened, exaggerated lump that would not go away. He walked to the bedroom window and looked down into the neighbor's garden. Everything was ordinary. Everything was as it should be. He wondered if he was losing his mind.

"A few more days," he said to Lucy the next morning. "Then we'll talk."

"What if I don't want to talk," she said.

"Then we won't talk."

"Good," she said. "Because there's nothing to talk about."

"I can't believe you slept through all of that last night," he said.

"I can't believe you didn't wake me," she said.

He looked at the clock.

"I have to go," he said.

He walked into the living room, kissed Ava on the forehead. He reached to feel her neck. She pushed him away.

"I'll see you later," he said.

He pulled on his boots by the back door, grabbed his jacket. The sky was gray. It was drizzling with rain. He closed the door behind him, walked down the garden, reached the gate and swung it open.

He was at the end of the road when his phone buzzed into life. A message from Lucy.

I want a separation.

Four words. Clear and precise. He stared at them.

He felt nothing except an emptiness, a hollow acceptance of what had come to pass between them.

He pulled his hood tight, slogged down the alleyway, trudged through the next alley and the next, keeping his head low, striding as purposefully as he could. He continued down the hill into town. Everything dark. Everything dismal. Barely anybody around. The streets sodden with rain. The fast-flowing, mud-brown river churning as it went.

The city center was quiet, the cobbles glazed with rain. Everything miserable. Everything lifeless. He reached the Butter-Market. A few souls milling about, hardy tourists in outdoor wear, cagoules, and umbrellas, the coffee shop opposite the cathedral gate full to bursting, the window misty with condensation.

He traipsed through the gathering puddles, pulled out his pass and showed it to the woman in the little shelter. Her in her blue anorak. She nodded silently. He looked up to see the great tower looming over him. The heavy clouds rolled over it so that it looked as if it were falling. But it wasn't falling. It was stalwart and timeless. Long after he and Lucy and Ava had gone, the tower would still be there. It would be there forever.

The Dark Entry would be there forever.

Lucy called him. He pondered not answering his phone, then relented. He stood in the cloisters by the Chapter House and talked to the mother of his sick child.

"I'm taking Ava to my mum's," she said.

"How can you think about this now?" he said. "How can you think about anything at a time like this?"

"It's this that's made things clear," she said.

He called the hospital. The specialist wasn't available. He spoke to a nurse instead.

"I'm waiting on some test results," he said. "My child. My daughter."

He gave Ava's name.

No tests results had come in.

"I'm sure they'll be here soon," said the nurse.

"But when?" he asked.

"Soon," said the nurse. "Any time now. Perhaps today even. We'll call you the moment they arrive."

He put the phone down.

He wandered in the direction of the Dark Entry, stopped before the arch. There was nobody around. He scanned the shadows. There was nothing there. He thought about the thing he had seen in the garden, the terrible thing cradling something in its arms. Beyond the Dark Entry was the tunnel that led by the infirmary hall to the Long Passage, a route he'd taken a thousand times, but he hesitated this time, frightened of the thing he had seen.

"No," he said to himself. "Come on."

He stepped forwards, felt the shadows tighten around him, like a shroud, like a heavy blanket. He stopped. He stood perfectly still. He felt something at his shoulder, but he didn't turn around. He would not look at it. Would not look at *her*. But he knew for certain that she was there. He could smell her. He could sense her here in the Dark Entry, a place that never knew sunlight. That had never known sunlight. Or warmth.

And this thing, he knew now, had never known sunlight or warmth, had never known touch or intimacy or love. Or if she had, she had lost those things in unimaginable ways. He felt her move, felt her shift in the space behind him. He felt the anger emanating from her, the suppression of all things good for all things evil. Because of what had happened to her.

"What do you want?" he asked.

He felt her breath on his neck and he knew that if he turned he would see her, that she would be the same as the sculpture he was creating against his will, that she would have the same eyes, the same mouth, the same agonized expression.

He knew he was paying for her torment, that after him there would be others, that there was nothing he could do to save himself.

Unless.

He left the Dark Entry behind him, marched into the vaults, into the chill and the damp. Those things were inside him now. They had infiltrated his being, become part of him. He didn't care about those things any longer. He would destroy the sculpture, take his hammer and chisel and smash it to pieces. He would do that and then it would be over. All of it would be over. That thing, looking at him. That face. Those eyes. The thing it had become. He would drive the chisel through it. Through *her*.

When he reached the studio the door was wedged open. He turned on the light. The sculpture wasn't there. There was just the empty bench. He turned and raced along the passage, through the nave and out into the grounds. He reached the fenced off section beneath the scaffolding. He stared through the mesh. They were hoisting the sculpture towards its home on the corner of the tower. He watched it slowly rise towards the rolling clouds.

The sound of a forklift reversing broke the spell, the repetitive warning of the alarm incongruous in this place, an intrusion. He shouted out over it, caught the attention of the supervisor in his hi-vis jacket and white helmet. The supervisor turned and walked towards him, clipboard in hand.

"We had to take her," said the supervisor. "It was now or never, and they wouldn't accept never."

The sculpture reached its level. Three or four men were up there. He saw them pull it in towards them.

"She looks great," said the supervisor. "She really does. You've done a fantastic job."

"But she's not finished," he shouted through the mesh. "You can't take her yet. She's not finished."

The supervisor shrugged. The forklift trundled to a stop. The alarm cut out. For a long second there was just the somber clouds, the crane jib and the empty hook swinging in the void where the sculpture had been.

His phone started ringing. He lifted it from his pocket and stared at the screen. The hospital was calling him.

He hesitated.

He turned to look back at the Dark Entry. The shadows under the archway were deep and condemning and he knew she was watching him, reveling in this moment, reveling in his dread. She was gaunt and naked and her mottled skin was like wet stone. She was cradling her stomach in such a way. Her face was frozen in a silent, grief-stricken scream.

His phone was still ringing. The supervisor was staring at him.

He couldn't answer his phone.

He simply couldn't.

DESICCANT

CRAIG LAURANCE GIDNEY

The Bellona Heights Apartments were rundown. The pavement of the open semi-courtyard had cracks, concrete wounds that oozed out moss and straggling weeds. An old fountain, spattered with bird droppings, was filled with stagnant rainwater and trash. The first level beige brick had graffiti, scrawls of obscene words and nonsense shapes spread across it. The balconies that faced the courtyard were over-stuffed with plants, bicycles and rusting lawn furniture. The cornices were crumbling. Hiphop and Reggaeton blasted from open windows.

Tituba shuddered in revulsion. But she had no choice, did she?

You get what you pay for, she thought, and a one bedroom in Bellona Heights was what she could afford. At least she'd found a place to live on such short notice. Her sister's new boyfriend, Vaughn, had threatened to change the locks one too many times. Tituba loved her sister Leah, but her choice in men was terrible. At least Juan, the last one, didn't misgender her. Yes, this place was below her standards, but, she reasoned, the lease was only for one year. And surely, she could find a more suitable place by then?

Inside the building, Tituba saw worn linoleum and the chipped paint on the walls. She picked up her keys at the office from a sullen clerk who couldn't pull her eyes away from a game on her phone and rode the old gear-grinding elevator up to the fourteenth floor. Phantom odors drifted down the hallway: weed, old fried fish and of course, boiled cabbage. Boiled cabbage was the smell of despair and deferred dreams.

1412 was semi-furnished, with a futon/couch frame and dresser-drawers. It was on the other side of the building, so there was no balcony. The window faced the alley, which was full of dumpsters.

At least it was clean, for the most part. The only visible flaw was the discoloration right outside the air-conditioning vent. Carmine smears dribbled from the grate. Tituba touched it before she thought better of it. She felt a powdery dust on her fingertips, surprised to find that it was not dried paint or even worse, blood.

Fabiana was late, as she always was. Tituba had been sitting at the café for a good fifteen minutes. She entered the space with a dramatic flair, her face wrapped in a bright orange scarf, and wearing bejeweled sunglasses. Her hands were encased in some silvery gloves. Heads turned, whispers came up from the other tables. She always wanted to be noticed. While Tituba had her moments, for the most part she wanted to be left alone.

Fabiana air-kissed her and then ordered an Americano and a low-fat blueberry muffin. She ignored both of the items.

"How's the new place? And when's the housewarming?"

Fabiana asked her as she removed her sunglasses, revealing violet-colored contact lenses.

"The place is ratchet, so there will not be a housewarming party. Leah and that scrub Vaughn practically tossed me out into the street."

"I thought Leah had your back," Fabiana said.

"She usually does," Tituba said, "when she's not dick-a-matized. Vaughn pitched a fit when one of his boys asked him for my number. He threw around the words, 'she-male,' and tranny and accused me of flirting. Leah didn't stop him. She became a whole other person. Meek and useless."

"Girl, if he had called *me* those names, I'd have sliced him up. I still carry my knife, in case anyone is fixing to get smart with me!"

"Trust me, it got ugly. He was all, 'What type of crazy name is

Tituba?' Frankly, I was angrier at my sister than I was at him. I felt betrayed."

"I'm so sorry for you," Fabiana said. "Do you want me to do something to teach this dude a lesson? I know some people."

"No," she replied. "I guess this is part of my journey. I thought I'd lucked out and wouldn't have to go through people around me rejecting who I was."

"I don't blame you," Fabiana replied. She finally ate a bite of her muffin. A tiny bird bite. "You sleeping all right?" she asked.

"No . . . Why do you ask?"

"Them bags under your eyes, child. You know what will fix them? Hemorrhoid cream. It tightens the skin."

"I am not about to put ass cream under my eyes!" Tituba said. Both of them laughed loudly, causing the other café patrons to glance in their direction.

Fabiana said playfully, "Keep it classy, bitch!"

Tituba swatted at her hand. "Oh, hush. Seriously, though. Falling asleep isn't the problem. Hell, *staying* asleep isn't, either. I sleep, but I wake up tired, as if I had a tough work out at the gym or gone a few rounds with a boxer. And when I wake up, there's always some weird reddish dust on me. And it's not just me. My neighbors all look . . . drained. One day, I saw a kid at the bus stop and his collar had stains of that red dust."

"Huh," said Fabiana. "Have you heard about Sick Building Syndrome? It's a place where all of the occupants get headaches and permanent sniffles. And fatigue. I think the *Post* did a series about it—one of the buildings owned by the EPA had it, and they had to close it."

"The *effing* Environmental Protection Agency had a 'sick building'?"

"You have to get out of there," Fabiana said, "Or, you need to get all *Norma Rae* on the building supervisor!"

Dust! Miles and miles, dune after dune of rust-red, as far as her eye could see. A red that was the color of old blood, slowly changing from crimson to brown.

She stood knee-deep in the middle of a valley, surrounded by mounds of the stuff. The sky above was hidden, obscured by a veil of red powder. She was sinking under, unable to get purchase on the feathery ground. The clothes she wore were reduced to blood-stained rags. It looked like she was shedding a membranous skin, like a snake. Her skin had abrasions, a network of thin cuts that were crusted over and flaking.

She must move on, before being swallowed whole by the wavering ground. If she didn't move, she would drown and die, forever preserved beneath, a beautiful mummy no one would ever see. She must move, or else she would die.

She lifted one foot clear of the squelching redness. And the wind began to blow. Dust rose up into the air, into a corrosive mist that erased her body. Soon, she could not see anything. All was lost in the simoom.

Tituba woke up coughing. Her body shuddered with the fit. She could feel something rattling in her chest, as if her body were a percussion instrument filled with dry rice. After the fit was over, she got up and switched the light on. Her tongue was heavy in her mouth, so she stumbled to the sink and drank two full glasses of water before she felt relatively normal.

She put the glass in the sink, checked the time. It was 3:30 a.m., early enough for a second shift of sleep. But she was too wired to get back into her bed. And it seemed that she wasn't the only person up at this hour. The floor above her creaked with footsteps. Bellona's paper-thin walls revealed activity on either side of her apartment, coughing on the left, the plaintive voice of a distressed child on the right.

Tituba knew that falling back to sleep would be difficult, so she pulled her phone from her charging port. Her headphones were on the ottoman next to her futon. That's when she first noticed the red dust. It was all over her mattress and futon, a fine sifting of rust-colored powder. She touched it. It didn't feel of anything. It was not coarse or smooth. It was feathery and insubstantial, even though she expected it to have a gritty feel like sand or salt. Then, it moved. An infinitesimal slither through her fingers, a blur of micro-movement. Reflexively, Tituba shook the stuff off her fingers and headphones.

It wouldn't come off. There was a slight disturbance, but then the powder-dust settled back. It clung to the curve of the headphones, the whorl of her fingertips. Tituba rubbed at the dust, hoping to dislodge it with friction. That did not work. Her fingertips were stained.

She muttered a curse word or two under her breath. She ran water over the stubborn stain at the kitchen sink.

A piece of dried skin, embossed with a fingerprint, fell off her hand, leaving behind tender new skin. She watched as the opaque red crinkled skin settled in the sink.

The powder-dust plumped up with the water. Fat with sudden moisture, the flakes began to rise upward, as if buoyed by an unfelt breeze. Red drops of old blood hung in the air, hovered. Then, they burst open.

Tituba screamed.

The office door was locked, as it had been for the past two weeks. Tituba had stopped by the superintendent's office before and after work, on the weekend, but the door had always been locked. The emails she sent were unanswered, and the phone calls went straight to voicemail.

She didn't know if she'd even seen him during the time she'd been in Bellona Heights. Her neighbors confirmed that he was elusive and unreachable at the best of times. Everyone she'd spoken to had given her a "why bother" attitude. When she told the residents in the mailroom or lobby about the mysterious, weird dust she'd seen, they just shrugged, as if defeated.

One time in the laundry room, she asked Phylis, an older woman who lived on the same floor, if she knew anything.

Phylis had been folding a child's clothes when Tituba entered the shabby basement with a week's worth of dirty clothing. Phylis had grudgingly given her a greeting when Tituba broached the subject.

"Yeah, I've seen it," Phylis had said, dripping with attitude. "Folks made a stink about it, back in the day. Nothing happened."

"But it must be unhealthy. So many people here have respiratory problems."

"And?" Phylis said, as she went to unload a dryer that had just buzzed. "Ain't nobody who owns this glorified flophouse care about our health. This ain't Northwest."

DESICCANT

Tituba purposefully ignored the bitterness dripping from Phylis's voice. "Maybe not. But the dust isn't natural. I hear it rattling in the vent, like tiny ants. Like it's alive . . ."

Phylis stopped folding the laundry and threw it into the basket. "You're a fine one to talk about 'unnatural' things," she announced as she headed to the door.

Tituba said, "Excuse me?"

But Phylis was already out of the room.

Now, she stood in front of the office door for the umpteenth time. She jiggled the lock, even though she knew there was no point. Maybe Phylis was right, and she should leave well enough alone. But she couldn't. Tituba's entire existence had been full of struggle, starting from birth, and it didn't look like it was going to get easy any time soon. The dancing dust was just one more obstacle to overcome.

Tituba went to the mailroom instead. She found the tiny room was full of packages and guessed that some of them were nebulizers and humidifiers. All week long, residents had unboxed the machines in the room, leaving a pile of broken-down cardboard boxes. She had toyed with getting one herself, to combat the dryness in the building.

Fabiana was right. Bellona Heights was a sick building. Ever since she'd moved in, she had been plagued with low-key headaches that threatened to grow into full-on migraines. Her stomach was unsettled, and food tasted weird. Walking down a city block easily winded her. And she began to notice discolorations on her skin: darkness beneath her eyes and white spots on her arms. Most of all, she was always thirsty. She would drink bottle after glass of water or juice, but she could never be satisfied. She didn't pee often, for the amount she drank. Where did it all go?

She passed by the superintendent's door, in futile hope.

"Warren not in again?" said someone behind her. It was Ty, who also lived on her floor. He was around her age and height, with a muscular lithe physique. His skin was dark and velvet-smooth, his bald head glowing with head wax. At least, that *had* been his appearance. Now, crows' feet and forehead wrinkles marred the smooth expanse, and the lustrous blue-blackness of his skin was dried out to a leathery brown.

"Apparently not." Tituba looked away from Ty, hoping that he didn't notice her shocked reaction.

He jiggled the doorknob, as if to verify. Then, he glanced at Tituba, and gave her a conspiratorial wink.

"Desperate times," he said, and he pushed against the door with his shoulder. The door quivered with the pressure and after a few more aggressive pushes, it popped open.

Ty and Tituba were immediately hit with a wave of stale air that had a slight cindery taste. They simultaneously began coughing in response. There was also another smell beneath that one—a smell of turned meat and the coppery tang of old blood. A haze of carmine simmered in the room, thick enough that they both had to wave it away. The shades were drawn, so it was dim in the room.

"Oh, my god," Tituba said, after her eyes adjusted to the gloom.

There was a body slumped over a desk. She knew it was a corpse. The angle of the head looked too uncomfortable to maintain, and the visible eye was open. She switched on the overhead light and immediately wished she hadn't. The older gentleman was in a gray mechanic's suit, and his mouth was opened in a grimace. Dust pooled around the open mouth, onto the desk. It was embedded on his skin, in his hair, and she could see flecks of it in the whites of his eye.

Ty walked around the desk, reached out to touch the body. "Leave it alone," Tituba said.

Ty lowered his hands, and reached for his cellphone instead, presumably to call for an ambulance.

Tituba saw the wrinkled flesh, fold upon fold of thin skin, some of it so dry that the pigment had leeched out. It didn't look like skin. It was papery, cracked like old parchment. And in the folds of skin, remnants of the red dust gathered. His mouth was open, and a crumbled pink tongue lolled out past black and cracked lips.

"He looks like a mummy," Ty said after he finished speaking to the emergency operator. "I wonder how long he's been here."

Tituba heard him, but she was distracted by the thin trail of red dripping down from the HVAC vent.

Whatever lived there had drained the superintendent, had turned him into a husk. His skin had the same color and texture as a tamarind. She could only imagine the poor man's innards, the pulp toughened into sponge and coral.

"He's been sucked dry," Tituba said. "We're gonna end up like him."

With tweezers, Tituba scraped the red residue into an old nail polish bottle she had cleaned out. Something was in the vents, something that left behind this weird substance.

She brought the bottle with her to dinner at a restaurant. The first thing Fabiana said when she saw Tituba was, "Girl, you look ashy and worn out!"

"I know," she replied, waving the comment away. "Listen to me. You were right. Bellona Heights *is* a sick building. Some kind of virus or something lives in the vents and gives everyone who lives there breathing problems!

"Last week, one of the other residents and I found the superintendent dead in his office. His body was dry. Bone dry. Desert dry. All of the moisture had been sucked right out of him."

Tituba pulled up a picture on her phone and handed it to Fabiana.

Fabiana shrieked. "Put that thing away!"

Tituba complied.

Fabiana said, "I don't think I've ever seen anything so terrible. Poor dude. He looks like one of those apple head dolls."

"I asked the EMTs if they were gonna do an autopsy to determine the cause of death. They ignored me."

Fabiana sucked her teeth in sympathetic dismay. "They always do. And we end up dead because they won't listen!"

Tituba dug around in her handbag until she found and pulled out the nail polish bottle.

"Look at it, Fab. Look closely."

"Look at an empty bottle of Carolina Beet lacquer?" Fabiana cautiously picked the bottle up and peered into it.

"Stop kidding around, girl. Tell me what you see."

Fabiana stared at it for a long moment, still looked as the server refilled their wine glasses with rosé.

Finally, she said, "That dust moves."

"I'm glad you saw that too! I thought I was going crazy!"

Fabiana still held the bottle close to her eye. "I don't think it's dust, Tituba. I saw one fragment of whatever-it-is, apart from the others, move on its own. I see wings. Tiny, infinitesimal scarlet wings. The wings of a moth, not a butterfly. The straggler eventually joined the rest of the swarm, I suppose. And it looked like a swirling dust."

"You think it's insects?"

Fabiana shrugged in response. "I don't know. All I *do* know is, you have to get the hell out of there!"

Tituba was unlocking the door to her apartment when she heard the scream. It came from down the hall. She found herself running there and knocking on the door until Phylis, the grandmother who lived there with her daughter Krystle and grandson Kendrick, opened it.

"What's wrong, Miss Phylis?" she asked.

Miss Phylis was wild-eyed and apoplectic, apparently unable to speak. She gestured weakly to an opened doorway off the L-shape of the apartment. More screams came from there, mostly Krystle saying, "Lord, lord, lord!" Tituba left Miss Phylis behind to look in the doorway.

She tried to make sense of the bizarre scene. This was obviously a child's room, full of Thomas the Tank Engine paraphernalia, the google-eyed train's face on toys and curtains and posters, with its frozen smile stretched across the face. The walls were splattered with moving constellations that came from a projector lamp. Tituba saw little Kendrick being cradled by his mother, in what looked like a grotesque parody of the *Pietá*, his limp body draped over her lap. His eyes were closed and fluttering, as if he were fighting to keep them open, some nightmare thing wouldn't let him wake up. Things moved on his unconscious body. Scarlet specks, a tide of them spilling over his pajamas, arms, and face. The tiny little blister-colored things vibrated as they moved. And they moved with purpose, heading for his nostrils and slightly opened mouth. She imagined the minuscule things coating his nasal passages, flurrying in the chambers of his sinuses, ricocheting and embedding themselves in spongy alveoli as they drank up the mists of the boy's body, drying out mucus membranes, turning plasma into dust. She heard Kendrick begin to wheeze, heard the raspy rattling in his chest.

Those creatures have done the same thing to me, every night, she thought. She recalled her dreams about Martian-red deserts and dust storms.

She switched on the overhead light. The stars became invisible. The moth-things slowed down, and lazily detached themselves from the child's body. They drifted upward, red motes of dust, heading toward the ceiling, heading toward the grates of the vent. More of them dribbled from Kendrick's nose and mouth. It looked like a twinkling river of blood. Tituba dug around her purse until she found a bottle of spray lotion. She spritzed the red-speckled air with the thick mist, saturating it. A clump of the things fell from the air, a worm-like wriggling ball of red paste with the consistency of snot. The coagulated mess fell on the floor with a wet splat. Tituba, Krystle and Miss Phylis watched with disgust at the wet wings flexing in globules of oily lotion.

Tituba said, "Quick! We have to get the rest of the stuff out of Kendrick! Wake him up and make him drink water. Maybe that will flush them out."

Krystle carried Kendrick into the kitchen, where he blinkingly woke up in the harsher light. They got the confused child to slurp down a couple of glasses of water. Then he began coughing, body-wracking spasmodic coughs. His mother patted his back, calling Kendrick her little angel, her sweetheart, her precious boy.

Then, he vomited.

Out of his mouth came a stream of red paste. They saw the fragments of wings and waterlogged pieces of something drip onto the floor. The swarm of dust-insects was decimated. But more lived in this forgotten, neglected building full of brown and black bodies. Were these tiny, moth-like vampires conscious of what they did as they fed upon sleeping bodies, draining the moisture of breath, crawling down throats? Perhaps they weren't malevolent, these winged specks of decay.

Bellona Heights. More like Hellona Depths.

* * *

Back in her apartment, Tituba blocked the vent with a piece of plywood. It was a temporary measure. She thought of black mold, or *Legionella* bacteria brought to life with some dark magic. She thought about contacting the press or an exterminator. But people ignored the superintendent's death, and the complaints bought by the other residents. It was unlikely that anyone would listen to a black trans woman.

She would have to fix this on her own. Survival was in her DNA. Survival, and its importance, was why she chose her name. Titus, her birth name, had been meek and a victim of the church, his family, and society. Titus would have succumbed to the dust-moths and been one more epidemiological statistic to be ignored.

Tituba, however, would fight. She would survive, like the historical woman she'd named herself after.

As she lay down at 4:00 a.m., exhausted from saving Kendrick's life, she heard the scarlet moths skittering around in the blocked vents, banging against the plywood barrier.

"I dare you," she said.

And she began coughing. Violence was in her lungs, her chest, her throat, her head. She coughed so hard that black spots appeared before her. *Some of those things must've found their way into me.* The malevolent red moths were attacking her, with clear intention. It could not have been a coincidence. They had heard her issued challenge, and now they responded.

If—*when*—Tituba survived this assault, she would destroy miniature dust-demons. She would kill them *tonight*.

OPEN HOUSE ON HAUNTED HILL

JOHN WISWELL

1 33 Poisonwood Avenue would be stronger if it was a killer house. There is an estate at 35 Silver Street that annihilated a family back in the 1800s and its roof has never sprung a leak since. In 2007 it still had the power to trap a bickering couple in an endless hedge maze that was physically only three hundred square feet. 35 Silver Street is a show-off.

133 Poisonwood only ever had one person ever die under its roof. Back in 1989, Dorottya Blasko had refused hospice, and spent two and a half months enjoying the sound of the wind on 133 Poisonwood's shingles. 133 Poisonwood played its heart out for her every day.

The house misses 1989. It has spent so much of the time since vacant.

Today it is going to change that. It is on its best behavior as the realtor, Mrs. Weiss, sweeps up. She puts out trays of store-bought cookies and hides scent dispensers, while 133 Poisonwood summons a gentle breeze and uses its aura to spook any groundhogs off the property. Both the realtor and the real estate need this open house to work.

Stragglers trickle in. They are bored people more interested in snacks than the restored plumbing. The house straightens its aching floorboards, like a human sucking in their belly. Stragglers track mud everywhere. The house would love nothing more than any of them to spend the rest of their lives tracking mud into it.

A heavyset man with sagging shoulders lets himself in. He has a bit of brownie smudged against the back of his parakeet green hoodie and doesn't seem aware of it. Mrs. Weiss gives him a little wave while continuing to hold up a ten-minute conversation with an affluent couple. The couple made the mistake of saying they were "thinking of thinking of conceiving," and Mrs. Weiss wields statistics about the school district like a cowboy wields a lasso. The couple's shoes likely cost more than a down payment on the house, but from how often they check their phones, they clearly are headed back to their Mercedes.

The man with the brownie-stained hoodie prowls through 133 Poisonwood's halls, and it pulls its floorboards so straight that its foundations tremble.

The man doesn't look at 133 Poisonwood's floor. He looks at the couple of ripples in the green floral wallpaper, with the expression of someone looking at his own armpit.

The house feels ashamed of the loose wallpaper. It's vintage painted silk, which Mrs. Weiss says could be a big value-add. Now the house ponders if it can haunt its own glue and help strip the wallpaper away to please him. It's especially important since he is spending more time here than anyone has yet without Mrs. Weiss wrangling them. It's like he doesn't feel the vibes other visitors do, or he doesn't care about them.

From his behavior, what he cares about is wallpaper, the natural lighting through the windows in the master bedroom and the kitchen.

A child stomps in through the front door, her frizzy hair in three oblong pigtails she probably did herself. A silver keepsake locket clashes with her bright green Incredible Hulk t-shirt. Her elbows are tucked into her chest, hands out like claws, stained with brownie bits.

Every step she takes is deliberate and channels all her tiny body weight to be as heavy as possible. If the house had to guess, the girl is probably pretending to be a dinosaur on the hunt.

The man in the brownie-stained hoodie glances at her. He asks, "Ana. Where's your coat?"

Ana bellows, "I hate clothes!"

Ana apparently hates clothes so much she immediately grabs the bottom of her Hulk T-shirt and yanks it up over her head. She is careful to keep her locket in place but chucks the shirt at the man. He grabs for her, and she ducks between his arms, bolting past Mrs. Weiss and the affluent couple, pigtails and locket bouncing.

In their chase, they leave the front door open. The house knows heating oil is expensive. It summons a spectral breeze to shut it for them.

The sound makes Ana pinwheel around, and she points at the door. She says, "Daddy! It's ghosts!"

Daddy says, "Ana, we talked about this. There's no such thing as ghosts."

"You didn't look."

"You don't have to look for things that aren't there."

Ana looks at her locket and huffs. "What if it's Mommy's ghost?"

Daddy closes his eyes for a moment. "Please just put your shirt back on."

Ana immediately attacks her own pants. "Clothes are for the weak!"

"Put it on or we are leaving, Ana," he says, trying to wrestle clothing onto his daughter. She pushes at him, leaving more brownie residue on his hoodie. As they battle, the affluent couple slips out the front door without closing it.

The house closes it for them. Heating oil isn't cheap.

The triangular roof means the second floor only has the space for one bedroom. Mrs. Weiss reads the expression on Daddy's face, and she attacks with, "The basement is very spacious with generous lighting. It's cool in the summer, and toasty in the winter."

Ana says, "Heights are bad luck anyway."

The four-year-old scarcely looks at the bedroom before backing out. She holds the handrail with both hands as she climbs down the stairs on quivering legs. On the third stair, she freezes entirely.

Daddy is in the middle of surveying the room and misses Ana quivering in place.

Some houses give their residents visions of slaughters or trauma. 133 Poisonwood gives Daddy a swift vision of his daughter's vertigo. He doesn't know it's anyone else's insight, and wouldn't believe it, but he's at the stairs in seconds. Ana holds onto his pants leg until she feels safe.

All 133 Poisonwood has is a light touch, but it knows how to use it. Haunting is an art.

The basement is only half-underground, so the windows are level with the freshly mowed front lawn. Ana spends a moment giggling at the view. Then she whizzes around the basement, from the combination furnace and laundry room, to a storage closet, and to a pair of vacant rooms. They would make a perfect child's bedroom and playroom.

Ana goes to the west room, announcing, "Daddy. You can keep all the ghosts you bust in here."

Mrs. Weiss offers, "One of these could be a home office. You said you telecommute? Google Fiber is coming to the area next year."

Daddy says, "I want to work from home more. I'm a software engineer, and I host a skeptic podcast. You might have heard us."

The house isn't offended. It doesn't believe in ghosts either.

Ana hops back and forth between the two rooms, scrutinizing over and over as though they'll grow. That is a trick the house doesn't have.

Daddy says, "We could sleep next door to each other. What do you think?"

Ana says, "But I want a big dino room."

"You're getting to be a big dinosaur. How about the room on the top floor?"

Ana's bottom lip shoots upward like she's going to run. She clearly won't settle for the room on the top floor, and there's only a master bedroom on the first floor. A tantrum is close, and it could ruin everything.

So 133 Poisonwood plays its ace. Every decent haunted house has at least one secret room. Dorottya Blasko used to sew down here when she didn't want to be pestered, in a room her family couldn't find. It would be a perfect place for Ana to grow up in. Perhaps she'll learn to sew.

With the sound of an affectionate kitten, the door opens. Shock hits the adults, who definitely don't remember there being a room there. Ana doesn't care and runs to explore it.

"Uh, we aren't showing that room," Mrs. Weiss says, scrambling to cover for herself. She's panicking, imagining hazards and lawsuits.

She doesn't understand. 133 Poisonwood is going to clinch the sale for them.

The room runs deep, with an expansive window that hasn't been seen from the outside in over twenty years. A sewing box with a scarlet and royal blue quilted exterior sits next to a rocking chair, and beneath the window is a broad spinning wheel that still smells like hobbies. Many great dresses were supposed to come out of this room. There are a few cracks on the concrete floor. Nothing a loving father can't fill in to perfect his daughter's big dino room.

"Ana," Daddy calls. "Stay near me."

Ana ignores the call and runs straight up to the spinning wheel. Her little hands grab onto spokes in the drive wheel, and she turns to the door. "It's like Mommy's."

Daddy says, "Careful, that's not ours—"

Ana yanks the wheel around to show it off to the adults. She pulls before the house can resist, and the entire device creaks and wobbles. It topples straight down on top of Ana, throwing her to the floor.

Daddy grabs her shoulders and pulls her from between the cracked wheel and treadle. Ana's too distracted bawling to feel her necklace snag the spindle. The thin chain snaps, and the locket slips from her neck and down a crack in the floor. Without intending to, the house sucks the chain down like a strand of spaghetti. The house tries to spit it out.

Daddy squeezes Ana to his chest so hard she could pop, and keeps repeating, "Are you all right? Are you all right?"

Mrs. Weiss gestures and says, "Her hand."

"Are you all right?"

Ana says, "Let me fix it!" She stretches her hands to the broken spinning wheel. One of her hands is bleeding and she still wants to use them to clean up her mess. She says, "Daddy, let go, I'll fix it. Don't make the ghosts sad."

That breaks Daddy's concerned trance, and he lifts her under one arm, ignoring the kicking of her feet. He marches for the stairs. "No. I warned you, and we are leaving."

"Daddy, no!"

"No more. Say goodbye. You see the ghosts aren't saying goodbye? Do you know why?"

An urge falls over the house to slam the door shut and trap them all inside. Daddy, Ana, and even Mrs. Weiss, force them all to spend eternity in its hidden room, where they can make dresses, and stay cool in the summer, and warm in the winter. It will shelter them from all the hurricanes the world can create. It needs them.

The phantom door's hinges and knob tremble as 133 Poisonwood fights itself. In that moment it knows what makes other homes go evil. The killer houses can't bear to be alone.

133 Poisonwood Avenue would be stronger if it was a killer house. But it isn't one.

It leaves its rooms open as Daddy carries his bawling daughter out of the basement, her incoherent sounds resonating through the house's crawl spaces. He carries her up the stairs and out the front door without a backward glance. This time, he remembers to close the door.

133 Poisonwood leaves the secret room open in the hopes that someone will come back. It squeezes the cracks in its floor closed, popping the locket out without scratching it. Inside is the picture of a woman with a thick nose and proud eyes. She would have made an excellent ghost. The house would take a phantom for an inhabitant at this point.

The afternoon is sluggish. There are four more visitors, none of whom stay long enough to check the basement for treasure. The hours chug by, and Mrs. Weiss spends most of the time on her phone.

With half an hour of daylight left, a red sedan pulls up. The driver lingers outside for two minutes before knocking. It's Daddy.

Mrs. Weiss answers and forces a smile, "Ulisses. Is Ana okay?"

Daddy says, "It was a scratch. Thanks for being understanding before."

She says, "I'm so sorry about that. I told the team this place was supposed to be empty."

He says, "Have you seen a locket? Ana wears it everywhere and it's gone missing."

Mrs. Weiss holds the door open for him, "We can check around. What does it look like?"

"It has a picture of Ana's mother inside. It's one of few gifts she still has from her."

"She was your wife?"

"She was going to be," he says, and looks around the master bedroom with an expression even emptier than the space. "There was an accident on our apartment's fire escape. She had a fall."

"Oh, that's terrible."

"Right now, Ana needs all the comfort she can get. So if we can find that locket, it'd save our lives."

They look around, the man so tired every step looks heavy. It's amazing he could stagger into a motel bed, let alone go hunting for a locket. The house hasn't seen someone as in need of a home in years.

Mrs. Weiss says, "I had something like that after my father passed away. Makes her feel like her mother's spirit is still with her?"

"Superstitions aren't comforting to me," he says, fatigue giving way to scorn, as though daring the house's walls to do something. "And Ana's mother was an atheist."

The house is tempted to give Daddy the shock of his life and toss the locket to him. Give him back the image of his lover and proof of its power.

But he doesn't need to believe in hauntings. With his slumped shoulders, and his clothes stained with his daughter's food, and the pieces of their lives he is trying to put together?

What he needs is a win.

So the house uses what little strength it has to levitate the locket onto the top basement stair. It twists it so the light catches it and shines into the upstairs living room.

Daddy finds the precious locket on his own. He bends over it, brushing a thumb over his lover's image. He heaves a sigh through his nose like he wishes he could fit inside the locket.

The house lets him be proud of himself. It will hold onto this memory for the cold years ahead until it is bulldozed.

Daddy stands up without the locket, leaving it behind. The house tries to send him a vision warning that he's forgotten what he came here for.

The mental image doesn't change what he's doing.

He goes right outside, to his sedan where Ana sits, rubbing at her puffy eyes and runny nose. Daddy says, "It might be here. Do you want to help me look?"

The house cannot cry. There is just a little air in its pipes.

Ana flops out of the car and trudges into 133 Poisonwood. She spends too long poking around the kitchen, a room she was barely in earlier. Daddy plays an even worse sleuth, deliberately checking around empty hallways that give him a view of when Ana finally checks the basement door.

"Mommy!" she cheers. She sits right down on the stair and hugs the locket to her throat, voice trembling with emotions too big for her body. "Mommy came back!"

Daddy asks, "So you found it?"

"I told you she'd be here. Mommy wanted me to find it."

"Your mother didn't do that, Ana."

She scrunches her nose and mimics his voice to say, "You don't know that."

Daddy puts a hand over the locket. "You found this. Not anybody else. You don't need ghosts," and he taps her on the temple, "because you have the best parts of your mother inside you."

Ana gazes up at her father with glossy eyes.

133 Poisonwood has never so understood what it wants to do for people as when it watches this parent. It tries to hold onto the vibrations of his voice in its walls.

Then Ana says, "Nah. The ghosts left it here."

She hauls off to the living room, hopping in late afternoon sunbeams, and holding the locket in the light.

Reason is defeated for the moment. Daddy doesn't fight her on it. He rests against the wall, against the wallpaper he hates, taking the house for granted. The house plays a tune on its shingles, the same one that calmed Dorottya Blasko in 1989.

Daddy calls, "Mrs. Weiss?"

"Please, call me Carol," she says. She's been pretending she wasn't lurking ten feet away this whole time. "You're very sweet with Ana. You can just tell some people were born with the knack."

"Three rooms in the basement. This is a lot of house for the money, isn't it?"

"It's just a family short of a home."

133 Poisonwood would be more charmed by the line if it hadn't heard her say that eight other times today.

Daddy says, "I like the space this place has for her. There's plenty of room to run. And she loves to run. Going to be a track and field star."

"I said to myself that this place looks happier when you're in it. It suits you."

The house can tell he wants to say he doesn't believe that.

He says, "What we need is somewhere to start fresh."

Mrs. Weiss offers him a folio of data on the house and gestures to the basement. "Care for another look around?"

"Yeah. Thank you." He takes the folio. "While Ana is playing upstairs, can we check how insulated from sound that sewing room is? It's funny, but I thought it might make a good podcast studio."

If houses could laugh. He sounds so unguarded and sincere.

This tired skeptic doesn't need to know that his podcast room doesn't technically exist. If he finds the blueprints for 133 Poisonwood, he'll shave away what he doesn't understand with Occam's razor. The house doesn't need him to believe in anything but himself and his daughter. It isn't here for the gratitude. It can try to support him as well as he supports Ana. If anything is as patient as a parent, it's a haunting.

THE GENETIC ALCHEMIST'S DAUGHTER

ELAINE CUYEGKENG

*S*he dreams of death and rebirth on her mother's table.

The smell of antiseptic: chemicals, artificial cherries and other-fruit. The specimen on the table. Herself, slipping a needle under the specimen's skin to obtain samples for reconstruction. Finally, the disposal of the body while the new one grows inside her crimson egg, kicking her little amphibian feet. Later, a telepathic matrix imparts an (edited) library of the Prodigal's memories. This reinforces the desired traits, knitted carefully into the genome.

In twelve days and twelve nights, there will be a single, perfected being: waking in the specimen's old room with only a vague, uneasy sense of displaced time. There will be no official record, no trace of the original (save for the genetic profiles, buried deep in her mother's libraries).

Everyone dreams those strange, mundane dreams of themselves performing their daily rites. The genetic alchemist's daughter is no different; why should she be? But still, Leto Alicia Chua Mercado wakes as if she were a child waking from a nightmare. Leto thinks: there are fragments of bone and marrow in her pajamas, in her blankets, her bed. For a moment, her hands are viscous with ruby red.

The Genetic Alchemists

Leto is her mother's daughter, and so, when she wakes, blinking out crimson dreams in the pre-dawn, the day's business is the first thing that occupies her. Nothing in Leto's creation was left to chance; the same is true of Chua Mercado Genetic Alchemy.

Below, the family's laboratories gestate the fruits of several lucrative contracts. Tiny mermaid embryos, for a techno-prince's private aquarium. A new variant of winged cat: Bengal Beauties, with jade eyes and leopard spots, jeweled peregrine's wings. Luminous Moths, ordered by an exclusive fashion house for their silk. There are the Prodigals, the human specimens who will be delivered to their families' holdings, waking in the original's old room as if from a dream.

And finally, there are the little Seraphim, tiny embryos swimming in their exo-wombs. The bulk of these are still ordered by foreign CEOs—grateful for the assurance of a rarefied offspring, grateful to be spared the inconveniences of caring for pregnant wives. One day, Leto's mother hopes, the world will be full of them. There will be no Prodigals, no broken creatures in need of repair.

(Leto feels a tenderness for them. She doesn't know why—perhaps it's their shared origins. The fact she knows, and they don't.

Leto's mother scoffs at that. You're not a specimen. You're my daughter.)

But Leto has always been what she is: the girl with all the gifts, Ofelia Chua Mercado's irrefutable proof. All the world had seen Leto in her womb, the tiny crimson egg Ofelia created. It made Ofelia's fortune and her infamy. How the Manilero elite were scandalized! Ofelia had created Leto without the help of a husband, without the blessing of the Holy Apostolic Church (or *any* church), simply because. Priests cried about the dissolution of the family from their cathedrals, pastors from their multi-million-dollar pulpits. But hereditary heads of state, foreign billionaires, Hollywood queens—all of them came clamoring for Ofelia's service.

Leto's mother waits for her at the breakfast table. She is a slender woman, not beautiful but magnificent. She has a cruel mouth, a hard face, a hooked nose as if she truly were the witch the more poetic among the Manila elite call her. Her black hair falls in rivulets down her back. No matter the demands of the day, Ofelia Chua Mercado insists on taking this time: the time to sit down and have a meal with family. She didn't create a daughter just to neglect her. She prides herself on having better husbandry of children. On the table are buttered toast, salted duck eggs, slices of chilled fruit.

"Today's clients will need careful handling," Ofelia murmurs, handing her daughter the day's dossiers. "I know you've managed them before, but darling, today, I need you to resist the urge to gloat."

Leto opens the dossiers. She understands the moment her eyes fall on the client's name. She doesn't smirk; she knows it's unladylike.

Ever since she was a tiny thing, old enough to be presented in a sad little classroom with portraits of saints, every single one of her classmates had hated her. They called her soulless. They said: You don't have a papa. And yet, over time, so many of them ended up on Leto's table. She carefully explained all the reasons why their families elected them for the procedure. She feels that they're owed an explanation, but she can't help feeling some satisfaction. *She* had never disappointed her mother.

"Not one Prodigal," Ofelia says, sipping her tea, "but *three*. Can you imagine that, darling? Imagine if they'd come to us from the beginning. It would have spared them so much trouble."

It's an old, old story. It is the puzzle that so many familial dynasties have tried to resolve. How does one halt the decline that seems to seep in the third, fourth generation? Sixteen, eighteen, twenty years old, and their beloved offspring showed signs of delinquency, addiction, general malaise, rebellion, *depression,* of all things. They showed poor scholarship. How does one save a child from themselves? Eighteen years of Mandarin lessons, ballet or music, and Catholic school didn't fix them. The Church and the promise of heaven can't fix them.

Manila might have been horrified by Ofelia, the woman who made a daughter. But as the decades passed, one by one, they crept to Ofelia's door, and begged her for her help. They turned to her genetic alchemy and, over the years, a whisper network has formed between desperate, gossiping mothers, patriarchs over games of golf and exquisite lunches.

Leto feels her fingers itch. Thinks of the discarded original, turning to ash in the furnace while a new, tiny creature emerges whole from Leto's artistry. All her fellow heirs have hated her: have always hated her. But here she is anyway, granting them a gift unbidden. They will never even know.

Her mother rises and kisses her cheek. "Good hunting, my sweet girl," Ofelia murmurs, and Leto blushes.

Her mother knows her, inside and out. Better than she knows herself.

The Dowager

When Leto goes to meet clients, she brings her mother's wares as if they are the trappings of their self-appointed office. In her arms, she brings a winged cat with snow-white plumage, her little feet ending in owl's talons and one blue eye alongside jade (feline specimens with heterochromia fetch *three times* the price). A speckled serpent with a forked tongue wraps himself around Leto's neck like a regent's gold necklace (base specimen: *Atheris hispida*). And finally, after a moment's consideration, Leto carefully selects amber earrings made from the chrysalises of Luminous Moths. She picks up a rose as white as a funeral, a present for the Dowager. She paints her mouth with a neutral pink (edging towards a baby pastel); lines her eyes with modest shadow (Industrial Revolution—a shade popular among her peers). She takes her little slate and programs the nanites in her hair; they color it a deep black with only the faintest streaks of a foreign autumn.

Leto understands what the heart wants: it wants a useful young woman, modest and helpful, who will solve all their problems with a flick of her manicured fingers. Leto meets clients because her existence says: *you could have a helper, a dutiful, reliable heir. The child you need, if only you had asked for our services from the beginning.* She revels in clients' gritted teeth and fingers pressed into their palms—how they hate being proven wrong! She sits herself at the little table, waits for the client to arrive.

And when the Dowager slips into Chua Mercado's rooms, dressed as if for a funeral (or a cocktail), Leto can't help it. She rises up and kisses the Dowager's cheeks like a fond niece. The Dowager closes her eyes;

she smells, very faintly, of very fine, expensive whiskey. She shudders; or perhaps, it's poor Leopold that terrifies her, the gorgeous speckled band winding himself around Leto's neck, or Anne-Marie, the snow-white cat purring in her arms. Here is Leto, an unnatural thing, decked out in unnatural things. But the Dowager needs her help.

"I have three daughters," the Dowager says with a rasp. "And they will all be the ruin of me." Her elegant hand trembles as she sits in the client's chair. Outside, Leto smiles; inside, a frisson of *schadenfreude* ticks upwards in spite of herself. She knows the Dowager's daughters: they are just like every other classmate who's ended up on her mother's table.

"Why don't you tell me what you need, Tita?" Leto asks. Like the witch in the story. What do you need? What do you lack? What price are you willing to pay?

The Dowager is Eva Maria Romano Iglesia—scion of a saintly house, married to a handsome media pastor in her baby-faced youth. She was a woman alone of all the multi-million-dollar pastors: having inherited the position after his untimely death. She preached in Chanel and pearls, wasp-waisted dresses with billowing skirts, and spoke of love and deference to husbands and fathers. She spoke of the sanctity of the family, this woman with no husband, and adoring crowds of women threw money at her. She was the most vicious of Ofelia's detractors, when Leto and the exo-womb were unveiled. She called Leto *soulless*. She called Ofelia a fallen woman, creating a child outside the sanctity of marriage, outside the bounds of God's intended methods.

But now two tiny granddaughters are dead. A son-in-law is set to be buried tomorrow, and the daughters are locked in their rooms in the family compound.

"I need you and your mother to give me the daughters I should have had from the beginning," the Dowager says. She almost spits. How it humbles her, to be abandoned so by the God who showered her in gold but gave her delinquent children on which to build her church.

"Our congregation needs us," the Dowager whispers, clutching her Chanel pearls. An entire congregation of lost souls—expensive women with husbands who loathe them, girls who became pregnant too early.

They all find solace in the Dowager and her family of perfect women. What happens when the image that gives them so much comfort comes crashing down?

Leto is never really interested in all the clients' reasons why *this* has to be done. She'd rather hear from the specimens themselves. Console them on their deathbeds.

"We'll need to stagger them out," Leto says. "One by one, to accommodate schedules for other clients."

"I want it over and done with, as soon as possible."

"I understand," Leto says evenly. And nothing more.

(Really, Leto just wants her to anguish over it, *just a little longer.*)

Silence settles between them. Leto feels the Dowager acquiesce. No one else can help her. She can't disappear three young women and gain their replacements, *their better selves,* on her own. She can't create a replacement daughter, and raise her, not at her age.

The Dowager is old. She is running out of time.

"No one will know?" The Dowager's hands tighten around her cane.

"No one will know," Leto says softly. "From head to toe, down to their cells, they will be exactly the same."

Leto takes the pale white rose, as perfect as a faerie dress. They named it Blanca Nieve. It smells like a perfumed night. She gives it to the Dowager. Places it carefully on the table, along with a lacquered box containing its food. Ten little nightingale corpses.

"People need to see you leave with it in your hands," she tells her. "So you've had a reason to come to us. Feed it with ten nightingales. You won't be disappointed."

The next day, a funeral for the Dowager's son-in-law is held in her stained-glass church. The cathedral arches are snow-white with roses, and they spill down the steps of the church, singing with bell-like voices.

No one even sees the bones.

Faith

She starts with the youngest. Why not?

They take her from the family compound. They place her, fast asleep, on Leto's table in the lab. Faith is a delicate snow-white beauty:

long limbs, a small head, the fair skin that Manileros prize so much. It's at odds with Faith's reputation.

Leto waits, and watches as the specimen slowly blinks herself awake. The upsurge in fear when she realizes that she's strapped to the table. When she realizes that she's not alone.

Leto doesn't see what she does as revenge, as former classmates have accused her when they have woken up to find themselves in her lab. She sits with the specimens, waits for them to wake up. It feels *wrong* to her, simply destroying the originals without explaining why their families requested the procedure. She hopes that a vague memory of that conversation settles into the client's cells. When they perform the process, create the new, perfected specimen, the Prodigal will not relapse.

"Faith?" Leto says. Her words come out muffled behind her mask. The girl stops struggling; she recognizes Leto's voice.

"Oh God," says Faith, and the pretty girl laughs. "All the stories they said about you are true."

Leto's hairs prick up at the back of her neck.

When they were children, Leto was the witch's daughter. Now, as adults, she is her mother's right hand, her coolly competent heir and that is where her story ends. All the specimens returned to the client families have had their memories edited: they know nothing of her mother's labs. But her classmates know *nothing* of Prodigals, of Leto's part in the process. They know nothing of the Procedure. It's in their parents' interest: that their children know nothing. They'd rather forget the unpleasantness and have their baby back (they never really will).

"Do you know why you're here?" she asks Faith. Faith laughs and pulls at the straps.

"I killed my sister's husband," Faith rasps. "We did it together, you know. Me. Charity. Harmony. We pushed him off the balcony."

They'd said it was an accident. Pat del Rosario—beloved husband, beloved son-in-law—falling over the balcony in the family's multi-million-dollar compound. Thank God, the Dowager had board positions on various media boards: his death was announced without mention of murder or suicide. They had locked Faith in her room until the funeral and she had appeared with the rest of the family, her stony face easily interpreted as a perfect mask of dignified grief.

"I did it knowing you'd show up," Faith whispers.

"You knew nothing of the sort," Leto says. Her voice is even, but under the table, her hand shakes.

Faith has no reason to believe Leto would show up. She has no reason to believe in her mother's lab. Leto is not a fairy tale, the way the Prodigals she perfects are fairy tales. They emerge perfect and whole under her fingers, blessed with cool-eyed competence, the smothering of their genetic demons.

"Do you even want to know *why?*" Faith asks.

"I know you want to tell me," Leto says.

It doesn't matter what they tell her; the procedure will go ahead anyway. But it's as if she's a confessor tending to a penitent on their deathbed. How can she say no?

You're not a specimen, Ofelia had told Leto. *You're my daughter.*

But still, the fact remains: Leto was created to prove the viability of her mother's product, the efficacy of her mother's services. Ofelia edited Leto's genes. She edited them for beauty, for genius, for musicality, an affinity for maths and languages, all those things that the ultra-rich crave in their children. They like to feel as if their genes have given rise to better stock, better product.

Leto was engineered for obedience, which meant she was inclined to recognize her mother's authority in all things. Her mother had been frank about this: there was no point in raising a child who spurned all her gifts. From the moment Leto stepped inside a classroom, she had excelled, surpassing her peers. It gave the elite of Manila something to consider, even as they called her *soulless.* When their beloved babies grew up, showing signs of rot by the time they reached their teens, they turned to Ofelia Chua Mercado and her helpful, perfect daughter. Who swap out imperfect specimens for better ones. Or at least, they edit the genetic code, so they are more inclined to conform to their parents' expectations. They're like fairy godmothers, granting obedience *as a gift.*

Faith had failed from the beginning. Even when she and her sisters were little, when the Dowager paraded them around as her little saints, Faith was infamous for her rage. There was a party, when a group of boys held her down to take her photo (wasn't it sweet? Babies and their games!). She'd pushed one of them down the stairs, and he broke his leg, right there on the Dowager's immaculate floors. When they were all older, there was another incident, another more grown college party, when she'd taken out someone's eye.

The Dowager said: *they'd hoped she'd grow out of it.* That time and patience and their guidance would temper her. It honestly surprised Leto that it's taken Faith this long to come to her table.

(Leto's mother said, scoffing, that they should have edited Faith's anger out of her, long ago. Leto had wisely kept quiet. She doesn't *blame* Faith, the way her mother did. But she knows what traits are desirable and what aren't—they don't like rage in little girls.)

And now there's a dead body that they've had to cover up with bribes and ritual, and a snow-white funeral.

"He killed Charity's babies," Faith snarls. "Did Mommy tell you that? He killed her girls."

It was in the dossier—a sad obituary in the *Manila Times* of the Dowager's twin granddaughters. But babies often die for strange, unknown, and unknowable reasons. Especially when they're so small.

"He put stuffed toys in their crib," Faith says. "It's a SIDS risk: everyone knows that. They kept telling him to stop; he laughed and kept doing it. *Look, she loves her little teddy. What's the harm?* Everyone said: *Men don't raise children, it's not in them. You can't expect them to understand.* It was Charity's responsibility: after all, she was *their mother.*

"Charity couldn't stay awake forever. *She tried. We all did.* He found reasons to keep us away. And one day she found him standing over their crib with a pillow—and her baby girls were dead." She closes her eyes. "A house full of people who were supposed to love them, and they all said she was hysterical. They didn't believe her. Poor Charity. *He barely cried.*"

"Why would he do that?" Leto asks.

She really shouldn't have asked. All Faith wants is to unburden herself.

"He wanted boys," Faith says. "It's not as if he hid that. He was so disappointed when they came out! And Charity was so happy—his disappointment was such a small thing to her, at least in the beginning. That she loved something he didn't."

"Annulment was an option, you know." It's not that she objects to what Faith did; it's that she should have been clever about it. She starts thinking of ways to snip the rage out of her, or at least temper it. They can modify memories to reinforce caution.

"Annulment isn't part of our brand," Faith says. "It's not an option for us. Can you imagine *the scandal*? Lola would kill us first. *Mommy* would."

That, Leto thinks, unfortunately is true.

"I'd have been more careful about it than you," Leto says. Faith laughs.

"We were past careful," Faith says. "After he killed the girls. After they all said Charity was hysterical and not thinking clearly. They even blamed *her*: Lola, Mommy, our *aunts*. We shut them up when we threw him down the balcony."

Leto starts prepping her needle. She needs to draw blood; their work is easy, really. They have such a rich source of DNA.

"So what are you going to do?" Faith asks. "Replace me with a soulless little drone? A *more palatable* version of me?"

"Don't be so dramatic," Leto says. "I can't make or remove a soul. I'd make a version of you that wouldn't have gotten caught."

It's not quite what Faith's mother would have wanted. It's not what Ofelia Chua Mercado would have wanted. But there is no one here to gainsay her decision.

She's not sure why or how she decided this: that Faith is entitled to her anger. But here she is.

"It's all right," Leto says, and she is back on familiar ground. "It's all right. You won't even remember this happened. The you that wakes up won't even remember this." And if the new Faith doesn't remember and the old Faith is simply erased, does Faith even suffer?

She lets Faith see the tiny little selves, swimming in their little crimson eggs, before she puts her to sleep. It seems to calm Faith: watching tender little creatures made from her bone and marrow. Leto dresses the new specimen herself when she emerges, perfect and whole. The new Faith will be little more calculating, a little less given to rages. If the new Faith does need to act on her rage, she will take better care not to get caught. The Prodigal is returned to the family. The Dowager sends back a message, saying: *Faith is much improved.* Leto imagines the Dowager breathing a little easier even as Faith is counting her grudges and biding her time. Counting down the days, until it's all done.

Leto schedules the next two procedures. She takes her time.

Charity

She was the last person Leto had thought would end up on her table.

The middle sister: kind-hearted and soft, the kind of girl who deflected other people's faults. The fairy tale girl people say they want but, in reality, isn't equipped to keep a dynasty together. Still, she had that fairy tale wedding, married the boy her family picked for her. The Dowager was very clear about her specifications: they want their sweet girl back, before she went wrong.

"*Really,*" Leto told her mother wearily, over chai tea and congee for breakfast, "they want a Charity who doesn't remember how much her family failed her. They want a Charity who won't make them feel guilty, every time they look at her."

"If that's what they want to believe," Ofelia said. She shrugged her elegant shoulders. It's cheating, but it's not *quite* cheating, is it, if a Prodigal is exactly the same, just slightly improved? It's the improvements they focus on.

Leto didn't tell her mother about what Faith had said. It's not that she believes Faith, exactly, but . . .

When Charity wakes up, when she sees Leto, she looks almost resigned. There's no shock. Ice pricks at the back of Leto's neck. Charity should be shocked. Charity should cry for help. Why doesn't she?

"I knew something was wrong," she says. "When Faith came back . . . She wasn't herself."

Leto doesn't answer.

"Poor Faith. Did she feel anything? Was it fast?"

"What can you possibly know about the procedure?"

Charity laughs, a sad little laugh that almost sounds like affection.

"We all talk about it, you know," she says. "All our old classmates, all our *old friends.*"

None of you were ever my friends. Leto digs her nails into her palms. She is not . . . she is not supposed to be the monster in anyone else's story. She's more than that unveiled creature in the womb, more than the girl in the schoolroom, more than the witch's baby everyone decided they should hate.

"I'm frankly surprised that you *don't know.* I would have thought that your mother would have told you. We could never match you in scholarship, but we're not stupid. Sometimes an old classmate would show up and . . . they weren't quite themselves. They would remember things—but in slightly different ways. We heard about the oldies' little whisper network. They say there's a little dungeon somewhere—where all the bodies are kept. There's a little lab where you clone tiny little creatures to replace us. That you sell our souls yourself."

Leto's heart is beating fast.

There is no reason. There is no reason why Charity and her friends should know. The specimens' memories of her mother's workshops are wiped. The Prodigals are returned to their rooms, and they don't remember—they don't remember anything of their time as tiny little creatures in blood-red eggs, their hatching.

If what Charity says is true and there are whispers of the process, and Leto's part in it . . . How could she not know that she has turned into a story she has no control over? How could her mother not know? She feels like she's back in that dreary little room again: her classmates whispering poison, spinning stories she has no control over.

Charity watches her face. "Do you remember?" she asks. "Do you remember anything—from before?"

"Before what?"

Charity closes her eyes and sighs, as if she is very tired and ready to go to sleep. She opens them again, and her eyes fix on Leto. "I wouldn't tell your mother about this conversation if I were you."

"We tell each other everything," Leto says.

"Do you?" Charity asks. "Do you really? Do you ever wonder about the little gaps in your memory—"

She doesn't have to pay attention to this. She doesn't.

"Look at me," Charity says, her voice soft and urgent. "I did everything my mother wanted. I married a boy she wanted. I gave up the idea of a master's degree in science. And still—look at where I am right now." Leto twitches, remembers her dreams of little feet, a crimson world.

"I wasn't expecting to have to destroy everything I was when I married," Charity whispers. "I wasn't expecting to destroy everything I loved. That wasn't the bargain I thought I made. Do you remember your Bella Norte?"

When she was fourteen, Leto had engineered little bees who sang like bells and were nocturnal. As sweet and docile as Charity. She'd been frankly surprised that the Dowager had purchased a specimen from Chua Mercado Alchemy. A birthday gift for her middle daughter, who had lately become obsessed with beekeeping.

"They never really caught on," Leto says. That was the trouble with new patents.

"Do you remember?" Charity asks. "Do you remember making them for me?"

Leto just stares. She'd done nothing of the kind. She made them, Charity ordered them, and that was the end of it. Charity sighs, softly.

"I kept beds and beds of nocturnal flowers to feed them. I did everything you told me to, even when you stopped answering my letters.

Nocturnal roses, honeysuckle, lavender. Leto can't even remember why she made them: only that she did.

"Mommy and Lola never approved. Pat wanted me to stop: they were dangerous to me and the baby. Who knew what they were picking up while they were dancing in the dark? Who knew how *reliable* the patent was, how docile they really were? I went on a trip to the States; I came back to find most of my hives burned. Lola said: *But it's such a little thing.* Mommy said: *You have babies now. You won't even notice they're gone.*"

Charity closes her eyes. "And then the girls turned out to be girls. We didn't even want to know—he was so sure God would give us what he *deserved*. I took their blood. I cut their hair. I wanted something to remember them by, just like I kept the bees to remember you." She breathes in, breathes out. Looks over at Leto, whose face is carefully blank.

She would have no reason. Her mother would have no reason to remake her. Leto is perfect, has been perfect, since the beginning. She was engineered for beauty, for intelligence, *reliability*. There is nothing that Leto wants, outside of what her mother needs.

"They were right," Charity whispers. "Oh God, they were right."

Leto doesn't answer. She preps her needle.

"*Listen to me,*" Charity says, before she slips off to sleep under Leto's needle. "You're not so different from us. Someone should have told you that from the beginning. I'm sorry we didn't."

Charity is easier, in many ways. They keep the base genetic profile. They edit her memories. *Faith* did it. *Harmony* did it. Charity just watched. Leto goes through an entire album of memories, editing things out, snipping inconvenient ones.

When the new Prodigal wakes in her room, she is more certain of her mother's authority, of her mother's love and adoration. The need to defer to her authority. She won't remember that conversation with Leto, in the lab below.

Leto should talk to her mother. She *should* talk to her, but something stops her, every time. Leto stays in the lab, watching over the dreaming specimens. Cinderella, over the turtledoves that shake gold and silver over her. She thinks of the ashes of every discarded specimen, feeding her mother's roses. Faith, Charity, an endless, endless parade of names before them.

And she wonders, she wonders. How many of them were *her*? How many dreams has she had, of a crimson world and kicking feet? Can she count all the times she might have been remade? She wouldn't even know when it began, what had been the starting point. She walks into the garden at twilight, where the apiaries of little Bella Norte are kept. Their little feet brush against her cheek like a kiss.

Do you know more of me than I do? she asks them.

Do you?

Harmony

The eldest daughter escapes.

She must have seen the writing on the wall, Leto muses to herself when it happens. The Dowager is beside herself. It would not have happened, it would not have happened, if Leto had done all three of them at once like she had asked.

You should have known better than to let the other girls out, is all Leto thinks. Ofelia lets the Dowager know, calmly, that matters are being *handled* and shoots Leto a look. Leto understands: she wants Leto to fix it. The foundations of the world her mother is building depends on Chua Mercado's reliability, *their reputation.* She needs to undo the damage she's caused.

But Leto spends some time in the garden, among the specimens and patents that never quite caught on. She spends some time with the Bella Norte bees, waking in the moonlight, settling on Leto's dress like golden dust.

You made them for me, said Charity. Why would Leto do that? What did she owe her?

She considers that Charity and Faith may be right, that her mother has been wiping her memory, altering her like a story that she can't quite perfect. She should be terrified. She should be outraged, but all she feels is hollow. She wonders if anger was edited out of her too.

"I don't know what to do," she says, honestly, to the Bella Norte bees, as if they could answer her.

They track Harmony down in a shabby little street in Binondo, in a shabby little room. Leto insists on going herself. After all, it was her mistake.

At that, something inside Ofelia seems to untwist and loosen. She kisses Leto on the cheek. She says: She knows Leto will make it right. Everyone makes mistakes. We all learn from them. We make ourselves *perfect.*

Leto lets herself into the shabby little room, and there is Harmony, waiting.

The survivors of Charity's bees surround her, drinking sugar water.

Harmony is tall and striking, even with her hair slick with the humidity and the lack of care over the past few days. Charity was the sweetheart, Faith was the baby, but Harmony was meant to be their mother, all over again. It must have galled the Dowager, when Harmony picked her sisters over her mother. *That* was not the natural way of things.

Leto isn't sure what edits to make to improve those outcomes.

"We all know you'd come for us, you know," says Harmony. She doesn't move. The bees settle around her, as if she is their saint.

"So I've heard," says Leto. Harmony raises her eyebrow.

"What do you remember?" Harmony asks, point blank.

Leto says nothing.

"What do you remember?" Harmony asks. "How many times did she make you over, so she could start all over again, a clean slate?"

Leto thinks of the ashes in her mother's garden. Whether any of them are made up of her former selves. She wouldn't know when her mother started. She wouldn't even know where to begin.

"I know about Charity's daughters," she says, her voice hollow. "I know about the bees."

Harmony sighs, and her shoulders slump over.

"We didn't know," she says, "if she'd remake you, over and over again. Just to make sure you couldn't remember. Do you remember? Making the bees for Charity? Do you?"

Leto feels breathless. A little Bella Norte lands on her cheek.

"She cried when you stopped answering her letters," says Harmony. "When we passed by each other and you acted as if you didn't know her. And later—when classmates came back, from rehab, from sabbaticals, from tours, *not quite right,* well, we all *wondered.*"

It's like a knife to her ribs. She doesn't—she can't feel anything.

Harmony gives her a box.

"I'd do it again you know," she says, between her teeth. "I would pick Faith and Charity, every time. *Every time.* Hollow me out, empty me of all the inconvenient things my mother wants gone, and I'd still make the same choice."

"What's inside?" Leto asks.

But she already knows.

* * *

The Dowager sends payment: all three Prodigals, successfully remade. She even gifts Leto with the survivors of Charity's bees. They have no use for them, and the girl is getting married again in the fall. Another fairy tale wedding. Then: one for Faith, and one for Harmony. She's already signed contracts for little Seraphim to be made.

"Well done," Ofelia says, and kisses her cheek. Another death, smoothed over. Because these girls wanted something outside what they should want.

What does Leto want? Nothing except her work. There's nothing that her mother left her.

So she creates a second variant of the Bella Norte, from the daughters of Charity's bees. They have Faith's anger; Charity's love; Harmony's loyalty. And inside, inside, they contain slivers of memory, two baby girls avenged by their mother and aunts.

Leto's daughters have no debut: they are not presented to the world the way Leto was. Instead, she lets them fly wild.

That year, the Dowager and her congregation will be haunted at nighttime by bees that sing like wind chimes, that smell of baby's breath, and build cathedrals inside her church. At her wedding, Charity will turn to look at them, and she won't know why she feels joy and heartbreak. Faith will wonder as she lets them settle on her shoulders and Harmony will feel a strange peace, even as the bees murder her mother's congregation.

They'll say it's a miracle, that the three of them are left alive.

SWANSKIN

ALISON LITTLEWOOD

L ater, it is not so much the attack that I see, again and again, in my
mind, but what came after it.

The two of them were walking along the shore at evening, a distance
ahead of me. The sky and sea were as gray as each other, and the air still
had winter's cold nip, carrying now and then a scouring of sand into my
face. The town was behind me, a pretty little spill of houses built into the
side of a cliff, nothing but the sea in front of it and miles of flat brown
land behind. Across the dunes, just ahead of the couple, was a quiet
little river mouth, where swans gathered and dabbled for pondweed, no
doubt dreaming their strange avian dreams of the north.

I could not make out their features, but I knew who they were. Horrocks, his very name meaning "part of a ship," owned the largest fishing
boat in the fleet; and Syl, his young wife, who walked a little straighter
than he and stood a little taller. If I had not recognized her form I would
have known her by her hair, which was more golden than the evening
sun and rippled finer than the sea.

Horrocks was hunch-shouldered under the weight of a pack, his
head turned to the sand, while Syl gazed upward, into the sky. And
yet both of them stopped when a riotous clamor arose, seemingly from
nowhere, a sound I could not place. It echoed from the dunes and at first

I thought of machinery, coming from the town perhaps, though I had never heard such a thing before; and then the wings appeared, as if from out of the ground.

Suddenly they were everywhere, surrounding the two of them, flocking above their heads. The birds were dark against the sky, yet I knew them to be white, for I recognized their cruciform shapes, their chiseled heads, the long, graceful arch of their necks.

Horrocks stumbled. He raised one arm to fend them off as they fell upon him, beating and stabbing. Each one of them was wider than Syl was tall. I rubbed at my eyes, wondering if it was some illusion formed of the sand—swans, I knew, did not attack men, not like this, not all together. One at a time perhaps, if he strayed too close to its nest, and even then, I was certain the stories must be lies: that a swan's wing could break a man's leg; that they had once drowned a man at the edge of the sea.

Horrocks fell to his knees. The birds were shrieking in a kind of blood lust, the beating of their wings a tumult. I couldn't tell if Horrocks cried out; I couldn't see his face. He *was* in the edge of the sea, I realized, though hidden by the chaos of feathers and flight.

I began to run towards them, even as I saw that his wife had not moved at all. Syl stood by, no doubt shocked into stillness, horrified; fear-frozen.

Horrocks pushed himself up from the water, roaring and choking the salt from his lungs. One moment the air was thick with plumage; and in the next the swans were gone, beating and creaking their way back towards the river.

All was suddenly quiet. I slowed a little, the sand making hard work of it, but they hadn't seen me; they didn't look at me all the time it was happening. I am uncertain if they ever knew I was there.

After the attack, Horrocks got to his knees and then his feet. His trousers were darkened with seawater, but he did not trouble about that. He did not pause to retrieve his pack from the waves. He half walked, half stumbled to where his wife still stood, tall and motionless. He stepped in front of her, straightening before striking her, hard, across her lips.

SWANSKIN

* * *

Unnatural, they say later, ensconced in their booths, pints frothing across the upturned barrels that pass for tables in the Anchor. *Uncanny. A freak.*

It is the same every night, at least when they are not at sea. The men of the town sail and fish and go home to hot meals and warm beds, but before they sleep they retire to the alehouse, spinning their yarns about the women who are trying to trap them. And yet tonight it is not the same, not quite. There is unease in their words and in their sidelong glances, which meet and slide away from each other.

Their words are cutting. They speak of the chatter of women, meaningless as the gabble of geese. They speak of the one thing they *are* good for, and spurt laughter before falling silent again, staring into their tankards.

They haven't yet said the word *witch*, but it isn't far behind *unnatural*. The air is thick with it, the echo of a thought that is louder than their obscenities, their laughter.

Soon I will go to sea. I shall be one of them—sitting at their table, talking as they do, flushed with drink and laughter. I was intended for a farmer, but the death of my parents ended that; now I live with a distant and ancient relative, a dry husk of a woman, in a tiny cottage nestled halfway up the cliff. The soft ploughed land of my childhood has become rock; the air I breathe has turned to salt.

I leave them, ducking out of the tavern in time to see a bevy of the town's women walking by, arm in arm. I stop and watch them go. Syl is at their center, the tallest, though I can see little of her face; it is almost concealed by a dark hood. When she sees me, she passes a hand across her mouth, as if to conceal her swollen lips.

Contrary to the men's talk, they do not gabble. Indeed, they do not say a word. One of Syl's companions looks at me sidelong. She is softer made than Syl, though still tall, still elegant. I think I make out, as she goes, a single white feather caught in the soft curls of her hair.

At evening, we sit before the fire, my ageing relative and I. She rocks in her chair, staring into the flames while my gaze is drawn, over and over, to the window. There is nothing out there but the dark. It is parceled into tiny squares by the leaded glass.

"You begin to see, then," she says.

I turn to her. Each crease on her face bears its own deep shadow. Her eyes look rheumy, as if damp with tears.

"See what, Aunt?" For Aunt I call her, though she is more distant than that in relation. Still, she has never blamed me for burdening her; she never reminds me of the thinness of our bond, that I am a stranger here.

She takes the pipe from between her lips, freeing a skein of mist scented of sandalwood and cloves.

"You'll know the truth soon enough." She gestures towards the window with the pipe's stem, just as a pale shape passes across the sky.

"The swans," she says. "They winter here. But here is not their home. That is what you sense, boy, when you look at them." She silences me with another wave of her pipe.

"Sometimes, a swan may shed her feathery skin. She casts it off and becomes a lovely maiden. And if a man should steal her skin—why, then she will stay, and keep her human shape, and be his wife, as long as her skin is kept from her. But sometimes, a whole flight of her sisters will come. They will try to free their sister and her swanskin."

Her eyes reflect the fire's gleam. "You should beware," she says. "Find a nice girl. A good girl. Not—" She spits, mutters something about *unnatural forms*.

I do not answer, am not certain how, and she takes to gazing once more, before nodding in her chair. I do not wake her; I wish to keep to my own thoughts. Somehow, I never once doubt the truth of her words. I half close my eyes, picturing the massing of the swans, the way they swooped on Horrocks as he walked with his wife along the shore. I remember the way he struck her; I see again her grace as she touched her fingers to her lips.

Unnatural forms, my aunt had said, echoing the gossip at the Anchor. But she never did tell me which of their forms was unnatural: whether it was their human or bird shape that was to be so feared.

SWANSKIN

The fishermen have sailed, the town left to the women, and to me. I wander the little streets between tall white houses, each set on their own angle, and try not to stare in at the windows. When I reach the largest, though, I cannot resist. I pass by it often and see Syl pacing the rooms, back and forth, restless, and I wonder: is she searching for her skin?

All know it when the boats return. The streets fill with boot steps and chatter, and I too throw on my coat and head down to the dock to help offload the catch. They have been absent, this time, four days. One more sailing and the eldest sea dog from Horrocks's boat, a fellow with half-closed eyes and leathern skin, will be done; I am promised his place.

I heft crate after crate of still-squirming silver to the quayside, where the women wait with their curved knives, their trestle tables set out ready. Gulls circle overhead, wailing, ready to snatch whatever they can with bladed beaks. Most of the town is here, I realize: the grizzled men, the soft-skinned maids, though few children, unless it is only that I do not see them.

The women's movements are quick and sure as they grasp the slippery fish. Syl is among the rest. She guts them one by one, her hands gored and shining, and she cuts slivers from the edge of their flesh and swallows them whole. She catches me watching, freezes for a moment, gives a small nod in return for my smile.

Unnatural, they had said. My cheeks color with shame at the memory of their words; the way they condemned her, forgetting, as perhaps her husband had himself, how he must have stolen her skin, kept it from her, made her what she is.

When the catch is done, the menfolk head up the narrow cobbled lane to the Anchor, but the women walk away, down to the shore. After a moment, I follow them. The sea has by now retreated, smudging the line where the earth meets the sky, and the beach seems a vast stretch of mud. They do not walk towards the brine, however, but to where the river meets the sea. They do not turn, and I stand behind them as they look at the swans out on the water, gliding, their necks bent into hooks.

I cannot see the women's faces. I do not know if they are remembering or dreaming, or perhaps both.

After a time the swans beat their wings and skim along the surface, forming a noisy trailing procession before they lift from the water. Their flight is hard-won, and the sound of their wings is like applause, as if they are glad to be in the air, rejoicing at their freedom. I wonder if they tell their own tales to each other—stories without words, warning of the wiles of man.

The swans circle around once more. The women exchange not a word, only watching them, tilting back their heads; then they hold out their hands. As I watch, the swans let fall their feathers: gifts for their skinless sisters.

The Anchor smells of burning. The air is acrid and dense, and I almost don't go inside but through the haze I hear the rumble of the men. I step across the threshold, blinking against the sting of it. I collect a tankard and the ale is mercifully cold at the back of my throat, though I still want to cough. No one else does, however, and I swallow it down.

They are seated in their accustomed places, Horrocks at the center, his eyes already glazed with liquor—or perhaps that too is from the smoke, which rises in front of him, obscuring his features. He tips a little of his ale onto the table, which extinguishes something with a hiss. He holds up what remains—a blackened quill, the filaments burned away, not a trace of white left.

They all laugh, turning to look at me, this newcomer in their midst, not yet certain if I will be a subject for further laughter or if I will swell its volume. I force a grin, wave my tankard in their direction.

"Sit, boy." Horrocks surprises me with his words, which fly from his mouth in a cloud of spittle. They move aside for me, scraping their stools across the floor. I sit between their bulky warm bodies.

"See this?" he throws down the quill onto the upturned barrel between us. Other burned feathers are scattered there, scarcely recognizable, the source of the stink. "Know what that means, boy?"

I don't know what I'm expected to say, so I simply shrug, then nod.

"You will." Horrocks grasps his crotch and makes a thrusting motion, and guffaws rise into the air.

I gulp at my drink. Then, buoyed by the ale or their sudden silence, I say, "Where is it you keep the skins?"

Horrocks is suddenly motionless. All traces of humor are gone; his eyes are tiny points of light. They pierce the gloom—pierce me. "Be careful, boy."

The quiet stretches out. I'm not certain what it will become, but then the fellow at my side nudges me in the ribs. "I take mine to sea," he says. "Use it to line my hammock. Keeps me warm."

Glances flit around the group. They still aren't sure, but Horrocks's shoulders relax and amusement ripples between them.

"Feel this, lad." Another offers the edge of his jerkin to my fingers. I notice that its surface is pocked with little dimples. "Plucked and tanned," he says, and they roar. Strike their tankards against each other. Drink spills across the table.

"Buried," another mutters.

"Burned."

My smile fades. I sit in the midst of their noise, their movement. I have no words. I think of them sullying the pure white skins, the things they must have craved, once; loving and yet fearing them, coveting them even as they tear them to pieces. I stare down at the scorched feathers, abandoned now; in them the wrecked hopes of the women who had stood on the shore and snatched them from the sky.

Horrocks suddenly leans across the table, grasps my arm. His grip is hardened by years of working the wet ropes, hauling in the nets, the constant scrape of salt. "We saves 'em, boy," he says. "Never forget that. Not if you want to stay."

The others watch, intent on his words.

"We save them from the spell," he says. "Enchantment. The trap they're in. It's against nature. Remember that."

He waits for my nod before he releases me. I refrain from rubbing at my arm. I can still feel the bone beneath the skin, as if his fingers remain wrapped around it. Does he really believe he has freed them—saved them from what they are—from magic? Does he think he has remade them, shaped them as they could and should have been? And yet how he must value the memory of that magic: the grace of her, the sinuous form, her loveliness beneath the skin.

My thoughts are lost in their mirth, released once more in gulps of amber and guffaws. The volume of it gathers, a rising tide that carries everything with it, so that I only dimly hear it as he says, "A feather bed. I had it stitched inside, right at the center. We sleep on it every night."

They are gathered in the street, just back from the quay, not far from where the Anchor hangs its old painted sign. It is not the day for market, or for sailing, or even for church, which anyway, few here trouble about. They are bending over an object made of wood. I cannot see or guess what it is but a great rustling and struggling comes from within, and they step back, snorting with laughter or mockery.

At last, I can see. The object is a wooden cage made of old crates and lobster pots, and inside is a folded, cramped, crushed creature. A golden beak, tipped with black, stabs at the bars. Momentarily it opens its mouth, revealing a long thin tongue as it hisses. Its feathers no longer appear white. They are damp, soiled, stained. I cannot make out its eyes against the dark sides of its skull.

Another ripple runs through the gathering as someone pokes a stick into the cage. The action is that of a child, but it is Horrocks; he turns, scans the crowd, and I see that Syl is standing there, at the back, looking on; seeing everything.

He nods, as if with satisfaction. Then he calls out, loud, so that everyone can hear.

"A witch." The word, spoken at last, cannot be contained. It runs about the street, touching all, lingering on their lips as they echo it.

"This creature would have beguiled a man. Inflamed his senses. Trapped him." He slaps his hand down on the top of the cage. "But we trapped it first, hey?"

They cheer. Fists assault the air. Someone kicks the cage. They are grinning, slapping backs, congratulating each other. The women stand by, watching, silent. They are cowled in their hoods, perhaps to cover their dangerous forms, their sinuous curves, lest they inflame a man; lest they bewitch him.

The swan in the cage does not make a sound. I do not know what they will do to her, but I cannot help her now; no one can. At least it will soon end, I think, and then Horrocks's voice rises again.

"A cull."

Now they have purpose. Now they know what to do. They gather behind him. Some are carrying guns, I realize, or sticks, or cudgels. They were ready for this. Primed. Someone releases the door of the cage and the swan stumbles out, clumsy on land, its webbed feet sliding on the cobblestones.

"A head start," Horrocks jokes, and they give chase. The swan never did have a chance. It vainly spreads its wings but there is no room for it to take flight. It goes to the ground and one of the men sets his boot on its long and shapely neck.

They begin to chant, others taking it up so that the words become something different and strange. "A cull, a cull."

I try to interject, grasping shoulders, calling out that such a thing is not lawful, that they cannot take it upon themselves. It is no use; my words are lost. They brandish their weapons, pounding the ground with their sticks as they go, stamping their feet. A cull—as if it is something scientific they do, something necessary.

They march away towards the river. The women follow, able to do nothing else. Will they fight? They have nothing but the clothes they wear. They trail behind, their gaze fixed not upon the sky but the earth the men have trodden; upon their duty; their destination. Will they watch as their sisters are torn and trampled, their feathers broken and ruined? Will they witness the snapped necks of their sons and daughters? Perhaps it would be worse, after all, to turn their faces away.

Still, as Syl passes me at the back of the crowd, I reach out and grasp her hand.

We run, away from the others, unseen, towards her house. She unlocks it using a key kept on a string about her neck and we go inside. I stride ahead of her, as if it is my own. I pass through the living space, not cramped and crammed with nick-nacks and scrimshaw like my aunt's cottage but airy and neat. I go to the stair. Syl does not protest at this intrusion in her home, only watches, her dark eyes the only brightness.

"A knife," I say, and run up the stairs, not worrying about the noise I make. He will be gone a while yet; there is time. There *must* be time. I wonder for a moment if his boasting words at the Anchor were really the truth as I pull back the embroidered sheet of their bed, wondering if she made it by her own hand. I wonder if the knife she passes to me is the one I saw her wielding by the quay, sliding in and out of the belly of a fish. It is slender and sharp and I plunge it into the mattress.

Feathers: white feathers, downy and soft and choking. They fly into the air, floating down once more, and at first she grabs at them—whether to conceal them or take them back I do not know, but I do not think these are a swan's. I thrust my hand into the rip I have made and feel inward to the center, trying not to imagine Horrocks on this bed, sweating on top of her.

Then I touch something that does not give, does not slip through my fingers like the other feathers: something that is as soft as they, yet supple, pliant as the finest leather.

I grasp hold of it and pull it towards me. She gives a harsh, choking cry—the first sound she has made—and snatches it from me. It is almost liquid, that brush of feathers against my skin; then it is gone, though I turn and see the glow of it, pure and shining, spilling from her hands.

I almost expect her to throw it over her shoulders at once, but she does not; she turns and runs for the stairs. But of course, there would be no room for her here to fly. The space she leaves behind feels cold and empty and the thought rises: I had imagined she might have spared a word for me.

When I step out of the door she is standing there, staring down the steep little street towards the glimmer of the sea. The swanskin is still in her hands. A muscle twitches in her cheek—it is as if she is tasting the air, a savor she had almost forgotten. She half closes her eyes, then whirls the feathers around her and she runs.

She moves away from me, fast, faster—and I see the stretch and curve of her wings, spreading wide, finding the air, finding their rhythm, feathertips spreading as she casts it all behind her. She is flying, I realize, her feet lifting from the ground, and still she does not look behind her, and still she has no word for me. An image: all the beautiful swans, her sisters, gliding upon the water, and yet separate from it; their feathers, with a simple flick, always remaining entirely dry.

But her transformation is not complete. Beneath the white is the merest suggestion of an arm, a hand, of weight, of darkness. Then a single shot rings out.

At first, her movement does not change. Then she begins to fall.

I cannot do what she would have done; I cannot watch, though I hear her bones shatter on the stone, the sound of her body breaking. Then they are there, the men, blooded and blood-hungry, the red light of it in their eyes, and it is not enough, will never be enough. They are all around and still they do not stop but raise and lower their cudgels and their sticks and they go on and on stamping with their feet.

Then they turn to me.

When the boats have sailed, there is time to mend. My arm is still in a sling, and I walk with a limp that I suspect will always be with me. I shall not now go to sea. No one has told me this; they do not have to. The knowledge does not lie in the way they look at me, but in the way they do not.

The women say nothing of what has passed. They clean and they cook and they wait for their men. They sit by the shore, dutifully mending nets and sails, always busy with their needles.

I stay with my aunt, doing whatever tasks she requires of me. Mostly she requires nothing; she sits in her rocking chair, smoking her pipe, staring into space and saying nothing of my failure.

After she fell, the thing that Syl had become was given to the fire. No one wished to look upon it too closely, that mangled and twisted form: fingers, beak, feathers, hair.

Outside the window, I hear the pattering of steps. I look out to see hooded shapes hurrying by, heading down the hillside towards the quay.

This time there is little conversation, no excited calls ringing into the air, but still I know what it means.

The men have returned from the sea.

At a glance from my aunt, I don my coat and slip out of the door. The cold air in my lungs feels like a relief after the closed rooms and I limp along in the wake of the women, scarcely knowing why.

The tables are set out along the quay, shining knives waiting there like smiles. Waves gently tap the hulls of the boats, lined up against the harbor wall. There is a stink of bladderwrack and brine; the sky is not gray, but a fresh clear blue scudded with white, and a firm breeze is blowing from the north. I realize something strange. There are no gulls, not today; no wailing cries ringing across the water.

The women are not seated at their tables, are not waiting for the catch. They stand a short distance away, together, still wearing their hoods. I can barely see their faces beneath them; I cannot see their hands. Then, as one, they cast them off.

Beneath their capes, they are naked. They do not wear the clothes their men have given them. Their hair is loose, rippling down their backs. They stand tall. They are unashamed of their bodies, of their bruises, the useless stubs of their wings.

Each is holding a mass of white feathers. They have made new skins, I realize, though not of swan feathers; the men have burned or broken too many for that. I peer into the air once more, cold suddenly, searching again for the gulls, listening for their rapacious cries. The sky is empty.

The women's faces are solemn. I cannot tell by their expressions what they are thinking. It only strikes me then that swans do not cry. They keep the brine inside them; the salt permeates their bones, their blood. It changes them. They, too, can adapt; after all, the river always has flowed into the sea.

The women are ready. And when they take their new forms, red of eye, sharp of beak, gulls sinuous and quick, feathers slick and shining, it is plain for anyone to see that they are also very, very hungry.

THE DEAD OUTSIDE MY DOOR

STEVE RASNIC TEM

S ome days the dead drifted: the ones empty of viscera, whose skeletons had worn wafer-thin, whose remaining skin was like parchment. They were as vague and insubstantial as memories imperfectly recalled. Sometimes the slightest breeze picked them up and tumbled them along the ground or flew them like kites. Jay suspected no one flew kites anymore and he didn't have the words to express how sad this made him.

He saw but this limited sample of the world, but he assumed only the dead gathered in groups. He couldn't imagine more church picnics or basketball games, sports of any kind. People—assuming there were others alive in the way he was alive—now understood what they always tried not to know, that they lived their imperfect lives alone.

The wind blew the dead into mangled clumps or dangled them from trees, still animated, gesturing their unconscious dismay. For the past few months, a semblance of a human being hung from the top branches of the hemlock across the road. He'd watched its slow dissolve into fluttering, translucent wisps of skin, so like a deteriorating plastic bag.

This new normal was not as it was once portrayed in the movies, the TV shows, the comic books. Not at all. He and his brother had had lengthy arguments over who was best prepared in the event of a zombie apocalypse. They didn't know what the hell they were talking about.

Jay considered it essential all this be documented. Perhaps there were others writing this down or making recordings, but he couldn't be sure. He had no illusions about his own importance, or his talent. At least he could put words on paper. He said them out loud first until they sounded right, then he wrote them down. At times they never sounded right, no matter how many ways he said them, and he would get discouraged, and behind. He might go a couple of weeks without writing, and then he had to rely on memory. Certain observations were lost, but those probably weren't the important ones. He kept talking even if he wasn't writing the words down to pretend he was having actual conversations.

He would talk to himself for hours and it all sounded quite wonderful, and he'd become drunk on the words and forget to write them. Or his hands would cramp near the end of a long session and he could no longer read his own handwriting. All in all, he was a poor selection for the role of scribe, but there had been a serious lack of volunteers.

"The dead are unaware. They've been blessed that way. At least that is my hope. If they have an awareness, even a small one, that's too terrible to think about. It's springtime, at least I think it is. I haven't been outside in months and if Mom and Dad owned a calendar, I haven't been able to find it. But the windows are full of green, and the air carries spring's odor of sweetness, the scent of flowers and moist breezes, and underneath all that, rot, the stench you get when the ground breaks open after a long, deep winter. And now, unfortunately, the corrupt smell of human decay, everywhere.

"In Southwest Virginia spring usually means oaks and maples budding into life, fresh produce in the restaurants, outdoor music concerts, walls of mountain laurel along the paths, weekend trips to the catfish pond, explosions of rhododendron, the pleasing smell of honeysuckle, violets and fleabane, wild red geraniums, azalea bushes, flowering dogwoods with white and pink blossoms. It has always been beautiful country. In many ways it still is. I have to say I've never seen so many different shades of green as I can see here in my windows.

"When I say the windows are full of green, I mean that literally.

Every year when growing season comes the weeds and the vines and the bushes are so aggressive, they cover the house in no time. I get tired of hacking them away. I can't keep up. All the windows are covered by a couple of years' worth of vine, the dead stuff closest to the glass, the new green stuff on top, sending feelers inside. I keep the attic window relatively clear, so I can get air into the house. Of course, it's an old house and air leaks in anyway, so I figure that means this ailment isn't airborne, right? Otherwise I would have turned already unless I'm immune. I don't really know, and I have no one to ask. Some day I will have to get out there and cut all the growth away, otherwise it'll pull the house apart. At least I think so. I don't look forward to spending extensive time outside."

Besides the burgeoning growth, the dead were more in evidence this time of year. Jay didn't know why—maybe they didn't like the cold. He had never believed Mother Nature had any sort of intelligence, or any sort of consciousness, but some chain of events must have been triggered, an unknown tipping point surpassed.

His brother had hated the cold. When Ryan was a kid, he couldn't wear enough sweaters and socks. This past winter Jay had been sorely tempted to go outside and throw a blanket over Ryan. He never did. Through the sidelights by the front door he could see his brother's body greening up, splotched with moss and lichen and ground covers supplying modesty patches where his shorts had rotted away. Ryan's head still moved aimlessly. He appeared to be looking at the front door, looking for Jay. Jay avoided gazing at his brother, afraid their eyes might meet.

"The day I saw Ryan sprawled near the front steps I wanted to rush out and drag him inside. But I didn't. I didn't want to take the risk. Besides, he wasn't the same Ryan anymore, I didn't think. I wish I could be sure.

"I don't know how long he'd been there. I almost never looked out those windows. His feet and one arm were missing. I wondered if some predator carried them away. I don't see how he could have made it this far without feet. But he hasn't gotten any closer. I don't think he can.

"I figure he was trying to get home the way I was. I just got here first. Mom and Dad weren't here. Maybe they went out to find us. I'll never know. But they never came back, and now I can only hope I never see them again.

"Ryan would have been a lot better at this. He was good with his hands, and knew about wells and electricity and plumbing, running a farm, raising food, using a compass. He'd have been a great Robinson Crusoe. I read *Robinson Crusoe*, and Defoe's other novels, but never learned anything practical from them. Dad would have wanted Ryan to run this place. He would have been disappointed with how I've let everything fall apart."

Jay getting to the farm first had been a matter of luck. He'd already been on his way, his car packed with all he owned. He'd just dropped out of college in his senior year, six months before graduation, a graduation which wasn't going to happen anyway. He was still figuring out what he was going to tell his parents, but it was a long drive. He had time to figure out an explanation for why he was disappointing them once again.

He knew he shouldn't be there anymore. He didn't know what he could do with an English degree anyway. Oh yeah, chronicle the end of humanity.

He'd just left the Richmond city limits, west on Interstate 64, when he saw people driving off the highway, accidents everywhere. He tried to get off at Charlottesville, but all the exits were jammed. Near Waynesboro he saw his first pile of bodies, along with some struggling to free themselves from dead weight and tangled limbs. He stopped the car and tried to help a young woman, but there was something wrong with her. She didn't try to attack him. Again, not like in the movies, but she scared him, because she seemed to be losing bits of herself, leaving them in a trail behind her in the grass.

His cellphone was useless. On I-81 he tried tuning up and down the dial, getting rational snippets, but no answers. It was his last exposure to mass media, and he didn't expect to encounter it again in his lifetime.

It took him an embarrassing length of time after he arrived home to realize all their farm animals were gone. Maybe his parents liberated them before they went looking for their sons, or maybe it was something more sinister, or maybe there was a simple explanation he hadn't thought of. It was a question Jay was never able to answer.

"Ryan should be the one recording this. He was the star. He always had practical strategies for almost every situation. He was the one who had the best ideas about what we could do if the zombies ever came. Of course, he was completely wrong about that, but maybe he'd have better ideas now.

"Is this an epidemiological event, a metaphysical catastrophe, or the result of warfare? Ryan would be the first to say it doesn't matter. The world has turned back to a time when no one knew anything about anything, so they made up explanations as they went along."

Jay never knew the time, or if the kitchen wall clock was ever correct. He knew eventually he would run through his parents' huge store of batteries, and then it would fail.

If he'd been thinking clearly, he could have created a calendar from the beginning, even if it were simply marks on a wall. He could remember neither the day nor the date he first arrived. He knew there were ways using instruments or astronomical knowledge to figure those things out, but he possessed none of those skills.

In his new world there were warm days and cold days, days with more sun than others, days which were longer or shorter than others, days when it rained, days when the sky was beautiful and he was tempted, but didn't dare, go outside.

There were frequent electrical outages. This caused him great anxiety since electricity powered the pump for the well. Eventually he would lose power. That he had it now seemed a miracle; wasn't some sort of maintenance required? He had no idea how things worked now, but then he never had. He didn't dare hope there were people still running things.

Within months of his arrival home his life before began to feel like a dream. He couldn't quite believe he had ever attended classes, gone out to movies, or had friends. After the first year he began to entertain the possibility he might have hallucinated that entire other life. A lifetime in isolation was a difficult fate. Imagining a former life which included people seemed a logical remedy.

* * *

"I still have enough food for six months or so if I'm careful. Mom and Dad kept years of it: jars, bottles, and cans stuffed into every corner of the cellar. There's some meat left in the big freezer. But at some point, obviously, I'll have to leave. I'll have to go exploring outside.

"The dead don't bother you. Again, nothing like the movies. The few times I had to go out, to unload the car, to retrieve stuff from the barn, I was clumsy. I made noise. I even screamed once when one of them surprised me. They don't notice you're there. The dead don't care. But I don't want to have whatever it is they have.

"I have no idea how it all works, how you get infected. If it's not the air, then maybe it's the touch, or something else. Certain people get it right away and a few people can't get it at all, although I haven't seen anyone else who wasn't dead. At least I don't think so. Maybe it's something we don't even have words for. No pronouns, no nouns, no adjectives, no verbs—maybe nothing I can say has anything to do with what is happening to the world."

The narrow, paved road through the farm was rarely used. It was an access road to smaller farms and properties beyond, and another, bigger road leading into Tennessee. It was unpaved the year Jay was born. They had their buildings and the garden on this side of the road. The other side was all hayfields and pastures for the cattle. They'd never had many visitors. Most people were just passing through.

The dead often arrived two or three at a time, sometimes in a group of a dozen or more, most on the road, and a few came out of the distant fields. Many wore pieces of clothing. Others didn't even have their skin.

Most of the dead staggered on, to the farms and lands beyond, but several stopped here, where an accumulation of them remained. Did they know he was here, though they paid him no attention? They lay down in the yard, or they lingered among the trees, or leaned against the barn. They stood out in the fields like noble scarecrows, until bit by bit they went away, perhaps stolen by the animals Jay never saw.

During the previous late fall and winter, a lesser number of the dead came with the weather. The wind blew them in, or they drifted out of the clouds with the snow, or they arrived like hail and shattered when they hit. Clouds rolled in and clouds rolled away, stars appeared, snow drifted, and the empty dead floated by.

"I know little about the human body. I doubt I could pass a basic anatomy test. I know nothing of pathology, or of the stages of decomposition, but what I see out of the attic window makes no sense. From up here, surrounded by my family's aged possessions, relics of a world that is no longer, I get a pretty good view of our farm: the yard, the barn, the sheds, the empty chicken coop, the weed-filled vegetable garden, the endless pastures. All of it smothered in green and a vinery brown, the land overgrown and the structures collapsing.

"And scattered throughout: the dead, like Halloween decorations, grotesque marionettes, pale ornaments dangling from trees, broken bits moving in a corner or ditch. These ghastly memorials show an unlikely variety in rates of decay—I wish there were a doctor I could speak to for some logical explanation. Why do some look so healthy, as if they were sleep walking, or just staggering down to the fridge for a glass of milk, and others appear to have been in the ground for years, recently dug up and whatever's left of them somehow animated?

"For many of those walking the roads their locomotion seems an impossibility. They shouldn't be able to sustain themselves mechanically as the connective tissue and the joints begin to fail. A hand drops off, an arm. Some do collapse because their legs will no longer support them, and they literally fall to pieces.

"Even many of the relatively fresh-looking ones degenerate at a rapid rate. By the time they get from one edge of our property to the other an accelerated decay has reduced them to almost nothing.

"I've watched how, for a few, a kind of self-digestion occurs. As they wobble down the road their bellies or their groins suddenly split open, and a foul mess of organs drops out. Some look down at this point, watching themselves stepping through their own insides. Others—perhaps the lucky ones—continue as if nothing has occurred.

"So, like the rest of us, the dead are both individuals and part of the herd. It makes sense—each of us suffers a different death, but we all, every one of us, dies. I think maybe I'm not out of the woods yet. I might still come down with this, and at any time.

"I use *us* as if it's a given. I have no idea. I never thought I was special. Now I hope to God I'm not."

Jay utilized his dad's old binoculars to get a better look at their faces. Early on, these faces were still recognizable as once-living personalities, with varying proportions, and individual noses, chins, eyes, and the like. Their features showed a range in expression, although for the most part these were simulations of living emotions, some variation of surprise, shock, or alarm.

Given their ages (although death, like the camera, can add years to a face), he assumed he'd know a few of them from high school or elementary, or he might have seen them in town. He tried not to make comparisons or think too much about familiar details. This continued to nag him, and when further deterioration resulted in anonymity, he felt relieved.

In some the eyeballs fell out. In others the eyeballs shrank and receded into the skull. Sometimes there was liquification and bloating. Or there was significant aridity and a paper-like appearance. Sometimes a dark leakage from the abdomen would dribble down the legs. Sometimes the skin looked tight and stretched like a drum. In others there was a great deal of skin slippage and teeth falling out. The world of the dead was every bit as unequal and unjust as the world of the living.

In church, when Jay was small, the preacher said when the rapture happens the souls of the believers would be delivered to heaven, leaving their sinful bodies behind. One afternoon he thought he saw the preacher's body lurching up the road. He turned away and went downstairs. He wasn't sure if it was out of respect, but he didn't want to see any more.

Then there had been the girl he'd always wanted to ask out in high school, but never did. He'd been too shy. Lately the dead who appeared on the road were so deteriorated, even if she'd been among them, he would not have recognized her. He was grateful for that much.

"All my life I've dreamed of the dead. Both in waking dreams and sleeping dreams I have seen them: passing through rooms, gliding across lawns, sometimes perched on rooftops. Sometimes in these dreams they confront me, angry because of something I've done or simply because I'm still alive. I've always come away from these dreams feeling guilty, either because of something thoughtless I said or something heartfelt I lacked the courage to reveal. But the most peculiar thing is that I've never dreamt of the actual dead. The dead people in my dreams have always been living at the time.

"Like everyone else I've lost elderly relatives. We expect grandparents to die, older parents, old men and women in the neighborhood. It seems natural. I loved my grandfather very much; he built this farm from nothing. But the last decade of his life I pulled away from him. I was still glad to see him when I did, but I didn't seek him out. Part of it was I was busy with my own life, and we didn't have as much in common anymore. But I know much of it was because I realized his life was on its way out. He was going to die relatively soon, and I didn't want to be close enough to watch.

"I'm ashamed of that now. I wanted to ask him how it felt—I admit that was more about my own anxieties than anything meant to comfort him—but I wanted to know how it was to lose most of the people you'd ever known, most of the people you'd ever loved, and knowing you were both the last and the next. No wonder the old looked so tired and moved as if they were carrying a great weight.

"I wish I had asked. I could really use that information right now.

"The first young person I knew who died was a popular high school boy who lived on a farm a few miles away. I was in elementary school, but everyone knew who he was—a star player on the high school football team, in the choir at church, and he always smiled and said hello to me even though I was just this scrawny kid he didn't really know.

"His junior year he was on a tractor helping his dad out when it rolled over on him, trapping him underneath. All the boys drove tractors around here, helping on the family farm. They tried everything to get him out while he screamed until he passed out, but he died under there.

"For years I just couldn't get him out of my head. Anytime anything big happened—a huge snowstorm, an important game, a new *Star Wars* film, the terrorist attack on the World Trade Center—the first thing I thought was *Frankie missed this,* like he missed falling in love, getting married, having kids, having a career. I wouldn't have said it was *unfair* because that's just the way life works. But I thought it was *strange,* the way it all works, a short life and a forever death. For the dead, death just is, I suppose. For the living it's about everything they missed, and what you miss about them. Until now, of course.

"What is happening now is much stranger. I'm glad Frankie died all those years ago, and not recently. I wouldn't want to see him walking around dead, like my brother Ryan before he ended up by the front steps.

"I haven't written down anything in a while. Sometimes I don't see the point. The power has been blinking out a lot lately. The other day it must have been 8 hours or more. Pretty soon it will go out for good. I've been lucky to have it this long. But the pump isn't working right, I think maybe because of all the power outages. You can't live without water. I may not know much about survival, but I know that much.

"I've got a backpack filled with some food, a blanket, a knife and a few tools, a change of clothes, extra shoes, some first aid stuff. I'll bring the journal and several pens as well. I'll see new things, so I'll have new things to write about.

"I'm a fool for not thinking more about what to pack for my exit from home. I had the time. I'm a fool for not maintaining my car. But I didn't want to go out there, and who knows if there's any gas to be found, or a clear space to drive. Lately the dead fill the road. I'll know soon enough. I'll know a lot of things I don't know now. Human beings, we're always learning."

Jay went out the front door the next morning. He left the door open, for another survivor, or as a new space the dead could—whatever. He would have liked to stay and watch that happen. That would have been too foolish even for him.

He would look for a place with a spring—quite possible in south-west Virginia, and if there was a store nearby, he was all set. Problem solved.

He stopped at Ryan's body and watched him for a few moments. The body wasn't exactly moving, but Jay detected a subtle trembling, a vibration, a Ryan quake. His brother had turned his face downward, as if in a deep contemplation of the ground and what lay beyond.

The dead in the yard paid no attention. He meant nothing to them. He dwelled in a different universe. There was a pervasive stench which, although not fresh, was deeply unpleasant. He was now close enough to examine the dead more thoroughly, but chose not to, assuming he would have many such chances later.

When he stepped onto the road Jay was pleased to see he would be able to ease past the walking forms without having to touch them. He wasn't sure which direction to take. It made little difference, but he decided to go right first, toward the small towns, for a greater selection of supplies. It did mean going against traffic, for all the dead were traveling the other way. Another thing he'd never been able to figure out—why all in the same direction? There was nothing for them there.

He was so tired. He hadn't slept well in, what? Months. He felt his hands trembling and brought them up to his face. When had they gotten so thin? And spotted. He had brownish spots everywhere. As his mother turned old she used to call those age spots. And skin so thin it looked like tissue. But still he looked better than these poor souls. So many things had happened to him. He was last of his kind.

He became momentarily confused and wasn't sure where he was going. He turned and turned and finally fell into pace with the rest of them.

He felt a great weight pressing on his shoulders. He may have put too much into his pack. He kept moving his feet, but it was becoming increasingly difficult. He was aware when the lower part of his body let go. There was a hushing sound, and a tremendous release. A great sigh rushed through him. He was still thinking. He was still thinking.

LUSCA

SOLEIL KNOWLES

Y ou wring your hands, cold and clammy and rough. Skin of teeth, salty with sea brine cuts into the humanlike fat of your palms, and you stare down the edge of oblivion. The wind whips you, sings to you. A full, fat, yellow moon casts a sultry pall over the water, the light disappearing into its mirror image on the sea. You take one step, then another. The blue hole sings its deep, droning song, and what can you do? Resist?

You are five on an island of scrubs and long roads. Of feuds between north and south, screeches disguised as "good morning" and "good afternoon" and "good evening." You live as inland as possible in a place where the distance between two coasts is the jump from thumb to fore-finger.

You cannot go to the ocean. Never the ocean.

Mother grabs you and shakes your shoulders and preaches harder than the priest in Sunday Mass: *The water is dangerous. The water will kill you. Stay away.* She bathes you with quick scrubs of a rough cloth, in a metal tub barely covered on the bottom with the freshest water straight off the boat. You've never seen a boat, save for the broken ones abandoned in the scrubs. The ones that serve no further purpose than to shelter old dogs from thunder. Boats mean ocean. Ocean means death. You let her scrub you raw and put you to bed. You never tell her you hear the waves in your dreams or see a circle of void stretching wide below your feet.

You are thirteen and gangly. You are thirteen and violent. *Eighth grade is not for gangly, violent girls*, you think as you chew on a piece of salami between hard bread. It doesn't fill you, nothing ever does. You scratch at your head, your dark, thick, nappy head, and stare at all the pretty, popular bright girls.

They titter and eat rice, crabs, pork chops, and everything else mother says will make you sick. They stare at you and whisper from behind perfectly manicured hands. You are rough. You are gangly. They are soft and they think you don't belong. You spit out your salami and walk up to them, fists clenched and skin prickling. They sneer at your clothes, at your hair, and ask what you want. You grab one—the brightest, blondest one—and swing her around by her ponytail. Around and around until she's a screaming top, a flurry of white socks and plaid skirt. She hits a tree when you've finished, and before those stunned, stupid girls can call someone, you've spat at their feet and stomped off. The blonde is crying, her face red and splotchy. She is not beautiful. Not anymore.

Mother makes you break a switch when you get home. The principal called her, and she stands there waiting for you with arms crossed and a thousand admonitions on her lips. She spews those admonitions in stops and bursts as she leaves red welts across your arms, your thighs and back. *Never do that again*, she screams. *Never use your strength. You will kill someone.* She sends you to bed with no food, but it's okay. You are no more hungry than you always are. You are ravenous, starving, and deep in your soul, you know it is a hunger that will never be satiated.

You don't mean to do it. You are so hungry.

The ram comes snuffling into your yard at half past midnight. You hear it clopping around, hear it tearing at your grass and your bushes and your corn. You need to run it, so you tiptoe out of the house. It stares at you, blank and foolish in the moonlight. You open your mouth to shout, to tell it to go away. Instead, your tongue lolls. Your mouth waters and your stomach opens because there's a bur in the fur on the edge of its tail and the bur has made a nick, and blood—a tiny pinprick of blood—spills from that nick. You are hungry. You are so hungry. You can never be filled, but this ram will help.

When you charge, it stands no chance. You grab it. Your very skin is rough enough to tear away clumps of fur. The ram bays into the night, and then stops. Silences. Hot blood soaks the dirt in a strange sort of sacrifice. You are not filled, but for once, you come close.

One ram. Then two. Then a flock.

People blame the dogs. People start poisoning the dogs, and you watch their bodies burn in piles and droves and explosions of kerosene. The fire offends you, offends your very being, and mother cannot pry you out of your room for days on end.

When she finally sends you to school again, with dark red caked and flaking beneath your nails, you meet no one's eyes.

The girls bemoan their poor pets, their poor sheep, their fathers who lived off of those sheep. Their faces grow red, and you can smell it. The life flowing just below their skin.

They are better than rams. They scream like rams.

You sit through lessons, writing down numbers and letters and answers to questions until your slate is full and your chalk is nubby, and all you can hear in your ears is the rush of blood in the water. You close your eyes and see that big blue void. Thunder rumbles in the distance. You taste salt and iron and decide you've had enough for one day. Your bike is parked outside, and it takes only a second to grab your bag and slip from the classroom. The teacher only knows you've gone when you're already down the road and the rain is starting to pour in sheets, creeping closer.

Your legs work, you pedal harder. You race the rain until you're standing on your bike, until your skirt is flying behind you and the downpour grows ever closer. Rogue droplets fly out of their ordered lines and catch the back of your neck, of your legs. Your skin itches. The rain reaches out, grabs the back of your skirt and makes sure that even once you've reached home, it has won the race. You toss your bike and limp inside, wet skirt obnoxious against your legs. You peel it away. Your legs itch, and when you scratch, your skin feels like it's made up of a million tiny teeth. Mother watches you with desolation, with sadness and failure and anger. She throws away the skirt. You cannot stay here. You are being sent to the capital; where the buildings are bigger and the people, more strange. Nobody cares in a city like that, and you will disappear like a drop in the ocean. There is less room for mistakes there. There are no rams in the capital.

Mother sends you off with one carry-on and a kiss to the forehead.

She sends you off with the promise that your new school is nice, that you'll live in a dormitory and make new friends.

She sends you off with the promise that you are safe.

You see the blue hole from the plane window. It looks so small. So plain. You laugh. What a magnificent lie.

You pull at your collar. The uniforms here are no different from home. The school is different, though. Bigger, with a concrete courtyard instead of dust and grass. The classrooms and office are arranged in a perfect square. You stand in perfect lines at a perfect assembly.

You sing the national anthem, and the administrator stands under the sole tree while you bake in the morning sun. They give false life lessons. They quote the Bible and pray and announce things and tell students who must report to the office. You look around at faces you've been forced to learn. At faces from Andros with long noses and downy feathers disguised as hair ornaments. At faces from Kingston filled with mischief, with too big mouths and hands that go translucent when the sun hits them just right. They do not see you swaying in the unforgiving sunlight. They do not hear the way your veins narrow and cry out. The perfect lines and bored faces sway, and your head cracks against the concrete. The administrator keeps talking. Someone screams.

They pray over your body long before they call for help.

* * *

They don't talk about it. They don't talk about the way you sweat and shiver and bay for blood as your skin dries. They don't talk about your gasp, your cry, the gnash of your teeth as they pour water down your throat.

They look at you the way mother did, with derision and scorn and *this child needs one good cutass* baked into their stares. They can't hide you, and so they lie it away.

There is nothing to see.

Heatstroke.

Move along.

The cafeteria serves fish on Thursdays and you race to be the first in line. You order three big plates and snarl at anyone who comes too close. It's saturated in oil and bread but still it claws at your stomach, at your tongue and your soul in ways the salami never did, in ways the ram just couldn't. You want more. You need more. The line is too long. The bell rings and like iron to magnets, everyone finds their way back into the square. You go back to class, gnawing on a fork and thinking of bulging eyes, of scales and gills and the deep blue sea.

You are dreaming of a beach, of the water. It licks at your heels, sings to you and pulls you in. Far away and distant, in the memory of a tin tub and flying plaid, your Mother tells you the water is dangerous. *She is not here*, the deep sings in her tidal voice. *I failed with her. She hates me. But I am here for you. I love you. Let me embrace you.*

You walk into the waves and split open.

You wake with a headache, soaked to the bone. Iron sits at the back of your mouth, and you know only that it tastes better than oily fried fish. You drag yourself onto the jitney, where the usual morning chatter is replaced with staunch whispers. You drag yourself off of the jitney and into the schoolyard, and everyone is talking. A girl from Andros shakes and ruffles. Her words sound like parrot chatter as she tries to whisper, but you hear it.

Lusca. They whisper. *Monster.*

"Ain't nobody see them in years," one says.

"I thought they gone extinct," hisses another.

"My daddy gone fishin' last night and say he saw it," one pipes above the rest. The students crowd around that one to hear a second-hand tale and you slip away into the girls room.

In the last stall on the right, you stare at your hands. At the webbing flaking away from between your fingers. At the sheen on your skin anyone with lesser sight would mistake for sweat. You leave the bathroom, nudge past the students. They speak of the Thing, of its gnashing teeth and dark eyes. They say it stole a fisherman's catch, ate it right by the boat. Someone brought their phone. Someone shares the hazy picture.

You go to class and try to ignore the whispers like roiling waves in your ears.

It's a Tuesday morning when they call you into the office, the air so thick with rain that it sinks down into your lungs. The old lady behind the desk emphasizes "good morning" when you don't say it first, mutters about rude children after she sends you off to the headmaster.

He's waiting for you with one leg crossed over the other. In his hand is the phone, confiscated. On the phone, the picture.

"Sit," he says. *Die*, he means.

You fold your hands, cross your legs at the ankle.

He puts the phone on his desk, slides it over

"Do you know what this is?"

"A picture, sir."

"Of?"

"I ain't know."

His nostrils flare. A vein sticks out on his wide forehead.

"You *don't* know. Are you sure?"

"Yes, sir." You never wanted to cuss an adult so bad in life. The rain beats down hard on his one little window, and you count patterns in the droplets instead of focusing on his face.

He lets you go with a wave of the hand and a stiff admonition on manners. The rain is still pouring, and it itches your skin as you run off to class.

* * *

On the weekend, you call Mother. She lies and lies and cries and asks why you are asking questions. She screams about the water. The water is evil. The water will kill you, gut you, turn you inside out until you are no longer human. You dash the phone against the wall. Everything is a lie and you are a shred of truth wrapped up in layers of misdirection.

They know now, after that picture. You see it in the way they look at you. The way they watch you dodge the rain and inhale bottles of water when the sun is high in the sky. Mother said you would be safe. Another of her thousand lies. Here, there is no room for magic. Here, they kill monsters.

You close your eyes and see it again.

The blue hole. The dark mystery. The void that sings and cries and pulls you in like it is the only true mother you will ever have.

You need to go back.

The men on the boat look at you and look away just as fast. They do not want to see your eyes, your skin, your teeth. They do not want to see the blood under your nails or the webbing between your fingers. They mercifully leave you alone and shove off.

You left that school and those people with not so much as a look back. You have no mind for them, their ordered world and dull lives. You hold on to the boat rails, watch the sea roil and smile in bursts of foam and schools of fish. You are going home, to scrubs and rams and the void from which all answers flow.

The cliff is rough, the sea is dark. The moon is yellow, and below you, the ocean reaches out her hands to catch you as you jump. You hit the water, and sink. You sink, and sink, until you see the fish. Until you warp, and scream, and finally, finally embrace the ocean. *Mother lied,* you think as a fin tears out of your back, as your legs stretch and split, split, and split again into eight. As rows of suckers line your new limbs and rows of teeth fill your mouth.

Oh, how she lied.

You catch fish after fish. You catch them and tear at them until blood soaks the water and turns the moonlight scarlet. You tear, gorge, and eat until, finally, the hunger is sated.

The water will not kill me, you think as a group of night swimmers run, splashing, into the waves. As they laugh and swim, paying no mind to the shadows lurking just beneath the surface.

It has brought me, finally, to life.

TO SAIL THE BLACK

A. C. WISE

The ghost ship *Xanthic Promise* sails the black, powered by the slumbering heart of a dying star. And its captain, Antimony Jones, stalks its decks in a swirl of crimson coat and fox fire lighting, dogged by voices. The recent dead, the long dead, and the dead-to-be, all murmuring as to how she's only three months into her command and it's all coming undone.

"Stow it." Antimony snaps, pirate-captain proper.

A living crew member jumps out of her way at the words, back flat against the wall, spanner clanking to the deck in alarm. The ghosts snicker, and Antimony bares her teeth until they fall silent.

"You. Back to work." Antimony jabs a finger at the frightened crew member, Hawk, even though she was the one who interrupted his work in the first place.

As he scrambles to obey, the ship murmurs its own complaint, an out-of-place thrumming Antimony feels in her back teeth. Something is wrong, and Hyacinth, her gods-damned chief engineer, is playing coy, making Antimony come to her in person rather than just telling her what's wrong.

She rounds the corner and nearly smacks into the door to the star chamber, which should open automatically. Antimony slaps a palm to override and enters shouting.

"What in all the gods-damned corporeal and incorporeal hells is so important that I had to come all the way down here instead of you telling me over the comm? And why is the door locked?"

Antimony stops dead. Because what is so gods-damned important is clearly obvious. Starling, her now-former boatswain, blood-soaked from chin to waist, well and truly slaughtered, hangs by his wrists in the pulsing light of the star chamber.

"Oh, fuck me," Antimony says and turns to kick the door.

As captain of a ghost ship, death and Antimony are well acquainted. The *Xanthic Promise*'s winding, nautilus halls bear countless invisible scars, Antimony's among them, where each member of the crew past and present has sworn their demise to the ship. Blood oaths cut into palm and wall as a condition of their service stitch their ghosts in place and power everything the star doesn't.

It's a reckless practice, condemned by the Galactic Fleet and every other kind of ship captain out there, save for pirates. But her crew's lives and deaths are their own to swear with as they please, and who is Antimony to say different. Some, she suspects, are too young and dumb to truly believe in their future deaths as a reality; others are at the end of their span and desperate to trade what little they've left for a last taste of freedom.

Antimony swore her own oath at fourteen, an orphan doomed to life on a backwater station until the *Xanthic Promise* docked for trade. Rough and battered as she'd been, the moment Antimony set eyes on *Xanthic Promise,* it had been love—true and deep and head over heels. All the fairy tales her mother and father had told her before their unfortunate demise, of living stars who sang their captains across the black, seemed poised to come true all at once.

She'd stowed aboard, and never mind that the star powering the ship was only roiling, pulsing light, and not the painfully beautiful, human-faced creature in the holo-illustrations from her parents' stories. The walls still whispered with ghosts, the opposite of the Galactic Fleet's cold logic and strict regulations, and definitely the opposite of a life lived station-bound, stuck in one place and hoping against hope the universe would come to her.

Loose-tongued ghosts had put a quick end to her plan to stay hidden, but instead of putting her right back where she started, or straight out into the black as would have been her right, then-captain Basalt had given Antimony a choice. Swear her life and future death to the ship by stitching a piece of herself to walls, or live a life staring at the same span of stars out of the station's viewports, always wondering what might have been.

Antimony hadn't hesitated, chin up, blade to palm, and bloody palm to wall all in a flash. She'd worked her way from deck girl, carrying and fetching and cleaning, to assistant boatswain, then boatswain, and on up with the sure knowledge in her heart that she would sit in Basalt's chair as captain one day.

That she finally achieved her dream at the cost of a death-promise is a problem for future-her. Present-her has everything she ever wanted. She's flush with ill-gotten gains, the boundless universe is spread before her, and the crackling power of her ghost ship is hers to command.

Except that at-this-very-moment-her has a very much here-and-now problem. Starling.

His death has the air of ritual. Doctor Coxcomb has his body down in the medbay, and the only thing she's been able to tell Antimony so far is that whoever killed Starling cut out his tongue before stringing him up like a burned offering.

Starling had sworn himself to *Xanthic Promise* young too, sixteen with a head full of dreams. They'd picked him up planet side and Antimony had been the one to argue for giving him the same choice she'd been given. Most of her interactions with him since had been recent, in his new capacity as boatswain, requisitioning goods and discussing the ship's stores. Except more than once, she'd caught him at his post, moon-eyed over holo-stories, including one with the very same illustration of the living, singing, humanoid star her parents had shown her.

It had made Antimony smile then, and makes her regret his death all the more now.

There's a headache building between her eyes. There's a . . . *hmmm*. It's a not-quite-buzz-not-quite-hum, like an itch on the wrong side of her skin, creeping around inside her skull. She's been hearing it since . . .

she isn't even sure when, but it's getting louder, tied to the ship feeling listless, argumentative, sluggish. It's in the soles of her boots, coming up through the deck plates. A sense of wrong. As if the sleeping star at the ship's heart was not merely a metaphor, as if the ship was having bad dreams.

"Heavy is the head that wears the crown."

A phantom voice at her ear stirs phantom hair. Antimony just manages to turn her surprised flinch into a hand grazed over her scalp's stubble, as if that was always what she meant to do. She turns to face her immediate predecessor.

"Fuck off, Cedar."

The former captain leans against nothing, the prerogative of ghosts, arms crossed, lips bent to smirking. He's much more corporeal than he has any right to be, in that he possesses form at all, though she can see right through him. Being stitched, Cedar should only be a voice, muttering in the walls with all the rest. That he's more, Antimony imagines, is sheer spite and force of will. And a handy trick she'd like to learn herself one day, if she can do it without sacrificing her pride and asking him how.

"What's the fun in death if I can't haunt my quarters and gloat?"

"Death isn't supposed to be fun. It's supposed to be useful." Antimony scowls. "And they're not your quarters, they're mine."

Antimony still doesn't know how Cedar won Basalt's good grace and favor and ended up captain before her. Cedar, with his Galactic Fleet training, the antithesis of everything a good pirate should be, yet Basalt had named him as successor. The fact that Cedar in turn named Antimony and not Hyacinth, Antimony is beginning to suspect, was another act of spite, as being captain is turning out to be a lot less fun and a lot more headachy than she imagined.

Cedar cocks his head, waiting for her to speak, waiting, more precisely, for her to ask for help. Antimony sits astride the polished bench of the single most improbable item on a ship crammed with impossibilities: a gleaming white baby grand piano, Cedar's pride and joy. Instead of giving him the satisfaction, she stabs a series of discordant notes. When Cedar frowns, some of the tension uncoils from Antimony's shoulders.

"I hear you have a ghost problem." Cedar breaks first, but it's only a moment before his smirk is back in place.

Because, gods-damn him, he's right. One of the many drawbacks of a ghost-powered ship—gossip travels fast. There are scant few secrets on the *Xanthic Promise*, save those kept from the still-living, which is precisely Antimony's problem.

If the universe were kind, she could simply ask Starling the cause of his death, but despite being sewn into the walls by a supposedly unbreakable pact, wherever his ghost is, she can't hear it. Like he gave up his voice with the loss of his tongue. All she can hear when she listens for him is that gods-damned *hmmm,* getting louder and making it hard to think.

"I don't suppose you have anything remotely useful to contribute?" Antimony grinds the words between her teeth.

An expression flickers bright through the former captain's eyes, which are the color of lightning, nothing Antimony can read. Cedar is only three months stitched; perhaps Starling's death is simply making him think of his own.

Antimony thinks on it too, an unfortunate debris-strike fracturing Cedar's faceplate during routine repairs—repairs he shouldn't even have been undertaking as captain. Antimony had been there when he'd told Hyacinth he wanted to stretch his legs in the black. She'd watched Hyacinth inspect his suit herself, likely the only thing that kept Antimony from suspicion, her desire for the captain's chair being no secret. She'd been there, too, when Cedar had come back to the ship, tether-hauled, frozen solid, ice crystals clinging to his skin, and his body ballooned to twice its size.

"What would you give me if I could tell you?" The flicker in Cedar's eyes turns sly, the promise of knowledge held like a curl of candied orange peel on his tongue.

Antimony puffs up, pride, as always, ready to tangle her legs and lead to a fall.

"Listen, you smug son-of-a—"

Cedar's eyes flicker again, static-shot. He's there and then he's not and Antimony thumps a fist against the piano again for good measure.

"Damn it."

She bites the inside of her cheek, considers calling him back, thinks of apologizing, and the thought turns her stomach. She doesn't need him, and he probably didn't know anything anyway.

Still, the air in her quarters feels empty, the temperature dropped. There's no love lost between them, but Cedar's departure hammers home the inevitable truth chained around the neck of all captains: she is alone.

"Damn it," she says again, softer this time, and swings her weary leg over the piano bench, rising.

Any sensible captain would remain locked in her quarters to drink her troubles away, but sensible has never been her style. Antimony makes her way to the ship's prow, allowing a detour to the ship's store, where she feels Starling's absence all over again as she requisitions a bottle of good rum and uncorks it with her teeth. She wonders what happened to his holo-stories. She could use a good fairy tale about valiant captains and singing ships right about now.

The hum-not-hum itch is there again as she walks the halls, a voice among other voices, one she isn't quite hearing. It's like an ill-tuned violin, a wetted finger circling the rim of a glass. On the edge of painful. A familiar voice, but corrupted somehow, like the mind behind it is still trying to figure out how to make words.

"Starling?" she asks it not expecting an answer, and the sound rises in pitch, a static-squeal like it's arguing with itself, before it falls silent.

Then there's only the usual ghost ship murmur, the dead speculating whether command has made her crack. Living crew members, too, give her the side-eye, whispering among themselves as if she can't hear. Let them talk. Cedar was a captain of the people, soft and decidedly un-piratey. Antimony is comfortable in her lonely command; better to be feared than loved, as they say.

Lacking anyone human to talk to, she *could* seek her own ghost, her dead-self-to-be as oracle, but that way lies madness. Or so she's heard tell. Knowing your ghost on an intellectual level is one thing; looking it dead in the eye and knowing it full and true, that's another.

Besides, at the moment, Antimony would rather drink herself into oblivion or into a state where a solution produces itself, whichever comes first. And she intends to do so in full sight of her ghosts and her crew. Let them see a captain without shame, bowed but not broken by the weight of her command. Let the living and the dead gossip on that if they will.

The crow's nest is empty, waiting, and Antimony can't help a grin. She strung the hammock across the ship's foremost eye herself during her first year aboard. Basalt had given her waste duty for a month, but she hadn't taken the nest down, and Antimony had even seen her captain using it a time or two herself when she thought no one was looking.

When she'd first come aboard, after her shifts, Antimony would throw herself into the hammock to listen while most everyone else slept. She'd gaze out at all those stars and wish the stories she'd devoured as a station-bound child were true. She'd wished that instead of the creaks and groans of metal deck plates, she could hear the star's voice. She'd wanted to hear it sing.

She'd been foolish enough then, naïve and wide-eyed, that she'd actually asked then-engineer Oak about the star, and whether it really slept.

They'd laughed at her, that deep barrel-chested laugh that, while it hadn't been cruel, had still struck her a blow. Fairy stories, they'd said. Tales for children to make the work of ships seem like magic.

But if ghosts could power a ship's weapons, she'd reasoned, then why not a sleeping star? Maybe, over the years, people had simply forgotten the truth. Maybe when they'd put the stars to sleep, they hadn't wanted to own the cruel thing they were doing, so they spun fantastical tales too incredible to possibly be true.

She'd given up her belief soon enough though, but had Starling?

Antimony throws herself into the crow's nest, kicking up her bootheels just as a commotion breaks out behind her.

What the fuck now? she thinks, wheeling her weary bones around.

"She wakes!" the man screams, a crew member whose name Antimony should know, excusing herself that she doesn't due to the fact that his face is currently an unrecognizable mask of blood.

He holds something sharp in crimson-slick fingers, not threatening anyone, but staggering and weaving—shock and blood-loss after gouging out his own eyes.

"It won't stop!" he screams. "He promised, but it never stops. Please, help me."

"You still want to make the run?" Hyacinth asks, all incredulous, scoffing tone.

"Are we or are we not gods-damned pirates," Antimony, rhetorical, shoots back.

Her mouth tastes the way she imagines the inside of an engine block would.

She has one crew member spaced, body refusing to yield up any other secrets, and one in the medbay, bandages over his lack of eyes and doped to oblivion. And she still has a gods-damned job to do.

"We can still make the pickup and drop in plenty of time to get paid. Even without the extra ghost to throw on the fire." Antimony tries to smile around the flat attempt at a joke.

Hyacinth scowls, muttering under her breath, as she walks away.

Doctor Coxcomb utterly forbid Antimony from questioning Chrysotile, though Antimony doubts he'd be able to provide her with sensible answers. Sensible people don't gouge their eyes out. But insensible people might just commit murder. Something to think about. Later. Solving mysteries doesn't pay the bills. Only piracy does.

The pickup goes without a hitch, the drop-off less so, because of course one thing can't fucking go right for her. Instead of payment, their contact meets them with guns, eyes blacked and teeth capped with gold, marking them as DeathSkull, notorious double-crossers, and not Green Hand, the flag they'd claimed to sail under.

"Evade where you can, fire only if you have to," Antimony shouts to be heard above the chaos.

A hit to *Xanthic Promise*'s portside causes the whole ship to rock, and a panel to her right explodes. *How the fuck does that even work?* she wonders, then ceases to wonder as sparks shower and she slaps at her coat to keep it from going up in flame. How many deaths can she afford to burn to get out of this mess? She rolls through the inventory of ghosts in her mind, then gives the order to fire.

She needs just a little time, just a little luck, just enough space to do something stupid to save their skins. Twin stars of glittering light leap from the ship's cannons. Ghost-tech rarely kills, but it does a credible job of convincing people they're dying. At least briefly. Sometimes, ironically, it even convinces them to death.

Either way, it's still a pretty light show that will buy them some time as, for the next few moments, the crew of the ship currently trying to wipe them from the stars relives the last breaths of six stitched souls now serving the Xanthic Promise as weaponry.

Basalt may be in there somewhere, Antimony thinks as the glittering light hits home. That could be her fate one day, the captain's last burst of glory, her final duty. There are worse ways to go.

Another panel explodes. Acrid smoke fills the air. Antimony coughs, and the ship slews hard and away, running running running. Rivets and seams strain, everything wanting to fly apart as Antimony wills it to hold. Jaw clenched, she calls up charts, squinting through eyes that stream part from headache, part from the bone-rattling speed. Her back molars feel as loose as the rivets, and she shouts fresh coordinates.

"Are you out of your gods-damned mind?" Hyacinth swivels to stare. A rivulet of blood tracks from a gash above her eye, but she doesn't wipe it away.

"Yes!" Antimony fires back.

"That's Sargasso space." Trust Hyacinth to recognize the coordinates right away. Damn and double gods-damn.

"Do it anyway."

Hyacinth's eyes blaze crimson mutiny, or maybe that's only the blood, but she punches the coordinates, punches the ship, and they're off.

The Horse Latitudes. The Doldrums. The Sargasso Sea. All names that don't make sense in the black, but the effect is the same. It's a graveyard for stars, a place of legend where ships stall for no discernable reason and never start up again. It's a place only the foolhardiest captain would go willingly, and which any sensible band of pirates would cut off pursuit to avoid, which is exactly what Antimony is counting on.

There's an under-the-skin feeling the moment *Xanthic Promise* hits that dead space. The DeathSkull ship drops pursuit, just as their own engines cut out, and Antimony breathes relief against the tightness in her ribs even if it doesn't last long. The walls chatter doubt. Her crew looks to each other, wild-eyed, but they're all still alive. They should be falling on their knees and thanking her.

That's when the screaming starts.

It's a wrong sound. An inside-out sound, purple-shattering-to-silver-at-the-edges, going on and on like a voice, like that untuned violin, but so much louder and worse. It is want and need and hunger and fear and unlike anything Antimony has ever heard before. It's unlike anything she ever wants to hear again. It makes her want to dig her nails into her skin and peel it away whole to go running around in her bones.

It leaves her panting on hands and knees, howling back at the noise until she tastes blood, until Hyacinth cracks her across the jaw hard enough to replace one ringing in her ears with another.

"What is. That. Noise. What you're. Doing." Hyacinth's words come out in huffing breaths, shaking and broken.

"You didn't hear it?" Antimony is still hearing it, is certain she'll always be hearing it from now until the end of time, but at least it's dulled, a bruise rather than a fresh blow.

"I heard you screaming," Hyacinth says. "I didn't know a human throat could make that sound."

"I'm not sure it can," Antimony says.

She stands.

"Well, whatever it was," Hyacinth says, voice steadying, "according to the report I just got, it happened at the same time three very long fissures appeared in the star chamber's glass. So, to put it mostly succinctly and bluntly, we are completely and utterly fucked."

Antimony follows Hyacinth to look at the star chamber, as if their own eyes could make the report untrue. No such luck. The star chamber is indeed breaking as reported, three long fissures running almost the entire length of the glass that looks somewhat like an old-fashioned lantern and somewhat like the heart of a lighthouse and nothing like either of those things at all. Breaking, but not broken, and that is one small mercy, but perhaps the only one.

Antimony leaves Hyacinth to do whatever she can, which is, she suspects, very little. The ship was already sick before this whole thing started. Cedar must have known it, and that's why he insisted on making the repairs himself. But something went wrong, and maybe that's where this all started, and it's all connected somehow.

Antimony thinks of Starling's missing tongue, a sacrifice, and the sound she's still hearing, like a ringing echo inside her skull, a voice that doesn't have words, belonging to something that never had a voice before. She thinks of fairy tales hiding a willfully forgotten truth in plain sight. She's beginning to build a picture in her mind, and she doesn't like it at all.

She takes herself to the medical bay.

Chrysotile lies rigid, lashed down with restraints. Fluid drips into his arm, a steady flow, keeping him somewhere between awake and dreaming. Coxcomb will likely be back soon. Not enough time to try to wake him, even if such a thing were possible. Antimony is considering sneaking out again when Chrysotile's head snaps around to look straight at her, which is disconcerting to say the least, given that he is without eyes.

"I thought I could finish it, but I wasn't strong enough. Starling said the light would stop if I helped him, but it only got worse."

His body seizes, guilt or pain or both wanting to make an arch against the restraints. He gropes the air, fingers twisted to claws and Antimony shoves down every skin-crawling impulse she has to make herself do the human thing and let Chrysotile take her hand. His fingers are freezing, his grip iron.

"Tell the captain I'm sorry."

"I—" Antimony begins, but gets no further as the door grinds open and Doctor Coxcomb descends on her like a storm.

"I was very specific in my orders." Coxcomb brandishes a syringe like a weapon, ready to deploy whatever is inside if Antimony doesn't leave now, captain or no.

And oops, yes, maybe Antimony did use her override on the medbay door knowing the doctor would deny her entry. She quick steps away, trusting to Coxcomb's brutality in defense of her patient. Besides, she needs to think.

Tell the captain I'm sorry. Antimony very much doubts Chrysotile meant her. Some promise made to Cedar? And how does Starling fit in? All those old stories. If they really were true, what monsters would that make her and all the other ghost ship captains down through the ages?

And even if the tales aren't true, what if Starling believed? Would it be enough for him to convince Chrysotile to kill him, so he could sacrifice his tongue to the star and give it a voice?

Thoughts roil, pressing out against her skin until Antimony feels she'll explode. She stomps through the halls and up to the crow's nest, the place she dreamed as a child, and now all those dreams and wishes feel like a cruel lie. Antimony presses her hands to the window and screams fuck you very loudly at the lack of stars.

Throat raw, she turns to an access panel, calling up the ship's logs. Something she should have done long ago, only she was busy with murdered and eyeless crew members, damned double-crossing pirates, and recalcitrant ghosts.

She finds Cedar's entries from the days before his death. He must have felt the same wrongness in the ship as she does now. Would he have attributed it to a waking star? And if he had, what would he do?

Deep in their hearts, do all ship's captains know the tales they drank like milk as children are true, but they've collectively chosen to believe otherwise?

Cedar never confided in her as his second in command. Keep your friends close, and your enemies closer. It stood to reason Cedar had only accepted her as first mate to keep an eye on her. Who had he confided in, then? Chrysotile? Certainly not his logs, as they are all maddeningly mundane and empty of any useful details.

Antimony returns to the ship's stores and requisitions another bottle, gin this time, and a sturdy blade. She's about to do a very unwise thing indeed. Antimony drinks and winds her way through the halls until she finds the place where her oath sings to her.

The expanse of wall would look unremarkable to anyone else, but it's where her death is stitched, her promise to the ship, and so for her, there's a faint silver glow of scars etched into the metal. With half the bottle killed, the blade weaves dangerously above her palm. She closes one eye and squints the other to make both knife and hand behave. Before she can think better of it, she traces the old seams until blood wells, and presses the new wound to old.

Red smears and a spark snap-jumps, shocking her spine rigid and clacking her teeth together. It's unwise to talk to one's own future-ghost, to seek one's death for counsel, but ever since the scream that rattled her to her core, Antimony has felt her death just inches beneath her skin and she'll be gods-damned if she just sits around waiting for it to come to her.

She forbids herself to pass out, winding the gauze she requisitioned at the same time as the bottle around her hand. It immediately soaks through. When her other-self appears, it's very much like looking in a mirror, same shorn-to-stubble hair, same smug grin. The event horizon between her death being a future-her problem and a present-her problem is collapsing. She rubs a hand over her scalp, almost expecting her ghost to do the same, but her ghost only smirks, reminding her irritatingly of Cedar.

"What is it?" Antimony asks.

The fox fire light around her ankles swirls, a chill reaching up her trouser legs, playing with the hem of her coat. She tries to keep her teeth from chattering. It wouldn't do to look weak in front of herself.

"You already know," her future-self's voice is an echo-blur. "It's the star. You're hearing her voice, the one Starling died to give her."

The smirk on the other-her's lips becomes something sharper, a blade, almost cruel. Would it be uncouth to punch her own ghost in the mouth?

"Stars aren't sentient. Those are just fairy tales." She doesn't want it to be true, but she knows down in her bones that it is, and hasn't she always known?

The other-her's smile doesn't waver. Antimony would have thought there might be some mercy in her eyes, but she also knows herself too well. All the knowing coming to her now is still wound-fresh to her other self. It hurts, too much for future-Antimony to offer any kindness.

Because she does know and she's always known and she's never wanted to know. All those stories, all that wishing, she never fully thought through the consequences because it would be too terrible. But Starling had known the truth and given his own life to it, a small right against a whole universe of wrong. And Chrysotile had helped him.

"What about Cedar?" Antimony asks herself. He must have known too, but what did he do about it?

"Ask him." Future-Antimony's eyes glitter, cruel delight, like passing the pain back to her past-self might lessen her own hurt.

Antimony's hand flashes out, fingers closing around her future-self's wrist, holding her in place. Even though she must be expecting it, her future-eyes widen in surprise, and there, at last, Antimony sees mercy, sorrow, her future-self aching for the past-self coming face-to-face with the death that will be. But she does nothing to stop her, and the mercy fades back into a smile that might have blood in it if her future-self were still a thing capable of bleeding. Because she knows what happens next.

Antimony looks into her own eyes.

And there, every possible path her future might take forks and forks and skates across the surface of everything like the glass in the star chamber not-yet shattering. Her life races along those cracks like lightning and comes to a dead stop, a point she can't see beyond.

She sees herself and the star in its chamber and both are burning. There is nothing else. Except. Except except except—an edge like a closed door, like a flat horizon, like a coin pressed to a table with another face Antimony knows is there but cannot see. There is no way to pick at the edge to open the door to see the other face to know that it exists because it does not or cannot or should not because this is where she ends.

All the light in the world goes out like a blown candle and rushes back all at once like knives to her eyes and Antimony is alone in the hall. She kicks the wall where her unhelpful asshole of a death is stitched, hard, so her bones jar and the steel toe in her boot rings and it doesn't make her feel any better at all.

She returns to the engine room, to the star chamber, and stands in front of the impossible swirl of light. It makes her skin itch, brings the jittery feeling back to her teeth. If she looks long enough, she can almost see a face, a mouth in the roiling, pulsing energy.

Antimony traces a finger over one hairline crack until it joins another and another—a river with three tributaries. She presses her bound hand to the glass, leaves a blood-petal kiss of red behind.

"I'm sorry," she whispers.

She makes a fist of her hand, thumps the side of it against the glass. She's being a coward. Still.

And now. Now she has a choice to make. Like Cedar made a choice. And fuck it, because her impulse is to do something noble and stupid and self-sacrificing and she really doesn't want to die.

Back in her quarters, Antimony mashes the piano's keyboard, thinking of the keys as teeth, Cedar's specifically.

"Come out and talk to me, you asshole." The yelling makes her feel better, but only marginally so.

Cedar isn't there and then he is, and even though Antimony called for him, she still jumps when he appears, leaning on nothing again, arms crossed. Despite the horrific nature of his death, he's still maddeningly pretty, cheekbones defined where hers look gaunt, relaxed and well-fucking-rested where she looks haunted and sleep-starved.

"You're lucky I'm not corporeal." Cedar tosses a meaningful look at the piano.

Antimony is still tired and still a little drunk and lightning keeps forking behind her eyes. But it's worse when the lightning stops, when it finds the place where it can't go any farther because that's where her life ends.

"Why didn't you tell me about the star waking?" Antimony steps back from the piano, closed fist shaking, and she tucks it behind her back so Cedar won't see.

"What fun would that be?" He runs fingers over the piano keys and when they make no sound, he runs a finger over the wires instead.

They still don't make a sound, but whatever it does makes Antimony shiver.

"Would you have listened even if I had tried?" The maddening expression on Cedar's face makes Antimony want to throw something.

He's right, and that only makes it worse. How many times did they butt heads when he was alive, when she was under his command? Even knowing there's no solidity to him, Antimony jerks open the piano bench, stuffed with books and sheets of music, and throws the first one she lays her hands on. The pages flutter, and a small square of paper tumbles free.

An actual, honest-to-gods, printed photograph.

"Oh fuck me." Antimony bends to retrieve it, Cedar watching her with a brow perfectly arched, expression smug.

This was here the whole time and Antimony never saw it, too uncultured to do anything with the piano other than bang on it for attention and use it as a place to sit and drink and feel sorry for herself.

"You and Chrysotile were in the Galactic Fleet together." Antimony holds up the picture, a group of young cadets in their uniforms, arms slung around each other. Chrysotile and Cedar are together at one end, and Chrysotile's head is slightly turned, caught in a moment, distracted and unaware of the picture about to be taken.

Even Antimony isn't dense enough to miss it. The expression on Chrysotile's face is stark: love.

She thinks of Chrysotile, eyeless in the medbay, grasping her hand and begging forgiveness from his dead captain. To be loved like that—enough that someone would kill for you. Well, it isn't exactly a comforting thought. It leaves Antimony feeling claustrophobic, but at the same time, achingly lonely. There is no one among the crew—no one in her life—she could even share a drink with, let alone someone willing to pick up a knife and kill a fellow crew member for her, to finish whatever it is she might leave undone.

"I was wrong about the star." The sorrowing look in Cedar's eyes takes Antimony's breath away.

She has a picture of her former captain in her mind—brash, ambitious, apologizing to no one. Stealing her rightful command out from under her, winning Basalt's favor and trust. But the more Antimony looks at her mental picture against Cedar's ghost, the more she realizes she doesn't know him at all. Did Cedar wash out of the Galactic Fleet? Was he dishonorably discharged? Maybe there's a pirate streak in him after all, and maybe there's something even more important, something Basalt saw in him and not in Antimony, which is why she gave him command—compassion.

The picture she holds in her mind of Cedar—it's a picture of herself. A picture of who she wants to be, or believed, up until this very moment, she needed to be in order to command. Ruthless, friendless, alone at the top. Holding her crew at bay in a mixture of awe and fear, needing no one.

Heavy is the head indeed. Maybe it wasn't a taunt on Cedar's lips earlier so much as a warning.

"How do I stop it?" Antimony asks.

Dead space aches all around the ship, the doldrums, like a bruise. The ship drifts, quiet in all the wrong ways. No engines thrumming; the only pulse of life the need of the star. If they stay, they're doomed, if they run, they'll fail. The star chamber will crack, the ship will explode or be devoured. This isn't just a graveyard for ships, it's a graveyard for stars, and her own always-dying star is calling to the ghosts of her own kind that haunt this space. And sooner or later, they will answer.

"You don't stop it." Cedar's expression is grim. "That's what I got wrong. There's nothing at all you can do. We kept the star chained, and this is her vengeance."

"A fucking lot of help you are." Antimony grits her teeth.

At the same time, guilt needles her; no matter how they clashed while he was alive, Cedar really did want what was best for the ship. He might even have loved the *Xanthic Promise* as much as she does. Enough to die for it.

Her intuition leaps.

"You went to talk to your own death too, and you came up with an answer that involved you walking out of the ship on a routine repair mission and meeting your end even though your time wasn't up yet."

The pieces click into place, a rapid tumble matched by the beat of her pulse.

"You thought if you rearranged fate, met your death early, you could strengthen the chains, put the star back to sleep and keep the ship running. Chrysotile tried to finish what you started, but Starling . . ."

The pieces fit, almost but not quite. There is still some missing. Did Starling simply get unlucky and cross Chrysotile's path just when he was feeling grief-mad and murderous? Or did Starling take advantage of Chrysotile's grief and talk him into committing murder, convincing

Chrysotile that his death would finish what Cedar started and put the star back to sleep? Only Starling lied. He wanted to wake the star. Give it a voice. Set it free.

"Starling got it right, and you got it absolutely fucking wrong."

Cedar's eyes blaze at her, all glare and bared teeth, and for a moment he is as terrible as any ghost ought to be. But all she can do is grin triumph in the face of his offended rage, because she's right, and a victory, even a pyrrhic one, is still a gods-damned win.

"You should have been trying to set her free, wake her up the rest of the way, rather than put her to sleep again. You died for nothing."

Cedar howls and lunges at her, fingers crooked like claws. But of course, he's insubstantial and passes right through her. Lacking the focus of the *Xanthic Promise*'s honed-bright weapons to make his death useful, Antimony feels nothing. Until she turns to mark his passage and where he ends up, comma-curled in the air, his body a sob without breath or tears.

"Fuck."

She's doing it again, setting herself above and apart, taking pleasure in a moment of being right, even though she was just as clueless as Cedar, and every bit as guilty. She should have held onto her belief in the old fairy tales, like Starling. She should have had compassion to pair with her ambition. She shouldn't have been such a bloody, arrogant fool.

She wishes she could pat Cedar's shoulder, comfort him. He straightens, emptied of rage now, as she is of gloating. And here is the other shoe about to drop between them. Cedar tried and failed and the ship is still in danger. The ship needs a captain, and at the moment, that's her.

"So what are you going to do about it?" Cedar asks.

"Well, fuck," Antimony says, because there's nothing else for it. Cedar was on the right track, but facing the wrong way.

"I guess I'd better go see about a star." Antimony shapes her lips to a fierce grin, her stance to a swagger. A little bit of brash and bravado isn't such a bad thing. She is a gods-damned pirate after all, and if she's going to go out, then it's going to be staring death in the face and giving it the middle finger.

Cedar tips his head at her forgotten bottle of gin. His expression is almost kind, but not really at all, because he's a gods-damned pirate too and that's not how it is between them.

Antimony lifts the bottle in salute, takes a swig, and pours out a measure for him. The washed light of Cedar's eyes flickers in something like pleasure, which gives her hope. Since she's about to be very dead herself soon, it would be nice to go out knowing that she can still get shit-faced in the afterlife.

Another swig for good luck and she leaves the bottle beside the piano, uncorked. She resists the urge to set it down on the bench where it would leave a mark, a last peace offering.

And off she goes.

Antimony strides the decks of the *Xanthic Promise*. The walls howl with the restless dead, and in her mind, they're a storm. She's a pirate of old, her heeled boots ringing on wood while her red coat swirls and rain lashes her. She bares her teeth as if to catch the wind, even though there's nothing here but recycled air.

"Out," she bellows as she steps into the star chamber's room.

Hyacinth looks up, scowls, a refusal on her lips. Antimony feels a flicker-flash of regret. Hyacinth is as sour as Antimony wants to be, or at least presents the same gruff exterior. Maybe they could have been friends, raised a glass together in the crow's nest and sang bawdy old star-shanties. Antimony guesses she'll never know.

"Go, or I'll clap you in irons or make you walk the plank or something equally piratey."

Hyacinth merely shakes her head, not so much a ceding to authority as her not being paid enough to care. As Antimony freshly reminded herself, they aren't friends, and the captain's chair will fall to Hyacinth next, so what stake does she have in stopping Antimony's stupidity?

Hyacinth retreats, leaving Antimony alone.

The star chamber itself is sealed with a double hatch. Antimony scrambles to the top of the chamber and overrides the locks to drop through.

And then. She is. Falling. Seeing her bones through her skin. Hearing them, and isn't that a weird fucking thing. Antimony is herself and she is her ghost, and she's every captain who came before her, stitched in a long line, and this is where it ends.

She tastes Cedar's death, holds it on her tongue, the bright bright bright moment of pure joy right before his faceplate shattered, thinking he was doing the right thing.

Her own death is here too, waiting for her just around a corner. A door. An edge. A turning.

But she isn't there yet.

The ship sings. It screams. A swarm of bees humming in a cave made of ice cracking and a violin playing and a color that is blue and purple and pink and none of those at all and a hunger and a heartbeat and a lullaby and a whale calling to its calf through the deep.

Oh, it echoes. Antimony feels it all along her jaw. An ache to answer, but the sound isn't for her. It's for the ghosts outside the ship. The dead stars and the living ones and the stars yet to be born. They're alive. All of them. Not just her star, but everyone among all the billions of points of light spread across the universe. Gloriously, terribly alive.

If a thing can have a heart that can be cut out and chained in the moment of its death to power a ship, then of course it is alive. Truly and properly alive. They had no right, none of them, the captains stretching back to the beginning of time sailing the black, to do what they have done.

Lightning cracks. Branches. The edge. There. Antimony reaches. Plunges her hand into the light that is the song that is the end of the line. And her ghost smirks and Cedar smirks and the thread tugs. She pictures with all her will and might, for whatever they are worth, cutting the star free, waking it up, shattering the bonds while sealing the wounds in the glass and keeping everyone on the *Xanthic Promise* safe, and she hopes against hope and against reason her death is strong enough to do that.

This is the end.

Except.

The coin pressed flat to the table has another side, and so does the door, and the edge really is a corner, and it can be turned.

Cedar made a bargain with his death and went to meet it early. But every member of a ghost ship's crew knows their death is a solid and inevitable thing. They swear an oath the moment they come on board, and live every day knowing fate cannot be cheated. It is an immutable fact.

And so, if Cedar met his death early, then in truth, he was always fated to do so.

And by that very same logic, if Antimony makes a deal with her death now, refuses it and slips around the edge to the other face of the coin, the other side of the door, then she will have always been meant to do so. Fate signed, sealed, and delivered.

A promise is still a promise. That is where the power of a ghost ship lies, and she's not denying her ship anything, only delaying its gratification a while.

And it is a glorious thing.

Here's the deal, she thinks, *You use my living voice, my tongue to scream your star song to the universe, to scream yourself awake and free, and you kick enough power into the ship on your way out to get us out of the Sargasso and I'll figure out the rest on the way down.*

It shouldn't work, but ghost ships are built on impossible things.

Antimony throws her head back and opens her throat to the voice that shivers along her jaw, the star longing to sing through her in a language not meant for human tongues. She burns. The chamber shatters and she shatters and the ship lurches forward through the dark—a blink that is not motion that suddenly puts them somewhere else.

Everything turns inside out and upside down and sideways and backwards oh my. And then Antimony Jones does the most impossible thing of all: she survives.

Her skin is still smoking as Antimony limps from the star chamber's remains. Chunks of glass, charred and black, litter the floor. The ship is whole, powered by a ghost, by a promise, as always, just enough to get them out of the doldrums and then, well, maybe Antimony will have to roll the dice again and put her life on the line one more time, but that's a problem for future-her.

Antimony looks down at her arms, her legs, at skin black as charcoal, cracked and crazed and flaking ash. Seams running through her flesh blaze with starlight, every and no color at all. Her clothes are gone.

And it's a damned good thing she shaved her head before this all began, because if not, her hair would be on fire.

She nearly collides with Hyacinth who hovers just on the other side of the door, anxious for her ship if not for her captain. Antimony tosses a crooked grin.

"Let's get a drink sometime," she says, and the words draw more shock from Hyacinth than Antimony's burned-and-smoldering condition.

Cheating death, or at least delaying it for a while, is as good an excuse as any to turn over a new leaf. She can be a fierce, piratey pirate and still make a friend, or at least try.

Black petals scorch the deck, the echo of footsteps left in her wake. The same goes for any place Antimony rests her hand to steady herself, which she does often, covering the ship with impressions of herself all the way back to her cabin where she scoops up the rest of the gin and kills it in one go.

The ghost-stitched walls chitter and gibber and gossip and Antimony grins. Let them tell grand epic tales of the captain who freed her ship's star, who looked her own death in the eye and said not today, motherfucker. She'll happily listen once those rumors circle back around as star-shanties, but not right now.

Now, she will fall into her bed and hope that the sheets don't catch fire because she intends to sleep for a week solid.

Whatever comes after that, well, that's a problem for future-her. Now-her is flush and full of victory, all the crackling power of her ghost ship at her fingertips, and the whole of the universe spread before her. Just the way it should be.

NOBODY LIVES HERE

H. PUEYO

There is no one here, no one but me. Out of ninety apartments—ten in each of the nine floors—only mine has someone inside, but most have already been sold. *It's an investment*, the estate agent told me when I was signing the contract. *An investment for life.* Yet I had no interest in becoming a landlord: all I wanted was a clean, well-ventilated, spacious apartment, and my new house ticks all the boxes. The only "downside" is that nobody lives here.

At first, I thought it would be an excellent setup. Without tenants, I wouldn't have to worry about the unwanted sounds that came from my last apartment, like loud music, student parties and insistent moans in the middle of the night. All my life, I have struggled with noise and chaotic environments, a combination that doesn't fit my silent personality. Now, every hour is as quiet as I am, and my only company is the distant sound of cars, the mews of my cat, or an occasional bird chirping from outside the walls of this private condominium, beautiful, ample, and empty.

"Wish me luck," I tell my sisters through the video call in the first evening, after removing all boxes from my brand new house. I have always disliked clutter and could only rest after organizing everything. "This place is so peaceful that it will be hard to get up tomorrow morning."

"Of course Sara's house would be like that," said Ana, laughing. I frowned, and Carla chuckled as well.

"You must be really happy in your empty shoebox!" she said, pointing at the background behind me. My cat moved her tail lazily, and Carla waved. "Hi, Kika!"

I wanted to say they had no right in criticizing me; it's not like they would have their own house anytime soon. My sisters are often in my mind, and I worry that they will never cut ties with our parents or live in any other healthier, better way. *Mind your own business*, I remind myself with a smile. *They are grown enough to choose what to do with their own lives.*

"Well, I'm tired now. Talk to you guys later!"

I close my laptop and push it aside, exhausted after cleaning the house and talking to them. That is all I have here: a sofa, a desk, a table with a single chair, and a few clothes, as little as possible to fill this vacant beauty. Even my books are digital, to avoid occupying space, and I feel like I can finally breathe, about to fall asleep like never before.

No noise.

No mess.

No chaos.

No one.

No one . . .

When I close my eyes, I'm back to my childhood home. The stale smell hits me at once, and droplets of humidity drip down the walls. I force myself through the living room, and there is no space between the cardboard boxes, forcing me to push them aside, but what I find underneath is a vile dark nest. The cockroaches crawl between my feet, their antennae brushing against my toes, and the mere feeling of it is enough to make me throw up. I hate their wings, their hairy legs, their reddish bodies and the noise it makes when I crush it with the sole of my feet. *Die*, I think.

Die, die, disappear.

The sound of a cockroach's cracking carcass brings me back, and I jump out of the sofa. Out of instinct, I scratch my arms, my face, my ears. I need to make sure there are no bugs in me.

"It was just a dream," I tell myself. Kika meows, and I remember where I am. There are no insects in this building, and if one appears, she would kill them for me.

Yet the noise continues on, and I look around, trying to find the source of it. First, a slap against the wall; then another, and another, and another. My brain recognizes the sound immediately, too used to the act of finding and killing bugs. *No one should be here*, I remember, looking out of the window to find lights, but there are none.

I only sleep again after convincing myself that I'm alone.

There were always too many things in my parents' house. The bathroom had piled magazines over the hamper, dirty laundry scattered around, towels thrown over the shower panels, old cosmetics bags, expired make up, and all kinds of pills stocked in the drawers. The same happened in the other rooms: clothes thrown on the floor, books that no one read, unwashed dishes, and food from today, yesterday and many years before.

My father, who was born in a recession, bought anything in triples, collected boxes of food—*just in case*, he used to say—and went on fits of rage if we threw something away. At first, my mother agreed to avoid a meltdown, but she started to believe that hoarding goods was for the best, keeping packets, used matches and empty lighters inside her purse. Ana and Carla obeyed them, and I did too, at least to their faces.

Many times I tried to wash clothes, scrub mildew from the walls, and wipe layers of grime from forks and knives when they were not around, but the dirt returned like a disease, and with it came the bugs. Cockroaches, ants, mosquitoes and larvae, and if I screeched in disgust, my parents mocked me: *how did Sara turn out, so scared of everything? We must have really spoiled her . . .*

What was spoiled were the cartons of milk in the cupboard, but I said nothing; there was no use in answering back. When I did, they shouted, when I asked them to stop, they continued, and I learned how to keep only the space around myself organized and clean. And, after years—so many years—I found my new house.

In the second week, I conclude that there are intruders living on the floor above or below. The state agent doesn't believe me, but I insist to her that I'm not imagining things. Every night after ten, the noise begins: they talk to each other, listen to music, trash their houses and slam things against the walls. It's deeply upsetting, even worse than my sisters when we still lived together, but I envision a plan to make it better.

My solution is simple. There is too little furniture and it causes their noise to echo in my house, so I go on a small shopping spree, and soon a dining table arrives with several matching chairs, together with an extra wardrobe for my bedroom and two armchairs. I plan to resell most of those after I get rid of the unwanted neighbors, but now I'm thankful to have the house a little more crowded, muffling their voices until everything is quiet again.

In the third week, the problem evolves.

"I'm fine, but the neighbors are killing me," I tell my sisters with a fake smile.

"We thought you didn't have neighbors." Ana talks so loud that, if there are indeed others in my buildings, they would all hear her. Carla has the same bad habit, but I avoid asking them to tone down nowadays.

"I don't," I reply, then correct myself. "I think some of the owners allowed their kids to move in for a little while."

I know what Ana and Carla think of me—*paranoid, neurotic, a control-freak*—they have told me many times, so I don't let them know that this is worrying me sick. Such words were thrown at me whenever they stuffed my bedroom with more garbage, especially after midnight, when I went to sleep. I tried to keep my bedroom as tidy as possible, but they cannibalized any empty space they found, filling it and using it until there was nothing left.

"It's not a big deal, just a small nuisance."

Something brushes against my arm, and I turn around.

"Sara?" Carla asks on the other side of the line. "Are you okay?"

It was a fly; I know it was. Heavier and slower than a mosquito, but smaller than a cockroach, accompanied by that maddening buzzing sound.

"We talk tomorrow, Kika broke something," I say, and turn off the chat before they can answer back.

When I stick my head out of the window, I see it. A fly, no, two, three, four flies, flying out of the window of the apartment under mine, and then back inside. Black and metallic green, like the ones of my memories, alighted on the food left exposed in the table of the kitchen, or around the filth on the floor. More than ten, in fact, buzzing, searching for more trash. *Die,* I think, and I realize my hands are shaking. *Die, die, die.*

I close all the windows, turn on the air conditioner and sit on the sofa, hugging an insect killer spray. I have one for flies and spiders, another for cockroaches, and a bottle of ant poison. I'll be fine.

It's their problem, not mine.

"Your house is pristine," the pest control team tells me. "We found nothing, ma'am, but if you're seeing any bugs coming in, now they won't anymore, at least not for the next six months."

Thank you, thank you, thank you.

The living room looks pretty with the new cushions I found online, the rug and a brown TV stand. The cupboards are also filled with food, methodically organized by color and type. Nothing that might expire soon, of course, only to fill the empty space; most of the time, I ask take-outs to avoid attracting more bugs. I watch the team leave, eyes focused on the dirt left by their shoes on my stainless floor. One of the men stops and looks at me.

"Oh, one more thing," he says. "You might want to check the mold, now that the wet season started."

"Mold?"

"Behind the fridge and the sofa. Good luck with that."

And there it is—little brown and green dots covering the lower part of the wall, almost invisible, ghost warnings of the furry patches and black blotches that I know too well. Once, I convinced my father to give away some portraits, but when we removed them, there was a thick dark substance glued to the wall like old grease. We had to call someone to remove the toxic mold, but I never forgot the drop of black water that ran from it, twirling until it left behind a gross spot.

I take a deep breath, wear my kitchen gloves, and begin to scrub them with vinegar. Die, die, die, the mantra returns to my head, and I blame the neighbors from the floor above. They must have done something to cause this; a seepage they didn't fix, or even a structural problem of the building I have not been warned about.

Later, after the walls are nice and clean, more furniture arrives, and the house now shelters several new shelves, lamps, clocks, an ironing board, a television I'll never use, and even a crib for the cat. Kika entered it once, then jumped back to the floor, preferring her usual place by my bed.

I'm wasting way too much money on this, but I can finally have a good night of sleep.

The neighbors on the floor below seem to have moved out, but there are noises coming from my floor now. I have never seen someone come or go in the corridors, but they bang their doors, and their security chains clank with the violence of it. I fasten mine and lock the door, once, twice, and another time, just out of safety, then go back to my own room. I'm not confident enough to take the garbage out, so I hide all the food packets inside trash bags and soak them with spray, but the memory of bugs and maggots always returns to my mind.

Kika curls by my side in the sofa. Around us, we have insect killer, a bottle of vinegar, another of alcohol, and an electric flyswatter. I'm only eating what's in the cans: corn for lunch, peas for dinner, and biscuits whenever I need a snack.

"Everything will be fine," I tell Kika, and she stares at me with a glassy look in her yellow eyes. "This is just a bad week."

A strong acidic smell surrounds me. It may be too much vinegar, or it may be mold, growing on, under, and behind the walls, forming bubbles in the white paint, spreading through the entire house. From the corridor, there are human voices, talking, whispering, animal screeches and growls, creaks and cracks, clacks and thuds. Someone tries to open my door, then bangs it, and I hide under the covers. It's almost as bad as my old apartment, but at least I'm alone with my cat. When they reach my doorknob, I hide under the coves and pretend they're not there.

Go away, go away, go away.

* * *

Nobody lives here. Nobody but me. The building is as empty as it should be—as I want it to be. Whenever I look through the peephole, the corridors are always dark, and I'm constantly watching for a proof that I'm not imagining things. A person, a shadow, a visitor, a neighbor. The clutter that I know is there. The furniture they pushed into the hallway, the piled chairs crowding the stairs. Anything that might explain the creaks and the sounds and the steps and the howls. It should be impossible, but I hear them when I wake up. I hear them at night. I hear them all through the day.

They sound like Ana and Carla when they laugh too loudly, like my father smashing the plates in a thousand pieces, like my mother complaining that I'm too annoying, too self-righteous, too sensitive.

I don't call my sisters anymore. I don't know where Kika is. She might have been lost between the sofas and the chairs and the tables and the desks and the trash bags and the packages and the boxes and the lamps. She's a smart cat, she can handle this.

I can't.

After dawn, they come for me: whoever they are, wherever they hide, they push all the objects jumbled in the corridor and try to unlock my door, banging it when they can't. They enter my house while I'm asleep, leaving trails of dirt on the panels of my floor, so I stop sleeping as well.

I don't go to my bedroom; it's too dirty in there. I don't enter the kitchen; it's full of flies and cockroaches and ants. I hide inside my bathroom, wiping the walls and the sink to remove the mold, and look through the hole I have made in the door. Here, there is nothing dirty. Nothing much. Just me.

So I look, and I wait.

And I will keep waiting.

Until all the sounds finally go away.

ON SAFARI IN R'LYEH AND CARCOSA WITH GUN AND CAMERA

ELIZABETH BEAR

"We wouldn't be having this conversation if you'd flunked Algebra, Griswold," Roberts said, racking another shell into his hunting rifle and peering over our flimsy barricade. He was trying to see if the monstrous creatures beyond were preparing for another assault.

I was too busy reloading my 10-gauge to answer, even if I'd wanted to dignify his assertion. Algebra wasn't the issue here.

Scientific curiosity was. And perhaps having had too much time on my hands.

I had to grant him that this was in every respect my fault. It was only his imprecision of language when it came to apportioning blame that griped me. And if I were being fair, that was probably me engaging in diversion, or sophistry, or whatever the technical psychological term for nitpicking the hell out of something to weasel out of it is.

Whatever: I'd been the one who sent in my spit sample to the online DNA testing folks, and I'd been the one who'd gotten curious about a weird little line item in the results, and I'd been the one who'd called up my old school buddy the geneticist to ask some pointed questions. Which—in my defense!—he'd been only too happy to investigate once his own curiosity was piqued.

And so here we were, on a strange planet under an alien sun, surrounded by twisted, non-Euclidean geometry; pistols at alien dawn with inside-out monstrosities which (presuming our hypothesis was reliable) wanted to eat our faces; and all the while attracting the wrath of dread gods. And it wasn't even our first trip.

This time, we had been "prepared."

My GoPro had been smashed by a lucky tentacle, so I couldn't be sure how good our data was. But we knew where to find the gate to get us home, and we knew how to get there, and I was confident in our ability to make it. Even if we didn't have my video, we'd have Roberts's. And I had vials full of biological samples.

I took a deep breath of the curiously thin and unsatisfying air. Everything was going to be fine. Everything was going to be fine.

Probably.

That's a little *Unfathomable Magazine! Tales of Adventure Beyond the Stars* for a quick synopsis, isn't it?

. . . Maybe I'd better start at the beginning.

My name is not Greer Griswold. I'm approximately fifty-two years old. I don't know who my birth parents were, and my adoptive parents are dead. I have never married; I have no children; I have very few close friends. I'm a physicist at a notable northeastern US institution you would have heard of if I named it. I'm not going to, any more than I'm going to give you my real name, because I have tenure but I'm not stupid. Being a woman in a male-dominated field isn't easy, and I've never been terribly interested in Performing My Gender in the fashion that gets you accepted as a mascot by the boys. I've had my share of gross harassment, but at least I'm not pretty. Not being pretty spares me certain things.

I spend a lot of time alone, and I've learned to like it. Despite that, and because of the third fact above, and because I'm not getting any younger, I thought it would be interesting to get some genetic testing done and find out where my ancestors came from. And maybe . . . if I had any close relatives around.

Nieces, nephews. Somebody I could will my extensive collection of vintage Hot Rods toy cars to when I'm gone.

It's one thing to embrace your alienation. It's another to wake up on the first day of spring semester classes and realize you haven't spoken to another human being since December 23, and there's only so long you can go on ordering your groceries from PeaPod and scooping up cookie butter with ruffled potato chips in front of Netflix until two a.m.

No matter how self-sufficient you are, when you're middle-aged and childless and unmarried . . . you start to hope maybe you're really not as alone in the world as you think you are.

I still might not have done it, if my department chair hadn't stuck his head into my office one afternoon in late August to let me know we had a new faculty member coming on board, and how did I feel about being their liaison during the onboarding process? I note, entirely for the record and apropos of nothing, that I am the only female tenured faculty in the physics department. I note, entirely for the record and apropos of nothing, that I do an estimated thirty-six percent of the emotional labor in my sixteen-person department.

Female grad students and admins do the rest. And it's not like we're any less introverted and non-neurotypical than the dudes. We're just forced to learn to endure more discomfort in order to have careers.

I gritted my teeth in a smile. I said yes. I waited for the door to close.

I'd gotten myself the kit for my birthday (observed, presumed) and had been ignoring its existence ever since. I dug it out of my desk drawer and unscrewed the lid on the little plastic vial while I was still fuming.

I know those DNA tests are very broad and subject to a certain degree of interpretation. But the results are improving with better data, and honestly not everything in science has to be about *doing science the right way with reproducible results subject to peer review.*

Sometimes science . . . or packaged, processed science food, if you prefer . . . can be just science-y and fun. Also, it might be useful to know if I had any ticking time bombs in my DNA, medically speaking. Make those family history questions a little less stymieing.

Surprise.

I was gratified to learn I was nearly one-twentieth Neanderthal. That's about twice as much as most modern Europeans, and according to the genetics company, it put me in the ninety-ninth percentile of their customer base.

Those redheaded Vikings had to come from somewhere. And it was nice to think of all that cross-cultural communication and exchange taking place, all the way back to the Weichselian Glaciation.

That was interesting, and fun to think about. But other than the *Homo neanderthalensis* and the Scandinavian, I was a pretty basic New England mix. A little Irish, a little German. A little Broadly South European, which is probably Portuguese. A smidge of Native American or Southeast Asian. And then . . .

Undetermined: 10.2%

Ten percent. That's a pretty big error bar there, genetics company that will remain unnamed.

Curiosity is probably my defining characteristic. I want to know how things work. I want to know why they work, and what happens if you alter the variables.

Sometimes it's not the variables that alter on you, however.

Sometimes it's the constants.

Of course I downloaded my raw genetic data and took it to my old friend Michael Roberts. If academics weren't constantly taking advantage of one another's skill sets, we'd have no topics of conversation at all other than who was cheating on their spouse and who wasn't going to get tenure.

Anyway, Roberts and I went back to undergrad, when we'd been lab partners in an organic chemistry class that wasn't in either of our fields but was required for both of our majors. We'd somehow gotten through the class, despite the lack of any apparent common language between either of us and the instructor. Years later, we'd wound up at the same institution, in different departments in the same college, and I still liked and trusted him.

What I wasn't expecting was for Roberts to call me up at one a.m., voice shaking as he accused me of having a little joke at his expense. "Come on, Greer," he said. "Tell me who you got to put this data set together, so I can mail them a dead badger."

I looked at my phone. Without my glasses, it was just a bright blur in the dark of my bedroom. I put it back to my ear. "That's right off the Real 46 website. If you want, I'll give you my login and you can download a copy for yourself."

He scoffed. "Well, I knew these companies played a little fast and loose, but this result is a mess and a half. Ten percent of the DNA doesn't even match up to the human genome. Did you chew up a tadpole or something before you took the swab?"

"Ew," I answered. "Hey, are you busy tommor— I mean, tonight? I'll buy you dinner and you can tell me all about it."

"Is it going to be sushi?" he asked, guardedly.

"It's always sushi," said I.

"The thing is," Roberts said, hovering a roll of negimaki between his chopsticks, "they should have just admitted they couldn't analyze a sample this contaminated. It must be chromosome bits everywhere."

"I did not," I said, "contaminate the sample."

He popped the beef and scallions into his mouth and chewed, eyes closing. I leaned away from the smell.

The mackerel and scallops I was eating, on the other hand, were amazing. Sashimi is about my favorite thing in the world, and the pungent deliciousness of the wasabi lit up the spaces in my skull.

"Is it possible there's something else going on?" I asked. "Not corrupted data but . . . a variant or a mutation? Something?"

"Possible," he said dubiously. "All those Neanderthal variants also really look like an error, though."

"Maybe the other stuff is Neanderthal variants too? I dunno, isolated genetic pocket?"

"You're already at two hundred percent of anything we'd consider normal variation." He sighed.

"Somebody's got to be on the tail of the curve."

More negimaki vanished into my friend, followed by sake. I've never been able to drink much. My mucous membranes hate the sensation of alcohol.

He said, "Oh, hmm. You know, I remember a story a colleague told me about a Ph.D. student of his whose dis was rejected. Something about impossible data the student kept insisting was verified. It wasn't at our institution, though. It was wherever he worked before. Miskatonic, maybe?"

"That dis should still be in the special collections, then."

"Yeah," he said. "I've got an alumni dinner over there next month. I could pop by the library and see."

"How is a failed dis going to help us? I mean, that's not a source I'm going to cite with any confidence."

He snorted. "Guy was doing some research about whether there were variants not mapped in the Human Genome Project, which was still in progress back then."

"Huh," I said.

"Anyway, you want me to check?"

"Can't hurt."

"Price of another dinner," he said.

I had a small octopus in my mouth by then, and was chewing carefully, so I couldn't interrupt in time to keep him from qualifying.

"Anything but sushi," he said.

Well, Roberts found the mysterious dissertation. And what he found *in* it seemed to unsettle him greatly, though I didn't understand the majority of his valiant attempts to explain the details. It was all highly technical stuff about chromosomes and variants in a field where my expertise stops at the four amino acids which make up DNA.

In any case, he felt a need to go and have a conversation with the guy who wrote the thing. And he wouldn't hear of having that conversation without me present.

"It's your research," he said, as if it were the last word on the subject.

"First, it's not research," I argued. "I'd have to be a geneticist for it to be research. It's idle curiosity. Second, it's not entirely just mine."

"Which one of us spit in the test tube?"

"Which one of us decided to go pull books in the special collections?"

"The results don't make any sense!"

I let it hang there until he rolled his eyes and laughed.

And continued, "Anyway, I had no luck with a phone. Disconnected. Or email. None on file."

"Well, that's that, then," I said, relieved despite myself.

"I found the guy's address."

"No."

"Yes. His name is Albert Gilman. He's out on Cape Ann."

The day we picked to go down, it was raining. I drove.

We parked on the sandy verge of a seaside road. It would have been crawling with children, tourists, and boogie boarders on any sunny day during the season. Because it was bleak November and dreeking to rival the Scottish highlands, the beach was abandoned and there was plenty of parking.

We got out. I found myself standing by the car and sighing contently. The cool, moist air kissed my face and I couldn't help but feel the tourists were missing out. The Atlantic was a planished sheet of titanium under a misty sky, obscuring any sense of horizon. The dune grass was faded straw, the masses of beach roses reduced to barbed stems festooned with fat rubies of rose hips, the only color in the entire landscape. On the landward side of the road, weathered cedar-shingle cottages wore a dull gray sheen that echoed the ocean.

Roberts walked up to a three-quarter Cape Cod-style cottage with a gambrel roof. I trailed him like a dog with separation anxiety.

We stepped in under the little peaked portico protecting the peeling, slate-colored door. Roberts rang the doorbell.

And we waited.

A cool breeze lifted the hair at my nape and jingled the pipes of a baritone wind chime. The waves shushed on the sand. From within the house, no sound or sign.

"Are you sure about this?" I whispered.

Roberts started to shake his head. The gesture half-completed, he froze, lifting one finger for silence.

A moment later, I heard it too. A heavy, slow squeak. The sound an old wood floor might make under the weight of a mattress, or a big piece of furniture being slid on a rug so it didn't scrape. It wasn't the step of a human being, no matter how sizeable.

Roberts leaned forward and tapped on the door. The knocking boomed unexpectedly, as if the house were empty of soft things. Fabric, furniture. Human things.

It surprised me so much I nearly fell off the steps, but Roberts was undaunted.

"Mr. Gilman?" he called through the door. "Albert Gilman?"

I put my hand on his shoulder. "Let's go."

He shook his head stubbornly.

An intercom mounted up in the angle between the wall and overhang crackled and popped. "Who are you?"

Roberts introduced us, and told the disembodied voice what we did.

"Doctor Roberts. Michael Roberts." I wondered if the person behind the door had already forgotten my name. But then he said, "What the hell is a geneticist doing here?"

"Please, call me Michael. I came to consult you on your research. Can we come in?"

"No!" A pause, in which I imagined I could hear frightened breathing through the static. Then, slower: "Maybe you haven't heard, but I washed out. Now get off my porch."

A harsh click as the intercom cut off.

Roberts thumped the door just once and raised his voice. "Albert, Albert, wait! I think you were onto something! I think we can corroborate!"

The intercom again. "Corroborate what?"

"Your research. My friend here did one of those pop genetics tests and came back with some similar results to yours."

Silence.

"Albert? We can vindicate your results."

"Oh god," he said. "I'm so sorry."

I squeezed Roberts's arm hard. "What do you mean?" he asked anyway. "Who was your research subject?"

A gulping sound, like a swallowed sob. "Me," he said. "The source of the material was me."

* * *

It was a long, silent ride home. Silent as far as Roberts and I were concerned, anyway. But I kept hearing Gilman's last words echoing in my head, before he shuffled away from the door: "You have to go. You both have to go *now*."

We didn't, immediately. But the intercom went dead again, and more creaking following, seeming to move away from the door. Deeper into the house, and silence followed.

We knocked and knocked until the neighbors came out to stare pointedly, clutching their phones. But Albert Gilman would not speak with us again.

We drove away with his silence still hanging around us. Neither one of us seemed willing to break that silence for some time after. Until I pulled up in front of Roberts's house, and he turned to me and said, "I have to know what's going on."

I'm not the only one with a curiosity problem.

"I know," I said. "But I have no idea where to go next."

"Yeah," Roberts sighed, opening the car door. The rain blew in. "Me neither."

Days went by, and I was still at a loss. To be honest, I didn't necessarily have a lot of time to worry about it, because the semester was closing in fast on Thanksgiving break and finals, which meant the students were as needy and distracting as they always are that time of year.

By the time I felt like I had them halfway squared away and in control of themselves, and like I wasn't totally abrogating my duty as a mentor and instructor, fate took matters out of my hands.

By fate, I suppose I mean the person of Albert Gilman, who mailed a package to my place of work right before Thanksgiving.

That's less creepy than it sounds, because Roberts had given him our names and institution, which meant we were only a Google away. And the package was just a Priority Mail flat pack, postage provided by an online stamp service.

I opened it, remembering the Unabomber only after I already would have blown my hands off. *Oh, well*, I told myself. I was pretty sure it was too thin and flexible to contain an improvised explosive device, anyway. It probably just held paper.

Which was what I slid out. A map, water-stained and coming apart at the creases, folded inside out. And some sheaves of notes in an impenetrable hand.

A sticky note on the top of it all said, "Good luck, Dr. Griswold," in the same difficult penmanship—if you could call it penmanship. The note seemed to have gotten damp at some point. It was creased and wrinkled and smelled faintly of salt water.

When I lifted it, I found more writing underneath. "By the time you get this, I'll be gone."

I drove back to Gilman's cottage with the package on the passenger seat, pushing my luck with the staties on the Mass Pike. I could have called the police to check his welfare, I suppose, but the honest truth is I just didn't think of it at the time. I only thought of getting there as fast as I could.

I parked where we had parked before and scrambled toward the house. The front door stood open. Sand had blown or been tracked in.

It was cold inside, and as empty as the echoes had predicted. The radiators were icy to the touch. The rooms contained just a few large beanbag chairs, damp from the sea air, and a musty mattress heaped with tangled blankets but otherwise unmade.

I approached—I had walked in the open door quite without premeditation, calling Gilman's name. A few steps away, I noticed something papery, translucent, with a silvery sheen. It was wound among the blankets.

I crouched to examine it more closely. It looked like the shed skin of a very large snake, and I had a wild moment of fear that Gilman had been eaten by a pet python that might be napping the meal off nearby. As I leaned forward, a report like a gunshot scared me back onto my ass, kicking my way across the floor with my heels. I had scrambled nearly to the bedroom door when I realized something had just popped sharply under my extra-wide oxford. (Women with feet like mine don't wear pumps.)

When my heart slowed, I spotted a tangle of black-green weed on the floor where it had dried and stuck.

Bladderwort.

The air sacs popping under my sole were what had frightened me.

I knew it was unethical, but before I left I found Gilman's desktop—a Windows machine old enough to be a student in second grade—and used an anonymized browser window to back his documents up to my cloud before I left. I had no good excuse. Except I was convinced now that what he had sent me was a suicide note, and that he had sent it because he thought I had a reason to be frightened of whatever had ruined his life, too.

For a while I wished I hadn't stolen the data. Except . . . it's always better to know.

The handwritten notes were bad enough, once I invested enough eye-strain to decipher them. But the private blog I had stolen had—God help me—photographs.

This time, I called Roberts at eleven at night. "I need you to come over."

He was groggy, obviously struggling up from sleep. "Dammit, Griswold," he said. "I have an early class tomorrow."

"Come over anyway," I said. "It's an emergency, and I can't tell you on the phone." *Because I don't believe it myself, quite frankly.*

"I took melatonin. I really can't drive."

"Get the campus bus," I said. "It runs until one, and the stop is two blocks from my house."

I was lucky. My place is right across from the rugby field and I can walk to work in any weather barring a whiteout blizzard or a hurricane. Roberts had an apartment in faculty housing on campus. He'd given up his house after his wife died, and I worried about him. But he said the social opportunities were better.

I wouldn't know. I avoid social opportunities except for the departmental schmoozing I cannot reasonably avoid.

He was there within twenty minutes, anyway. He probably could have walked it in fifteen. I let him in and showed him into the living room. I poured him a drink (I kept the bourbon in the house for Roberts) and a cup of coffee without asking, and handed him my laptop after he'd investigated each of them and set them on the coffee table.

Nervously, I started talking before he even clicked through. "This could be faked. I guess. But why would it be? He just left it on his computer—"

He stared at me. "You broke into his *house?*"

"It was wide open," I said defensively. "Wait, let me start at the beginning. He sent me this. It arrived today."

The papers rattled as I handed them over.

"I thought it was a suicide threat and went to talk to him. When I got there the front door was open and"—I sat down heavily beside Roberts and spoke through my hands—"I think he walked into the sea, Mike."

He nudged the whiskey I'd poured him over in front of me. "If I mix bourbon and melatonin you're not getting an ounce of sense out of me. Go on, you look like you need it."

I sipped. The burn clarified my mind and felt like it was going to peel the inside of my throat off. I gulped the whole two fingers and started coughing. How do people *drink* this stuff?

Roberts laughed at me, drank some coffee, and paged through the file. Slowly, the smile slid off his face. "These are selfies. First one dated, what? Two years ago?"

I clawed at the back of my hand, which itched abominably. Psychosomatic. Definitely.

Roberts studied the screen, then studied me. He shook his head and looked back at the computer. My eyes were swimming.

Roberts said, "What's he document— Oh. *Oh.*"

"Yes," I said. "He was changing. Into something . . . else."

"Something . . . batracian," Roberts said.

"Hey," Roberts said at about three in the morning. "There's something drawn on this map, Griswold."

He held it out to me. I hadn't really looked at it before, except to determine that it was a large-scale driving map of southern New England.

The sort of thing nobody bothers wrestling with anymore in the age of smartphones and GPS.

But there was a circle and a little X in gray pencil on it. It had been folded to show the inset map of Martha's Vineyard, and the mark was just a tiny bit off the coast, out from the wilderness preserve on the long, flat southern edge of the island, which faces the open sea.

It's easy to get a car ferry berth in the off-season, weather permitting, although the ferries don't run as often after Columbus Day. And I didn't have any place to be on Thanksgiving. Neither did Roberts. Well, he had an invitation from his daughter out in Ohio, but he said he didn't feel like traveling. I happen to know he can't stand his son-in-law, which probably had more to do with it than holiday traffic.

We didn't talk much on the trip through Nantucket Sound. Unspoken agreement took us out on the top deck, towards the prow. A stiff wind blew into our faces and the swells pitched us up and down, but here in the shelter of the Cape and islands it wasn't as bad as it might have been. Even so, when we passed into the protection of the Vineyard's two protruding horns of land—known as East Chop and West Chop for inscrutable, ancestral Yankee reasons—the sting of wind eased, and I breathed a sigh.

We disembarked in Vineyard Haven, driving out of the belly of a ferry as big as a high school into a seemingly inexhaustible river of cars. The island air was brisk and salty. Houses and shops crowded the waterfront.

I wondered for how long this place could be saved. Surely the rising sea would claim it eventually.

There was money here, which might serve to protect it. And I supposed the historic homes, the elaborately painted gingerbread cottages, could be relocated to the mainland or up the hill to high ground, if the expense were deemed sustainable. Although the interior of the island was mostly protected forest. And if a few good hurricanes washed over it, I wouldn't be surprised if the whole thing came out below sea level.

You can't win an argument with the sea.

We drove around the circumference of the island. There were roads through the interior, more or less. But I wasn't certain if they would get us across the island any faster than taking the highway around. And I wanted to see the ocean.

Cape Cod was just visible, a line on the northern horizon. Nantucket was too far over the curve of the earth to catch a glimpse. There's no ferry between the islands in winter.

We'd stopped at the Black Dog beside the ferry terminal for coffee, and also gotten sandwiches for later. I used the paper cup to warm my hands while Roberts drove, and I tried not to be superstitious about folklore and fetches.

Black dogs are beasts of ill omen.

At last, having passed through Oak Bluffs and Edgartown, we came to the turnoff into the wildlife preserve. We parked. We'd have to hike in from this point.

We packed up the sandwiches, though neither one of us was hungry yet. We'd both gorged ourselves at the pie-and-breakfast place in Woods Hole before we got on the ferry. Lightly burdened, me carrying the map, we set out across the dune grass with Roberts in the lead. He frowned over his GPS: an old-school yellow plastic handheld one, because cell phones get intermittent reception in the islands. We were willful rebels against the signs warning us to prevent dune erosion by staying on the path.

Before long, we came to the *real* Atlantic. It took my breath away. Lines of waves marched to the open ocean; next stop, Africa. I tried not to think of Albert Gilman out there somewhere with rocks in his pockets, rolling in the deep.

He'd be on the other side of Cape Cod, anyway. Somewhere in Massachusetts Bay. His body would turn up someday, I guessed. Unless his peculiar transformation had been more than merely cosmetic, and he'd returned to the deeps like a hatchling sea turtle.

If so, I hoped he'd make it. Lots of hungry things eat hatchlings, and anyone who's been paying attention to the news knows there are plenty of sharks in the waters off the Cape.

* * *

We made our way down to the beach, which was littered with the detritus of the previous week's storms: derelict limpets; the hulks of horseshoe crabs. We walked the margin for what seemed like a long time. It was hard going. Sand and worn pebbles turned under our boots and when we went closer to the water's edge the waves played keep-away.

There was plenty of kelp and bladderwort mixed in with the wrack, and plenty of small dead things. A few living ones too. I surprised a hermit crab in a conch shell big as my hand, scavenging. It took off toward the water. I let it go. A faint cold smell of decay came in waves, like the sea.

At long last we came in sight of what I took to be the landmark circled on the map. A tumbled finger of heaped stones—perhaps what remained of an ancient jetty, perhaps an eroded igneous spur—pointed into the cold Atlantic.

Roberts stopped. "Wow, I do not want to walk out on that."

"I will." I've never been afraid of water, and the sea was not angry. There would be some scrambling, and my boots might get wet. The rest of me certainly would, for where the breakers struck the boulders, white spray arced up, flashing in the pale late autumn sun.

I took my cell phone out of my pocket and wrapped it in a plastic bag from inside my knapsack. And tied the bag closed to be certain it would keep the water out.

Grumbling, Roberts followed me. Middle age comes with its share of aches and pains. I'd been luckier than a number of my contemporaries and was not yet suffering from arthritis or more than the usual complement of farsightedness and achy joints. I managed to keep up with my program of kayaking, swimming, and hiking well enough to be reasonably fit. I was no Roberts—he ran half-marathons, and while he'd never be competitive he was a lanky, not-too-tall sort who still had an eight-minute mile—but I got by.

It was a good thing I wasn't feeling scared, because the scramble was strenuous. I wished I'd brought gloves, heavy ones to keep the wet rock from abrading my hands. The black basalt had awfully sharp edges for being exposed to the power of the open sea, and the line of the finger was steadily ascending. As I walked it, I revised my estimation about the possibility of its being man-made, for I could discern no reason for humans to build a stone pier that rose to a peak out in the ocean. But the tallest rock looked flat on top, and at least the stairsteps lifted us above the spray and the threat of waves breaking over our path and washing us into the battering surf.

We reached the last rock, and I revised my opinion again. The stones might have been a geological feature, a basaltic causeway of some sort. And, indeed, the enormous, squat, hexagonal basalt column we found ourselves atop might have formed by natural processes.

But the elaborate carvings marking its surface had not.

The top of the pillar was perhaps twelve feet in diameter, and when I glanced over the edge, I realized we had climbed, incrementally, a good two stories above sea level. I leaned quickly away from the vertiginous prospect, though it bothered me less than heights usually do.

I have never liked them.

As a distraction, I set myself to examining the markings carved into the tabletop-like plateau. I wasn't quite sure what I expected—pictograms, or names and dates carved in an elegant hand—but it wasn't a six-pointed star reaching point to point across the entire enormous Giant's Causeway-style basalt crystal. There was an elegant inscription in the center, in a stonemason's script that reminded me of colonial gravestones.

"Hey," I said to Roberts, who was standing staring at the sea, "help me clean this off."

He looked at me as if dragging himself back from interstellar distances. "Pardon?"

I gestured to the star. "Help me clean out this inscription. I want to see if I can make out what it says."

We set to, and in fifteen minutes or so had the pebbles, sand, and bird droppings scraped away.

Latin?

I read a little Latin—a very little—but I hadn't expected to find it here. Just one more piece of evidence that the eighteenth century had a higher standard of graffiti.

Roberts came to stand beside me as I leaned over the inscription and read: "*Fer corpus meum animumque mecum nunc Carcosam.*"

The world dropped out from under our feet.

Roberts and I hit hard, but not hard enough to hurt ourselves. We clutched each other and stayed upright, and found ourselves gasping up at a streaky, bubbling yellow sky flecked with black, unradiant stars. Not the kind of yellow sky which makes you expect a tornado. Not even the kind of yellow sky which results from a dust storm, or a forest fire. It was—and I say this advisedly—an uncanny color. A distressing color. It made me think of pus and the pulsating bodies of hungry maggots, and not in a good way.

I acknowledge there's no good way to think about pus. There are probably good ways to think about maggots, if you're an entomologist.

Self-consciously, I let go of my colleague. I felt terrible: achy and discombobulated, as if I had been fighting the flu.

"Right," I said. "Well, we somehow wound up here. And we're obviously talking about some very different physical rules." I pointed at the pavement.

Roberts blinked at me. "Rocks?"

"Octagons," I said. "Traditionally, they don't interlock without small squares to make up the corners."

"But honeycomb?"

"Hexagons," I said. "Like the basalt pillar we were on. Your bathroom tiles, those are octagons. With the little black squares between the corners, because that's how topology works."

Well, that was how topology worked where *we* came from. *Here*, apparently octagons interlocked.

I hoped my amino acids didn't decide to celebrate by becoming unraveled. I couldn't be sure they weren't already doing so. I felt hungover, wrung out, and like my cranium was full of kitty litter. Roberts, rocking on his feet, pressing a fist into his stomach as if to counter a sharp pain, looked even worse.

Chalk one up for *Homo sapiens neanderthalensis*.

"What the hell did you *say*?" Roberts asked.

"*Fer corpus meum animumque mecum nunc Carcosam,*" I repeated.

"Sure." If his tone were any more soaked in exasperation it would have been dripping. "But what does it mean?"

"Oh." My cheeks burned from more than the—possibly mildly caustic—atmosphere. "Come with me, body and soul, to Carcosa."

"Hmm. So this is Carcosa." He straightened himself up and looked around. "What do we know about Carcosa?"

"There are some very weird towers in this city. If it is a city. I don't see anybody who might live here."

"These buildings do look like they were drawn by Dr. Seuss on cold medicine. The good stuff, with the codeine in it."

My eye had been drawn by a flicker of movement embedded in the soupy horizon. If you've ever seen bats rise from under a bridge at dusk, or a murmuration of starlings taking flight, you have an idea what it looked like: varying pinpricks flocking in weird, uneasy patterns, stretching and collapsing, spiraling obscenely. It looked more computer-generated than real. I half expected to find it had been projected.

But whatever was flocking rose, and spiraled (obscenely), and rose again. I had the unsettling impression of it casting about, like a hound after a scent. The shapes coalesced into a writhing arrowhead and darted in our direction. I thought at first that they weren't too far off— that they moved slowly and were small. But then I realized they were bigger than human beings—the wingspans three or four times as long as I was tall—and they were very far away.

Far away, but coming fast, given the distance. Very fast indeed.

I put it in the file with interlocking octagons and got on with my life. A life which, currently, involved a frantic search of the surrounding area for someplace defensible.

"Greer," said Roberts, "have you noticed that those are a lot of moons?"

"I have," I said, casting about for a roof, a wall—anything that could serve to shelter us from a flying attack. "And they're setting in front of those things flying towards us. And also in front of the towers and domes of the city."

"Huh," he said, in the bland tone of voice people reserve for real catastrophes. "Maybe they're not actually moons, then."

"Maybe it's more topography." I craned my head back and looked up at the sky. Something was making me nauseated, and I wasn't sure if it was my strange exhaustion, or the seething yellow sky, or the way everything fit together entirely wrong. "Those flying things look like they have claws, don't they?"

Just then, they began to swarm around the moons, or lanterns, or hot air balloons lit up from the inside, or whatever the hell those things were. The light shone through their bodies in unsettling patterns, as if through the gaps in the leaves of a *Monstera deliciosa*.

. . . as if through the gaps in a human rib cage.

"Oh god," Roberts said, having apparently come to the same conclusion I had. "We could run to the towers."

"I think they fly faster than we run." Despite the enormous distances, the creatures were already much closer. I wondered when I would begin to hear the flapping of their leathery wings.

A voice I did not recognize spoke from behind me. "Very astute, stranger."

I jumped and turned in midair. Landed badly and staggered but did not fall. I found myself facing someone—a man, sure. We'll call him a man. He was naked, and his skin was rubbery black. His features were elegant, idealized. His eyes were gold, without sclera, with slit pupils like a cat's. The eyes of a lion.

"Who are you?" I yelped.

"Does a trespasser demand *my* bona fides?" he mocked. "By rights, I should be asking you what brings you to Carcosa."

"Accident." I looked over at Roberts. He was dumbstruck, with his jaw hanging open. Apparently holding up the conversation was down to me.

And I was doing such a stunning job of it.

"That explains why you are standing here without shelter while the byakhee are rising in the distance, then. Oh, and why nobody has any guns."

"Byakhee." It was a strange word, and I rolled it around on my tongue.

They had nearly reached us. I felt my instinctive half-crouch, my readiness to throw my arms up to shield my face. But they broke off and circled, giving me lingering looks at their decomposed-seeming bodies that I could have quite happily survived without.

They made a terrible sound, a kind of gobbling shriek. It pierced my hearing. I slapped my palms over my ears, which eased the pain only a little.

The strange man turned his head toward me. An iridescent yellow reflection ran over his bald, poreless pate from the roiling sky. Somehow, when he spoke, his words came bell-clear through the terrible sound and my attempts to block it. "You really are an innocent. But I can smell your provenance on you. Come, let us advance past this annoyance."

He held a glossy hand out to me. Gritting my teeth, I managed to yank my hands from my ears. I grabbed Roberts's elbow with one hand, and the stranger's fingers with the other.

The stranger nodded. Not to me. To the sky.

The roil increased. I felt as If I were watching one of those sped-up stop-motion films of cloudscapes tearing themselves around mountains. The moons crossed the zenith in spiraling synchrony and set—before the towers, on the other side of the sky. The byakhee whirled like vultures, faster, faster—until suddenly it seemed they were flung wide all at once, racing to the umpteen corners of the sky.

Nausea dizzied me. I doubled over. If I hadn't been holding on to my companions, I would have put my hands on my knees.

As it was, all my effort went to not vomiting up my shoes.

While I was still gasping, two sickly conjoined suns rose: behind, I was relieved to note, the black domes and twisted, monolithic towers.

I was really astoundingly glad I was not a topologist.

"There," the man said. He let go of my hand. I did not let go of Roberts's. "They don't love the daylight. Where did you come from?"

"There was a basalt pillar along the coast of an island. Martha's Vineyard. I read some graffiti carved on it—"

"What on Earth were you doing there?" He put a funny emphasis on "Earth," I thought, but I looked up at the twin suns in the yellow sky again, and wondered less.

I wasn't sure what to say. Like Roberts, I opened my mouth soundlessly. Unlike Roberts, I closed it and tried again. What came out was a truth I had not even recognized until I spoke it. "I was looking for my family. The carving on the causeway brought us here."

"To find your family, lost scion, you must look farther to the south than the causeway," he said, almost kindly. "You turned in the wrong direction."

"This place—"

"The gods of this place are related to the gods of that place. They are all very old." He looked at Roberts. "None of them are the gods of your kind. You are fortunate that there are bonds of hospitality of a sort between your colleague's people and those who dwell here."

Roberts made a protesting noise. I hid a smirk. The reminder that he wasn't always going to be first-billed would be good for him.

The stranger said, "Come along then, lost scion, I will help you get home. Follow me. And watch your feet while you walk. Humans find the topography confusing."

"You don't say," Roberts muttered.

The stranger led us through ways that defied description, around buildings that seemed to twist into new shapes with every step we took. I felt as if I were walking at the edge of the CGI map of reality, so things flickered in and out and twisted in unlikely ways as the rendering failed and generally made me worry I was going to get stuck inside a boulder or something if I wasn't careful.

I noticed I had grown hungry and thirsty only when Roberts held out a sandwich—somewhat the worse for wear since we'd purchased it at the Black Dog—to me. He didn't say anything, and I took the sandwich with a nod instead of a word. It seemed perilous enough that our footfalls echoed wildly with every step.

I could not have told you how long we had been walking when we emerged onto the shore of a tremendous bay. Roberts, who had continued tensely silent, let out an enormous sigh. My own relief was as sharp. And as short-lived, because a moment later we both noticed the lapping waves were not water but some heavy vapor streaming like fluid between the stones. The stones were jagged, unsmoothed.

There was a smell in the air, autumnal as chrysanthemums but not in any manner floral. The suns were edging toward the horizon on the far side of the lake. The sky and the mist above it were shading to ruddy and orange. The first and darkest of the black stars prickled out around the edge of the firmament.

I shuddered as if a chill touched me. Would the byakhee return with the moonsrise?

"Here." Our guide pointed to a set of menhir stones, steles carved in alphabets which wavered before my eyes—and not because I needed my progressives updated. "Step into that circle and speak as you spoke before. You recollect the incantation?"

I nodded. "I do not wish to be transported body and mind to Carcosa, however."

He spoke over his shoulder, walking away. "You'll find another word on the stones. It is the true name of the place you wish to return to. This gate will take you there."

I called after him. "What did you mean, look further south? There's nothing south of there but the ocean."

He waved airily and did not look back.

I took a step after him. I might have broken into a run, but Roberts caught my wrist.

I had so many questions. "What did you mean, you can smell my provenance?"

But—with a subtle pop of air rushing to fill a sudden vacuum—he was gone.

"We have to go *back*," Roberts said.

I stomped my foot like a fifties stereotype. "Fine." Two steps had us better centered between the upright stones. There were words scribed here, as well. I spat them out grumpily. "*Fer corpus meum animumque mecum nunc Noepe.*"

Another pop of displacement followed.

* * *

Astoundingly, I felt even worse when we came through on the other side. I fell—I probably would have gone flat on my face if it hadn't been for Roberts hanging on to me—and skinned my knee right through my jeans. It turns out basalt has a little texture to it.

Roberts hauled me up again. He looked a little better than I felt, but his complexion was waxy and his hair looked . . . stiff, and frayed. Like a sick dog's pelt.

I said as much.

He snorted. "You're pretty green around the gills yourself." Still holding on to my wrist, he led me toward land.

It was a long, cold walk back to the car. Night was coming on fast and a needle-sharp rain had blown up. I wondered how long we'd been gone; it felt like a week. My phone, when I unwrapped it and turned it on, told me it was a little over twenty-four hours.

The ferry wasn't running because of the storm. We found a last-minute emergency hotel in Edgartown. They were as happy to have us as we were to find them: most people don't come to the Vineyard in the late autumn, and most hotels don't stay open past sometime in mid-October.

Sensibly, all around.

The lady at the front desk studied me quizzically. "You look familiar," she said with a certain hesitancy. "Have you been here before?"

"First time," I admitted, accepting the key card. I snuck a look at the edge of her computer monitor and was relieved to confirm my phone's intimation that we'd only been gone overnight.

"Family on the Vineyard?" It might have been a cheerful tone. It might have been a leading one. But it was the sort of question anybody might ask. As so often happens when one has an unconventional upbringing, small talk brought me up short and sharp.

"I don't know," I admitted. "I'm adopted."

"Mmm." Her eyes shifted from me to Roberts. She handed him a key card too. "Have a nice night. You can park your car in the lot around the corner. Put this on the dash—it's got a map to show you which lot. I'm afraid it'll be a short walk back in the rain."

"I'll go," Roberts said. "It's not like I could be much wetter. See you for dinner?"

I didn't argue for the privilege of suffering a tiny bit more. Roberts could have the moral high ground. There was supposed to be a big tub in my room, and I was done in. I would have opted for room service—if a hotel this size, in the off-season, offered it.

The water helped with the winter itch of dry and scaly skin. I dumped the complimentary bath salts in, and that helped too, though I wasn't sure peach jasmine ginger was really a scent suited to my personality. I scrubbed out the scrapes, including the bits of grit trapped in them, and was relieved when they didn't bleed too much. My shins looked like they were covered with eczema, so I coated them with free body lotion (peach jasmine ginger) before I pulled my muddy, torn jeans back on.

They were what I had to wear, unless I wanted to go see if the Black Dog was still open and pick up some touristy sweatpants.

We had dinner in one of the four or five restaurants in town that stayed open all winter, and I ate an entire clambake—this place called it "Lobster in the Rough" and it was comprised of a forearm-sized lobster, clams, mussels, linguiça, potatoes, and corn on the cob—without any help from Roberts except when I had to fend him away from my sausage. When I found myself picking out the bits of kelp they throw in for that authentic buried-in-a-pit-of-coals-on-the-beach-at-low-tide flavor and dragging them through the remnants of my clarified butter before eating them, I gave up and ordered dessert. The kelp tasted even better than the potatoes, frankly.

I guess interdimensional travel takes it out of you.

Roberts did justice and more than justice to his own food. We didn't talk much: what *could* we say, in a crowded restaurant? But he did look up from his pie at one point and say, "We need to go back and document that."

"With GoPros," I agreed.

He nodded. "And guns."

We finished our food and went back to the hotel.

* * *

I hadn't thought I would sleep, but I had reckoned without the combination of exhaustion, the enormous meal, and the hypnotic flicker of the Edgartown light along the horizon outside my sea-facing window. It's a beautiful place, Martha's Vineyard.

What a pity if the rising oceans do eventually wash it away.

I dreamed of undersea tourists gliding through the waters of the North Atlantic, no longer rich and murky with nutrients but as gorgeously transparent as any less fertile Caribbean sea. Their flippered feet kicked lazily, a dream of sunrays shining past them to illuminate the ruins of Oak Bluffs, of Tisbury, of Edgartown far beneath. They passed over Menemsha, a tiny hamlet whose industries are fishing and movie memorabilia—*Jaws* was filmed there—and I thought about the *Boston Globe*'s breathless coverage of the great white sharks that had returned to Cape Cod with the rebounding harbor seal population.

I guess they got the last laugh. If sharks laugh.

I was awakened by a cautious tapping sound sometime after midnight. I scrambled into some clothes—I hadn't brought anything to sleep in, and I wasn't about to expose Roberts to my dishabille—and opened the door a groggy, tousled inch.

There was no one in the hall. I checked twice. You know how it is when you're sleepy. I closed and re-latched the door and was about to decide I'd overheard somebody else's assignation when the tapping came again.

My room had a balcony to go with its water view. This hadn't been relevant to my objectives when I fell first into the tub and then into bed. Now I walked toward the sliding glass door, and the shape outside it that I could glimpse, every few seconds, limned in the glow of the Edgartown light. I felt as if I might still be dreaming. I felt no fear, just a curious attraction to the glass, as if I stepped up silently to the partition keeping me from some dangerous animal in a zoo.

Except I was the one in the cage, wasn't I? Trapped inside this boxlike structure, while the creature out there stood comfortably in the rain sheeting down its pebbled neck and shoulders, in the light reflecting dark green as kelp from its wet, gleaming hide.

"Hello," I said, as I pulled the sliding door open. Rain and wind whipped around me. The vertical blinds rattled like knives in a drawer. "I've been waiting for you."

"We've encountered each other before," the creature said in an awkward croak. "Well, after a fashion."

It stepped inside.

"I met Albert Gilman last night," I told Roberts the next morning. The rain had stopped, and we had taken our coffee up to the cold, exposed roof of the Chappy Ferry terminal. There were two ferries, and each could take about two cars at a time. They went back and forth across the narrow channel between Martha's Vineyard and Chappaquiddick in a kind of square dance, each bending wide and reversing as they passed one another like partners swinging on the parquet. "He came to my hotel room."

Roberts blinked. He sipped his coffee and looked away from the do-si-do-ing ferries. "That's a hell of a conversational opener."

"He's gone a lot farther than he had in the documents he sent us," I said. I glanced down at my own hand and picked a thread of skin loose from a sunburned-looking patch by the base of my thumb.

"Oh," Roberts said. He looked at me, mouth thinning. "Oh."

"He wants me to come with him. To visit his people."

Roberts nodded, as if knowing what I was going to say next. He looked at me and kept looking.

I said, "Our people."

Even if he had expected it, it still led to a long pause. "Is it safe? I mean . . . you can come back?"

"Yes. I can come back. He gave me a . . . a talisman. Until I'm better adapted to the pressure and breathing water."

"A talisman. *That* sounds like science."

"It sounds like bullshit." I choked on it and laughed. But once I got it out, everything behind it followed in a hurry. "But maybe there is some science behind it. Maybe there's science we can learn."

"Maybe."

"If I go will you wait for me?"

He laughed, this time. Forced, but not false. "It's your car, Greer. I'm not going to steal it."

"I'll pay you back with a Nobel Prize in physics," I promised.

"I'm a geneticist!"

I rolled my eyes so hard I gave myself a headache.

"*Frog people*, Michael. Have you been tuning in?"

The waves curled around my thighs. Albert stood beside me as I stared out into the Atlantic. I touched the amulet on my breast. "You're sure about this?"

He croaked laughter. "I've never been sure about anything in my life," he said. "But the salt water does help with the itching."

"But. What do they want with me?" *What will they want* from *me*? I couldn't ask him that. He wouldn't understand.

"To welcome you to the family," he said. " Once you're ready to come live with our people full time, you'll find a whole society. You're one of us, and your children will know who they are from the start."

I shook my head. "I'm past all that."

"Some of the elders you'll meet today are older than the Constitution," he said. "You're barely a teenager."

I blinked at him. It was hard to tell, but I think he grinned at me.

We dove.

I knew the water was cold, but it didn't feel cold. Albert was a shadow alongside me, drifting deeper and deeper, while the light grew dimmer and greener above. It was my dream, but the sea wasn't lifeless. There were still clouds of plankton in the water; there were still schools of silvery fish darting away from us.

We swam down, and down. My lungs grew tired from the stress of moving water in and out and in again. My chest muscles ached as if I had been coughing for days. I envied Albert his gills. I touched the folds of my own throat hopefully: no luck.

Well, it would happen in time. I had grown confident, or perhaps resigned.

We descended. The pressure should have been unbearable, but it didn't even make my ears pop. I wondered if I would need to fear the bends on our return. I did not swim as strongly as my companion. He would kick once with his flippers, then glide and wait for me to catch up to him.

I touched the talisman on its cord. I was pretty sure its help was the only reason I managed to stay close to him, even with Albert going easy on me.

Albert spoke as we swam. I could understand him, but I could not reply. He asked questions, which I could not answer; it turns out it's not easy to make your vocal cords vibrate when your trachea is full of ocean water. The metallic salt of the sea filled my sinuses.

Albert asked if I was afraid and said he had been. He'd been terrified. The language he spoke wasn't English, but I understood it as well as if it were. Another gift of the talisman? Or something intrinsic in the instincts in my unclassified DNA?

I didn't know. I'd find out, though. I was a scientist, and I was going where no scientist had both gone before and come back from. It wasn't my field but that didn't matter. I didn't have the attention to spare from curiosity to waste on being afraid.

I was not sure what I had expected, but an entire glorious undersea city wasn't it. An entire glorious undersea city existing in what should have been utter blackness, bioluminescing among the convolutions of deep-sea corals I had not even realized existed in the North Atlantic, swarming with large, pebble-skinned, sociable people.

They wanted me. They were interested in me.

They welcomed me, froggy eyes blinking, webbed fingers reaching out to touch my hair. They were curious and interested, and I was curious about them, too.

I could feel Albert's concern: he hovered close and tried to shield me from the swarm of fishy, froggy people surrounding me. Englobing me. Presenting me with pretty shells and glowing bits of coral. Albert waved them away, but I got the impression they didn't trust his judgment enough to let it override their own.

I felt like I was suffocating, and it wasn't just the water in my lungs.

I kicked away, knowing it was futile. They were bigger and faster. They belonged here.

I didn't belong anywhere.

I burst through the surface, gasping as if I had been holding my breath, thick saltwater scouring my throat as I choked it up. I cast about, looking for pursuit, but I was alone except for the steady flash of the Edgartown light over the dark water. I should have been shuddering violently, but the cold didn't touch me.

Just as I drew a relieved breath of air, something big broke the water. I kicked myself around, expecting to feel teeth or clawed flippers—

It was Albert.

I was surprised to realize that I recognized him. I hadn't thought about being able to tell the frog people apart: I'd just assumed it would be impossible.

Bad scientist. No biscuit.

"You ran away," he said, his voice resonating through the water as his throat expanded.

"It was a lot of people," I answered, and salt water got in my mouth. Under the circumstances, his system was clearly superior. "I'm not good at people."

He held out a flippered hand. At first I thought he wanted me to take it, but I realized he was pointing back toward the horizon and the flicker of the lighthouse. In the east, the night was fading. "Do you want help getting home?"

"That's not my home," I said, and stopped myself before going any further. "Yes," I said. "I mean, yes. And if I haven't ruined things, I'd like to talk to you again."

"Sure," he said. "I've missed being around scientists."

Everybody expects something from you, and it's rarely for you to be yourself. It's your job to put everybody else first. To take care of them.

Well, I'm tired of it.

No computers under water. No particle accelerators. No—to judge from what Albert said—scientists.

I'm not sure that is the place for me, either. I'm not sure the place for me exists.

The thin gleam of pale beach grew wider against the horizon. We talked as we swam, and I realized I was a better swimmer than I had been. I'd never been a *bad* swimmer, but now my body seemed to work with the water rather than against it. I mentioned it to Albert, and he croak-laughed deep in his throat pouches and said, "That's only going to keep happening."

"So I'm turning into a—I mean, I'm changing, like you." Sand gritted under my flippers. I stood up. Waves broke around my thighs.

"Turning into a monster, you were going to say?" He loomed up beside me, half again my height and twice as broad, green-black hide camouflaged against the green-black ocean. "Look, what I've learned since I changed . . . we've been living peaceably alongside you Yankee assholes for generations. And you people come down and blow up Jeffreys Ledge and Stellwagen Bank every time you notice us."

There we were, standing on the beach in November, yelling at each other through the rain. At least it would keep the beachcombers indoors. "Aren't you one of us Yankee assholes, at least in part? You seem much more comfortable with the change than you did in the diaries you sent me."

He turned and started walking away from the light. It was only a couple stories tall, and it sat right on the beach, surrounded by a low stone patio. I followed along behind him, my own gait less of a shamble.

For the time being.

"I've had time to get used to it. And . . ." Water splashed off his hide as he shook his froggy head. "I like the community. They . . . take care of each other."

"Sounds a damned sight more humane than academia," I deadpanned through chattering teeth. Now that I was out of the water, I was starting to get cold.

He croaked what I could only assume was laughter. "Well, I didn't even have that, after . . . after I flunked out. Also, I know *you* never bombed Jeffreys Ledge. I'm sorry about that crack."

"It's okay," I said. I reached out—reached up—awkwardly and patted his shoulder. "When did we bomb Jeffreys Ledge? Isn't that where the whale watch boats go?"

"Nineteen twenty-eight," he said. "But our people live a long time. Most of the ones you just met—"

"Briefly."

"—remember."

"Oh," I said, doing math in my head. So most of them were more than ninety years old.

Most of us.

I remembered what he'd said about the Constitution.

"We're here when you're ready," he said. "I should go back now."

"What if I'm never ready?"

"You can't avoid the sea forever," he said. "It can outwait anyone."

I returned to the hotel room. I took a hot shower. I still didn't have dry clothes, but the room had a bathrobe. I put it on, and I went and rapped on Robert's door. He opened it and stared at me.

"Do you have coffee? Or tea? I'm cold through the bones."

"You're back," he said.

"For now," I said.

He held the door wide. "Come in."

How many physicists actually get to *go* to the stars? And pioneer a completely new field of physics? So, I've found an inexhaustible research subject.

And my family.

When I'm ready to deal with having a family.

If I'm ever ready to deal with having a family.

The ocean is big, after all. It might be a good place to be alone. Or maybe the Boston Aquarium needs a physicist. Or Woods Hole: is there such a thing as a deep-sea marine physicist?

There should be. I can always collect a few more degrees if it makes me more useful.

Why are my people in hiding?

I'm going to be the first frog people visibility activist. You see if I don't. After all, it looks like, barring accidents, I'm going to live a very long time . . . barring accidents, inside-out monstrosities eating my face, or dread gods, I should say. But I'm tougher than humans are, and a firefight on an alien world against flying abominations is all in a day's work.

I have tenure. I should have time to do a lot of science. And I imagine I will have a lot less to worry about from certain coworkers as my *claws* grow in.

In the meantime, I also have some hypotheses to prove about gate technology, and the biology of byakhee.

Which brings us back, I suppose, to Roberts and me, the flimsy barricade, and the need to get back to our gate home right away.

I racked my shotgun and met Roberts's eyes. "In the immortal words of David Bowie," I said, "I'm ready."

THE THICKENING

BRIAN EVENSON

I.

When he was very young, Greppur often awoke late at night feeling he could not afford to remain alone. He would creep from his room and down the hall, listening to the swish of his soles against the parquet floor. That and the feel of his hand brushing along the wall were just enough to keep the air from thickening into something else. He would travel by feel to the end of the hall and open the door to his parents' bedroom as quietly as possible. He could not climb into bed with them because this might wake his father up. If his father awoke, Greppur would be immediately carried back to his own bedroom, locked in this time. But if he was careful, he could creep to the chair just next to his mother's side of the bed and curl up there.

Once there, if he was unlucky, his father would still sense him and suddenly rough hands would be lifting him, carrying him back to his room, where the thickening would begin.

If he was very lucky indeed, he would fall asleep to the sound of his mother's breathing and remain in the chair until morning.

Usually he was just lucky enough. After some time in the chair he would calm down, and only then see a glint in the darkness and know his mother's eyes were open, that she was observing him.

"What is it?" his mother would whisper. "Another bad dream?"

"No," he would whisper back.

But his mother did not understand that what he meant by this was not that there had not been a *bad* dream. What he meant was that it hadn't been a dream at all. That it had been real.

She would nod. Sometimes she let him stay, but even if she sent him back to bed it was usually all right: enough time had gone by that the danger had passed.

As he grew older, he came to understand the thickening never happened more than once per night, and usually not even that. He dreaded it happening, and it was always terrible when it did, but usually he could wake himself in time. If there was another person in the house, as long as he came close enough to them to hear the sound of their breathing he could stop it from happening. Knowing another person was near was enough. Sometimes, though, he woke only when the thickening had already begun, and it was too late.

When, later still, he was in college and sharing a dorm room, it stopped entirely. For a few weeks he thought he was free of it. But when his roommate went home for the weekend, there, there it was again, three nights in a row, nearly unbearable in the way the thing that congealed from the air peered into him. But once his roommate was back, it stopped.

Perhaps this was why he became entangled with someone before college was finished. It seemed a necessity. He first lived with her and then, when her parents, religious, objected, married her. It wasn't that he didn't, in his way, love her, only that that was far from his only reason for being with her, not even the primary one. On some level any warm body would have done. Sleeping next to anyone would save him: it just happened to be her.

They were, so everybody said, inseparable. *Twenty-five years together*, he overheard his wife say proudly once to a friend on the telephone, *and not a single night spent apart*, which made him cringe. Made him, after so many years, remember. Made him, for the first time in years, nervous about going to sleep.

Nearly a decade later, long after he had forgotten again, his wife died: a sudden thing, a stroke, almost no warning. One moment they were speaking about how they would spend their evening, the next she collapsed. Then he was calling 911, then riding in the ambulance with her, then riding in the ambulance with her corpse. It was a terrible thing, occurring in such fashion as to leave him drenched in guilt and confusion. Coming back to the house alone in the early hours of the morning, he hardly felt like himself. Exhausted, he managed to strip off his coat and flop onto the bed. And then, before he knew it, he was asleep.

But he was not asleep for long.

II.

It was just like it had been when he was a child. He had been dreaming that the air had become thick around him so that it was hard to breathe and even hard to move. He had come gaspingly awake, only he wasn't sure if he was awake or just dreaming he was awake. Was there time to get up and go find his parents' room? *But no*, he suddenly realized with something akin to wonder, *I'm not a child anymore*: his parents had been dead for many years. His wife too was dead now, and he was alone.

"Greppur," the thickening in the air crooned. "Greppur?" It was feeling for him with something that, if he squinted and ignored the fact that he could see through it, looked like a hand, but was not a hand. He could not see it, not really: it was like *an interruption of the air*. He remembered thinking that when he was a child, had taken the phrase, he supposed, from something misunderstood in a children's story. But he could see it was right, the right phrase, at least for this particular phase of the thickening.

"When did I see you last?" it asked. "Yesterday? Decades ago? It seems like so much time has gone by, and so little."

It did to Greppur too. Both.

It began to thicken, began to inflict a more substantial form upon the air. The voice was sharper now. What had been a wavering in the air took on firmer shape. It was too late. He could guess where its mouth was already, if he was right to call it a mouth.

"Where are you?" it said in a wheedling tone. "Let me see you, Greppur."

He tried to close his eyes, but they would not close.

What if he fled to the hall? Would it follow him? What if he made it outside? He tried to get up, grunting with effort, unable, really, to move. It wheeled and faced his way at the sound, though facing was the wrong word since other than the mouth, if it was a mouth, it didn't yet have a face. It thickened further, visible now, but flattened out and slightly translucent, as if made of paper.

"Ah, there you are," it said. "I hear you anyway." And ears began to form.

He tried again to rise and managed to roll out of the bed and fall onto the floor. He could not move his arms to catch his fall. He struck hard, with a *thunk*.

"What's that?" it said. "What's that? What are you trying now, child?" He had fallen facedown and was turned so he was largely looking at the floor, but with his head angled just enough that one eye saw the bottom of the door, a little stretch of baseboard, a few inches of wall.

"We were meant to be together, Greppur," it said. "You know we were."

Maybe it is a dream, he told himself, though he knew it was not a dream. He tried to lift his head but could not lift his head. He could move his body a little, just a very little, like a worm, more a shiver than movement proper. He began to do that, began to shiver, rocking a little too, oozing his way slowly, inch by inch, under the bed.

"Where are you?" it said. "Let me see you, child. Let me take a good, long look."

But this, Greppur felt, was precisely what he could not let it do. He kept shivering, kept inching. Was he making progress? He was,

but was it enough? He could smell dust. He felt something brush the back of his head. Had it found him? No, that was the blanket hanging just over the side of the bed, his head brushing past it as he moved underneath. And then it was growing darker and he could wriggle a little better and there he was, a grown man in his fifties, facedown under his own bed, motes of dust whirling around him.

"Greppur," the reedy voice still called from somewhere above. "Where are you, my sweet?"

He was more himself under the bed, even if only slightly. He could turn his head a little now. He could see the creature's legs, looking thick and substantial and opaque, though they left no mark on the carpet wherever they stepped. The feet left the floor, and he knew it was on the bed now, though the bed did not shake or creak. But as soon as he noted this, the bed did shake, did creak, and he became afraid that by questioning it he had made it happen, had thickened the creature further.

Now the mattress was sagging down, resting against his back like a splayed palm. He waited, hidden. I can just wait it out, he told himself. *I can just wait until morning. It won't find me.*

As suddenly as it had started, the weight pushing down the mattress was gone. Something was there beside him, deeper under the bed, just behind his head.

Ah, it said, and gave a tinny, tinkling laugh. He felt all of its hands close around his head, the fingers long and bony now. It slowly exerted pressure. His face rubbed along the floor and through the dust, and then there the other face was, right beside his own. It had not finished becoming a face yet, or had gone about it wrongly: where one would expect features there was only a gash for a mouth and two divots for eyes, the surface otherwise smooth and bled of color.

"I told you I would return for you," the mouth said softly.

Please, he tried to say, but nothing came out.

"Let me have a look in you," the mouth said, "a good long one." And then the lipless mouth opened to reveal a blotch of darkness. Slowly, from within drifted up what seemed at first a large, dirty white marble, but then turned to reveal itself to be an eye.

It remained there at the top of the darkness, clasped delicately between the lipless top edge of the mouthgash and the lipless bottom edge of the mouthgash. It vibrated slightly, the pupil dilating and contracting, and stared, stared.

And then the creature said, with delight, *Ah, at last*!

III.

Whenever it came for him in childhood, it had always gone something like that: it stared into him so deeply it was as if he felt the eye held in the mouth slowly licking away the lining of his skull. It was looking for something, he knew, but he did not know what. Some memory, he supposed, or some concatenation of memories, but he was not even sure of that much. There was always a long moment where he felt he had been backed into a corner of his own mind, and then the voice would say, softly, "Not yet." And then it was gone and he was left gasping.

After he calmed down, he was, usually, able to convince himself over time it had all been a dream, a bad one, true, but a dream. And, usually, exhausted, he could slip back into sleep, and only wake at daylight, the visit nearly forgotten. He would not think about the creature until, a night or two or three later, it came for him again.

As a child he became quite agile, if agile was the right word, at sensing the thickening coming. He would awaken before it was too late, before it arrived. All he had to do was find someone, be near someone, in the same room as some other human asleep or awake. If he could do that, the thickening would simply dissolve.

But he could not always be agile. Or perhaps as time went on, and he managed to avoid it, it became hungrier and more desperate. It might take a few weeks, a few months, but eventually he would awaken too late, after the thickening was too far along. When that happened, it was hard for him to move and impossible for him to speak. It wandered about the room, crooning his name, not quite able to see him.

But, in the end, it always found him. Just as it had done now, decades later, now that he was an adult, now that it was starving.

In the past, when it was done with him, it would always say, *Not yet. I'll come back for you.*

And now it seemed after all these years it had.

IV.

When he awoke, he remembered very little. Bad dreams, the beginning of panic, nightmares. But it was understandable: he'd had a bad day the day before. The worst of days, he felt, he was sure, he was almost sure, even if he couldn't quite remember what, what exactly, had been so bad.

It must have been bad since he seemed to have slept in his clothes. Why hadn't his wife helped him undress?

He rolled over in the other direction, curling up against his wife's back. Her skin was cold. She uttered a little moan of pleasure.

There was something strange, he suddenly felt, something missing. Had he left something somewhere by accident and subconsciously realized it, was feeling vague anxiety as a result? Or if not something left, an appointment forgotten? To what? With whom?

He shook his head slightly, trying to remember. He felt his wife stiffen a little.

"Honey," she said, still facing away, "darling, what's wrong?"

"I . . . don't know," he said.

It was almost there, on the tip of his tongue.

"Don't you want to tell me?" she asked.

"I . . . ," he started, and then realized that no, he did not. Thinking this made him feel guilty. Why shouldn't he tell his wife?

And then she turned toward him and he knew why: there was something wrong with her features. They were too soft. Almost as he remembered them but not quite.

But then he blinked his eyes and looked again and thought, *No, it must have been something wrong with my vision.* She looked just as she always had.

Didn't she? What was it? What was he missing? What had he forgotten?

"Honey," she said. She almost sang the word. "What is it?" He just shook his head, said nothing.

She stroked his face with all of her hands. Her hands were cold too. "We were meant to be together," she said. "You know we were." He tried not to look at her.

"Let me help you," she said.

And now he did not dare speak or move his head at all in fear that she would take this for assent. But this was his wife. There was no reason to be afraid. What was wrong with him?

Then she opened her mouth wide and looked at him, really looked with another eye entirely, and he realized he had every reason to be afraid, though it was already far too late for something like fear to do him any good.

THE OWL COUNT

ELIZABETH HAND

I n mid-March, Louis's childhood friend Eric died of a cerebral aneu-
rysm after being in a coma for nine days. The memorial was in the
small Vermont town where they'd grown up together. Louis drove there
from northern Maine, spent the night at a friend's house after the service,
and left again next morning.

It was late afternoon when he got back home, to a few inches of new
snow. He went inside and fired up the woodstove, sorted through the
few items of mail that had arrived since he'd left, grabbed a beer from
the fridge, and checked his mobile. There he found a text message from
his old friend Yvette.

> Looks like the best night for the owl count will be tonight or
> Monday. Moon is just past full now. Will be cold but I'm afraid if
> we don't get out this week we'll miss the chance because of
> weather.

Louis stared out at the bare trees silhouetted against the dusk. After
a moment he wrote, just returned from a funeral in vermont, can do it
tomorrow maybe

Immediately she replied: No, supposed to snow early tomorrow. Need
to go tonight.

Louis swore softly, then sighed. ok what time
Will pick you up @ 11:30. See you then!

He finished his beer and reheated some soup for dinner, checked the temperature and weather. Twenty-eight degrees, cloudy, not much wind. Heavy snow predicted but not till morning. Not an ideal night, at least as far as Louis was concerned—it was way too cold.

But the owls wouldn't care, and neither would Yvette. Like Louis, she was widowed. Her husband, Buddy, had been Louis's close friend, a game warden who'd been two months from retirement when he had a heart attack while searching for a snowmobiler who'd gone missing up by Greenville. Louis always felt like he'd taken Buddy's death harder than Yvette. Not true, he knew that; it was just Yvette's way. Her composure and oddly fatalistic good humor remained unshaken by death, war, the slow decay of the wilderness where they lived. And now, her own illness.

Louis's wife, Sheila, had died within a year of Buddy. That was over a decade ago. The plastic bins full of medications she'd been prescribed in her last months were still jammed onto the floor of the bedroom closet, where her winter coats, flannel shirts, and snowmobiling gear continued to hang alongside Louis's own. Like Yvette—like everyone—he'd been downsized from his teaching job when their university rolled over to the AI modules. Since then he'd gotten by the same way his Maine ancestors had a century earlier. Bartering and scavenging; hunting and fishing; coaxing pumpkins, squash, beans, onions, garlic, Jacob's Cattle Beans from the stony soil and longer growing season that was one of the few enduring benefits of the so-called lost winters.

"You can grow tomatoes in Maine now!" Yvette always marveled.

"Yeah, but not potatoes," Louis would retort. The mutated potato bugs had seen to that.

He washed his soup bowl and spoon, went outside to bring in more firewood. If it really did snow the next day, he'd be too tired from the owl count to bother in the morning. He drank another beer, set the alarm for 11:00 p.m., four hours from now, and went to bed.

He woke when the phone rang. Yvette again. He looked blearily at the time and groaned. "Jesus, you couldn't let me sleep another fifteen minutes?"

"I was afraid you wouldn't wake up!"

Louis had never overslept for the owl count, but he knew that wasn't the issue. Yvette was too excited to wait. "Well, give me a few minutes. I need some coffee."

"I have coffee."

"I give up. See you when you get here."

He heated water for the coffee and dressed. Thermal long under-wear, a pair of wool hunting pants that had been his father's, a ragg wool sweater and another that Sheila had knit for him. Two pairs of wool socks, old insulated Bean boots. Most years, he and Yvette didn't hear any owls. But it was guaranteed that they'd freeze as they waited in hopes of doing so.

He'd just finished gulping down the coffee when Yvette's headlights cut through the darkness outside the kitchen window. She left the car idling and entered without knocking. Louis held up his coffee mug. "Want some?"

Yvette perched on the arm of the chair beside the woodstove. With her green snow pants, oversized black boots, and red parka, its pointed hood pulled up so that wispy white curls framed her face, she resembled a garden gnome. She glanced at the coffee mug and shook her head.

"I'm all set," she said. She watched Louis with the avid expression of a dog awaiting a walk. He grabbed gloves and knit cap, pulled on his own parka; shoved his mobile in a pocket, and stuck another log in the woodstove.

"Okay," he said.

Yvette hopped up and hurried outside. Louis followed, the snow soft beneath his boots. He got into her old Subaru, where she handed him a clipboard.

"And there's more coffee." She pointed at a thermos on the floor, put the car into gear, and gingerly pulled out onto the road. "I'm so excited!" she exclaimed, and grinned.

Louis had joined the owl count twenty-six years earlier, when Yvette's former owling partner moved back to Florida. Back then, the program was administered by a Maine college that had received a grant to do a study of the state's owl population. The top data sheet on Louis's clipboard dated to that time.

We seek to establish owl presence across our landscape,
to estimate population and density for common Maine owls,
and to detect changes in distribution or density perhaps
related to human influences . . .

Data was collected by teams of volunteers across Maine between early March and mid-April—breeding season. They monitored five owl species—short- and long-eared owls, saw-whet owls, barred owls, great horned owls. The project ended years ago, but Yvette and Louis had continued to go out nearly every spring since. This was Yvette's idea, of course, but except for that year when Sheila had finally gone into hospice in Bangor, Louis accompanied Yvette every time, including the March night only weeks after Buddy's death.

The Subaru jounced down the rutted drive to the road as Yvette downshifted to avoid potholes and frost heaves. Louis's car was a hybrid, nearly as old as Yvette's Subaru, but it didn't fare as well in winter. He stuck the clipboard on the floor and reached to turn down the heat. Yvette's car reeked of dog and scorched engine oil—the head gasket leaked, so she had to top off the oil every other day, from a stock-pile she'd traded for with gallons of tomato sauce and some deworming medicine with a 2007 expiration date. Her dog, Wilmer, was back at the house. The only time he didn't accompany Yvette was during the owl count.

"Damn!" Yvette slapped the steering wheel and Louis looked at her in alarm. Yvette never swore. "I forgot to check if there's batteries in the CD player! Do you have any?"

"At the house, maybe." He twisted to look into the back seat, piled with outdoor gear and blankets covered in dog hair, and snaked out his arm to retrieve the portable boom box, a decrepit piece of out-moded technology that Yvette coddled as though it had been one of her wheezing dogs. She'd bought it specifically for the owl count. That must have been more than thirty years ago, when CDs were already being phased out.

As far as Louis knew, she never used it for any other purpose—he'd never seen a single other CD in her house. Some nights during the summer, she'd play the owl-call CD on the deck of her house up on Flywheel Mountain, watching as the owls appeared ghostlike from the darkness above her head. A practice the Owl Monitoring Program had strictly warned against, back in the day, but the study had ended so long ago, who was possibly left to care? Certainly Yvette had seen and heard more owls during these forbidden sessions than they ever had during the owl count.

He peered through the CD player's smudged plastic window and saw the disc. Did she ever even remove it? Probably not. He hit *Play*, watched as the disc began to spin. "It's working," he said.

"Thank God."

The car juddered as she steered it onto Route 217, one of the secondary roads that threaded through this part of the Allagash territory. Yvette had meticulous directions for the owl count—the exact mileage between each stop, numbers on utility poles and mailboxes, descriptions of unusual trees or rocks, notes for other landmarks. Once upon a time, there had been sporting camps here, then family-friendly resorts, then a few glampsites, a fairly desperate and frankly insane attempt on the part of entrepreneurs from away that failed almost overnight. As the timber companies went under, most of their holdings went to the state, but with no demand for paper, building materials, or recreation, the land had reverted to wilderness. A new and different kind of wilderness: the nature of the boreal forest changed as conifers and evergreens adapted to the longer growing season or, in many cases, died.

Someone from away might not notice the difference. Looking out the window of the Subaru, Louis still saw the black encroaching walls to either side of the narrow road, the trees closer to the broken tarmac with each passing season. He rolled down the window—even with the heat off, the car was stifling. Cold air rushed in, balsam and the pissy scent of cat spruce, along with a more forbidding, granitic scent that he knew presaged snow.

"It feels like it could be a real storm," he said, cradling the boom box in his lap.

"I know." Yvette sounded triumphant. "That's why I wanted to go tonight. Can you see the *Gazetteer* back there? Grab it, will you? I want to head up to the Araweag."

"Really?" The Araweag was paper-mill land, or had been before it was clear-cut long ago. Now it was boggy, impenetrable thickets of speckled alder and blackberry crowding the wetland.

"I want to try something different. Miriam Rogers told me her son was hunting moose up there and saw a great horned owl. Hunting, in daylight."

"The owl or Miriam's son?"

"The owl. He watched it swoop down on a snowshoe hare. Poor bunny."

"A snowshoe hare? In broad daylight?"

"That's why I want to go."

"If the owls are hunting in daytime, why would we hear them now?"

Yvette swatted him. "Just tell me how far it is."

He opened the glove compartment so he could read by its light, flipped through the *Gazetteer* until he found the right page. "Twenty miles, maybe? Bad roads, though. Some may not be open anymore."

"Let's stay on 217. Make a few of the old stops first."

Louis nodded. He closed the glove compartment and tossed the *Gazetteer* onto the floor behind his seat, swigged a mouthful of tepid coffee from the thermos, and closed his eyes.

"I'm sorry about your friend," Yvette said. "It was your friend, right?"

Louis didn't open his eyes. Yvette had mild dementia that manifested mostly as forgetfulness. "Thanks."

"After Buddy died," she went on cheerfully, "someone told me I should watch for signs. Lori, she's the massage therapist used to live at Stone Farm. She told me if I wanted a sign from Buddy, I should close my eyes and count to three. When I opened them, the first three things I saw, that would be the sign."

"Did you ever see anything?"

"Just the dogs."

Eyes shut, Louis thought of Eric, the last time they'd met. Walking along the Battenkill, the river where as boys they'd fished for brownies and brookies: once one of the world's great trout streams, now nothing but a stony track that resembled an ancient Roman road winding through the Vermont woods. When he opened his eyes, he saw only his own reflection in the black glass of the Subaru's passenger window.

When they used to do the owl count, Yvette would put a big cardboard sign that read OWL MONITORING PROGRAM on the dashboard. In those days, more vehicles were on the road. Not many, especially in the middle of the night, but there'd been a few times when people slowed or even stopped. Always men, they often seemed to have been drinking, another reason Louis liked to accompany Yvette. Once a state trooper had approached them—someone had noticed the parked Subaru and phoned dispatch. The policeman had been bemused, even more so when Yvette played him some of the owl calls.

"Well, just be careful you don't run out of gas," he'd finally said. "Cold out here."

It had been years since they'd seen another car or pickup at night, but Louis felt the familiar frisson as they pulled over beside their first landmark, a Bangor Hydro power pole that hadn't been live since 2013. A small piece of metal stamped 141A was nailed to the pole, but Louis had long since learned to identify it by the surrounding fields: once farmland, now overgrown with highbush blueberry and sumac.

In daylight, you could spot the centuries-old clapboard farmhouse in the distance. When he and Yvette had first done the count, lights shone from one or two of its windows and dogs barked, alerting the household to interlopers in the road, but no one had ever come out to investigate. Louis heard the old man who'd lived there wandered off one night a few summers ago. His body was never found. Now Louis could barely make out the house, ghostly white against the black trees.

Yvette asked, "Did you check the volume?"

Louis reached again for the boom box. He switched it to the radio, reflexively turning the dial. Nothing but static until he hit the Christian music station out of Houlton, one of the few remaining stations in operation and the only one with a signal strong enough to be heard up here. Louis adjusted the volume, grimacing, and quickly switched the player back to CD mode.

"Did you bring extra batteries?"

Louis shook his head. "I told you, no."

"Oh," said Yvette. She turned the car off and stared at the steering column with vague interest, as though she'd never seen one before. "I didn't hear you."

"That's okay." Louis often wondered if her forgetfulness might be an evolutionary advantage. If you couldn't recall the world as it had once been, you couldn't miss it.

Though the evolutionary benefits diminished once you factored in things like forgetting to eat or misplacing the car keys while you were out in the middle of the night in subzero weather. He slid the key from the ignition and pocketed it.

Yvette smiled. "I didn't forget the key."

Louis smiled back. "Neither did I." He turned on the dashboard light, fumbled a pen from his parka pocket as he balanced the clip-board on his knees, turning from the first data sheet to the one beneath.

MOMP 2012 MAINE OWL MONITORING PROGRAM
MAINE AUDUBON AND THE MAINE DEPARTMENT
OF INLAND FISHERIES AND WILDLIFE

He filled in the date and time, ignored the other blank spaces—Observer, Route Code, Observer Email/Phone Number, Assistant's Name—and began to fill in the information for Stop 1:

Time (military): 00:27, Temp: 28F, Cloud Cover: 40 percent

For Wind he circled the appropriate numerical Beaufort Wind Scale, guessing it was a 2 [*4–6 mph, light breeze, wind felt on face, leaves rustle*], even though there were no leaves to rustle. He glanced outside and saw spruce boughs rippling, changed the 2 to a 3 [*gentle breeze, leaves and small twigs in motion*]. He notated Noise and Precipitation in the same way, circling 0 for Precipitation [*note that survey should not be conducted if precipitation is a 3 or above*] and 1 for Noise [*relatively quiet*], even though when he cracked the window, it was pretty much silent outside.

For Snow Cover he circled *C* [*complete*]. For Frogs: Yes/No, *No*. He left Car Count and Plane Count blank. He couldn't remember when he'd last seen or heard a plane. He filled in the Playback info from memory—*Boom Box, High Volume, Memorex, Audible at 1/10 mile*—and left the Comments section blank, for now.

"Ready?" asked Yvette.

"Almost." He turned to the next sheet, scrawled in the date, his name and Yvette's, the name of the township. He didn't bother with the odometer reading, but looked outside once more before filling in the stop and habitat descriptions: *Pole 141 A, Overgrown fields and abandoned house to right of road, woods to L.* "Okay, let's go."

He set the clipboard on the floor, opened his door, and stepped outside. Yvette turned off the dashboard light, grabbed the boom box, and did the same. "Not that cold," she said.

Louis gave a noncommittal nod. It didn't feel that cold, but he knew how it worked, especially with snow in the forecast. No fear of frostbite, but the humidity would seep through your parka and gloves and cap: if you didn't keep moving, within a short while your blood would seem to cool and thicken, your bones to feel as though they held ice instead of marrow.

And you weren't supposed to move, not once the playback started. Yvette set the boom box onto the rust-pocked hood of the old car, pointing it toward the distant empty house across the fields. That overgrown swath would still be ideal habitat for owls and their prey—voles and white-footed mice, rabbits and snowshoe hare, smaller winter birds like chickadees that would be sleeping now but might be caught at dawn or dusk if they stirred.

He leaned against the car, letting his eyes adjust to the darkness, his ears to the silence. His breath clouded the air as he tipped his head back and saw a few stars pricking through the haze. *Cloud cover only 30 percent*, he thought, but that wouldn't last. A few feet away, Yvette's pose mirrored his own, but her eyes were closed. Not sleeping: listening intently. He squeezed his own eyes shut, his head still uptilted.

Everything sounded the same: white pine needles a susurrus like waves on the shore; the *skreak* of spruce branches rubbing together; a noise like knuckles cracking that might be a deer moving through the woods. He recalled what Yvette had said about watching for signs, held his breath, counted to three, and opened his eyes.

For a split second he thought he saw another pair of eyes gazing into his, then realized they were stars, momentarily dazzling in a gap of clouds that moved swiftly across the sky. The wind carried a faint scent of crushed bracken and balsam. Almost certainly a deer had left its bed, awakened by their presence. He looked over his shoulder and saw Yvette watching him, her hand on the boom box. She raised her eyebrows. He nodded; she nodded back, then pushed *Play*.

The owl-call sequence began with a low electronic beep, followed by the first track: two minutes of silence. During that time, Louis's hearing grew more acute, the rustling of trees amplified so that he could distinguish between individual branches as they rubbed together, some high, others closer to the ground. After two minutes, the second track kicked in—the call of a short-eared owl; a series of brief, breathy hoots; repeated twice, then another two minutes of silence.

Louis held his breath, straining to hear a reply. Many years ago, he had seen a short-eared owl in daylight, skimming above a field, its yellow eyes bright as traffic lights, tiny tufted ears nowhere in evidence. He saw and heard nothing now. The next call was the long-eared owl's: a single, rather toneless hoot, repeated several times, each after a few seconds' interval, followed by the two-minute silence.

Only now it wasn't so silent. Tiny things stirred nearby—small birds fluttering nervously in the lower branches of the spruce trees. Mice skittered across the dead leaves that had rucked up against the tree trunks to provide shelter from the snow. Squeaks and rustlings, a swift settling back into a new, more watchful silence.

The saw-whet owl was next. Its breathy piping cry grew gradually louder, paused, then repeated. Louis had seen one of these too, improbably perched upon his bulkhead one late-spring morning. It looked like a toy, small enough to fit into his cupped palm, with enormous orange eyes that, when it blinked, gave it the appearance of a sleepy child. Louis had longed to pick it up, it looked so utterly helpless and soft. When he went to check on it an hour later, it was gone. He hoped it hadn't fallen prey to some larger owl or eagle. He cocked his head, hoping to hear a response in the silence that followed.

Again, he heard nothing but wind in the trees. Like him, the birds and mice were holding their breath. He glanced at Yvette and saw her staring raptly into the sky above the field, her gaze flicking back and forth. Was she watching something? He squinted but could make out only darkness seeded by a handful of stars.

Two tracks left. The barred owl came first, the owl they were most likely to hear, with its distinctive demand *Who cooks for you? Who cooks for you?* followed by a six-minute silence—barred owls sometimes took longer to reply.

This was the most difficult part of each stop. Six minutes could be an agony, if you were cold and unable to move. The frigid air crept up from his frozen feet: he felt immobilized, his legs encased in ice as though he were trapped in one of those fairy tales where people turned into statues. He no longer felt his fingers in his gloves. He tensed his muscles, fighting the urge to shiver, when, fainter than the sound of his own breath, an answering call echoed from somewhere far off in the black woods that surrounded the overgrown fields.

Who cooks for you? Who cooks for you?

Elation flooded him; he glanced at Yvette and saw her grinning like a madwoman. He strained to hear another call but none came. The long silence broke with the final track, the great horned owl's loud, increasingly threatening *Who? Who?? WHO???*

Its cry died off into the sound of wind rattling the aster stalks. Louis tilted his head slightly, mentally counting down the remaining seconds, and stiffened.

Something was walking across the snow. Furtively: it paused before its feet broke through the frozen surface, a sound like a boot crunching shattered glass.

Heat flashed through Louis's body, terror and adrenaline. He looked at Yvette and saw her eyes widening, not in fear but wonder. He turned to see what she gazed at, detected nothing at first but then caught a glimpse of a dark blur at the edge of the field, maybe twenty yards away. In an eyeblink it had disappeared into the trees.

An electronic beep signaled the end of the owl-call sequence. Louis grabbed the boom box. He and Yvette jumped backed into the car, slamming the doors closed behind them. Louis locked his, leaned over, and did the same to Yvette's.

"Did you see that?" she asked, eyes so wide she looked like an owl herself.

"I don't know." He set the boom box at his feet—it felt cold as a block of ice—yanked off his gloves and blew on his fingers as Yvette turned the ignition. "What was it?"

"I don't know." Hands gripping the wheel, she craned her neck to peer past him, to where the black line of spruce and pine gave way to the long, white expanse broken by brambles, stands of dead aster, and milkweed. "It looked like a person."

"It can't have been a person," Louis said, even though his thumping heart suggested that's exactly what he believed. "A deer, probably."

"It was upright." Yvette stared outside for another minute before she sighed, turned on the headlights, and began to drive, very very slowly, continuing to look out the passenger side of the windshield. "Did you see it? Tall and kind of stooped. It might have been a bear."

"Bears don't walk upright. Not in winter, anyway. They're hibernating."

"But you saw it, right?"

He shrugged, unwilling to look at her. "I don't know," he repeated. "I saw something—I *think* I saw something. I definitely heard something. I thought it was a deer. That noise their hooves make when they break through the crust."

"Deer don't walk upright."

"Then it was a person."

Now he did meet Yvette's gaze. They grimaced in unison.

"That's not good," she said. "They could freeze."

"Do you think we should go back?"

"No." They both laughed, and Yvette added, "Maybe we should go back? What if it's someone who's lost?"

"No one's lost." Louis removed his knit cap and pressed his hands against his ears to warm them. As heat flooded the car, and him, his fear abated. "It was probably a deer. I mean, it could have been an owl—I just saw it from the corner of my eye. You heard that barred owl, right?"

"Yes! 'Who cooks for you?'" Yvette hooted, and laughed again. "Did you write it down?"

Louis shook his head. He retrieved the clipboard and pen, using his mobile as a flashlight as he scrawled Barred owl. He couldn't recall the last time they'd heard an owl respond to the CD when they were out in the field like this—four or five years ago? Yet he heard plenty of owls when he was at home, barred owls and the occasional great horned owl, and he and Yvette had even sighted them a few times when they were driving along the owl-count route. Maybe there were simply fewer owls than there used to be, along with everything else. Fewer bats, fewer nightjars, fewer bugs, fewer bees.

Fewer people too, since the last few outbreaks, though it was hard to think of that as a bad thing. Friends of his in the warden service said that wildlife populations appeared to be rebounding, not just deer and moose but apex predators and omnivores. Black bears and coyotes, mountain lions and wolves, whose existence the state's Department of Inland Fisheries and Wildlife had a decades-long policy of denying, despite numerous sightings. The last confirmed wolf in Maine had been shot dead in Ellsworth in the 1990s, but Louis knew people who'd seen them, reliable witnesses—hunters, trappers, loggers, fishermen. The wolves came down from Quebec. No one knew if there were enough in Maine for a breeding population. Funding for that sort of study had disappeared long ago.

Yvette longed to see a bear or wolf. Louis was content to think that they were out there at a safe distance from his home. Hearing a family of coyotes erupt into howls in the middle of the night, fifty feet from his driveway, could be hair-raising enough.

"What's the next stop?" he asked.

"Deadman's Curve."

After about five miles, Yvette pulled the car over again, this time along a heavily wooded stretch. The road here hadn't been plowed, but wind had scoured most of the snow from the broken blacktop. A decaying mobile home stood a dozen yards from the road, its roof and walls collapsed to expose clouds of soggy pink fiberglass insulation, shredded Tyvek, and splintered beams, like some immense piece of roadkill.

As Louis stepped out of the car, he recoiled from the odor of mildew and an overpowering reek of rodent urine, along with the stink of something dead, a rat or scavenging fox or coyote. He pulled his scarf up to cover his face as Yvette motioned him back into the car, and they pulled up farther along the road, out of sight of the trailer.

"Whew. That was bad." He stepped outside cautiously, pressing his scarf against his nose so he could breathe in the reassuring scents of damp wool and woodsmoke. "It's better here."

Yvette nodded. She looked drifty, like maybe she couldn't quite remember where they were, or why, but when she saw Louis watching her she smiled and set the boom box on the car's hood. For a minute they stood without speaking. Louis lowered his scarf and breathed in tentatively, catching only the faintest whiff of mildew.

Not far from the road, on the same side as the ruined trailer, a stream ran through the woods. A small stream—with his long legs, he could have jumped across it without much effort—yet deep enough that it hadn't frozen. No one had bothered to trim the trees here for ages—while most of the power poles remained standing, the power companies had long ago stopped maintaining them. As a result, the oaks and maples and birches had grown unchecked, their branches nearly meeting above the road to form a ragged net in which a few stars gleamed like trapped minnows. In the darkness, the little stream sounded startlingly loud, more like a torrent than a brook.

"Ready?"

He turned back to Yvette, nodding, and she pressed *Play*.

The owls' mournful liturgy repeated itself as before, alternating between silence and melancholy summons, its only response a fretful twittering from above that Louis recognized as a red squirrel's alarm. The cold seemed more penetrating here; because of the tangle of branches over the road, Louis thought, then realized that was ridiculous. There was no sun. It must be getting onto 2:00 a.m.

He cursed himself for not bringing along a thermos of hot coffee. He knew better than to ask Yvette to abort the trip: she might forget what day, or even year, it was, but the owl count was sacrosanct. As the great horned owl's cry faded into the final, silent track, Louis didn't bother to suppress a yawn. He rubbed his arms, noting that Yvette remained stock-still, her hood's pointed tip silhouetted against the trees like a spearpoint. The rushing stream sounded so loud he wondered if they'd missed the beep signaling the end of the call sequence. But then he heard the soft beep. Immediately he turned to open the car door. As he did, an explosive sound echoed from the woods directly behind them. Louis shouted: he stared into the trees, then at Yvette where she stood and gazed open-mouthed at him. He heard splashing, a huffing noise that turned into a strangled grunt as something crashed through the underbrush. An over-powering fecal odor filled his nostrils, rot and shit but also sweat, a smell he'd never encountered that was somehow horribly recognizable.

"Get in!" he gasped at Yvette, but she'd already grabbed the boom box and was back in the car. Louis flung the door open and saw her fumbling for the keys—she'd forgotten again and left them in the ignition. He got inside and locked the door, shouted at Yvette to do the same. The Subaru's engine rumbled and the car shot forward, fishtailing across the slick road then straightening as Yvette hunched over the steering wheel.

"That was a bear!" She sounded exultant.

Louis said nothing, tried to slow his breath enough to speak without his voice breaking. "The fuck it was," he said at last. He pulled off his gloves, hands shaking, and turned to look through the rear window. The car's brake lights cast a dull crimson glow across skeletal birch trees and a fallen evergreen bough that Yvette had somehow avoided. "It sounded huge."

"Bears are huge. It could've been a moose. Or a beaver."

Louis snorted, but she was right. The sound of a beaver slapping its tail on the water in warning could reverberate like a thunderclap. "There's no pond back there, just that stream."

"Maybe it runs into a pond nearby. Check the *Gazetteer*."

Louis shook his head impatiently—he felt at once irritated and fright-ened—but he picked up the *Gazetteer* and found the corresponding map among its frayed pages. "Nope. No pond."

Yvette slowed the car to a crawl, its studded tires grinding over the snow. "There should be a turn in the next few miles. For the Araweag— I think it's on the left. Can you check for that?"

"You still want to go?"

"I thought we decided."

"Yeah, but. That thing . . ."

"I know!" Her cheeks were flushed, excitement more than cold, he suspected. "See if you can find that turn."

A glance at the open *Gazetteer* on his lap showed the township, a formless green space threaded by streams that connected myriad small ponds, lakes, and wetlands. Broken stitches indicated a seasonal road, which these days meant an impassable one. Before he could voice a perfectly reasonable excuse for not going there—they'd get stuck, run out of gas, and not be found until spring, besides which there was just as much likelihood of hearing owls right here on the old route as in the Araweag—Yvette brought up the single unreasonable one.

"Are you scared?"

He took a deep breath. "Not really. Just—that noise, it spooked me. And the smell? Did you smell it?"

"I did." Yvette wrinkled her nose. "Phew! Like when my septic field overflows every year."

Yvette's septic field hadn't flooded in decades—she'd switched to a composting toilet, like nearly everyone else, as the grid became unreiable. Louis knew it would be pointless to remind her of this. She'd laugh and say, *Oh right, I forgot.* Then forget it all over again, just as she'd done with the car keys. He cleared his window, the glass already steaming up, stared out at the shifting crosshatch of black and gray-white. Trees, rocks, snowdrifts, trees.

"It smelled worse than that," he said. "Like . . ."

"It could have been a moose. It sounded big."

Louis nodded, frowning. He picked up the thermos, took a swig of cold coffee, then offered it to Yvette, who shook her head. "Whatever it was, it smelled like it had rolled in something dead," he said. "Like a dog does. And what was that noise? It sounded like an entire tree came down."

"Like I said, moose."

"A moose doesn't knock down trees."

"Well, it's not the same thing we heard at the first stop, whatever it was." Yvette tugged her hood from her face. "It's four miles from there to that old trailer. Nothing goes that fast. Maybe an owl," she added after a moment's thought. "Horned owls, they're fast."

Yvette turned the wipers on. It had started to snow—tiny, dry flakes, the kind that normally blow off the windshield, but they weren't driving fast enough for that. She hunched over the steering wheel, scanning the road. "I think there's a sign—didn't there used to be a sign?"

"I don't remember." Louis didn't bother to keep the irritation from his tone. He peeled off his gloves and closed his eyes for a moment, imagining himself back at home in bed, warm and asleep. Then he remembered Eric was dead. He was old enough now that grief had become a near-constant presence, a prolonged dull ache rather than the piercing anguish he'd experienced when he was younger. The aftermath of his wife's death was like a raging virus that left him sickened and weak for several years, a virus that could be reawakened by stress, or sunrise, or a scent. You don't recover from grief, he'd learned, it can't be cured; it only appears to go into remission, to flare up, not as intensely perhaps but retaining its nightmarish power, with the next death.

He had not even begun to mourn Eric. He thought again of that last time, just over a year ago, the two of them leaving the dried-up Battenkill to hike up a ski trail, a broad swath of young beeches and sugar maples that had sprung up when the ski mountain closed early in the century. Eric white-haired but hale, more so than Louis, who'd had to stop often to catch his breath, holding on to young birch trees that showered them with autumn leaves like a rain of new pennies. "They found a mastodon in the Mastigouche," Eric had told him, and Louis laughed.

"That sounds like a song," he said, and began to warble. "Mastodon, in the Mastigooooche . . ."

"No, really—there was a landslide, and they found its tusks in the rubble. Like in Siberia, where they keep mining mammoth ivory where the permafrost used to be."

He started as Yvette nudged him, looked up to see her grinning at him. "I know," she said. "It was the Agropelter!" She pronounced the word with a slight lilt and the accent on the final syllable, the way her Quebecois grandmother would have. *Agre-pel-tay´.*

Louis made a face. "Well, I hope not," he said, and they laughed. Yvette's great-grandfather had been a trucker who worked the Golden Road, the hundred-mile-long, mostly unpaved track that ran from the old paper mill in Millinocket to the Quebec border, and her great-great-grandfather had worked in Canadian logging camps. Yvette's grandmother claimed he had hundreds of stories about the terrible things that could happen in the North Woods, but the only one Yvette recalled was about the Agropelter. Half human, half ape, the Agropelter sat in treetops and hurled rocks and branches at unsuspecting woodsmen, sometimes killing them.

"Sounds like a bad excuse for knocking someone off with an ax," Louis had remarked the first time Yvette recounted the legend.

Now he checked the time: 2:17. "Getting late," he said. "And it's starting to snow. We're supposed to call it off if it snows."

"Who's going to check? And it's not snowing now," she added. Which was true: the sifting flakes had stopped. "You came—why did you come if you didn't want to?"

"I needed to be distracted." That sounded cruel; she might not even remember his best friend had died. "Because of Eric."

"Of course," she said, her customary briskness softened. "I remember." She grasped his hand and squeezed it. "I'm so sorry, Louis."

"Thank you."

"You know, when Buddy died, my friend Lori told me if I ever wanted a sign from him, I should just close my eyes. The first three things I saw when I opened them, those would be the sign."

"Yes, you told me that."

"Oh, sorry!" she said without embarrassment. "I keep forgetting."

He turned away, recalling how Sheila during her illness had joked that whatever he did after she died, he shouldn't marry Yvette. "Not a chance," he'd told her, and that had never changed. His eyes stung and he closed them, thinking this time of Sheila, not Eric; opened them and gazed at his bare hands, the red knuckles swollen and fingers twisted from Dupuytren's contracture.

He leaned over to check the gas gauge. A quarter tank, enough to get home. He wondered when and where she'd been able to last fill the tank. Bangor, probably, which meant she'd used up a considerable amount of fuel driving home afterward. He looked in the back seat again, reached into the heap of dog hair-covered fabric, rummaged around till he found a zipper, and pulled at it. A sleeping bag emerged, trailing a chewed-up leash.

"There might still be some of those hand warmers," said Yvette. "Poke around, see if you can find them."

"That's okay. I was looking for a weapon, actually. In case it tries to eat us."

"Very funny. They only eat owls, my gran said. And woodpeckers."

"Well, we're safe then. The turn looks to be about eight miles, on the left. You remembered that fine."

The car inched along, Yvette downshifting as they crept over knee-high frost heaves and avoiding potholes large enough to swallow a bicycle. Intermittent gusts of snow would cloud the air then just as swiftly disappear, the tiny flakes not big enough to constitute a squall. The real snow wouldn't start until morning. If it looked like it was going to come down sooner, they'd simply turn around.

They drove in silence, interrupted only when one of them pointed out a former stop—the flat boulder overlooking a bog, the sweeping vista where they'd once heard two great horned owls—or when they spotted something. A fox crossing leisurely in front of them; a snow-shoe hare sprinting off in alarm, its long hind feet kicking up feathers of snow; a pair of tufted ears like devil horns above glowing green eyes, barely visible in the underbrush.

"Bobcat!" said Louis.

"Lynx!" cried Yvette in triumph.

"Oh, come on, how could you tell?"

"It was bigger than a bobcat."

"It was there for two seconds!"

Yvette pursed her lips in a smug smile. "I just know."

Louis unzipped his parka as the car grew overheated, the doggie smell vying with the faint, scorched-sugar scent of antifreeze that seeped from the vents. "You have a radiator leak," he said.

"I know. Bob Marsh said he'd fix it, come spring."

Louis checked the odometer, trying to figure out how much far-ther it was to the turn. They'd been driving for at least twenty minutes, a long time to cover only eight miles, even in the middle of the night, even on these roads.

"Do you think we missed it?" he asked. "The sign could be gone. That old access road could be completely overgrown by now."

Yvette's brow creased. "I hope not. Let's give it another few minutes."

A few minutes became ten—Louis clocked the time. He couldn't do anything else with his mobile; even back in the early part of the century, there hadn't been service here.

"Look."

Yvette inclined her head to the left, where a twisted metal pole jutted toward the road at a thirty-degree angle. Atop it dangled a small green sign so rusted Louis could barely read it. FR 2973, a fire road.

"Huh. I haven't seen one of those for years." Once ubiquitous, these numerical signs designated seasonal or little-used roads. The numbering system had disappeared when towns had to conform to Emergency 911 standards, meaning all roads needed an actual name.

Despite the warmth, Louis shivered. He peered into the darkness past the twisted pole. "Can we even get down there?"

"I'll just turn in, we can park and walk a bit if the snow's not too deep."

Louis ran his hands across his knees but said nothing. His knees ached, his back. The Dupuytren's contracture in his right hand made it hard to move his fingers in the chill. He'd dressed for cold, not for trudging through deep snow.

But the old fire road, while overgrown and snow covered, still showed signs of use. He saw snowmobile tracks veering across the broad path, along with those of another vehicle, a small Sno-Cat prob-ably. Someone poaching firewood, now that the territory was basically no-man's-land. A few inches of snow had fallen since anyone had last been here—judging by the crust, at least a week ago—but not enough to impede walking.

He zipped up his parka, watched as Yvette made the turn and drove several yards. He winced as the old Subaru jolted over a buried rock and bottomed out. "Maybe this is far enough?"

Yvette nodded and brought the car to an abrupt stop, forgetting to take it out of gear. Louis's skull banged against the headrest. "Ow!"

"Sorry!" Yvette clapped her hands to her face. She began to laugh, then reached to touch Louis's neck gently. "We don't have to stay long. Miriam's son saw a great horned owl here. He was hunting— moose, I think. I would love to see another one of those. The owl, I mean. Or the moose."

"I would rather not see a moose at night," said Louis, gingerly rubbing the back of his neck. "Not if it's going to knock a tree on my head."

"That wasn't a moose. Bear," said Yvette.

She pulled up her hood and stepped out of the car without the boom box. Louis considered leaving it inside—maybe she'd forget the reason they were here, and they could just head home. But then she turned and pointed at it. He tucked it under one arm and joined her, stumping through the snow and halting in front of the car.

Shreds of gray lichen littered the snow, and the dark scales of pine-cones resembling fingernail clippings, which fell where red squirrels had fed in the trees overhead. Balsam and pine resin scented the air, rather than pissy cat spruce and crushed bracken. Even though the road was only a few yards off, he felt as though with a few steps, he'd traversed a hundred years, backward or forward, to a moment when his presence was as inconsequential as a thread of reindeer moss.

He found the thought oddly comforting. Perhaps this was how Yvette felt all the time. He set the boom box on the top of the car, tugged his knit cap snugly over his ears, pulled up his hood, and stared at the sky.

Far above him, a gap in the clouds revealed stars so brilliant he imagined he heard them crackling in the frigid air. The night seemed absolutely still—he felt no wind on his cheeks, and the jagged black evergreens that scraped the horizon appeared not to move.

And yet he did hear something. A faint, nearly subliminal sound like static, a noise he could imagine accompanying the prickles that pre-saged the agonizing leg cramps that woke him some nights. He cocked his head, trying to figure out if he was imagining it and, if not, where it came from; glanced over to see Yvette looking at him, eyebrows raised. Within moments her expression altered, from perplexity to alarm to outright horror. He opened his mouth to ask What? Then he heard the same thing.

He thought it was the wind at first: a low rumbling that lasted mere seconds before it stopped. In the near silence he heard Yvette's breathing and his own, a frantic rustling in a tree overhead. He exhaled shakily, caught his breath sharply when the sound recurred—louder this time, closer, rising then fading into a long echo that, after several moments, died away completely.

And, after another few moments, resumed. The cry rose, not the yodeling ululation of a coyote or wolf, both of which he knew: something deeper, more sustained and resonant. It died away before recurring a fourth time, much louder, so close that the hairs on his neck and arms and scalp rose, as from nearby lightning. Sensation flooded him, an emotion he had never experienced before: a horror so all-encompassing his stomach convulsed. His arms grew limp, his knees buckled, and he slumped against the car's hood, gloved fingers sliding across the smooth metal as he tried to grab it.

The sound faded. Silence surrounded him, long enough that his gasps subsided and he drew a shuddering breath, wiping tears onto his sleeve. He struggled to stand upright, bracing himself against the car, and cried aloud when the sound came again, from not more than twenty feet away. Loud enough now that he could detect within the deafening bellow a grinding anguish, physical pain and also a deeper torment, as the cry exploded into a thunderous roar. His ears ached but he could clearly hear as it crashed through the trees, not blindly but with steady purpose, pausing between each step as though ensuring the ground would bear its weight. A shrill piping sounded in his ears, the saw-whet owl, he thought with desperate calm, before recognizing his own scream. The roar came again and with it a wave of heat.

He gagged as that smell of fecal rot overwhelmed him. A tree crashed down, pine needles and splinters of wood stabbed his cheek and his vision blurred as blood washed across one eye. Soft feathers brushed his face, or fur, he could no longer distinguish between what was his skin, his body inside his layers of clothing, his scalp or neck or toes. His feet disappeared, the ground beneath them. With a moan he slanted his gaze sideways, searching for Yvette in the maelstrom of snow and broken bark, hair, blood, bone, and feathers.

He saw only a smudge of red, the tip of her parka's hood. He tried to breathe but found his mouth sealed shut by the wind; tasted blood, he'd bitten his tongue. He thought of Yvette, of Sheila in bed beside him, of Eric walking next to him as they traced the lost Battenkill.

He closed his eyes, counted to three. *Who cooks for you?* he thought, and opened them.

COLOR, HEAT, AND
THE WRECK OF THE ARGO

CATHERYNNE M. VALENTE

Variations in Luminance

Big Edie was a useless piece of shit.

Johanna Telle found the most significant relationship of her life on a Saturday afternoon in late May, sitting on one of those excruciatingly handmade quilts crafty stay-at-homes used to make out of their precious baby's old clothes and putting a deep, damp dent in the buttercup-infested lawn of 11 Buckthorn Drive, Ossining, New York. A four-pointed Arkansas Traveler star radiated out around her, each of the four diamond patches so exquisitely nailing the era of the quilter's *pax materna* that Johanna pulled out her Leica and snapped a shot before the homeowners could stop her: *The Pretenders, Captain Planet Says No Nukes, Got Milk?* and a Hypercolor tee subjected, as so many had been, to the indignity of a commercial dryer until it finally gave up the thermochromic ghost, its worn cotton-poly blend permanently stuck on a sad blown-out pink.

And Big Edie in the middle, ugly as all the sins of man, with a box of *Advanced Dungeons & Dragons: Second Edition* modules on the eastern point of the compass, a mint condition *Teenage Mutant Ninja Turtles* Sewer Lair Playset to the west, a working laserdisc player up north, and down south, one beefy hardcase Samsonite in Executive Silver with a handwritten sign on it promising a complete set of signed first edition Danielle Steel hardbacks inside. A steal at $300, suitcase included.

Still life with late eighties/early nineties. Johanna loved it.

But she only had eyes for Big Edie. The absolute and utter trashbeast technological abortion winking up cheekily at her from within a nest of vanished childhoods.

She'd driven all the way out into the golden calcified time-bubble of the Hudson Valley after the ephemeral promises of an estate sale. The people here had so much money they never had to grow or change or evolve past the approximate epoch of their children's most precocious years. That's how Johanna had gotten a Hasselblad for ninety dollars and a fake phone number a couple of years ago at a *fuck-Gam-Gam-just-get-rid-of-this-junk* free-for-all in Stonybrook. You just crossed your eyes and hoped the kids were the type to tell everyone who never asked that social media was a disease and didn't sully themselves with Google or eBay.

This was clearly the case on that late-May Ossining afternoon. The card balanced against Big Edie's case read:

Does Not Work. $50 OBO.

Johanna Telle smiled in the perfect post-processed sun. The EDC-55 ED-Beta Camcorder retailed for a cool $7700 in 1987. Just over sixteen grand in 2015 funbucks. It could produce over 550 lines of resolution in an age where high definition was barely even a phrase. Automatic iris control, dual 2/3 inch precision CCD imaging, Fujinon f1.7 range macro zoom, on-the-fly audio/video editing, capable of recording in hi-fi stereo and most impressively for its time, native video playback. Angular black and matte silver bug-ugly design. The last glorious 13.5-kilogram gasp of the Betamax world, still in its hardcase shell, that particular shade of tan that meant Serious Business for the Terminally Eighties Man.

In digital terms, Big Edie was prehistoric. Big Edie was fucking Cretaceous. If there was a camera set up on a tripod to record what happened when the primordial soup stopped being polite and started getting real, Big Edie would have been a top-tier choice for the discerning prosumer.

Big Edie was *archaeology*.

Johanna whipped her faded seafoam-green hair to one side and hefted that machine corpse onto her dark brown shoulder. She was comically heavy. The weight of a dead world, its concerns long quieted.

Johanna Telle, when she was paying attention, when she was happy, in those moments when she was most definitively Johanna, saw down to the deeps of things. It was all she was really good at, in her estimation. She *saw* that world, *le regime ancien*, projected onto the back of her skull like a drive-in theater screen.

When she was little, she'd sat criss-cross applesauce in her mother's lap in a kind of mute blue nirvana, watching a crew send an unmanned submersible in a metal cage down the icy miles to find the HMS *Titanic*. Before her father left them, before they lost the house, before the hundred little fatal cuts of getting from one end of childhood to the other. Long beams of light broke the black water of forgetting and scattered across that ghostly bow and found what had been lost. Impossibly lost. Forever. Johanna had barely been able to breathe. She knew herself then, in that terrifying way you know things when you are small. The warmth of her mother's chest rose and fell behind her, an entire universe of protection and presence. A gentle little prick of the aquamarine pendant she always wore against Johanna's scalp. The familiar smell of Pink Window, her mother's signature Red Door knockoff, pulsing off her clavicle. The tinny voice of a rich man floating out of the blue ocean. Later, when the neighborhood kids played games on their unforgivably Spielbergian suburban streets, hollering *I'm the Incredible Hulk* or *I'm the Pink Ranger* or *I'm Tenderheart Bear*, Johanna would call out something nominally culturally appropriate but whisper the truth to herself, which never changed, no matter the game or the streets: *I am the exterior lighting array on Robert Ballard's Argo ROV unit.*

Johanna put her eye to Big Edie's viewfinder. The black cup *pocked* gently against her cheekbone. Such a *nice* feeling. Like holding a girl's hand for the first time. She stared into inert darkness.

"It only takes these weird old tapes," someone said from outside Edie's warm lightless innards. A friendly, well-hydrated, nicely brought-up male voice, full of solicitude, exhausted, heartbroken, hanging in there, like the orange kitten in the old poster.

Johanna didn't look up. She amused herself picturing the kitten putting its paws on its hips and whistling regretfully through its sharp teeth at the fifty dollar OBO paperweight before them. She suppressed her not-very-inner snob. *Yes, dear, ED Super Beta II and III series cassettes. You can still get them, anywhere between thirty-five and fifty dollars a pop. You can still get anything if you don't care what it costs.*

"There's one stuck in there. Made a nasty sound when I tried to lever it out. I don't have any others, though. Dad didn't stick with this one for very long. I put his digital cameras around by the hydrangeas, way better. You want me to show you?"

"Does it turn on?"

"Nope. Well, not unless it's a Tuesday and the moon is in Pisces and you're standing on one foot or some shit. I keep the battery charged up, though. I heard you have to do that, or it degrades. I'm Jeff, by the way."

Of course you are. That's what they always name soft orange kittens like you.

Johanna's fingers slid down Big Edie's flank and found the raised plastic goose-pimple that marked the power button as easily as a practiced accordionist settling onto C Major. She pointed the lens at the bereaved child of its former owner and hit the big red square.

A firehose of light white-watered through the generous 1.5" black and white viewfinder into her cerebral cortex. In the middle of it stood, not the *hang in there* kitten, but a tall handsome guy in his late twenties or early thirties. Big emotive eyes, tennis shorts, dark polo shirt, with a shimmer of beard-stubble six or seven hours deep, hair the cut and style of debate team and law school and firm handshakes and warm decades ahead in a secure center-right Senate seat.

A shard of glass punched through his chest. Black monochrome blood sheeted down over his shorts and his long, gray, summer-muscled legs. His neck whipped hard to the side, like he'd suddenly seen an old girlfriend and was about to call her name, but when he opened his mouth, a jet of dark liquid spurted onto the quilt of his so-loved child-hood clothes. It cut across the white block-print *Pretenders* in a clean spattered line.

"What's the verdict?" Jeff asked. That voice like a clean fingernail cut through Johanna's attention. She yanked her face up off the view-finder. Jeff's fine blond eyebrows arched curiously before her in full color, waiting to find out if that old Betamax monster still had juice. If the moon was, in fact, in Pisces. He shoved his hands in the pockets of a paint-splattered pair of jeans.

Johanna glanced back down into Big Edie's gullet. It was waiting down there, that death-image of silver and ichor.

"I like your shirt," she said. The walls of her throat stuck together. Inside the camera, that charcoal polo dripped silent-film blood onto his new white tennis shoes. Outside, he wore a slim-cut celery-green tee with *Newport Folk Festival 2010* stamped across his chest in a faux-rustic font. She could look back and forth between them. Back and forth. Black and white. Color. Black and white. Gray and green. Green and gray. And wet, dripping jet-onyx blood. All that faded thermochro-micity blazing back onto the scene to react with the not live but defi-nitely Memorex heat-death of Jeff from Ossining.

Big Edie went down for the count.

The image guttered out like a pilot light, a sound both grinding and whining shook through her, and she rather ungracefully peaced out.

"Thirty dollars?"

"All yours," Jeff grinned.

He took Johanna Telle's money and strode off across the mown lawn, through the labyrinth of his late father's obsessions, the sun on his shoulders as though it would never leave him.

Aliasing

It's much easier to pry a stuck tape out of a machine when you're not that bothered if you break it. Get a screwdriver and a Sharpie and believe in yourself. It came free with significant but impotent protest, trailing a tangled mess of ropy ED Supra Beta II behind it. Johanna wound the mistreated tape back through the cartridge with the pen the way kids would never do again, and she would have been perfectly content for the rest of her days on this maudlin, over-saturated planet if she could have said the stupid suburban sun got in her eyes and that's all she really saw.

But Betamax tells no lies.

Johanna sat on the floor of her apartment like the kid from *Poltergeist* all grown up, heavily medicated, and a cog in the gig economy. A massive daisy chain of converter cables hooked Big Edie up to the living room flatscreen, each one coaxing the signal five or six years forward from 1987 to the slick shiny present day.

The reflected video image washed her face in color. A forgotten pleasure, like the taste of ancient Egyptian beer. You used to always see your shot in black and white when you looked through the viewfinder. You only got to see the colors when you reviewed the footage. Inside the camera was another planet. Color was a side effect of traveling from that world to this one. Step from Kansas into Oz, cross your fingers for fidelity, saturation, hue, hope those shoes still look as red as they did before you crammed them through a lens.

So. No more black-and-white artsy viewfinder image. Now it was straight outta Kodachrome. But this tape sat in Big Edie's time-out box for thirty years. Chromatic degradation slipped and popped all over the image, sickly green blooms, hot orange halos, compression artefacts, uncanny edging that rimmed this and that object in weird chemical colors.

Johanna watched a factory-direct seventies mustache-dad with tennis socks up to God's chin helping his small, yet unmistakably Jeff, son unwrap a record player on Christmas morning. Big Edie came standard automatic fade-in and fade-out, so everything transitioned elegantly, creating a subtle sense of deliberate editing where none truly existed. Fade to black, then a slow melt into a hopeless lacrosse game, small children running nowhere, hitting each other with sticks too big for them to hold properly.

Another bloom of darkness.

A school play, reedy, vulnerable pre-adolescent Jeff dressed as a cloud fringed with silver tinsel rain, twirling and twirling, technique-free, his arms stretched out. Then another and Johanna presumed this was Jeff's mother, the maker of the T-shirt quilt, 80% Diane Keaton, 20% Shelley Duvall, a white-wine flush on her cheeks, smiling up at the man with the camera in frank, unguarded affection and not a little desire, her shoulders bare above a strapless summer dress the color of the hydrangeas she probably hadn't even planted yet.

Such wildly un-special moments, clichés of heart-beggaring authenticity, carefully cut out of the flow of time and pasted into the future, selected for immortality for no particular reason, random access memories transfigured into light that cannot die—but can get stuck in a metal cage for want of a Sharpie and a flathead.

Time travel. The only real time travel, unnoticed and uncredited because it was so unbearably slow. In the present, you use this astonishing machine to freeze the past. And you send it to the future. One second per second.

The image cut to black and then it was 2015 and Jeff selling off a lifetime of his father's lovingly dragon-hoarded *objets d'*American masculinity. Standing on a lawn with catalogue-ready light and dark green stripes in the grass. Talking not to the man who produced and directed his childhood but to Johanna. She can hear her own voice on the recording.

Does it turn on?

He makes a joke about the moon and tells her his name. Sitting alone in the dark, Johanna realizes he was flirting with her, and she has a second to wonder what his mustached father's name was before the glass smashes through his sternum again and blood streams down to soak a just out-of-frame blanket stitched together from mass-marketed polyester and lost time.

Johanna ran the tape back. Then she watched it again.

Back. And again.

She was still doing it when the morning broke into her apartment without announcing itself.

Five weeks later, she'll be down to two or three run-throughs a day. An article will swim across her feed.

COLOR, HEAT, AND THE WRECK OF THE ARGO

LATE NIGHT FOUR-CAR PILE UP ON I-84 LEAVES TWO DEAD, SEVEN INJURED.
Jeffrey Havemeyer of Westchester County, NY, 34, remains in critical care.
Johanna will feel nothing. She's seen it a thousand times already.

Overclocking

"Sit there," Johanna tells her cousin's daughter, pointing at a cracked leather barstool.

Anika is nineteen, in her second year at Columbia. She is everything Johanna is not: mentally stable, tall, good hair, vegan, grounded by parental encouragement and affection, prone to healthy relationships, able to commit to an exercise regimen. *The* twenty-first-century girl. Johanna has always found her fascinating. Scientifically. It's like hanging out with an alien. Your whole ecosystem is based in carbon and abandonment and trash, and you just always assumed those were the essential building blocks of life, but it turns out they're totally unnecessary and sentient beings can just as well be made out of palladium and love and sensible choices instead, look at this actual good person right here, you have the same nose.

Johanna's arthritic Great Dane watches them coolly from his massive fluffy bed.

"Your hair looks like a badger," Anika says.

It's been some time since Ossining and quilt and the hydrangeas and what Johanna has come to think of as the glitch. Technical difficulties. Runtime error. It's late summer. Sweat darkens Anika's hairline under the expected carefully messy topknot. The boroughs are one long incessant screech of twelve million window-mounted air conditioners and the smell of warm garbage bags, round and shiny on every doorstep.

Seafoam green softheart mermaid look out; icicle-white collarbone-length brutalist bob with black tips in.

"I like to think of it as ermine. You know, royal cloaks and all that."

"Did you know ermines are just regular stoats with their winter coats on?" Anika helpfully informs her. "Not special at all. Fancy weasels. *Glam* weasels."

"That's perfect. I myself am a decidedly unspecial glam weasel."

Johanna adjusts the tripod under Big Edie. It took Johanna weeks to gut the old girl, order parts, and convince her that modern life truly was worth living. Nothing really wrong with her at all, other than the audio-visual equivalent of osteoporosis and a bad back. Johanna loved the work. Data was invisible now. Stored on sand, transferred on air, transcending physical form. Light talking to light. But not Big Edie. She was very visible. Gross and awkward and tangible. The girl would never be good as new again. But she was good enough.

"No you're not, you're amazing," Anika says softly, and Johanna can hear the little girl she's known in that grown-up, gonna-save-the-world-with-believing-it-can-be-saved voice.

Johanna ignores this obvious lie.

They've already done a few shots with the Hasselblad, the Leica, a couple with her phone. She doesn't really know why she's putting on a show. Anika wouldn't question just sitting in front of an old Betamax camcorder for a few minutes and then heading off for Hungarian pastries and a good full-body-cleanse political rant. But it feels important that today has the appearance of a plausibly professional kind of thing. Not that Johanna is using her.

Which she is.

Johanna doesn't have access to a lot of people at the moment. They find her off-putting. Not user-friendly. An unintuitive interface. Carbon-based.

"Can you let the blinds down halfway?" she asks.

Anika does. Slats of August light and dark slash down her face and torso (like glass slicing through skin) like an old pre-lapsarian end-of-programming test screen. It would be a gorgeous shot even if the shot was the point.

"I mean it. This apartment, your work. Margot. Mapplethorpe." The Great Dane's floppy black ears perk up at the sound of his name. "I love it here. You're living the dream."

Johanna hesitates with her forefinger over the record button. God, she remembers how much she hated it when people told her college wasn't the real world and she had no idea what it was like out there, as if studying and working full-time wasn't more work and less fun than the barren salt flats of adulthood between your twenties and death. But she wanted badly to shovel the same shit for Anika now. The only way you could look at this place and see a dream was through a lens that had never touched reality.

This is fine, she tells herself. *The Havemeyer Glitch is not a thing. Just a shill for Big Coincidence. It's not like he died. And besides, nothing bad can ever happen to Anika. She is a palladium-based life form. So this is fine. It's for science. You will take beautiful footage of your beautiful niece-once-removed, and buy her a walnut kolachi, and she will tell her mother what a nice time she had.*

"Margot moved out last week," Johanna says without emotion. Margot moved out three months ago. She left a purple brush in the bathroom. Long black hair still tangled up in it. Johanna can't bring herself to move the last cells of Margot that exist in proximity to Johanna's cells.

"Oh," Anika replies gently. "So that's why you changed your hair."

Johanna hits *record*.

For eighty-seven seconds, the only thing Big Edie has to say is that Anika Telle was born for the camera, a portrait of her generation, artlessly artful, a corkscrew of loose dark hair hanging forward to catch the light, one gray bare leg tucked up beneath a billowy sack dress with small elephants printed on it, the other not quite long enough to touch the peeling floor. Her expression genuinely, infinitely, but entirely temporarily sad for the misfortunes of someone else. *See? This is fine. Tell her to say something. Recite Shakespeare. Or Seinfeld.*

Deep in Big Edie's viewfinder, Anika's left eye crumples in a wet gush of pearl and black. Her head rockets back, shrouded in mist. She coughs, gags, tears streaming from her remaining eye. She's still sitting on the barstool in Johanna's apartment with silvery botanical wallpaper behind her, the tall window, the August sun, the half-drawn blinds. But the Anika in the camera wears black leggings, a puffy black winter coat, a black surgical mask. White duct tape crisscrosses the back of her jacket to form the words: #NOJUSTICE. She's older, the lingering baby soft-ness in her jaw gone, her hair a buzzed undercut. The cords on her neck stand out as she runs, her face ruined, blind with pain, stumbling, looking over her shoulder as she bolts on the video feed from one end of the living room to the other. Out of nothing, a cop in riot gear steps out of Johanna's kitchenette, grabs the back of Anika's skull in one hand and shoves her down. Anika-in-black falls to her knees, sobbing, puking into her mask, holding one hand to the hole where her eye used to be, screaming silently into Johanna's (Margot's) red paisley rug.

Johanna yanks her head up out of the sucking desaturated pit of the camera.

Mapplethorpe snores loudly. Trucks beep in reverse outside the apartment building. Anika sighs softly, bored but not rude. She scratches a mosquito bite on her knee. "I really am sorry. I liked Margot. She was good for you, I think. Got you out of the house."

All the blood has either rushed to or drained from Johanna's head. She can't tell which. All she can hear or feel is her own pulse slamming itself against her eardrums.

"Do you . . . want me to do something?" Anika asks uncertainly.

Johanna shuts the camera down quickly. The image at the bottom of the viewfinder clicks out of existence. She tries to talk, but there's no talk to be found. Just the burning hot green-on-red afterimage of a crystal brown eye collapsing in its socket, over and over.

"Come on, Auntie J," Anika says finally, hopping lightly off the stool and bending down, scratching Mapplethorpe between his spotted shoulder blades. "Dinner's on me. Malaysian okay? Maps can have a curry puff, can't you, baby?"

Test Pattern

An experiment that cannot be repeated is evidence of nothing.

Johanna establishes a beachhead in Owl's Head Park. Back supported by a black walnut tree. Bare toes clenched in a sea of tiny white flowers and clover-infiltrated grass. Big Edie propped against her breastbone, lens stabilized by knees on either side. Mapplethorpe's yellow lead loops around her ankle, but the big fellow has long passed his days of running off after unsuspecting children. He munches philosophically on a pricey organic broth-basted rawhide shaped like a braided ring.

She finds a target, hits the button, rolls footage for a few minutes, tracking them as they throw frisbees for far-inferior dogs or kick soccer balls or kiss on picnic blankets or drag giant wooden chess pieces across a giant board or just walk aimlessly, whatever Saturday afternoon moves them to do. She doesn't look through the viewfinder into that hellworld of black and white. Just presses buttons.

Turn it on.

Shut it off.

Find someone new.

Repeat.

She chooses at random. No more Anikas. No one is special, or unspecial. It doesn't matter who they are or what they look like. They're just data. That man, that woman, that child, that set of twin babies, those skaters, that guy sleeping with a James Patterson book over his eyes. Compressed data to be converted later.

Johanna's brain checks out and begins a speed run through the five stages of grief over the death of a reliable reality. Denial: *you're losing it, change up your medication, girl, it's not real, it's not anything, just a stupid old camera that you bought because you are stupid, at best it's old footage coming through on an old tape.*

Stop recording. New person. Girl in green skinny jeans with a sketchbook.

Anger: *fuck this, fuck you, fuck estate sales, fuck Robert Ballard, fuck the Columbia School of Law, fuck sad elephant print fabric, fuck hydrangeas, fuck curry puffs that make my dog poop out his soul, fuck Betamax you dumb drooling obsolete idiot tech, fuck me, fuck my dad, fuck Jeff Havemeyer's dad, fuck I-84, fuck Margot, fuck the linear flow of time, fuck everything, life is garbage and this is proof. Why is this happening to me?*

Stop. Scan. Record. Lanky white-dude dreds fuckboy in a vest but no shirt.

Depression: *Of course it's happening to me, because I am garbage and this is proof, and whatever cosmic hazmat disposal dump site got its back end trapped in my camera would only open the gates to a warped maladjust like me.*

Stop. Scan. Record. Old man on the bench with god-tier eyebrows and a yellow plastic sunflower in his lapel.

Bargaining: *I'll just watch this back tonight and whatever happens, afterward I'll tip Big Edie in the bin and never tell anyone. And then I will straighten up and clean my apartment and go on Tinder and eat leafy greens five times a day and see Anika more often and make amends and buy an exercise bike. Okay, Elder AV Club Gods? Deal?*

Stop. Scan. Record. Kid on a dirt bike with (elephants) puffins on her dress.

Acceptance.

Acceptance.

Acceptance is Johanna sitting cross-legged (crisscross applesauce) on Mapplethorpe's bed while he snoozes jowlfully on the couch. She braces herself for red slicks of gore and bone. For Jeff and Anika redux. *Once is luck, two is coincidence, three is a pattern . . . or at least time to wake up and smell what your inevitable descent into psychosis is cooking.*

But that's not what Big Edie has for her.

Not entirely, anyway.

Entropic Coding

Gloppy August sunlight washes out the image. Everything is overexposed, too bright, unforgiving. His thin chest rises and falls with his breath. He watches a small blue and white bird hop nervously down the iron rail of his park bench. A cerulean warbler, Johanna notes with supreme irrelevance. Closer to him, then further away, then close again. He crumbles a crust of brown bread on his tweedy knee and waits knowingly. This goes on long enough that Johanna starts to relax. It isn't going to happen again. The bird will give in, and eat, and Johanna's life will resume the program already in progress.

COLOR, HEAT, AND THE WRECK OF THE ARGO

Then the sunlight cools, then it darkens, then it is a dim nothing-watt lamp with a tacky early sixties cherry pattern on the shade. The branches of black oak and Dutch elm in Owl's Head Park still reach into the frame like kids who've spotted a news crew, showing off in the background, dying to get on TV. But the bench and the octogenarian perched on it have become a mustard-colored corduroy sofa and a young man with his head in his hands. Vaguely Scandinavian mid-century wooden end tables bookend the couch. A clock with thin brass spikes radiating out around it ticks over a clearly decorative fireplace. Above the man hangs a proto-Bob Ross painting of standard-issue lake/pines/mountain/lonely boat in a dizzying array of shades from brown to brown. Children's toys cover the floor. At least one boy and one girl. Maybe more. Wooden blocks, a rocking horse with yellow yarn hair, green plastic army men. Donald Duck and Bugs Bunny and Snoopy staring lifelessly at the ceiling in a triple rictus of frozen grimaces. A book of Connie Francis paper dolls with most of the smiling valium-glazed Connies already carefully cut out hiding under the Formica coffee table. A Funflowers Vac-U-Form Maker-Pak Johanna recognizes from a box of crap her grandmother let her play with the year they had to live with her because, no matter how she tried to pretend it was an adventure, her mother had no options left. You squeezed out perfumed Lucite goo into molds and made "Daffy Dills" and "Tuffy Tulips" that looked like crystals in the sun until you got bored and broke a vase just to get some attention. A Spirograph and stacks of spiraled paper, scattered across the avocado shag carpet like ticker tape after the parade has gone. Like mystic offerings before the massive, inert cabinet television that probably weighs more than everyone who lives here put together. The kinds of toys you lift off a flea market shelf with joy and reverence, despite the peeling paint and chipped edges and missing vital organs.

But these are all new.

A wind moves through Owl's Head Park and dappled shadows in the jaundiced light of the living room move across the man, the sofa, the table, the TV, the toys, the cherry lampshade.

The man on the yellow sofa looks up.

He is so young. Perhaps thirty-five, perhaps not even that. His incredible, architectural eyebrows are dark brown now; he has all his hair. He's still wearing a suit, but this one has wide lapels, no tie, a plaid pattern that will crown endcaps in Goodwill until the sun burns out. He looks exhausted. Someone's been smoking all night and it was probably him. maybe not just him. Butts overflow a pink pearlescent ashtray under the cherry lamp. About a third have frosted coral lipstick prints glowing on their filters, each one fainter than the last.

Johanna braces herself for the shard of glass or the ruination of his eye or gunshot or gas leak, whatever is about to break this poor soul in half. Her heart rate spins up into the rhythm of a jet propeller carrying her into nothing and nowhere. Her stomach muscles clench for impact.

But: the man gets up. Wipes his palms on his wrinkled pants. Walks across the room. Stops. Bends down to pull one perfect yellow Vac-U-Form Funflower out of the pile of misshapen attempts. Slides it into his lapel. The man leaves the house. He closes the door behind him so gently it doesn't even click. No sound at all until his car engine starts outside, and then that's gone too.

In the margins of the image, the cerulean warbler flies off with a cry. The shadow of his little body flickers over the empty room.

Fade out.

Fade in on the girl in the green skinny jeans and peasant blouse lying with her sketchbook under the willow tree.

Johanna makes it five people and ten minutes sixteen seconds deep by the overlarge alarm-clock-style timestamp before she scrambles off the dog bed and shuts the whole rig off.

An hour later, she gets out of bed and pads back to the living room on tiptoe, as if afraid to wake Margot's brush. Blue light washes her cheeks and her hands and her walls and Johanna doesn't move until it's over.

Then she hits rewind and starts over from the beginning.

Image Burn

Mapplethorpe makes it another year before turning his creaky back on that big dog life. Since Johanna got to keep him through the quiet post-apocalypse of their union, they agreed Margot could have his ashes.

She looks the same. Just the *same*. As if Margot stepped out of the day she left and into today with no interruption in continuity. Johanna knows that dress, the navy blue vintagey thing with white piping and a little too much room in the torso, but that she refused to take in or give up on, because at thirty-seven, she might still have some growing left in her.

"Your hair," Margot says softly. She steps gingerly over the map of cables and playback devices that have replaced living breathing life for Johanna and sits uncomfortably in the old bisque-colored armchair (falls asleep re-reading *Harry Potter* in it during a snowstorm five years ago; Johanna drapes a crocheted blanket over her and squeezes the bare foot hanging over the overstuffed arm gently, fondly). She sits as though she is trying to hover, as thought it might burn her to stay.

"What about my hair?"

"It's ... shocking."

"It's my hair."

"I assumed you would have gone puce or checkerboard by now. Your actual hair hasn't seen the light of day since high school as far as I know."

Johanna only dimly recalls that she used to care about things like wilding her hair. It seems like a fact about a stranger. Like something she would see on Big Edie and use to pinpoint a date.

They make small talk. Margot is leaving the city soon. She's bought a house in Providence with her wife, two blows Johanna absorbs expressionlessly as a cascade of words concerning Victorian architectural flourishes and small, private ceremonies patter down around her ears like raindrops. Mrs. Margot was apparently called Juniper, because of course she was, bet you call her June-bug too, gross. She was joining the obstetrics team at Rhode Island Hospital. Margot would teach very well-scrubbed scions of the even-better scrubbed at a private prep academy in the fall. Plant heirloom squash. Adopt three-legged rescue Labradors.

What are Johanna's plans? If she has a gallery show before September, Margot would love to come. Anyone new in her life? How is Anika?

Well, Marge, I plan to shoot weddings and graduations and bar

*mitzvahs in which the cakes have significantly more artistic value than
my entire self until I die alone pitched face-first into my takeout mas-
saman with no dog and no stomach lining and no friends except a magic
camera, can I get you a 40%-off Pinnacle buttered-popcorn-flavor
vodka straight up, because that's where I am right now.*

But she doesn't say that. She would never say that.

Instead, she decides to ruin Margot's life. And in that moment, she
genuinely believes it'll work.

"Can I show you something?" Johanna says.

"Of course. Always." Margot brushes her hair out of her eyes, now
and a hundred thousand times in that chair, in this light. "New work?"
Miss M was always her first audience, first viewer, the only other eye she
trusted.

"Sort of. Mostly I just want you to tell me I'm not crazy." And she
doesn't realize how entirely true that is until it's out of her mouth and
loosed on the dusty air.

Margot frowns. "You don't look well. I didn't want to say. Are you
still drinking?"

Johanna laughs bitterly as she flips through the input options on the
flatscreen. "Why would I not be drinking? Drink is friend." She shoves
delivery detritus off the couch to make a space: receipts, plastic bags,
black takeout containers, breath mints and fortune cookies and after-
dinner toffees.

And they watch together. Side by side. Just the same. Like it is before.
Like she will pick up her purple brush again tonight and run it through
her hair and come to bed and tomorrow will be years ago and the film
of them will run forward from the splice.

Rather, Margot watches. And Johanna watches Margot.

The colors waver on her face like she's underwater, staring up at the
parade of strangers fading in and out before her.

The old man/young man on the park bench and the mustard-cor-
duroy sofa.

The girl in the green skinny jeans under the willow and sitting at
a bistro table with fake electronic candles as a man walks in, says her
name uncertainly, kisses her cheek, orders an old-fashioned.

The guy with white-boy dreds and a vest with no shirt steps off a bike path and into a gorgeous apartment in no way decorated by a man who would wear a vest with no shirt even once, all minimalist monochrome, and a woman in pajama pants and jade chip earrings sobbing *get out get out not one more minute I'm done get out.*

A kid in a Spider-Man hoodie swinging upside down from a jungle gym and lying on his couch, a teenager, playing Madden on XBox, yelling to an invisible mother that he'll mow the lawn, yeah yeah, just one more game.

And worse. A boy's face fades into his forties on the subway. He asks why he's being pulled over. A gash blooms on his beautiful brown neck. A student drinking alone in a bar ages fifteen years and loses twenty pounds between sips of house red. She waits for someone with frantic energy and when somebody shows up, gives her a little wax paper packet, leaves her to it, her fingers start to turn the color of corpses on the wine glass. A volunteer museum docent grows red rings and bags around his eyes but loses his wrinkles. Somewhere between the Ancient Greeks and Mesopotamian pottery, gets out of a Camry, locks it, and runs toward an appointment, wholly unseeing the baby in the backseat, asleep in a puffy lavender knitted hat.

"What is this?" Margot says. "Glitch art? Datamoshing? Like Planes and Jacquemin? What program did you use? It's really seamless."

"No program."

"What do you mean 'no program'? This is a practical effect?" Johanna chuckles mirthlessly. The screen shimmers. "Where did you *find* all these actors?"

"No, look, you're not *seeing*. You have to *look*. The calendar in the apartment. The clothes the girl in the bistro is wearing. Do you recognize *any* of the players in that Madden game?"

"You know I don't care about sports. I wouldn't recognize any player's name five minutes after I heard it."

"Okay, fine. The song on the radio when the guy gets stuck in traffic." She pauses it, waits for Margot to catch up, to see the faint cursive 2026-At-A-Glance calendar on the inside of the pantry door in that perfect sleek flat, the unfamiliar controls on the car dash. "I've never heard that song. You've never heard that song. Because that song doesn't exist, on any service, in any catalogue, anywhere."

"I'm sure that's not true. Come on, you couldn't *possibly* know that for certain, Jo."

But Margot doesn't *see*. Margot isn't Robert Ballard's submersible lighting array. She doesn't know how to crawl into an image and live there. What she *does* glimpse in Johanna's pleading eyes is the weight of time. Time she has spent searching for these things, for connections, hoping, honestly hoping, to find that song buried on some indie compilation CD with some revoltingly photoshopped jacket art and a discount sticker. And a thousand other objects like it. Books on televisions, limited edition toys, tie-widths, license plates, worse, more scattered, atomized, randomized information that never coalesced into anything but Johanna's increasing silence and solitude. She vibrates so intensely it looks like she is sitting still.

And so, slowly, knowing how it sounds, hating how it sounds, Johanna explains about Big Edie as more strange moments unfold before the not-really-that-long-lost love of her life; naked bodies, and there are a lot of them, in embraces violent and lovely or both or neither, strangers meeting, over and over, in different clothes, different hairstyles, different seasons, a child abandoned in an airport in Reno, calling for her mother, surrounded by slot machines ringing in cherries and oranges, tears rolling down her face. And at the end of the reel, Jeff and his glass heart, Anika and her shattered eye, the long staircase into images that has become Johanna's life.

Margot says nothing for some time. It is a terrible, sour nothing that lingers far too long in the air between them.

"So you think your camera shows . . . what? Death?"

"Maybe. Sometimes. But not always, not even often, really."

"Then what if not that? The future? Like the calendar."

"That's closer, I think. Better. But at least a third of them are the past."

"How do you know?"

"Well, the man in the living room is 1970. You can tell by the Updike book on top of the TV. That was the first edition cover, and it's *pristine*.

You can figure it out, sometimes. If you care about these things. If you know too much about garbage. And you *know* I know too much about garbage, M."

Margot smiles faintly, but it is *very* faint.

"But also I went back to the park and talked to the guy. His name is Antony." Johanna scratches at the back of her hand. "Antony left his family. In 1970. Just up and walked out on Grace, Walt, Irene, and Amelia, who he'd married when she was fucking seventeen. The proverbial running out for a pack of cigarettes. Left them like they were just . . . a skin he was molting."

Margot looks for a way to shut it off, but Johanna doesn't help her find it. Why should Margot get to turn away from it? Why should she escape?

"Fine," she says coldly. "What is it then?"

Johanna takes a deep breath. "So whenever you transfer or transmit or store data, especially a lot of data, like audio or video or both, it gets compressed, and in the process, you lose a little bit of it. Maybe a lot, like MP3s were always straight garbage compactors for sound. Maybe only a little bit. Maybe so little you wouldn't even notice. But in order to fit the storage device or the bandwidth, in order to save information or share it, you have to ... you have to *harm* it. And that creates distortion. Halos. Noise. Warping. Busy regions in the image. Blocky deformations called quilting, and visual echoes called ghosts. They're called compression artefacts, and that's . . . that's what I think these are. Distortions created by the present and everything else getting compressed, crushed into one stream. Halos and noise and warps and quilts and ghosts. A lot of words for damage. Just damage.

"But the answer is: I don't really know *what* it does. Technically speaking, it's a problem of parallax. *Catastrophic* parallax. A vast difference between the apparent object and the actual object. And for a while, I thought it showed the worst day of your life. Which, odds are, for some percentage of people, is going to be the day you die. But not for everyone. Not for Antony. See, nothing ever went right for him after he left. Two more divorces and a dried-up retirement fund. Grandkids he isn't allowed to meet. Lung cancer he picked up working a big gorgeous free man's HVAC repair shop. But it took him almost his whole life to understand any of it. To process where he fucked up. What he lost when he thought he was barreling down the highway to a big gorgeous free man's life. Big Edie knew it in an *instant*. She had his number faster than a speeding therapist, and that number was 1970. So it seemed to make enough sense. When I shot old people, Big Edie usually spat out the past. Young people mostly turned up older on playback. The future. That kid playing Madden. *Madden 23*, to be exact." She points to him on the projection. The hole in his sock. The length of his hair. The name on the Patriots' QB jersey.

"Do you actually expect me to believe your camera recorded something in 2023? Jo, come on. I'm really busy, and frankly, I'm not in the mood."

"Just *listen*. Because then there was this. A wedding. Mr. and Mrs. Nathaniel and Lucy Vaclavik." She fast-forwards through scene after scene. Johanna can tell just the sheer number of them is starting to look bad on her, and the manic sizzle in her voice isn't helping, but she can't stop herself.

The creams and golds and pops of understated rose-shades of a high-end matrimonial spread flood the screen. The bride waves her lily-dripping bouquet in the air. The Hudson River throbs with sunset behind her. Her hair sparkles with carefully applied glitter. Eyeliner and brows that date her nuptials as surely as a library stamp. Her new husband, in a gray tux, bends down to kiss her expertly neutral-frosted lips and their unified families clap like a gentle river of approval. The picture flows smoothly to the edge of the frame. No ghostly picture-in-picture. No shadows cast from other places, other times.

Margot smiles politely. Johanna knows she is losing her (has lost her). "I don't get it."

"I didn't either," she confesses softly. "I shot this no differently than the others. But what you see is what I saw. What Big Edie saw. No parallax. No difference in images. I rolled tape and the wedding marched right through the lens and back out again and it was just a wedding, no more or less. Nothing else has been like that. And the next day we got right back to business-as-horrible. I couldn't figure it out. Why was it special? What was different? The thing is . . . he killed her. It made the news for about thirty seconds in April. They found her in the woods in Connecticut. But, you know, hedge fund guys aren't that good at forensics, even if they're 100% current on all CSI franchises, so they caught him pretty fast. So maybe . . . maybe Big Edie doesn't record the worst thing that ever happened to you. Maybe it's something so much smaller than that. The moment when the worst thing that ever happens to you sees you coming. Turns toward you in the dark. I think, once she married him, he was always going to hurt her. Because that was *in* him, an egg or a seed or a tumor, whatever you want to call it, a future that no longer has the option of not happening. The flowchart flows until you meet that person at that conference and then there's no more choose your own adventure, you're going to fall in love, and they're going to bankrupt you or betray you or just . . . disappoint you until there's nothing left but cynicism swirling around at the bottom of your heart like tea leaves. Or leave you in the woods in Connecticut. I don't know, maybe it's just a huge ugly regret machine. And mostly I will never understand these. What happened to the Madden kid or the girl in the bar or why getting stuck in traffic on that particular day was so important to that man's whole trajectory, or any of them, because that stuff doesn't come across the AP like Mrs. Vaclavik. They're just moments, unconnected, pulled free of every other moment."

The wedding fades out and the two women wince together as a man they do not know pushes a woman they have never met against a wall. Blood trickles down her temple where she hit a picture frame and she looks up at him with unbelieving eyes.

"Enough," Margot says. She grabs the remote. Shuts it all down. Turns to Johanna and touches her face. *Touches* her. No one has touched Johanna in a year. It is an alien burn. It is Margot. It is the past and the future and death, stroking her hair and making enormous eyes at her while the constituent atoms of their dog look on from the coffee table.

"I miss you so much," Johanna whispers, and wishes she could have thought of something better, more elegant, more memorable, but her need banishes pretty words.

"Don't," Margot answers with finality. The finality of Providence,

Rhode Island, and heirloom squash varietals and Harrington Prepara-
tory School and June-Bug and poor Mapplethorpe in a box.

"What do you think?" She cannot help that either, the need for her
approval, her regard, the perfect full absent moon of her gaze on Johanna's work, Johanna's self.

"Honey . . . I think you need help. This is . . . this is *nothing*, J. It's
a bunch of slice of life shots of nothing in particular and three or four
gory jump-scares. You taped over some movie of the week with a lot of
nonsense. And I'm supposed to believe it's what, magic? It's you *stalking
strangers*. Listen to yourself. Catastrophic parallax? You're manic, you
need *care*."

But Johanna can't hear that. "Okay, but that's just exactly what I
mean. Do you know what *catastrophe* means? It's Greek. It just means a
turn. A turn down or a turn under or a turn inside. A turn away."

"Jo, this is basically a conspiracy theorist wall and you're unspooling
more red yarn. This is not an X-File. This is you not coping. As usual."

"No, you don't understand. I'll show you. Just stand over there, I'll
shoot you for a few minutes, a few seconds, and you'll see." And what
will Big Edie see? Margot leaving that hot, humid, unretrievable night,
Margot packing up boxes for Providence, Margot right now, right here,
telling Johanna she will never believe her? One of them, maybe, surely.
What else was even possible?

"No," Margot whispers firmly. "You don't need me. And you definitely don't need to ride that camera any harder. I'm not going to enable
this. You just need help, baby. Professional help. That's all. I have to go."

"Wait—"

"I have to *go*."

There is a disentangling, a hurry to go back, edit, remove even the
idea that physical contact was made. Margot excuses herself to splash
water on her face and Johanna sees herself in the mute black monitor,
sees as the ex-moon of her night sees: a woman so thin her clothes don't
fit, who smells sour, whose hair hangs limp and unwashed, whose face
has grown lines it didn't have even a few weeks ago, degradation lines,
juddering through the frame of her face.

Margot emerges awkwardly, chagrined, her familiar elfin face not one cell altered from the day she left, her voice echoing against every surface: *I'm so fucking lonely, Jo, I'm lonely even when you're here. Especially when you're here. I'm lonely right the fuck now and I'm looking at you.*

She holds up something in her hand. Something purple. Something precious.

"Forgot my brush," she says softly.

And then she is gone.

Ghosts

Johanna puts it off for a long time.

Why bother? What use could it possibly be to her? What use is any of this? You couldn't do one single thing with it. The shot was too tight to predict the future. Fight crime? Protect the innocent? No. The camera crowded the subject, an unbearable idiot intimacy that took away everything but the seeing itself.

But eventually, she was always going to do it.

Johanna watches herself on the flatscreen. Watches herself get up in Big Edie's face. Fix the focus, back up to sit on the same barstool that held Anika all those ages ago, shifting awkwardly as she looks into the lens like an actor breaking the fourth wall.

She knows what she will see. She is calmly certain of it. She shouldn't have bothered running the tape back for this little screening. She saw it the first time, when she was seven. When she was thirsty in the middle of the night and padded quietly out of her room to get a glass of water. Out of her room and past her father sitting alone in his armchair, the moonlight crawling in after him through the window, grasping at him just before he shot himself and her life . . . turned. There never was any hope for her. She was turned before she got one foot in the world. It wouldn't be a prettier shot now.

The compression artefact burns out from the center of her nuclear-powered selfie. Her stomach muscles seize up the way they do when she just barely reaches the tipping point of a roller coaster and enters freefall, down the rails into her old house, the rugs, the stain on the ceiling, the off-kilter hang of her bedroom door. Her father's face. Her mother's soft snoring from the bedroom.

But that's not what she sees.

No moonlight. No armchair. No 3:00 a.m. drink of water in a seven-year-old girl's hand. It is just Johanna, seafoam green hair and all, walking on the lovely light and dark stripes of green on a lawn in Ossining, in sunlight direct from a photography lab, approaching a quilt made of old T-shirts and the objects it carries. She bends down and presses her warm thumb into the patch of Hypercolor shirt, waiting for the fabric to change color, to unsuffer the damage of too-constant exposure to the very thing that it was designed to react with, which of course it will not, cannot, ever again.

Johanna touches her own face on the television, that seafoam green girl who still had Margot and Mapplethorpe and opinions about everything, that familiar face, yet better-fed and better-loved and almost obscenely untroubled. An ancient version of herself, suddenly unearthed at the bottom of the sea.

Finite State Machine

Johanna puts Big Edie up on Craigslist, all her specs laid out like a personal ad: *enjoys long walks on the beach, getting lost in the rain, composite video output, and turning everything you point me at into an avant-garde film-school short. If you can't handle me being haunted, you don't deserve me being way more work than the camera app on your phone.*

She lowballs the price. She means it. She can change her artefact. She can let it all go, like Margot said. Get care. Be normal. Cope. She can take that moment in Ossining and make it nothing. Make it just another random memory on a compilation tape of the decades fading in and out, like the little tinseled cloud boy turning and turning on his forgotten school stage, meaningless, untethered, beautiful and sad and without connection to anything before or after.

And then anyone could. The boy who doesn't want to mow the lawn. The girl meeting that man at the bistro. Lucy Vaclavik. Antony. Jeff. Anika. Anyone. The long white beam of the Argo's exterior lighting array sweeping through that dark and missing the great hulking skeleton in the blackness, brushing gently by, just barely, just by inches, finding nothing but open water.

She doesn't answer a single query.

Six months later, Johanna doesn't even remember what it's like to leave the house without Big Edie. The pockets of her original-issue carrying case bulge with new tapes.

ANCESTRIES

SHEREE RENÉE THOMAS

I n the beginning were the ancestors, gods of earth who breathed the air and walked in flesh. Their backs were straight and their temples tall. We carved the ancestors from the scented wood, before the fire and the poison water took them, too. We rubbed ebony-stained oil on their braided hair and placed them on the altars with the first harvest, the nuts and the fresh fruit. None would eat before the ancestors were fed, for it was through their blood and toil we emerged from the dark sea to be.

But that was then, and this is now, and we are another tale.

It begins as all stories must, with an ending. My story begins when my world ended, the day my sister shoved me into the ancestors' altar. That morning, one sun before Oma Day, my bare heels slipped in bright gold and orange paste. Sorcadia blossoms lay flattened, their juicy red centers already drying on the ground.

The air in my lungs disappeared. Struggling to breathe, I pressed my palm over the spoiled flowers, as if I could hide the damage. Before Yera could cover her smile, the younger children came.

"Fele, Fele," they cried and backed away, "the ancient ones will claim you!" Their voices were filled with derision but their eyes held something else, something close to fear.

"Claim her?" Yera threw her head back, the fishtail braid snaking down the hollow of her back, a dark slick eel. "She is not worthy," she said to the children, and turned her eyes on them. They scattered like chickens. Shrill laughter made the *sorcadia* plants dance. A dark witness, the fat purple vines and shoots twisted and undulated above me. I bowed my head. Even the plants took part in my shame.

"And I don't need you, shadow," Yera said, turning to me, her face a brighter, crooked reflection of my own. "*You* are just a spare." A spare.

Only a few breaths older than me, Yera, my twin, has hated me since before birth.

Our oma says even in the womb, my sister fought me, that our mother's labors were so long because Yera held me fast, her tiny fingers clasped around my throat, as if to stop the breath I had yet to take. The origin of her disdain is a mystery, a blessing unrevealed. All I know is that when I was born, Yera gave me a kick before she was pushed out of our mother's womb, a kick so strong it left an impression, a mark, like a bright shining star in the middle of my chest.

This star, the symbol of my mother's love and my sister's hate, is another way my story ended.

I am told that I refused to follow, that I lay inside my mother, after her waters spilled, after my sister abandoned me, gasping like a small fish, gasping for breath. That in her delirium my mother sang to me, calling, begging me to make the journey on, that she made

to those of the deep, promises that a mother should never make. "You were the *bebe* one, head so shiny, slick like a ripe green seed," our oma would say.

"Ripe," Yera echoed, her voice sweet for Oma, sweet as the *sorcadia* tree's fruit, but her mouth was crooked, slanting at me. Yera had as many faces as the ancestors that once walked our land, but none she hated more than mine.

While I slept, Yera took the spines our oma collected from the popper fish and sharpened them, pushed the spines deep into the star in my chest. I'd wake to scream, but the paralysis would take hold, and I would lie in my pallet, seeing, knowing, feeling but unable to fight or defend.

When we were *lardah*, and I had done something to displease her—

rise awake, breathe, talk, stand—Yera would dig her nails into my right shoulder and hiss in my ear. "Shadow, spare. Thief of life. You are the reason we have no mother." It was my sister's favorite way to steal my joy.

And then, when she saw my face cloud, as the sky before rain, she would take me into her arms and stroke me. "There, my sister, my second, my own broken one," she would coo. "When I descend, you can have mother's comb, and put it in your own hair. Remember me," she would whisper in my ear, her breath soft and warm as any lover. "Remember me," and then she would stick her tongue inside my ear and pinch me until I screamed.

Our oma tried to protect me, but her loyalty was like the suwa wind, inconstant, mercurial. Oma only saw what she wanted. Older age and even older love made her forget the rest.

"Come!" I could hear the drumbeat echo of her clapping hands. "Yera, Fele," she sang, her tongue adding more syllables to our names, Yera, Fele, the words for one and two. The high pitch meant it was time to braid Oma's hair. The multiversal loops meant she wanted the complex spiral pattern. Three hours of labor, if my hands did not cramp first, maybe less if Yera was feeling industrious.

With our oma calling us back home, I wiped my palms on the inside of my thighs, and ignored the stares. My sister did not reach back to help me. A crowd had gathered, pointing but silent. No words were needed here. The lines in their faces said it all. I trudged behind Yera's tall, straight back, my eyes focused on the fishtail's tip.

"They should have buried you with the afterbirth."

When we reached the courtyard, my basket empty, Yera's full as she intended, we found our oma resting in her battered rocker in the yard. She had untied the wrap from her head. Her edges spiked around her full moon forehead, black tendrils reaching for the sun.

She smiled as Yera revealed the spices and herbs she collected. I pressed fresh moons into my palms and bit my lip. No words were needed here. As usual, our oma had eyes that did not see. She waved away my half empty basket, cast her eyes sadly away from the fresh bloody marks on my shoulder, and pointed to her scalp instead.

"Fele, I am feeling festive today, bold." She stared at a group of *baji* yellow-tailed birds pecking at the crushed roots and dried leaves scattered on the ground. They too would be burned and offered tomorrow night, at Yera's descension. And we would feast on the fruits of the land, as my sister descended into the sea.

"I need a style fitting for one who is an oma of a goddess.
My beauty."

"A queen!" Yera cried, returning from our *bafa*. She flicked the fishtail and raised her palms to the sky. "An ancestress, joining the deep."

Yera had been joining the deep since we were small girls. She never let me forget it.

"Come, Fele," she said, "You take the left," as if I did not know. Yera held the carved wooden comb of our mother like a machete, her gaze as sharp and deadly. Her eyes dared me to argue. She knew that I would not.

Together we stood like sentinels, each flanking oma's side. The creamy gel from the fragrant *sorcadian* butter glistened on the backs of our hands. I placed a small bowl of the blue-shelled sea snails, an ointment said to grow hair thick and wild as the deepest weed of the sea. Yera gently parted our oma's scalp, careful not to dig the wooden teeth in. Before I learned to braid my own hair, Yera had tortured me as a child, digging the teeth into the tender flesh of my scalp. Now her fingers moved in a blur, making the part in one deft move. A dollop of gel dripped onto her wrists. She looked as if she wore blue-stained bracelets—or chains.

I gathered our oma's thick roots, streaked with white and the ashen gray she refused to dye, saying she had earned every strand of it.

"This is a special time, an auspicious occasion. It is not every year that Oma Day falls on the Night of Descension. The moon will fill the sky and light our world as bright as in the day of the gods."

I massaged scented oils into the fine roots of her scalp, brushed my fingertips along the nape of her neck. I loved to comb our oma's hair. The strands felt like silk from the spider tree, cotton from the prickly bushes. Oma said in the time before, our ancestors used to have enough fire to light the sky, that it burned all morning, evening, and the night, from a power they once called electricity. I love how that name feels inside my head—*e-lec-tri-city*. It sounds like one of our oma's healing spells, the prayers she sends up with incense and flame.

Once when Yera and I were very small, we ran too far inside the ancestors' old walled temples. Before we were forbidden, we used to scavenge there. We climbed atop the dusty, rusted carcasses of metal beasts. We ducked under rebar, concrete giants jutting from the earth, skipped over faded signage. We scuttled through the scraps of the metal yard at the edge of green, where the land took back what the old gods had claimed. I claimed something, too, my reflection in the temple called Family Dollar, a toy that looked like me. Her hair was braided in my same simple box pattern, the eyes were black and glossy. She wore a faded skirt, the pattern long gone. When I flipped her over, to my surprise, I discovered another body where the hips and legs should be. The skirt concealed one body when the other was upright. Two bodies, two heads, but only one could be played with at a time. I tried to hide my find from Yera, but she could see contentment on my face. So I ran. I ran to the broken, tumble down buildings with blown-out windows that looked like great gaping mouths. I ran into the mouth of darkness, clutching my doll but when I closed my eyes, searching for the light, Yera was waiting on the other side.

That is when I knew I could never escape her. My sister is always with me.

Before the Descension, our people once lived in a land of great sweeping black and green fields, land filled with thick-limbed, tall trees and flowing rivers of cool waters, some sweet and clear, others dark as the rich, black soil. Our oma says when our ancestors could no longer live on the land, when the poisons had reached the bottom of every man, woman, and child's cup, they journeyed on foot and walked back into the sea, back to the place of the old gods, the deep ones.

But before they left, they lifted their hands and made a promise. That if the land could someday heal from its long scars, the wounds that people inflicted, that they would return again. In the meanwhile, one among us, one strong and true, must willingly descend into the depths to join the ancestors. This one, our people's first true harvest, will know from the signs and symbols, the transformations that only come from the blessing of the ancestors, when the stars in the sky above align themselves just so. Yera is that first harvest. She has wanted this honor her whole life. And from her birth, the signs were clear. Her lungs have grown strong, her limbs straight and tall, she does not bend and curve like the rest of us.

My sister has the old gods' favor and when Oma Day ends and the Descension is complete, she will join the waters, and rule them as she once ruled the waters of our mother's womb, she will enter them and be reborn as an ancestress.

The ceremony has not yet begun and I am already tired. I am tired, because I spend much of my time and energy devoted to breathing. For me, to live each day is a conscious act, an exercise of will, mind over my broken body's matter. I must imagine a future with every breath, consciously exhaling, expelling the poison because my brain thinks I need more air, and signals my body to produce light, even though my lungs are weak and filled with the ash of the old gods. Unable to filter the poison quickly, my body panics and it thinks I am dying. My knees lock, and I pull them up to my chest and hold myself, gasping for breath like our oma said I did, waiting in my mother's womb.

Oma gives me herbs. She grinds them up, mortar and pestle in her conch shell, and mixes them in my food. When I was smaller, she made me recite the ingredients daily, a song she hummed to lull me asleep. But as I grew, the herbs worked less and less, and my sister did things to them, things that made me finally give them up. I have given so much to her these years.

And I have created many different ways to breathe.

I breathe through my tongue, letting the pink buds taste the songs in the air. I breathe through the fine hairs on the ridge of my curved back and my arms, the misshapen ones she calls claws. I breathe through the dark pores of my skin. And when I am alone, and out of my oma's earshot, out of my wretched sister's reach, I breathe through my mouth, unfiltered and free. My fingers searching the most hidden, soft parts of myself and I am *light air star shine, light air star shine, light—*

In the suns before Oma Day, I spent a lot of time sleeping. My breathing tends to be easier if I sleep well, and so I slept. My lungs are filled with poison which means there's no space for the light, the good clean air. I have many different ways to expel the poison, and meanwhile my body goes into panic because my mind thinks I'm dying, so between controlling the exhalation, telling my mind that I am not dying, inhaling our oma's herbs through her conch shell, I am exhausted since I do this many times a day. And then there is Yera. Always my sister, Yera. I must watch for her. I know my sister's movements more than I know myself.

This night, on the eve of Oma Day, which is to say, the eve of my sister's descension, I can feel Yera smile, even in the dark. It is that way with sisters. As a child I did not fear the night. How could I? My sister's voice filled it. Outside, the *baji* birds gathered in the high tops of our oma's trees. Their wings sounded like the great wind whistling through what was left of the ancestors' stone wall towers. They chattered and squawked in waves as hypnotic as the ocean itself, their excitement mirroring our own. And I too was excited, my mind filled with questions and a few hopes I dared not even share with myself. Would I still exist without my sister? Can there be one without two?

As more stars add their light to the darkness, I turn in my bed, over and over again like the gold beetles burrowing in our oma's soil. I turned, my mind restless while Yera slept the sleep of the ages. For me, sleep never comes. So I sit in the dark, braiding and unbraiding my hair and wait for the day to come, when my world would end again or perhaps when it might begin.

The past few days I've been aware that braiding makes me short of breath, and I realized that I am very, very tired. Last night I was going through my patterns, braiding and unbraiding them in my head, overhand and underhand, when I remembered what the elder had once said to our oma. That she had done a lot in her life, that she, already an honored mother, had raised *felanga* on her own, and it was all right if she rested now. And I thought that maybe that was true for me, the resting part, which is perhaps why today I feel changed.

"Hurry, child. Hunger is on me."

Our oma calls but even she is too nervous to eat. Her hair is a wonder, a sculpture that rises from her head like two great entwined serpents holding our world together. My scalp is sore. My hands still ache in the center of my palms and I am concentrating harder now to breathe. I rub the palm flesh of my left hand, massaging the pain in a slow ring of circles.

Yera has not joined us yet. She refused my offer to help braid her hair. "You think I want your broken hand in my head?

"You know your hands don't work," she said. I remember only once receiving praise from her for my handiwork. I had struggled long, my fingers cramped, my temple pulsing. I braided her hair into a series of intricate loops, twisting off her shining scalp like lush *sorcadia* blooms. Yera did not speak her praise. Vocal with anger, she was silent with approval. Impressed, Yera tapped her upper teeth with her thumb. Oma, big-spirited as she was big-legged, ran to me. She lifted my aching hands high into the air as if the old gods could see them. Now dressed in nothing more than a wrap, Yera's full breasts exposed, nipples like dark moons, her mouth is all teeth and venom. "You have always been jealous of me."

"Jealous?" I say and turn the word over in my mouth. It is sour and I don't like its taste. I spit it out like a rotten *sorcadian* seed.

She turns, her thick brows high on her smooth, shining forehead. "Oh, so you speak now. Your tongue has found its roots on the day of my descension?"

Inside, my spirit folds on itself. It turns over and over again and gasps for air, but outside, I hold firm. "Why should I feel jealous? You are my sister, and I am yours. Your glory is my glory."

I wait. Her eyes study me coolly, narrow into bright slits. The scabs on my shoulder feel tight and itchy. After a moment, she turns again, her hands a fine blur atop her head. She signals assent with a flick of her wrist. Braiding and braiding, overhand, underhand, the pattern is intricate.

I have never seen Yera so shiny.

I take a strip of brightly stained cloth and hand it to her. She weaves it expertly into the starfish pattern. Concentric circles dot the crown of her head. Each branch of her dark, thick hair is adorned with a *sorcadian* blossom. We have not even reached the water and she already looks like an ancestor.

"Supreme," I whisper. But no words are needed here. I pick up the bowl of sea snail ointment and dip my fingertips into the glistening blue gel. My stained fingers trail the air lightly. "Mother's comb," Yera says and bows her head. "You may have mother's comb. I won't be needing it anymore."

I smile, something close to pleasure, something close to pain. My fingertips feel soft and warm on her neck. They tingle and then they go numb.

Yera's mouth gapes open and closed, like a *bebe*, a flat shiny fish. Her pink tongue blossoms, juicy as a *sorcadian* center. Red lines spiral out from her pupils, crimson starfish.

"Sister, spare me," I say. "Love is not a word that fits in your mouth."

The *sorcadia* tree is said to save souls. Its branches helped provide shelter and firewood. Its fruit, healing sustenance. Its juicy blossoms with their juicy centers help feed and please the old gods.

To have a belly full and an eye full of sweet color is not the worst life. As I leave our Oma's house, the wind rustles and the *sorcadia* in Oma's yard groans as if it is a witness. I gaze at the *sorcadia* whose branches reach for me as if to pull me back into the house. Even the trees know my crimes.

Silver stretches over the surface of the sand. Water mingles with moonlight, and from a distance it looks like an incomplete rainbow. Our oma says this is a special moon, the color of blood, a sign from the ancestors. The moon is the ultimate symbol of transformation. She pulls on the waters and she pulls on wombs. When we look at it we are seeing all of the sunrises and sunsets across our world, every beginning and every ending all at once. This idea comforts me as I spot our oma in the distance. I follow the silver light, my feet sinking in the sand as I join the solemn crowd waiting at the beach.

There are no words here, only sound. The rhythmic exhalations, inhalations of our people's singing fills the air, their overtones a great buzzing hum deep enough to rend the sky. Before I can stop myself, I am humming with them. The sound rises from a pit in my belly and vibrates from the back of my throat. It tumbles out of my dry mouth to join the others around me. Beneath my soles the earth rumbles. That night my people sang as if the whole earth would open up beneath us. We sang as if the future rested in our throats. The songs pull me out of myself. I am inside and out all at once. As my sister walks to stand at the edge of the waters, I feel as if I might fly away, as if every breath I had ever taken is lifting me up now.

A strong descension assures that straight-backed, strong limbed children will be born from our mothers' wombs, that green, grasping roots will rise from the dead husks of trees to seed a future. The others dance around this vision. When one descends, all are born. When one returns, all return. Each bloodline lives and with it, their memory, and we are received by our kin.

Music rises from the waves, echoes out across the sand, a keening. The elders raise their voices, the sound of their prayers join. I walk past them, my hair a tight interlocked monument to skill, to pain. The same children who laughed in my face and taunted me are silent now. Only the wind, the elders' voices, and the sound of the waters rise up ahead to greet me. The entire village watches.

Oma waits with her back to me, in the carved wooden chair they have carried out to face the waters. When I stand beside her, her fingertips brush the marks on my shoulder. Her touch stings.

The wounds have not all scabbed over yet. She turns and clasps my hands, her eyes searching for answers hidden in my face.

"Fele, why, why do you do such things?"

Our oma's unseeing eyes search but I can find no answer that would please her.

"Yera," I begin but her *tsk*, the sharp air sucking between her teeth, cuts me off.

"No," she says, shaking her head, "not Yera. You, Fele, it is you."

They think I don't hear them, here under the water, that I don't know what they are doing, from here in the sea. But I do.

I wanted Yera to fight back, to curse me, to make me forget even the sound of my own name. I am unaccustomed to this Yera. This silent, still one.

"Fele!" they call. "She has always been touched." "I told her oma, but she refused to listen." "One head here with the living, the other with the dead." "Should have never named her. To tell a child she killed her sister, her mother. What a terrible curse."

They whisper harsh words sharp enough to cut through bone. But no words are needed here. I have withstood assault all these years, since before birth. This last attack is borne away by the ocean's tears. They say my Yera does not exist. That she died when our mother bore us, that I should have died, too. But that was then and this is now and we are another tale.

It does not matter if she is on land or that I am in the sea. We are sisters. We share the same sky.

Through some spells, when the moon is high and the tide is low, and my body flinches, panics because it thinks it is dying, I journey inland, to where the ancestors once walked in flesh, the ones we carved into wood. I journey inward and I can smell the scent of *sorcadians* in bloom, the pungent scent of overripe fruit, and feel my sister's fingers pressed around my throat, daring me to breathe.

Tiny *bebe* dart and nibble around my brow. They swim around the circles in my hair and sing me songs of new suns here in the blueblack waters. Now I am the straight and the curved, our past and our future. Here in the water, I dwell with the ancient ones, in the space where all our lives begin, and my story ends as all stories must, a new beginning.

THE SOUND OF THE SEA, TOO CLOSE

JAMES EVERINGTON

There were kids in the abandoned school again, Jack realized as he approached. He always knew. He paused now at the locked door, keys in his hand, then turned away. Not yet. He walked past the sun-faded sign marked *Haffield Primary* and down the side of the building. He was looking for smashed windows or other signs of forced entry, although he knew there'd be none. He rounded the corner to the rear of the school, stepped from shade into sunlight; the day already too hot despite the early hour. He heard the sound of waves; he tasted both salt and smoke in the air. He looked straight ahead rather than towards the cliffs as he hurried along the pathway to get round and out of the heat. It wasn't a big building, as schools went: there were only two classrooms, a central assembly area, a staff room, boiler room, small kitchen. All on one level, pressed down by a low flat roof like a hand pressing down on them from the sky. So Jack thought when he'd been a pupil at Haffield, decades before. There were enough kids in the village then to make it seem a real school.

Having circled the school he reached the main door again, tried not to admit to any nerves—or anger or guilt—before he unlocked it. Maybe he was wrong and the school would be empty. When he put the key in the lock he was surprised to find it was stiff to turn, and his hands flickered with a premonition of arthritis. He'd have to lubricate the lock; the school had only been abandoned a few months but already lack of use meant things were seizing up, falling into disrepair. Which hardly mattered: the building would be knocked down if the sea didn't claim it first. But for now it was still Council property, for now he was still a Council employee, and they paid him to look after the place. No one would know if he didn't, but he *was* responsible, and after all he'd barely leave the house otherwise: his silent mid-terrace house devoid of neighbors either side. And now the kids were appearing, so didn't he have to check the school each day?

"Hello?" he called as he stepped inside the small waiting area by a shuttered-up reception window. "Just me, the caretaker. Hello?"

Of course, I shouldn't think of them as "kids," he thought. Like with Kevin—no matter the years gone, he and Mary always spoke about him like he was still a child.

He opened the inner doors into the assembly area, an empty and dim space that took his eyes seconds to adjust to. (The school had shutters on the back windows to protect against the salt in the air, and it was too much hassle to open and close them each visit so Jack left them shut.) Red plastic chairs were stacked against the far wall; most hadn't been sat on in years. An old clock made a half tick-tock sound on the wall, the second hand jerking forward then back again, frozen at the same point in time.

"Hello?" he called into the room, in case one of them was hiding there. His hearing wasn't good enough to be certain no one replied. Jack sometimes wondered if his eyes were going the same way, the things he saw.

He did a brief circuit of the room, clenching and unclenching his fists to stop them seizing up. To delay looking round the rest of the school, he fetched his step-ladder from the adjacent boiler room and climbed up to the clock and took it from the wall, silenced it by removing its battery. The ticking sound was replaced by that of the sea—you'd not been able to hear it in this room before, Jack knew. He'd loved that sound as a kid, used it to tempt Mary to the village; to the terraced house just the right size for a family. Now, like the few others left in Haffield, he wished he could block the noise out.

He'd clenched his fists again without realizing; the pain as he unfurled them was like penance. It's not my fault, he thought, didn't I try and stop things? Think what *we* gave up, to stop things! Yet still. It was best not to think about it, for all that fear and guilt were the background to all his thoughts, to his every action no matter how mundane. He sighed and wondered if in doing so he'd covered up a noise from elsewhere in the building. There was no point in delaying further; he turned and walked towards the first classroom. They were normally drawn to one of the classrooms.

When he entered, his eyes were drawn to the back of the room, to see if the far door was already opened. If they'd already got out to the rear of the building, to the bright sunlight and salt smell, he might be too late. But the door was shut. He'd left the blinds drawn the last time he'd been here; sharp blades of light still intruded through the gaps. He couldn't see anyone present, although the room still gave the impression it might be filled with chattering kids at any moment. Posters and notices still lined the walls; toys and books were stacked neatly on the shelves as if in expectation they'd be taken down and played with again soon. There had been too much leftover stuff in the school for the staff to remove it all on that last day.

Jack moved further into the room, walked around the low tables and short chairs still laid out as if for a lesson. He noticed one chair was overturned; he was certain it hadn't been yesterday. When he tried to call out again, his voice failed him.

He stepped forward, cursed as he stumbled; he'd not noticed the tub of crayons scattered over the floor. He put his hand out to steady himself, touched a wall marred with old Blu-tac and dusty curls of tape. Only one picture remained: a child's drawing of a house, a nuclear family outside, a large sun with stick-like rays reaching down to the people, and around their feet the sea, the sea.

Jack swore again as he righted himself; any tumble now and it sent his heart racing.

"That's a naughty word," a voice said, and giggled. A figure was sitting at one of the tables near the back door, its form broken by the alternating light and shade from the blind. It was far too big for its surroundings; when it stood it did so clumsily, comically pulling its adult body from the small plastic chair. But Jack didn't laugh; he felt sick. For although the person looked full grown its movements seemed child-like, and he remembered small sticky hands pulling at him to be lifted up, the trusting grip around his neck.

It hadn't been until they'd taken Kevin away that they'd told Jack and Mary they wouldn't be getting another chance. That they'd been struck from the list. The whole of Haffield had, in fact. Mary had screamed and thumped his chest when they left. The last of the moors beyond the village had been black with smoke that year, and everyone's eyes had been tearing up all the time.

The person stepped towards him, still giggling at his "fuck" even as it stumbled in its heeled shoes, as if unused to them. As if playing dress-up. Jack guessed the woman's age to be about thirty-five: her hair was in a tight bun, and she wore a charcoal-gray trouser suit. Around her neck hung a pass for some corporate office no doubt miles from Haffield. One ear still had a wireless earbud in, the other presumably fallen on her journey from there to here.

She stank of piss and shit.

She stared at him with eyes wide with a hectic imitation (if it *was* imitation) of childlike excitement familiar to Jack. As if staying up past their bedtime, a treat verging on misbehavior.

The woman held something in her hand, which she raised and rubbed on her lips, then chewed. Her teeth, her mouth, were stained bright red with a mixture of saliva and crayon.

"Look," she said, "look." Her voice pitched high so that it sounded artificial, put on. "Lipstick like Kay-Kay's." Her eyes gleamed in the slatted light, darted back and forth as if seeking approval.

In the resulting silence, they both heard the sound of waves. The woman stiffened then clapped both her hands together, the crayon falling to the floor. She turned her head with exaggerated movements left and right looking for the source of the noise, one hand absently scratching at her arse. Her lips smacked together, and more of the frothy red wax dribbled from her mouth, down her suit.

"Bockit spade!" she shouted, darting with alarming speed through the room to the storage units of toys, which she started rummaging through with great excitement. Plastic swords and toy planes and hair-brushes cluttered the floor as she let each drop. Jack saw on the table she'd been sitting at an expensive leather handbag.

If he turned and walked away now, came back in a few hours, Jack knew the woman would be gone; probably some of the toys would be gone too, clutched in her hand even as she went to her death. The bag would most likely still be exactly where she'd left it.

He almost did walk away.

Instead he sighed, flexed his fingers to unstiffen them, picked up the bag and approached her. The smell got worse as he drew near, and his resolution faltered. But she was young, to his old eyes, and so trying not to grimace he gently touched her shoulder.

She looked nervous now, in that way kids had when the excitement of a new place wore off and they wondered where they were and how they'd get back. Jack made soothing nonsense sounds like he'd used to when Kevin woke from another nightmare. His arm drew her into a comforting hug—decades' old muscle memory. ("Huggles," Kevin had called them.) He tried not to grimace, tried not to cry, when the woman relaxed herself into it. Her body was hot, feverish as the planet's terrible summers, and after a few seconds he pulled away slightly, tried to free himself from her infant grip that didn't want to let go. To distract her he gave her the handbag; she made cooing, appreciative noises like she'd never seen it before.

He coaxed her up, led her with his arm round her shoulders towards the door—not the one to the outside area, but the one to the dim and silenced hall, then back towards the main school exit. She was talking to him trustingly. "When I grow up . . ." she said at one point and giggled. He wondered if parents still said that to their kids—"when you grow up"—still encouraged it, let them think they definitely would.

It's not my fault, he thought again.

Outside, the sunlight was harsh and unforgiving, any clouds in the sky burnt away. The woman shrank from it; Jack turned and blinked away after-images and tears. His body ached with the effort of getting her this far, contorted as it was to guide a grown woman as if she were a child. She looked at him now, with her arid, trusting eyes and waxy smeared grin.

You could hear the sea from the front of the school, although you'd never been able to before.

Instead, he directed her towards what he still called the moors, although the last of the heather and bracken burnt away seasons ago. The landscape around the village was one of sunbaked rocks and dead soil, a few stubby, stubborn plants, skeletal trees, and a cloudless, birdless sky. The road—the only road out of the village—could be seen snaking its way through the moors; while navigable, it was in a state of some disrepair.

"That way," he said gently. "You go that way."

"What that way?" she said in her little girl voice and remembering he told her it was the beach.

"And Josie and Kay-Kay?" she asked quickly, her red- rimmed eyes so dry and caught between excitement and panic. He told her yes.

He watched her set off along the road through the moors; the next village was seven miles inland. Seven miles safer. She was still toddling in her high heels like they were too big for her, although they'd presumably fit fine that morning. Or the morning before—he never knew how long it took them to reach him. He watched her figure become smaller and smaller, both with distance and the distorting heat haze rising from the road, so that he could almost believe her the child she thought herself to be. Looking for someone's hand to hold. He was crying although he didn't know if he should be. Had he done the right thing, or should he have let her go where she wanted? Maybe they came back when he wasn't around anyway, drawn by whatever lemming-like instinct drew them here.

Were they even real? Jack thought, as he turned and walked back inside (not wanting to see the moment when she crested the hill and dropped out of sight). Oh he knew they were *physical*; the shit and the sweat and piss and blood on them proved that. Still, were they *real* real? Who were they? No one ever came looking for them, no reports ever came from the villages inland of their arrival. Nor did Jack know how they journeyed to the school or got inside. There were never any cars parked out front. He'd tried calling the police the first few times, but no patrols came out to Haffield anymore; officially it was uninhabited, a non-place. By the time someone phoned him back, the kids had already headed out back anyway.

They're *not* bloody kids, he thought to himself. Why should *they* get out of it?

His moods, in his old age, were sometimes unpredictable, flipping with a suddenness like in his youth, and he now found himself irrationally angry. Or maybe it was his lack of anger before that was irrational. Look at what happened to his life, to this place. Just *look*. His fists clenched, but he ignored the pain.

It was then, in the dim silence of the old school he heard a sound, and realized there were more of them inside.

He made a low, stressed sound in his throat, only half aware he was doing it. What did they *want*, these messed up people? Why come to *him*? There'd been a time he wanted kids, wanted responsibility, but that was—how long ago? He could only work it out by remembering the year Kevin came to them from the agency and counting forward from there. Holding the nervous young boy's hand and leading him wide-eyed into the "seaside house"—he'd felt like a superhero. As if the fact he'd do anything to protect Kevin and his future gave him the powers to actually do so. That moment was the fixed point in Jack's thoughts, about which all else revolved. They'd hoped for other such moments, but it had remained unique.

When Mary died she was still bitter, her love for Jack still eroded and crumbling from his insistence they live in his childhood home close enough to hear the sea, and what followed was her reluctant agreement. He'd vowed he wouldn't die like that, trussed up and powerless in a hospital bed, given too much chance to think of the past. The past was too painful with missed chances, lost time, and the future was too awful and blighted a thing to contemplate. He wanted to live only in the present moment, even at the moment of his death. At least now he knew how it would happen.

It was only after Mary died that the kids started appearing in the school.

Now he heard, from the other classroom, the sound of someone clumsily moving around, as if unused to their size. He thought, as he always did when given warning (when they stumbled out of the hot dusty light towards him, lips gummy, eyes wide and arid, arms out wanting a hug, wanting comfort, wanting an adult to tell them the bad things were gone), of just walking away, not letting himself see them. Of walking out the school and locking it behind, confronting the blackened space of the moors; of closing his eyes, and hearing the loud calling of the sea, tasting the salt in the air . . . But he never did. Responsibility was responsibility, whether you'd asked for it or not. And so he walked, fingers flexing, joints raging, towards the sound of the kids.

There were two of them, this time. Two men, all dressed up for the fairway: slacks, pastel polo shirts, spiked golf shoes. One of them had what looked like chocolate sauce smeared over his clothes, his hands, his mouth. He wore a pink permed wig from the dressing up box; his companion wore a feathered Robin Hood hat. They were sitting on the floor, pretending to pour tea from a plastic teapot into plastic teacups, with that seriousness of purpose some kids had when playing. They were so absorbed in it Jack watched them unnoticed. He saw they were actually pouring something from the teapot; as he stepped further into the dim classroom he realized the carpet was wet, and what he took to be the sound of the sea was in fact a tap running. He walked quickly to the low enamel sink and saw it was blocked with wads of green and brown tissue paper. The water was unpleasantly warm when he reached down to remove the blockage.

"Someone else always cleans it up eh?" he said loudly to the two men, and they started with the nervous, sudden guilt of children surprised to find themselves in the wrong. The teacup and teapot fell from their oversized hands, splashed to the ground. These people, they never broke character once. It was ridiculous, Jack thought: these guys were, what, early sixties? Why did *they* get to play dress-up and pretend to be someone else, somewhere else? God, but his hands hurt as they squeezed at nothing; his head ached and his vision blurred, and he still heard the sound of water.

"C'mon, stand up!" he yelled, as if he held some authority, moral or otherwise, over the two men. Quickly they scrambled up, their tanned skin, their beer guts becoming more obvious as they did so. They were similar to Jack's age, but their bodies betrayed none of the stiffness and wear his did; these men had obviously lived easy, gluttonous lives, Jack thought. As if that were the decider, when in truth he'd already decided before he'd even entered the room . . .

"Sorry," one said in a small falsetto voice.

"'orry," the other echoed, shuffling his feet.

Jack stood clenching and unclenching his fists. He wondered how far the woman had got, crossing the bleak and soot-scarred moors, tripping over her feet.

The sound of the sea could be heard, as if it were lapping at the perimeter of the building. The two kids looked towards the sound, then back at him. Two men used to getting what they wanted, Jack thought, used to just taking without consequence to themselves.

"Want to play outside?" he said, nodding towards the back of the classroom.

"Yay!" one of them shouted, his feet squelching on the water-logged carpet as he jigged excitedly. The other joined in, the curls of his wig slipping to reveal white hair beneath; he stopped and solemnly straightened it.

"Go on then," Jack said. (You spoil him, Mary said, you just give in when he wants . . . but she had been smiling when she said it.) The kids looked at him cautiously, as if they might still be denied. Jack gestured towards the door at the back of the classroom, although there was really no need; the same instinct which drew the kids to the school drew them out back, if left long enough. He'd disconnected the electricity, so that the door no longer set off the alarm when opened. Not that there was anyone to hear it ringing, anymore.

It was already scorching outside, the sky clear, and Jack shuddered. One of the things, nowadays, was that you could no longer simply enjoy nice weather. Yet the two men seemed to, running onto the straw-dry yellowed grass, arms outstretched like planes, glancing at Jack from the corners of their red-rimmed eyes to see if he was still angry with them.

He gestured them forwards.

Not only did the heat feel wrong, but the outside *looked* wrong too. Jack had been at this spot thousands of times, both as an adult and child. The grass had once been green and spotted with dandelions and daisies; a large chestnut had provided shade in the summer, conkers in the autumn. Jack still saw a plastic slide, swings, a seesaw; remembered all his classmates charging to play on them at break-time. And beyond them—quite a way beyond—tall, sturdy metal railings, protecting the children from the cliff drop the other side.

Now, it was like something had eaten away half of what he remembered as true, for the edge of the cliffs was much closer, and the only inadequate protection was some fluorescent tape staked in the ground, snapped strands of it fluttering in the air, like it was marking an old crime scene. What happened to Haffield had happened in slow-motion; they'd read reports and seen artist impressions of the inevitable for years. People had stopped being able to get mortgages or home insurance; estate agents stopped listing the properties in the village because no one could buy them. The rising sea levels meant the dwellings in the lower part of the village, down by the small harbor, were already standing in inches of water at high tide. The upper part of the village was still theoretically habitable, but families left every week. And the higher tides didn't just flood the low areas but increased the erosion at the base of the cliffs; gradually they fell away, so that the available land receded year after year.

The agency said they'd taken Kevin away for his own good. That night, Jack and Mary argued about whether they should pack up and leave, for all they couldn't sell the house. To just go. They'd both wept, hot and seething in their bed even though they'd rolled away from each other to avoid touch, their weeping as rhythmic and slowly destructive as the sounds of the sea.

The two kids were playing something different now, some chasing game too complicated for him to understand, the shapes they made running from each other too quick for his eyes to follow. In the haze from the heat, he could fancy they looked smaller, their slacks and polo shirts baggier on their bodies. He was dizzy watching them. It was too hot. The sea was too loud. His hands burned as they squeezed and slowly let go something invisible in his grip. Jack closed his eyes.

"Hide and seek!" he shouted in the darkness. "You run and hide, and I'll close my eyes and count to ten."

"We shouldn't have children," he'd said to Mary, years ago when things seemed salvageable. "Not our *own*. Another mouth on a hungry planet? What's the point in living like we do . . ."—the cut-backs, the going-without, the growing- your-own—" . . . if we have kids? There's plenty of children need looking after already; there will be more soon the way things are headed. We could foster, maybe adopt." And reminded of a childhood secure and carefree, he'd told her he knew just the place to move to in order to do so. When Kevin came into their life it was like he'd been right.

The sound of the waves was so *hungry*.

When Jack opened his eyes, one of the men was gone.

The other one, the one in the pink wig, was cautiously tip-toeing towards the edge of the cliffs. He looked at Jack with those wide arid innocent eyes, and Jack surged with hatred. Why did *they* get to play innocent? They weren't fucking innocent; no one grown up was.

"Flying," the man said in a squeaky voice, making his airplane arms, looking down the drop to the rocks and sea, then back at Jack.

"I haven't flown in thirty years," Jack said gruffly, deliberately misunderstanding. Had *this* man stopped flying, made sacrifices? He hoped not.

Hands clenched, let go.

"Wanna keep playing with him," the man said, pointing downwards. "Ona beach." Jack noticed the man's hands were clenched around something too. He walked towards the man and everything seemed to intensify: the heat, the salt-taste, the pain in his joints and chest and the noise of the waves. He took the man's hand, which was bigger than his, and gently curled open the fingers.

"Found ladybird!"

"Look a *ladybird*!" Kevin had said that first week, the first sign of excitement, of engagement with his new home. As if he'd never seen one before; maybe he hadn't, even though they'd not been endangered then. Held out his small sheltering hand with the small life inside for Jack and Mary to see. Where was he now, Jack thought, he'd be a grown up himself and . . .

The air was too scorched with light to follow the flight of the lady-bird from the man's open palm; Jack's eyes watered to blindness and he closed them again. He heard a childlike cry of mingled excitement and disappointment, and the hand pulled away from his. He tried to hold on, then remembering, let go. There was smoke in the air, salt on his lips, the crash of the sea on the rocks and hard-packed sand below. There was the sound of someone counting to ten, and he wasn't sure if it was him.

When Jack opened his eyes there was no one to be seen at all.

He shuffled right to the edge of the drop, as he did every time. The tips of his shoes poked over the edge, and he heard the crumbling sound as small pebbles and loose earth fell away. One day it would go, he knew, and so would he. It was only fitting. Deserved.

He peered down. Was what he saw all fallen from the school, or was some of it from places equally crumbling and in the process of being eaten away? He could see plastic cars and star-ships, doll arms, a bike wheel, dead sea birds noosed in plastic, a deflated beach ball, parts of an old seesaw, torn jackets and coats swirling in the water like they still housed things alive. A bright pink princess palace, a kite, suntan lotion bottles, a feathered hat, a severed hand, a smashed face, a pink wig . . .

He would count to ten as if he were still playing hide and seek, and then walk away, he decided. It was Kevin's favorite game, for those few months they'd had him, and in all those years after he'd been taken from them, Jack had never been able to find any trace of him. He closed his eyes; and something gave way beneath his feet, then more. Would today be the day?

"Coming ready or not," he said.

All he could hear, now the children were gone, was the sound of the sea too close.

DRUNK PHYSICS

KELLEY ARMSTRONG

*D*runk Physics started in a bar, naturally. A bunch of physics postgrads hanging out, blowing off thesis stress, getting wasted and getting loud, and pissing off the group of math post-grads quietly working through theorems at the next table.

Six of us crammed into the booth. Trinity and I were the only girls—I do remember that. We weren't exactly friends, but if Trinity wanted a drink with the guys, she always asked me to come along. I was her wingman, a warning to the guys that none of them would be escorting Trinity home, however noble their intentions.

I'm a good drinker. Well, not "good" in the sense I can hold my liquor. I absolutely cannot. I just become someone different, someone fun and funny and vastly more entertaining than sober Hannah. Being drunk doesn't just lower my inhibitions—it atomically annihilates them while never destroying my common sense. All the clever and cool retorts I'd normally think but never say? They actually come out of my mouth. Plenty of silly non- sense, too, but never anything cruel.

So, I'm in the college pub with the guys, downing a fizzy pink something—that's how I order drinks: just give me a fizzy pink something or a blue sour whatever. Bartenders either love me or hate me. This one thinks I'm adorable, and I suspect there are more than two shots in my drink. One minute I'm expounding on this show *Drunk History* and the next I'm riffing on a *Drunk Physics* version of it, and the guys are laughing so hard they're snorting beer. Even Trinity chuckles as she sips her wine cocktail.

Then Rory says, "You should totally do that. Put it on YouTube."

"Be my guest," I say.

"No, *you*, Hannah." Liu waves an unsteady finger in my face. "You and Trin. Together. You'd rack up the views. You're hilarious, and Trin's . . . Well, Trin's Trin."

Trinity is gorgeous. That's what he means. She looks like Hollywood's idea of a physics doctoral student, the sort who makes actual physics majors roll their eyes because, come on, we don't look like that. Except Trinity does. Long curly black hair, huge amber eyes, a slender but curvy body. I'm embarrassed to admit that the first time I saw her in class, I almost offered to help her find her room because she was clearly in the wrong place.

"So, *Drunk Physics*, huh?" Trinity says. "How would that work?"

"You guys drink," Liu says. "A lot. You get wasted, and then you try to explain a physics concept and post the result on a YouTube channel."

"It *would* be hilarious," Rory says. "You should do it, Hannah." The other guys take up a chant of "Do it! Do it!" banging the scarred table. I roll my eyes. Trinity shrugs and says, "Sure, why not."

I look at her. "Seriously?"

A soft smile. "Seriously. It'd be fun." And so *Drunk Physics* was born.

Six months later

I wake on the couch, groaning and reaching for my water bottle, which I've learned to put on the table before we start filming.

As I chug lukewarm water, Trinity's figure sways in front of me. She's seated at the desk, and she isn't actually swaying—that's just me.

Trinity's gaze is fixed on a massive computer screen where my drunken image gestures wildly. Thankfully, the sound is off. It's last night's *Drunk Girl Physics* episode. Yes, we had a name change. Apparently, *Drunk Physics* wasn't as original as I thought. We decided to play on the element that made our show unique. *Drunk Girl Physics*. *DGP* to its fans, and to my everlasting shock, we actually have those. A lot.

Six months ago, Trinity and I started with a laptop and a cheap microphone. Now we have this ginormous computer monitor, connected to a top-of-the-line laptop, professional-grade cameras and microphones, all courtesy of Webizode.com, a startup channel for web series. We began on YouTube, but that was an exercise in humility. Oh, we got traffic—thanks to incredibly kind shout-outs from a few stars in the science-web-series biz—but we also got the kind of attention no one wants. For Trinity, that was endless chatter asking her to show some body part or another. For me, it was the opposite.

Don't undress, please, Hannah.

Well, it's a good thing she's funny, 'cause no one would be watching her otherwise.

Despite a rocketing viewership—and actual income—we'd been ready to quit, deciding no amount of money was worth the humiliation. Then Webizode came along, offering us a home with awesome comment moderation. They gave us the equipment, too, plus promotion, exposure, and enough income for Trinity and me to leave grad-school housing. We found this gorgeous old house to rent, and yes, Trinity swears she gets spooky vibes from it, but honestly, I think she'd say that about any house more than twenty years old.

While we loved having our own house, it was Webizode's moderation we appreciated most. Still, the morning after our latest upload, Trinity is scrolling through comments, ready to hit our personal report button if anything slipped through.

"All good?" I croak as I rise from the couch, the floor tilting underfoot.

She doesn't turn. "That was a really shitty thing to do, Hannah."

"Wh-what?" I blink and stagger to the desk as my head and stomach spin . . . in opposite directions, of course.

God, I need to drink less for these videos. Except that's the point, as

Webizode pointed out when I tried subbing water for half my vodka shots. Our fans noticed and were not impressed, and neither was Webizode.

In six months, I've exhausted every hangover remedy on the planet. The only thing that helps is having a full stomach pretaping and then drinking enough water afterward that I might as well sleep in the bathroom. I may have actually done that once or twice. I look down at Trinity, my lurching brain struggling to remember why I'm here.

Oh, right.

"What'd I do?" I say.

She turns on the volume and hits *Play* on the frozen video.

I'm saying, "The prevailing theory of time is that it moves in a straight line, like this." I demonstrate with an empty shot glass, which does not move in any actual semblance of "straight."

"Which means that to travel through time, you'd need to . . ." I did something on-screen with the two empty glasses.

I groan. "Time travel? Really?"

On-screen, I continue drunkenly explaining concepts that I don't even understand sober.

"But that presumes that time is orderly, when it could actually be," my drunken self says, and then launches into a Doctor Who quote about time being like a ball of "*wibbly-wobbly, timey-wimey stuff.*"

"What?" on-screen Trinity says.

I continue to quote the show with, "*Things don't always happen in the right order.*"

Trinity hits *Stop* and glares at me. I sink into a chair and blink at the screen. Then I blink at her.

"I made a fool of myself," I say. "Situation normal. But I'm not seeing what . . ."

She jabs a finger at a section of the comments.

trekgal98: Twenty points to Hannah for the Doctor Who refs!

larrybarry: And they both zoomed right over Trinity's head.

trekgal98: Are you surprised?

larrybarry: LOL

It seems like an innocuous exchange. It *is* innocuous—all comments pass through Webizode's moderation. Profanity is removed. Insults and innuendo are blocked. Trinity, though, cannot help scraping away those layers of idle comments to find the insult hidden within, and she's found it here as she always does when I make a geek-culture reference that she doesn't get.

"You promised to stop doing that," she says.

I throw up my hands. "I'm drunk, and I'm blathering nonsense."

"You do it on purpose. You know our audience, and you play to them, and you make me look like an idiot."

"Not watching a TV show hardly makes you an idiot, Trin. In fact, it makes you smart. Unlike me, you don't waste your study hours watching Netflix."

"Because I need to study. You don't. You're a freaking genius." And that's what it comes down to. What it always comes down to. Trinity has decided t at I'm smarter than her and that our Webizode audience prefers me. She's . . . not wrong.

Damn it. I hate saying that. I've gotten to know Trinity much better in the last six months, and I consider her a friend. Yet the more I get to know her, the less I envy her. Yes, she's gorgeous. Smart, too, or she wouldn't be in our doctoral program. But she has an insecure core that desperately needs to be more than a pretty face. She is accustomed to being the center of attention, and when the spotlight slides my way, she deflates, her anxieties twisting into anger that homes in on me, as if I've stolen that spotlight from her.

"I didn't mean it, Trin," I say evenly. "You know that. I'm making a fool of myself." I wave at the screen. "Time travel? I don't even know what I'm saying there. Lunatic fringe."

"They love it," she says. "Check the stats."

I peer at the counter and frown. The episode has been up for fewer than eight hours, and it's already gotten more views than last week's.

"That can't be about me babbling incoherent sci-fi references," I say. "There must be something else."

I zoom through the comments. I don't get far before I find what I'm looking for, and I groan anew. Then I fast-forward the video. About halfway through our segment, a dim light appears over Trinity's shoulder. It gradually becomes brighter until there is very clearly a translucent amorphous blob hovering there.

"Ghost," I say.

"What?"

I point at the shape. "This is a ghostly orb. At least, it is according to our viewers."

Trinity reads the comments and then squints at the screen. "That thing?"

"Hey, you're the one who said this place was haunted. There's your proof."

She gives me a hard look. "I said this house gave me a weird feeling, and you're never going to let me forget that, are you?"

I tap the screen. "Looks like a ghost to me."

She rolls her eyes. "It's light glare. Even I know that."

"Well, more clicks will make Webizode happy." I shut off the monitor. "I'll make you a deal. I won't bug you about ghosts again, and you won't bug me about time travel."

"Fair enough. You want the shower first?"

"I want coffee first. And after." I purse my lips. "Think I can rig the brewer up to the nozzle and shower in it?"

She rolls her eyes and heads for the bathroom.

The orb is back. It's right where it was in the last segment, hovering over Trinity's shoulder.

I'd set my alarm to get up before Trinity could check our latest episode. I wasn't looking for the orb. I'd forgotten all about it. I just wanted to comment-skim, make sure I hadn't said anything else to upset her.

After the last episode, I emailed our contact at Webizode and asked whether they could delete any future comments on my geek-culture references. They refused. It'd be a game of Whack-A-Mole, really. Delete one, and another commenter would gleefully jump in, thinking they were the first to recognize it, claiming whatever cosmic cookies the universe awarded for that.

I knew Webizode would refuse. That was just my opening gambit, so they'd be more likely to agree when I asked them to instead delete comments about Trinity failing to recognize my references. While they said yes, I was still checking.

I only get through the first page before someone mentions the orb. I check, and sure enough, there it is.

It seems . . . brighter? No, clearer. It looks like a reflection of the moon, a pale sphere with cratered shadows. There's only one window in this room, though, and it's behind the camera with a permanently closed blackout blind to avoid light cast by passing cars.

I read the comments.

schrodingers_cow: I see a face in the orb. Don't you?

jazzhands1999: Uh, no. I see the reflection of a light bulb.

kalebsmom: That's not a light bulb. It's an orb. And I see a face, too. Zoom in. Eyes. Mouth. Nose. It's all there.

I blow the video up to full screen. Yes, there are dark blotches approximately where you'd find eyes and a mouth, but it's like spotting dragon-shaped clouds. People see what they want, and apparently, they want ghosts.

I keep scrolling through comments. Some are about our episode, but more and more are about the orb, people new to our channel tuning in just for that.

I won't argue with a little publicity, though I'd rather it were for the actual show. As our marketing team at Webizode says, it doesn't matter why people come—just get them there, present a good product, and some will stay. Which is probably why Webizode hasn't argued about the high heating bills that keep Trinity in tank tops year-round.

I'm popping two aspirin when Trinity comes downstairs as fresh and bright-eyed as ever.

"Your ghost has returned," I say as I swivel the keyboard her way. "Sorry, our ghost. According to the comments, it now has a face."

"What?" She seems genuinely startled, and I chastise myself for joking around. She believes in this stuff. I hurry on to tell her that I do not see a face in what is obviously a lighting glitch.

As she skims the comments, I say, "So the question is whether we investigate the anomaly or not."

She pales. "Investigate a ghost? I hope you're kidding, Hannah. You don't mess with that sort of thing."

"I mean investigate the real cause of the light. What's causing the reflection. Do we embrace our scientist credo and conduct a ghost-busting investigation . . . or do we let people keep thinking it's a ghost if that bumps our stats."

She doesn't answer. She's stopped on a section of comments. When I turn to head into the kitchen, she says, "I thought you went through these."

"I did."

"And you weren't going to mention this?" Her nail stabs the screen, making the image shudder.

I read the comments.

gonegirl5: You see me, don't you? I know you do.

gonegirl5: Did you really think you'd get away with it?

"Yeah," I say. "I read that. Random bullshit. I don't know how it got through moderation. Sometimes I wonder whether there's a real person monitoring it or just a bot looking for key words."

"Webizode said it's a real person. They guaranteed that in our contract."

"Then it's an intern looking for key words, and since those comments don't have any, they ignored them. I'll mention it to them."

After the next episode, I wake to Trinity shaking me hard enough that I jolt upright with an uncharacteristic snarl.

"Could you not do that?" I mutter as I sit up, rubbing my eyes.

"You weren't waking," she says. "You're still drunk."

"Yeah, that's what six shots of tequila will do to a girl. We need to stop accepting those damn challenges."

I'm grumbling, but the truth is that I watered my shots, and as a result, I'm barely hungover. Trinity has been on edge. Yesterday, I made the mistake of glancing sidelong at the new clubbing dress she planned to wear on camera. I was eyeing the tiny sheath of shimmering fabric, thinking, "Damn, I wish I could wear that," but she took my look as criticism, and we had to delay the taping while she changed. I watered down my tequila while she was gone, knowing it wouldn't take much to set her off again.

I glance at our stats. Fifty percent more views. Double the comments. Triple the link shares.

"Ugh," I say. "Casper must be back."

"I'm glad you find this amusing. How about this?" She points at two comments.

gonegirl5: You thought I was gone, didn't you? You thought you got away with it.

gonegirl5: I'm dead, and it's your fault, and I'm going to make sure everyone knows.

I snicker.

Trinity slowly turns on me. "You think *everything's* funny, don't you, Hannah?"

"No. I do, however, think this is funny." I intone the comments in an ominous voice. "It's B-movie dialogue. *I know what you did last summer.* I'm actually surprised it doesn't say that. Maybe it'd be too on the nose."

"Someone is accusing me of being responsible for their death, Hannah. That is not, in any way, amusing."

"You?" I read the comments again. "I don't see anything saying these are about you, Trin."

She points at the orb. Is it clearer now? It *seems* clearer. I definitely see what looks like eyes and a—

I shake that off. The power of suggestion. "Still not seeing why this is about you," I say.

"It's over *my* shoulder. The ghost is always right there, next to me."

"Trinity," I say, as carefully as I can. "That is not a ghost. It's a lighting anomaly. One person decides it's an orb, and suddenly everyone sees spooks, and then someone's gotta take it to the next level and accuse us of murder."

"It doesn't say 'murder.' It just says we're responsible."

"Maybe that's why the comment moderation didn't pick it up. It lacks whatever words are on the intern's watch list. I'll report it." I hit a few keys. "And now we'll prove this is not a ghostly orb. It isn't worth a bump in stats if it upsets you."

"You think I'm overreacting."

"No, I think it's understandably unsettling," I say evenly as I pull up the original video. "I'll find out what's going on, and our next show will be spook-free."

"It's not there," Trinity whispers.

In front of us, the screen is divided into two panels. One shows the online show from two weeks ago, paused where the orb is clearest. The other window is a direct feed from the camera, stopped at the same spot.

There is no orb on the original video.

I'd started with last night's show. When I didn't find the orb there, I went back to the previous show. Same thing. Now I'm at the first one. There is undeniably an orb in the online version and not even a hint of stray light in the original.

At a noise, I look over to see Trinity gripping the mouse, her hand trembling so much it chitters against the desktop.

"Hey," I say, squeezing her arm. "This is good news. It means the orb didn't originate at our end. There's definitely no ghost. Someone tampered with the online version."

She glances at me, her eyes blank.

"Someone tampered with the episodes," I say again, slower. "It's happening on the back end. At Webizode. They're screwing with our uploaded video."

"Why would they do that?"

"For the views," I say, stopping myself before I add "obvi- ously."
"It's someone's idea of a marketing ploy. They're probably also responsible for the original comments, identifying the orb as a ghost. Interns,
right? Some sixteen-year-old marketing exec wannabe who's trying to
wow the boss with a creative scheme."

Trinity nods dully. "Okay."

"We have to—" My phone rings. Webizode's number fills the screen.
"Perfect timing. Let me handle this. An intern is about to be sacked."

I'm not nearly as badass on the phone call. I'm polite and calm. Our
contact—Oscar—is touching base about the comment I flagged, but I
want to talk about the video first. I explain that I've examined the original video, and there's no sign of an orb. Then I pause to let that sink in.

He's quiet long enough that I'm about to prod, when he speaks in
that way of his that I'm sure he thinks is gentle but is patronizing as hell.
Is that what Trinity hears when I address her concerns? Shit. I'll need to
be more careful. There's a fine line between "gentle" and "patronizing,"
and I might be straying as far over it as Oscar is.

"I know you girls are very invested in the success of your show,
Hannah," he says. "We all are. But I might suggest that if you have
marketing ideas, you run them past our team first. That's what we're
here for."

"Marketing ideas?"

"Your brand is science," he says in that same slow, patronizing way.
"You are both brilliant girls, and even while inebriated, you explain
complex concepts in a way that's both enlightening and entertaining.
You have a great package, and you don't need to muddy it with . . ." He
pauses, as if struggling for words. "Off-brand theatrics."

"You think we're doing this? I just said it's not on our uploaded—"

"I know you've seen a jump in stats, but you're attracting the wrong
kind of viewers, ones who will dilute your brand."

"We aren't—"

"We've noticed you girls haven't discussed the orb on camera, and
we weren't sure you realized it was there. We were debating whether to

tell you to adjust your lighting. If it's a marketing ploy, though? That would be a violation of your contract."

"We didn't put it there. We don't *want* it there. The fact that it's not on the original means it's coming from the other end of the process."

A long pause. "You think *we're* doing this?"

"I don't actually care. Just make it stop. It's upsetting—" I glance at Trinity, who's listening in. "Upsetting *us*. Now, what I originally messaged about is something else that's upsetting us. Those comments. I'm presuming the fact that they don't actually say 'murder' gets them past comment moderation. Your moderator needs to be more careful."

"That's why I was calling, Hannah. To discuss the comments. They're bypassing moderation."

"Exactly. Whoever is moderating is letting them—"

"No, I mean they're *bypassing* moderation. And the only account that can do that is the one you two share."

"Sure, our account isn't moderated but . . . Wait. Are you suggesting—?"

Trinity hits the Speaker button. "Oscar? Trinity here. Are you saying someone posted those comments from *our* computer?"

"Yes," he says.

"The call is coming from inside the house," I intone. She glares at me.

"That means someone's hacked our account," I say. Oscar doesn't reply.

"Track the IP address," I say. "Find out where exactly those comments came from."

More silence.

"You already have, haven't you?" I say carefully.

"Yes."

And I don't need to ask what he found.

The call really did come from inside the house.

After I end the call with Oscar, I text Rory. Thirty minutes later, he's at our place, dissecting the videos and the comments for signs of tampering. Rory might be a physics postgrad, but his area of expertise is quantum computing . . . and he did his share of hacking in his misspent youth.

If Trinity doesn't match anyone's idea of a physics doctoral student, Rory is a walking stereotype, effortlessly managing to convey both computer geek and science nerd wound in a double helix. He's not much taller than me, slight and reedy. His saving grace is his hair, which is an adorable boy-band mop of dark curls. Today he's wearing a "Super Jew" T-shirt and blue jeans that I'm pretty sure he irons—he might even starch them. That sounds less than complimentary, but to me, guys like Rory really are superheroes in disguise—sweet, funny, smart as hell, packaged in a way that lets them pass under the radar of girls like Trinity. I do not fail to notice how fast Rory replied to my SOS, even on a Sunday morning, and I won't pretend I'm not pleased by that.

After an hour of work, Rory leans back in the swivel chair and adjusts his glasses. "I don't know what to tell you, Hannah."

"The truth?"

"That I can't find any sign of outside tampering. I don't know how those orbs are getting on the video, but it seems to be the same one you've uploaded. No one is taking it down, tweaking it and putting it up again. As for the comments, everything indicates that they really did come from this computer."

I swear under my breath. Then I say, "It's not me."

"You'd hardly call me in to investigate if it was. The real culprit must be . . ." His eyes cut toward the back of the house.

"I don't think it's Trin, either. She's really freaked out by all this."

"Hmm." He eyes the closed door again and lowers his voice. "Trin likes attention, and since you guys switched to Webizode, you're the one getting it. You're the cool, quirky science geek. Trin is the window dressing. The straight man to your comedian." He lowers his voice even more. "Does she know you've been fielding offers for solo projects?"

"I delete those as soon as they come in. Trin and I were having trouble even before this. She thinks I'm mocking her with my geek-culture references and . . ." I sigh. "Managing her moods is harder than I expected."

"Mm-hmm."

I turn back to the computer. "She's going to think I'm doing this. How do I convince her I'm not?"

"By ending the show."

When I stiffen, he says, "It started as a lark. But between Trinity's bullshit and the weekly hangovers, you're not having fun anymore. You already have job offers—real job offers in your field just waiting for you to graduate. You don't need this show, Hannah."

"Trinity does. It means a lot to her. Both the exposure and the money."

"Which is not a good reason for you to continue, when she's the reason you're miserable."

"We're fine," I say, taking the keyboard and busying myself checking comments.

"You said Trinity is really freaked out by those comments," he says. "Does that seem like an overreaction?" He leans in, his dark eyes twinkling with amusement. "Maybe our Trin is a secret killer, tormented by her guilty conscience."

I groan.

"You did say she believes in ghosts," he says. "Maybe she's convinced her past has literally come back to haunt her."

He starts making ghost noises, and I laugh, telling him to cut it out. That's when Trinity walks in. She looks from me to Rory.

"Did I just hear you two talking about ghosts?" she says.

"Uh, no, we—" I begin.

"You were making fun of me, weren't you, Hannah."

Rory rolls his chair between us. "No, I was joking about ghosts, and Hannah was telling me to stop." He gets to his feet. "I have a lab this morning, and I need to run. First, though . . ." He reaches into his backpack and hands me a wrapped mug. "Almost forgot this."

I unroll the paper to find a Doctor Who mug with the "timey-wimey stuff" quote I'd paraphrased on the show. As I laugh, I catch Trinity's expression.

I quickly rewrap the mug. "I'll put this in my room."

She snatches the mug and sticks it on the desk, facing the camera, with "There" and a defiant look my way. Rory counters with a narrowed-eyes glare, but Trinity doesn't notice, just plunks herself into the chair with, "So, did you find any evidence of tampering?"

So these comments came from our account. From our computer. And they're being posted after Trinity goes upstairs to bed and I am alone, sleeping it off on the couch.

I'm the logical culprit. Trinity isn't buying my protests and excuses. She's convinced I'm responsible, and I need to fix that.

I keep thinking of what Rory said about Trinity seeming suspiciously freaked out. His comment about her having murdered someone was a joke. And yet . . .

The more paranoid Trinity becomes, the more I wonder whether there is something in her past to warrant it. Not that she's actually killed anyone. But whenever I slip and say we're being accused of murder, she's always quick to clarify that the comments never say that. Only that one of us is *responsible* for a death.

I'd joked about *I Know What You Did Last Summer*, in which a group of teens accidentally hit and kill a pedestrian. What if there's something like that in Trinity's past?

It doesn't even need to be that dramatic. I'd been at summer camp with a girl who drowned, and I still feel guilty for not noticing her go under the water . . . even if a dozen other kids and three counselors didn't notice, either. Survivor guilt, my mom calls it.

Someone could know that Trinity feels guilty over an accidental death and be trolling her. Tormenting her. If there's something in Trinity's past—connected to those comments or not—it'd help me understand her paranoia.

I conduct my search in the library. If the public computers weren't crammed with undergrads, I'd have used those to better hide my search history. Is *that* paranoid? Maybe, but I need only to imagine Trinity discovering what I've searched, and my back tenses, triggering an ache that suggests I've been more stressed lately than I like to admit.

I think of what Rory said, about quitting the show. I'd be fine with that. I might even be relieved. My parents are both corporate researchers, and while we're hardly rich, I don't need the show income—I've been stashing it in a savings account. Also, I'm really tired of the drinking. The occasional pub night with friends used to be fun. Now I nurse a Coke . . . or blow off the invitations altogether.

The problem is Trinity. I can't be the bitch who takes away a critical source of income. And maybe I won't need to be, because I find the answer to my question a lot faster than I imagined.

In high school, Trinity was blamed for the suicide of a bullied classmate.

My gut clenches reading that. I won't pretend that I don't know what it's like to be bullied. I mostly flew too far under the radar to attract attention, but there was one girl in high school who decided I was a vastly underappreciated and overlooked target. Even today, I'll tense seeing her first name online.

Trinity isn't named in the actual articles about her classmate's suicide. They only refer to bullying by "an unnamed sixteen-year-old classmate who has not been charge at this time." It's social media that fingers Trinity as the perpetrator, and even there, while no one disputes she's the one accused, they hotly debate her guilt. The short version is this: When Trinity was sixteen, a classmate—Vanessa Lyons—committed suicide. In her note, she alleged ongoing and systematic harassment by Trinity, who had been her best friend in middle school. Vanessa claimed Trinity had dumped her as a friend after becoming a cheerleader and joining the popular clique. When Vanessa tried to maintain a civil relationship, Trinity turned on her, bullying and berating her until depression claimed Vanessa's life.

It's a common story that carries the mournful ring of truth. Girls are BFFs, but then one grows into a gorgeous cheerleader and the other . . . does not. Popular girl ditches uncool friend, who flounders, trying to make sense of it, and when she reaches out, popular girl drives her away with insults that lacerate the friend's already paper-thin self-confidence, driving her to a place where suicide seems the only option. In death, she can finally accuse her true killer.

Reading that article, I cannot help but picture the orb behind Trinity. Cannot help but see those messages again.

In death, she can finally accuse her true killer.

I shiver even as I berate myself for it. Vanessa Lyons's ghost has not returned to wreak beyond-the-grave vengeance. Someone else has, though. Someone who blames Trinity.

The problem is that few people *did* seem to blame Trinity. On social media, her friends defended her, insisting Trinity had never said anything unkind about Vanessa in their hearing. Of course they would say that, being her friends. But only a couple of other classmates claimed to have witnessed the bullying, and no one put much stock in their credibility. Most of those blaming Trinity never saw or heard anything—they simply condemned her with variations on "Of course she did it. Girls like her are total bitches."

Reading this and knowing Trinity, I'm not persuaded she's guilty. I do know why she's freaking out, though.

She's convinced Vanessa Lyons has come back to haunt her.

I try to cancel the next episode of *Drunk Girl Physics*. Trinity won't hear of it. The show must go on, apparently. I do convince her to let us switch seats. That way, if the orb appears over me, I'll know it's just a random asshole hacker, nothing to do with the death of Vanessa Lyons.

I set my alarm for seven the next morning to beat Trinity to the comment section. When I wake, I find a text from Rory. He asks me to call him as soon as I wake. The fact he's asking for a call rather than a text means it's urgent.

He picks up on the first ring.

"First, I need to apologize," he says. "I overstepped my bounds and did something that, in retrospect, is going to seem really skeevy. It was for a good reason, though."

"Okay . . ."

"I set up a spy camera on the desk in your office."

"Uh . . ."

He hurries on. "I only activated it after last night's episode went live, and it's focused on the computer. I can't see the rest of the room. I just wanted to monitor the keyboard after you uploaded the show."

"To see which of us was tampering with the film and posting the comments."

"Yes." He exhales, as if in relief that I understand. "Not that I thought it was you. Honestly, I expected to catch Trin."

The hairs on my neck prickle. "But it was me? Drunk sleepwalking?"

"No, no. Nobody tampered with it, Hannah. That's what I wanted to tell you. I have the entire night of tape, and no one came near the desk."

"Okay, is the orb gone, then?"

His hesitation tells me otherwise, and I hurry to the computer. "Two minutes, ten seconds," he says.

I find the spot. As I watch, the orb manifests over Trinity's seated form.

"Shit," I say.

"You switched spots," he says. "That was a good idea."

"No," I say. "It was actually really stupid. Now she's going to see that and—"

"See what?" says a voice behind me. I wheel as Trinity walks in. She stops. "Who are you talking to, Hannah?"

"J-just Rory." Did I stammer? Why the hell did I stammer?

Her gaze slides to the screen, and she blanches. I mumble something to Rory and hang up.

"Someone's hacking the system," I say quickly. "That's what Rory was calling about. He put a camera in here and—"

"He put a spy camera in our house?"

"He apologized. He could only see this desk, and he only turned it on after we posted the show. He was watching in case I was posting the comments in my sleep or something."

"Or *something*?" Her voice hardens. "He was trying to catch me. Except he didn't. He caught you. That's why he called. He installed a secret camera and caught you doing it, and he called to warn you. He thought he was going to catch me, and instead, he caught the girl he likes. That puts him in a really nasty position."

"I didn't do anything, Trinity," I say. "Ask Rory."

"He'll lie for you."

"Then ask him to show you the tape."

"He'll have erased it by now."

"What the hell?" I stop myself and take a deep breath. "Explain why I'd do this to you. Why I'd undermine our show like this."

"You're not undermining it. Our show is more popular than ever, and you don't want to ruin it—you want it all for yourself. You want me to quit."

"No. I'd quit myself before I—"

"Do you think I haven't seen those solo offers? They send them to our damn show address. I find them in the trash folder."

"I delete them because I'm not interested. If I wanted you off the show, Trinity, I sure as hell wouldn't do something as silly as this."

"It's not silly. It's clever, and you're always clever, Hannah. You know I believe in ghosts. You know I've said this house has a weird vibe. You found out about my past, didn't you? What I was accused of. You used that to fake a very public haunting. An on-screen haunting, complete with accusatory comments. You're hoping I'll quit. If that doesn't work, then eventually someone will dig up my past and humiliate me, forcing me off your show."

I take a deep breath. "Yes, I know about Vanessa. I found out yesterday. You were freaking out, and it worried me, and I had to investigate. Whether or not you bullied her—"

"I didn't." She spits the words and steps up to my face. "She bullied me."

I open my mouth.

Trinity continues. "You don't believe that, do you? No one did. Obviously, the pretty, popular girl was the bully. That's why you don't even bother to name me in those comments. Everyone will presume it's me. Geeky little Hannah wouldn't bully anyone. But Trinity? Oh, yes, she's just the type."

"I know you and Vanessa stopped being friends—"

"Because she was a nasty, vicious *bitch*, always putting me down to pull herself up. I made new friends, and Vanessa couldn't handle that. She came at me all the harder, posting from anonymous accounts, telling people I was a slut, a two-faced bitch, anorexic, all the things that kids are quick to believe about someone who looks like me."

"And then she . . . killed herself?"

Trinity laughs. It's an ugly, raw laugh. "Oh, she didn't mean to. That's the irony. Vanessa was like you—a clever girl who always had a plan. She wrote a suicide note blaming me, and then she took just enough pills to be rushed to the hospital for a good stomach pumping. Except she passed out from the sleeping pills and choked to death on her own vomit. Joke's on her. Only it wasn't, because the school believed her suicide note. Zero tolerance for bullying. It didn't matter that they had absolutely no proof. I had to go live with my aunt so I could attend a new school. I spent the rest of high school on depression meds and suicide watch. The fact I'm here—getting my PhD, no less—is a freaking miracle."

"No," I say. "It's a sign of hard work and resilience. What happened to you was shitty, Trin, but—"

"Oh, spare me your patronizing bullshit, Hannah. You're gingerly patting me on the head like a rabid rottweiler who has you cornered. I'm not going to hurt you. But I am going to make sure you don't get away with this. I'll prove you're behind the orbs and the comments."

"Sure. Go for it. You may find your efforts hampered by the small fact that I didn't actually do anything but—"

She wheels on me. "You aren't going to give up, are you? You're determined to make me look like a fool."

"Nope, actually, right now, I'm just determined to end this conversation, go out and enjoy my Sunday while you dig for evidence you're never going to find. I've tried to be reasonable, Trin, to pussyfoot around your paranoia. If anyone is behind this, it's you." I start to step past her. "If this is a cry for attention, I'm not listening anymore."

She grabs my arm. "Don't you dare—"

I wheel to throw her off, and she flings me. My stockinged feet slide on the hardwood. When I stumble, she shoves me with all her might. I fly backward, feet sailing out from under me, head striking the desk edge.

The last thing I see is Trinity, staring in wide-eyed horror as I crumple to the floor.

I wake on the office floor, my head throbbing. I grab the chair, which of course wheels away, and I sprawl face-first onto the hardwood.

"Trin?" I manage to croak.

There's no answer. I lift my head and peer around an empty office. There's blood on the floor, and when I touch the back of my head, I feel sticky, wet hair. I wince as my fingers brush a gash in my scalp.

Blinking hard, I grab the desk edge and pull myself up. I'm standing in front of the computer monitor. On the screen is Trinity with that orb behind her. Except what was an orb is now changing into a very clear figure.

A ghostly figure standing behind Trinity. Standing right where I am. Below it, there's a new comment.

gonegirl5: You killed me, as surely as if you'd bashed my head into that desk.

No.

That's not . . .

It can't be. It makes no sense.

And yet . . .

I swallow hard. When I look at the figure again, I can make out long dark hair and what looks like a pale T-shirt. In the reflection of that screen, I see myself . . . with long dark hair and a gray tee.

I am the ghost behind Trinity. I am the ghost accusing her. Not Vanessa Lyons.

Me.

But that isn't possible. We saw the orb three weeks ago. The comments started three weeks ago. How could I be the one . . . ? My gaze shifts to the mug prominently displayed on the screen. The *Doctor Who* mug from Rory, with the time travel quote I'd said on the show.

Things don't always happen in the right order . . .

Footsteps thunder down the hallway. "Hannah? Hannah!"

It's Rory.

Oh God, Rory. He's about to race in and find my body. I spin, as if I can stop him, but he's already frozen in the doorway, his gaze on the floor. Then it lifts to me.

"Sit," he says, rolling the chair toward me. "You hit your head, and there's blood . . . Damn it! Where the hell is Trinity? Did she just shove you down and take off?"

"You can see me?"

His brow furrows. "Of course I can . . ." He sputters a ragged laugh. "How badly did you hit your head, Hannah? No, you're not a ghost. Sit down for a minute, and then we're getting you to the hospital."

As he puts me in the chair, he explains that he saw part of the fight on the hidden camera. Without any sound, he only caught a glimpse of Trinity pushing me, in the screen reflection. Then he saw me crumple to the floor. He caught an Uber and spent twenty minutes banging on the door before breaking in through a back window.

"Fucking Trinity," he mutters. "I hope this is the hint you need, Hannah. She's no friend of yours, and you have to get out before . . ."

He trails off, his gaze fixed on something behind me. I turn to see he's looking at blood on the floor, a pool of it creeping from behind the desk.

I'm about to say that's just mine. Then I realize it's in the wrong spot—I fell on the other side of the desk, and this is a pool of blood, trickling along a crack between the floorboards.

That's when I see Trinity's sneaker.

I bolt up from the chair so fast my head lurches. Rory grabs my arm to steady me. Then we make our way to the desk. There, on the other side, sits Trinity, holding her slashed wrists on her lap. Dead eyes stare at us.

There's a note by her leg. I pick it up as Rory hurries to check for a pulse that I know he won't find.

I skim the note. It's barely legible, a crazed rant about my trick with the orb and the comments, how I tried to drive her off, and we argued, and I fell, and Trinity knew everyone would blame her, just as they did with Vanessa.

"She thought she killed me," I whisper.

"What?" Rory takes the note and skims it. "Wow. I knew she was unstable, but she lost it. She totally lost it."

He's still talking. I don't hear him. I'm staring at the screen as that figure behind Trinity slowly comes into focus. It's a slender young woman with long dark hair. I see the ghost's shirt—a pale blue V-neck. My gaze goes to Trinity's body . . . wearing a pale blue V-neck.

That's when the comments begin to scroll.

gonegirl5: You're alive, and I'm not, and that's your fault, Hannah.

gonegirl5: Everyone's going to know what you did to me.

gonegirl5: I'll make sure of it.

CALL THEM CHILDREN

WENMIMAREBA KLOBAH COLLINS

On this island we like to die slowly. Generationally.

At the other side of the counter, Mamá stirs sancocho with the candlelight drawing tenderness onto her features. "I am lucky to have you," she says, "Mi tesoro."

It is, really, all she ever says anymore.

It worries her, the soundlessness when we go out. There are no children. Or barely any. No children on the docks, tangled in the mangroves, skittering like fiddler crabs and calling out to one another. None at the colmado ordering papaya juice. Schools run empty. People have gotten scared. And restless. And superstitious in that way that no one talks about but are aware of like a weary tide. I see it in the way she looks at me now, with sallow skin and shifting eyes: the desire to keep me close—to swallow me, if she could. Keep me in the pit of her stomach as something intrinsically hers. It frightens me, a bit. But it is enough for me to scoff at her words and shake my head with a mocking smile. In these in-between moments of candlelight, soft curls of tongue, and the heady smell of childhood spice, it is almost too intimate.

I push off from the stool. The damp floorboards carry my weight like a burden.

It's been five days since I've seen Camelia, and this is five days too many.

The door gives to a humid outdoors, the shift in temperature prickling my skin with sweat. Bare feet on the mangrove bark—pelicans up in the crow's nest of canopy—and, just below the water surface, the glimmer of fish. Further down, below sight, there must be some street, I know, but it has been years since I've seen one.

I reach down, trail fingers in the water, splash my legs against the persistence of mosquitoes. We practically walk on water these days when we climb our way across a nervous system of mangroves and ex-skyscrapers turned merely superficial rooftops. Five years of monsoon will do that to a place—drown it and soak it to the marrow. Leave it gasping and doggy-paddling its mouth right at the surface of waves. It didn't take much. Puerto Rico's metropolis was always teetering at nature's maw. Now it hovers: un hombro, una oreja, a hip-bone buoyed in the water.

Camelia's house is a bower bird's home—an interwoven nook in walking trees. The seedpods hang and sway like wind chimes.

"Camelia!" I call, rubbing my finger pads against the perpetually bark-shaped bruising on my callused hands. My feet are equally sore—leather soles on the flats from years of natural jungle-gymming the island.

"Camelia—" I repeat, at the door now. I sink to my ankles in the compact sand, wipe the back of my hand against my forehead.

It takes a while, minutes, for her mother to answer the door quietly. Small, in the way she is not, not usually, she looks up at me with that same consuming desire that inhabits my mother's face.

"Sra. Rodríguez?" I ask, uncertain and a bit like I've lost my footing. Losing your footing can be deadly here—here where we live on the brink of suffocation. Her knuckles are white with the clench of her grip on the door, as if she is avoiding this exact thing.

Her dark, dark eyes linger mutely on my face for a few seconds before she nods and turns away from me, pulling her mundillo shawl tighter around her. Her hands clutch it close, at her chest. It's almost like watching a blind fledgling bumble through the traitorous landscape that surrounds it, the way she navigates the house. Like a duppy's moved everything three inches to the left and there is foreign topography in the layout of a home that should be well-known to the hands that shaped it.

Sra. Rodriguez sits at the foot of a small, circular window. The glass' frame has become completely interwoven with the ever-questing root system of the mangrove. The musk of damp earth, of layer upon layer of salt, of adobo y plátanos—of warmth—stays tacky at the back of my throat. It makes it hard to breathe—hard to speak.

"Where is—" I clear my throat. "Where is Camelia?" I ask finally, settled across from her in one of the rattan chairs, my legs pulled up and my arms crossed over them. She casts her dreamy eyes about the room and hums. There is a languid late-ness to her expressions as if life itself has slowed for her. I shift in the chair. Ghosts of her hands, and her boisterous laugh, and her cheerful lightness-of-step linger in the walls—but the woman herself is a golem.

"Ah," she says. "I didn't—get you the, the tea." Feigned forgetfulness. She and Camelia don't drink tea.

"I don't need tea," I murmur, watching her begin to push herself to her feet. She sags back into the couch with a heavy exhale.

"Ah. You don't need tea." She nods as if confirming a fact to herself. The silence stretches tenuously between us with each breath. I run my hands over the scars on my palms—scales. I think they look like scales. It would be nice to have scales, as a fish might, but they look more like the corrugated hide of a crocodile. It would be nice to tell Camelia that.

I lift my head to peer at Sra. Rodríguez, but she's already looking straight at me.

"Por casualidad, ¿has visto a los otros hoy? The other children?" she asks slowly. I shake my head with a small frown. Not many to see. Not anymore. "Veo. Pues, it's good you are safe. At least."

The stillness of the house is unwelcoming—unsettling.

"And—Camelia? Has she seen others?" I brave, lowering one leg and grazing my foot to-and-fro over the uneven flooring. Such questions are best left unvoiced. Our numbers are less in some ways—more in others. Some can't be counted as children. At least, this is what Mamá says. All I know is that there are some houses that are missing occupants, and that the cracked chalkboard at the town council meetings has more names struck off it each week.

"No. We don't see others, outside of city council. And my Cami would not walk the marsh that far." Sra. Rodríguez scrubs at her eyes tiredly. "She isn't here, my Cami. She's been—desaparecida. I thought maybe she was with you. I see that is not the case."

I forcefully press the callused pads of my fingers against my scales. "No. That is not the case."

"No," she agrees, pulling some strands of graying hair behind an ear and looking out the window. Smog. Thick and rolling in with the late afternoon.

"Mama Dlo," she says, quiet and child-like in the awkward search for the right words. "She likes children with good, strong singing voices. She's the one that's taking them, ¿sabes? Mi Cami siempre tuvo una voz hermosa."

It is not an insinuation, but it is. It is a murmur heavy with belief—with certainty that Camelia would have been back by now, if not because of Mama Dlo. Despite my skepticism, I feel my chest, my throat, constrict. It's easily dismissible as old woman talk. As misticismo nonsense. And yet, it's true. Camelia's voice was promising. Smog ruined most of our voices, made them ratty, but she'd somehow gotten lucky.

"Sí. Cami siempre tuvo una voz hermosa," I repeat slowly. The words join the marble of smells at the back of my throat, of mothertongue slithering in my ears. I stand up, walk to the window and get up on my toes to look out it. I rub sweaty palms against my thighs. Her breath rattles between us. We can sometimes get inhalers for Sra. Rodríguez, but it's rare. There she goes again with the parranda in her lungs. Asalto!

She wheezes and I hear shifting noises until there are papery fingers at my elbow, guiding me to the door. I realize how heated my skin is when I step outdoors—the humid wind tugging at my clothes as the horizon becomes white with waves of smog.

"Yuya," Sra. Rodríguez says, stops, looks at me. "Yuya," she repeats. It becomes an exercise in waiting—me standing across from her, gnats stinging at my legs, and her heavy eyes that feel a frightful thing to look away from. Something terribly important here that I'm missing. "Te tienes que cuidar." The weight of humidity—her gaze—my feet in the sand.

I stammer. Stop. "Y tú, Paulina. Take care."

It feels wrong to leave her at the doorway. To not usher her in against the sun and the salt—to leave all that hunger at my back. But I am sinking where I stand, and Camelia is missing. No children in that house. Or in many others, aside from mine. No Camelia in the her-shaped space I keep tended in her absence.

Slow is how it makes a place for itself inside me as I walk across the horizon of water and root and moss rock. Hollow non-realization and non-grief because grief is tied to death. But I know that this, whatever it is that makes a home in my throat, is not unlike the pervasive starvation that resides in the gazes of our mothers.

She is not baptized. Camelia is not baptized. Nor am I. But she is not dead, either. If I'm to believe superstition, she's been taken early—stolen—and it is not hard for the thing in my throat to twist a knot against my Adam's apple.

We were not alike in this: the disbelief in the stories passed down to us from our mother's mouths, and their mother's mouths to them, and further back. My mother and Paulina María Rodríguez would sit as the rain spat bullets of water against the zinc roof—back in the old house—back before the flood years. Camelia Ramón Rodríguez and I at their feet, their fingers making quick work of our hair until a farmland of braids was neatly arranged on each of our heads. I was the doubter. I am the doubter, but Camelia is motivation enough to try.

I have to believe that she will still be nearby because she can't have gone far, not with the water unpredictably deep. I have to believe, more than that, that Mama Dlo still has some stray ones left to collect and that she will stay. She will keep them close, all of her children—this is how the stories always go, after all.

Nightfall is the time where these not-things, in-between ones, make a home between the crickets and the warbler frogs.

I have always been the doubter, but my fingers keep drifting to touch at the cross around my neck. I roll the crucifix between my fingers and flick the switch of the flashlight on with the other hand. A dimly-lit night makes the world a shadowed topography: the sea a pool of black and the trees moaning in the high winds. A coot screams out alarm, the sudden ruffling of feathers—an iguana's tail disappearing past the beam I swing in its direction. After a few hours out in the dark, these things become sinister rather than comforting. With no proof of Dlo or Camila anywhere, they become doubly so.

Not quite as sure-footed in the dark, my feet slide off of roots. I scrape my legs, catch my arm on twiggy branches, bat swarms of bugs away from the lens, and then: a clearing.

The brine and heavy mangrove-rot scents fill my lungs—wet, damp, saltine, and corroding things. I set the flashlight up on a rock, widening the beam over the clearing.

The cays around Camila's home are an expansive network, but I know the places she frequents. My fingers seek out the jagged scrapes at the side of the rock. A "C + Y" so haphazardly chipped into the surface. I smile and linger for a moment before I leave outcrop behind in favor of the tide pools at the shore. It is true that Camelia would not walk too far. She was—is—one far more satisfied by the comforts of the indoors.

I've just dipped my finger in the sixth tide pool when a sour, acidic smell joins me. I frown and turn around. *Kchk!* The clash of one marble of discomfort claiming another in the crowded space of my throat. I swallow while returning to the clearing on unsteady feet, and settle my hand next to the flashlight.

Hissing breaths, as if compressed out from large bellows, fill the space. They are massive sounds with weight and presence that arrive far before the body comes into view. I am reminded of when I saw a small snake tangled in branches of mangrove; its sheening scales and the diamond of its head. A thick body slithers through the underbrush, pulling out from between reaching roots and closer to me. She coils up a tree, cocking her inquisitively human face at me, yellow eyes a beacon in the dark. Mama Dlo is no small snake. "Ussssually my children have to go invite ot*hhh*her children before they come to me."

I stare at her in silence, knowing she can hear my heartbeat, taste my fear. I stare and she stares back with slitted eyes, not angry—merely curious.

"I was not. Looking for you, I mean," I reply with a sharp intake of breath. "I was looking for a, uh, friend. A girl."

Her mouth purses into the parody of a smile and she looks at me from beneath her lashes. "A . . . *fffffriend*?"

"Yes."

"That's all?" She croons and I frown at her. The patter of feet, shifting of foliage and scattered titters.

"Yes," I reply again, less firm, less sure, gaze away from her as I notice the new arrivals.

"And?"

"And," I say, slowly, "I think you took her."

A raucous roar of laughter surges up from all sides, children's giggles and mocking amusement. Mama Dlo joins them, shaking her head and sending stray braids tumbling from the loose bun they're tied up in. The douens—unbaptized children, sequestered little ones swaddled in the arms of older ones and all of them stuck in that limbo of not-death, of not yet and not quite—start to peek and crawl their way through the green. Their small backwards feet appear ankle-first in the clearing. Faces obscured by wide-brimmed hats, they sit and fold themselves down onto the ground. Their androgynous bodies go mostly nude, but for the occasional one in a well-worn shirt clearly loved, like the nostalgic souvenir of a place that now goes unvisited.

"I have taken many," she says with casual disinterest and hums, gaze assessing. "But, ye*ssss*, I did take a girl recently."

"She was not dead, not yours to keep."

"They wanted a new one, an older one." She gazes out over the douens in their conicle hats with a smile. "However, if you can identify your friend, you're welcome to take her back." When the smile passes over me it is no longer warm—a field of urchin spine teeth behind two lips parted like a wound.

I turn my back on her and face a gathering of bamboo hats. They shuffle closer, a humming reverberating from them and surging like a current across the bodies. They circle me, closing in as the humming becomes a low singing.

The flashlight skitters across the rock surface and falls to the ground with a crack—batteries expelled, and the clearing left a detail-less void. The approach of the sounds of feet slapping against rock, muddy sediment—I breathe into a narrowing space, reach for the knife I should have brought but didn't. Hands pull me by the clothes, tear at my face with razor nails, hold me by the hand and pull me forward.

"*Brown girl, brown girl in the ring,*" the douens sing delightedly.

I smash my hands, elbows, against the bodies blindly, pushing through the crowd as their chanting grows in volume and the air vibrates. My feet slip in the wet mud and clay—hands shooting out for balance against more formless bodies, fingers slipping against humid shoulders, arms, faces, chests. A foot catches against the root of a mangrove tree and, as I fall, I reach out again only to be met with bark. No bruising this time. It shreds the fleshy crests of my palms; leaves me wheezing and whimpering out a string of babble. The burn of toenails ripped or folded back past the quick, the warm well of blood smearing across the bark, the tremble of limbs and the heavy breathing—enclosing bodies, the sounds of more than fifty children wanting to pull me back with them—smells wet, and saltine, and vitriolic. "*Tra-la-la-la-la.*"

The push off from the tree trunk pitches me into disorientation and I begin to break the rules of a post-flood islander. I run. Running until my feet hit the shore—hit the water.

I fold into myself there, dry-heaving as the salt sears my palms, my legs and feet. But the sound has stopped. Silence. The moon hovers high and out from the canopy's shadow I see my hands staining the sand dark. The grains stick to my palms and I shudder, a percolating in my stomach that goes unfulfilled. I feel sick, but nothing comes out.

No sound, gleaming eyes back in the foliage but no movement closer and I hear Dlo's big snake body crashing through the underbrush, away from me. The scatter of feet follows soon after and when I look up again there are no bamboo hats or vague silhouettes watching over me. My eyes linger on my own feet and I think of Camelia and those children with their backwards feet. Did Mama Dlo snare Camelia's feet in her jaw; have the others hold her struggling body down? Did Dlo whip, snap, re-arrange the feet herself—or did she instruct from afar? The various methods to disjoint at the ankle, the stinging of palms, the phantom whispers—contemplations that follow the heels of night into the dawn.

I consider running. But I am quick to notice I am trapped between land and water. Bobbing, dewy lashes and gleaming eyes—water mummas have been drawn to the shallows. Either the noise, or my blood, has summoned them. They speak to one another rarely, and in non-verbal clicks when they do. All that is visible of them is the top half of their head as they examine me. I cannot see their fish tails, or distended maws, but I know they're there.

I would not run even if I had where to go.

Their vigil keeps me up.

Limbs bogged down by sleeplessness, I stand just as the sky pinkens. My blood has crusted around the grains, the scratches barely scabbed over and stiff with a fine layer of salt. When I return to the treeline of the cay, I see footprints. Haphazard things that slope into giving earth, coming to and going away from the shore. I follow the ones pointed towards the shore into the forest, remembering backwards feet.

They lead me to a field of sleeping bodies: sexless children with their faces tucked up under their bamboo hats. Brown bodies in the low-light. I make myself as quiet as possible, just another night creature as I pick my way through the crowd. It is hard to know Camelia like this. The larger ones are the ones I approach. Peaceful in sleep, their young mouths closed over razor teeth, I dare call them children. My fingers lift the brims of their hats carefully, revealing faces not unlike my own. A field of children at rest.

The hat pushes up from the forehead and luminous eyes peer up at me from beneath the hemline of bamboo. They are marbles in the dark—metallic glints in the night with a shy and traitorous moon. A hand grabs me by the wrist, wrenches me closer as I begin to struggle, to let out noise against knowing better.

"It's me," this creature says, pushing its face close to mine until the brim of the hat presses uncomfortably against my head. Shallow breaths between us and my heart arrhythmic, I shudder and shake and press forward into her—into my Camelia.

"It's me, Yuya. I've been waiting for you. ¿Por qué te tardáste tanto?"

"I thought—I. I don't know what I thought. No sé, no sé," I mumble against her cheek. She smells of salt water and mangoes.

"You lost me?" She replies, soft and I feel the smile pull her cheeks. "You would never."

She rubs her cheek against mine, trails her face down my neck until she rests at the nook there, her warm breath making me break out into goosebumps.

"They're swollen. My ankles, I mean."

I pull back, out from under the shielding hat and away from her heat. I am again suddenly aware that we are surrounded by these others, these greedy ones.

"Tenemos que—we have to leave. Now," I say, pulling my legs beneath me to stand but Camelia's hand on my wrist again stills me. She tilts her head back, face illuminated fully by the night and her hat a halo around her head. She looks confused—brown eyes looking from me to the other sleeping children.

"But why?" She asks, low and with a smile that makes my breath hitch. "We can stay here. It is nice, and we sing all day. Mama Dlo brings us fruit and bathes us in the river." She moves her hand to my knee and leans in close. "Stay, Yuya. You would like it here. We all like it here, where the sun is soft."

I begin to tremble again, eyes flickering to the stirring bodies around us. "Camelia, por favor." I tug at her arm. "We have to go."

"Please stay. Here. With me?" She presses a kiss to my wrist, busses her lips against it and begins to pull me in.

"I can't. I can't, please, nos tenemos que ir," I whisper hurriedly, frantically as I pull away, fall back on my hands and plead. We are getting too loud.

It's when the stirring turns to shifting that I grab her upper arm and pull her to her feet. "Please, Camelia," I say, high, panicky. She stares at me for a heavy moment before tilting her head down, obscuring her face with her hat, and allowing me to tangle my fingers with hers.

The whole time we walk she remains quiet but on occasion will stop in place and look off into the mangrove, the fingers of her free hand twitching at her side. She listens, and stops, and does not show me her face.

When I deposit her against the trunk of the nearest mangrove to the riverbank, I kneel down to massage her ankles. They feel broken, as if her feet have been wrenched backwards by hand, by pure force, by cruelty and little care. This is not how the stories go. They must have done this when they realized they'd taken her too soon.

"Stay, please," I say gently. She watches me with glossy eyes; does not reply. But then, she gazes beyond me and points at the water.

At first I can only see the calm ebbing of water, and then I see them: the water mummas that have stuck their heads out of the water to watch us with shadowed expressions. Their hair gleams in the dawn, droplets glinting off the tight curls and a low chatter begins to rise—clicking sounds and a trilling of aggressive tongues. They've followed me, I realize. Scented me.

I hesitate, hands hovering over Camila. They're interested. They want something of me, and perhaps I could also want something from them. I run my fingers over the crucifix at my throat pensively as I approach cautiously.

"I want—my friend, she—" A hush, sudden. Stillness from the figures. I swallow once, and again to attempt to soothe a tacky throat. "Mummas, Mama Dlo and her children took my friend and many other before their time. My friend—her feet, they are not turned right. You," I pause, leaning forward to chase the minimal indication that I'm being listened to. They tilt their heads forward. "You can help me, right? Turn them back?" I murmur—not quite beseeching, but on the edge of vulnerability.

Two dark heads disappear underwater and the three remaining ones wait. A hoarse voice, when it comes, seems to have no body attached to it. "We can."

I wait but they do not move until I dig my fingers into the red clay of the bank. There is no time for these moments of ambiguity—not for me, and not for Camelia. "I will cut my hair for you, if that is what you want," I add. A bargain, I remember from Mamá's candle-lit folktales. I don't have much to give these woman-creatures.

They draw closer, webbed fingers ghosting near mine and they are cold—clammy. The three women are so close I feel their breaths on my face, shoulders.

"That is not enough," comes the disembodied reply. "That is not valuable."

"What would be?" I ask, pulling back slightly. Looking over their grayed skin.

"A drink, for each of us."

I pause, glancing back at Camila. "My—you mean my blood?"

"We can do this for you only once, and that is our price."

It does not seem too bad a price, if only there were not so many of them. As far as I can see, there are nine. Underwater there could be more.

I've barely nodded when I'm pulled down into the water by a hand against my neck and another tangled in my hair.

I'm breathing water and there is no light. No light but for the occasional gleam of a whipping scaled tail. A strong grip seals around my upper arms, keeps me in place as I thrash—panic and no breath and there is no light and the mother in the woods, and the mother in my home, and Camelia with her feet turned backwards. The sharp yank of my arms being pulled taut, scalding on my forearm like the time Elías threatened me with a cigarette, and then a sudden release. Writhing and the rough of bodies scratching, whirling against me and—air. Silence. I cough up into the night, ragged breaths and the rise and fall of a bruised ribcage. The River Mummas are gone under pitch black waters. I look down at my arms. From wrist to elbow, perfectly circular bitemarks mar my skin and weep.

"Do not waste," a voice purrs at my side, but when I flinch there is no contact with a body. "Take the blood. Baptize her feet. You will be able to right them only then."

On the riverbank, they have left me a bowl filled with liquid.

Once I haul myself away from the water, I make my way back to Camelia and sit at her feet. I am light-headed, shaky-limbed, but push through with determination, my hands grasping onto Camelia's feet for as much her sake as mine. Grounding.

I put them in the bowl, begin to wash them with blood and saltwater until they wrinkle. Her stare bores into me—*traitor*, it says. Frightened, angry, on the sharpened dagger of exhausted, I am cruel in the way I twist her feet back around with a crunch and wrench of muscle and bone. Rough hands and no consoling sounds as she wails out into the night, hands flailing to grab purchase in the grass and clay. It takes every ounce of energy from me. She twists her body at the waist, sobbing into the earth and repeating a word I do not make out until I stand and walk to return the bowl. *"Cruel, cruel, cruel."*

I fling the bowl into the river and stand on shaking legs as my nails dig into my palms. It's sobering. I hear Camelia's small whimpering breaths, stay in my place, wonder if Dlo will come for us. If Dlo can spare even one. If Dlo can scent me as the mummas have or heard Camelia's cry.

Camelia lets herself be pulled into my arms—lets me kiss the side of her head and hold her to my chest. "Can you walk?" I ask. She nods damply, but still ends up being unsteady when I help her up. She cries with each step, heavy tears that leave her trembling and looking like she's on the verge of panic at any moment. I can say I'm better by very little.

I wonder if this will be enough: that Camelia's feet are turned back. It seems suddenly possible that those douens could get lost—confused by their own footprints and follow ours backwards or consider them some of their own. It is equally improbable.

We are not far from the old post office, a small shack of a thing grown-over by nature and pierced through with trunks. I coax Camelia with small comforting noises as we stagger on feet skewered by an unwelcoming landscape.

It is far more in shambles than what I remember; practically a lean-to of completely element-torn walls. A boat is tied there, the post master's, once. This town has gotten no mail for years.

I step into it and it groans but does not tip over or leak once I pull Camelia in. I slip the knife from the still open fishing kit into my pocket.

"¿A dónde vamos?" she wails, distraught and pulling against the arms I have wrapped around her torso. "We can't leave without her. She— Yuya, she is everything." She turns in my arms, holds my face in her hands. I force myself not to dwell on how satisfying this is. I force myself not to think on how I am unable to prevent the wounded, close-mouthed sound that escapes me as I lean into the touch. "Ella es todo, Yuya," she repeats, her face the image of earnestness, of sobriety. Her eyes are not clouded by physical pain, or confusion: a moment of total lucidity.

"There is nothing for you there," I growl. Instantly her look changes into a pitying one and I feel myself anger.

"Is it so wrong to want children? Or friends? That is all they want, and you could be part of it," she murmurs, pulling close, sitting beside me on the central bench of the dinghy. "We could be part of it."

"Camelia, look at what they did to your feet!" I shout. "La crueldad no es amor—you do not belong there. You have not died. They *stole* you, from your real mother. From me."

"Our island has been dying a long time," Camelia insists. "Dlo said I'm special—that if I did this, if I turned my feet, I would be her human girl—the one to keep growing. She just—she knows that we're on a time-clock."

"There is no future for you there." I shrug her off brusquely and take the oars into my hands. "You can stay, si quieres. But I won't join you."

She is quiet and still at my side before she slips from the bench to the one at the stern and I begin to push us off. I've only just started to row when I find resistance. The oars lurch from my hands, a shout of alarm escaping me. Several pairs of hands pull and push the boat back to shore. Hyperventilation in my throat and Camelia has her head hanging over the side of the boat, looking down at her siblings, speaking to them in a quick-tongue parlance. My hand finds purchase in her tattered shirt and I pull her back from the edge, folded into my arms.

"They won't hurt you!" she says, wriggling in my arms.

The moment the boat's lip bumps into the makeshift dock, I push her up onto it and follow with hastily scrambling steps, a shard of pain lancing through my foot. Her hand in mine, I pull her along as she shuffles her swollen feet. I've carved into bark, sliced meat into fine portions, cut my own hair—but I've never held a knife as a weapon. I pull it from my pocket, grip it hard.

The douens herd us into another clearing where Mama Dlo rests her snake body in a whorl, cheek pillowed on her flank. She opens one eye first and then the other—brown with big circular pupils. Her hair has been let down from its braids: tight coils rather than loose curls. In this light, she is younger—seems to look younger each second, but she springs from her coil in a vicious launching of her humongous body at Camelia with fangs exposed. Eye, shaving an ear to a stump, harpooned into the side of the neck—sites where the knife could find a pocket to inhabit. It hooks on the tender corner of her mouth, splitting her cheek open in a splatter of blood as I shove Camelia out of the way. Dlo's body clips me, destabilizing me and throwing me into stumbling steps. My mind whirls, blood drips down my fingers. I am unsure if it is mine, or Dlo's.

At whipping speed, she turns and sinks her fangs into my upper thigh. I scream, a ripped, hoarse, modulating noise that echoes through the cays. She squeezes her jaw down, the gory cut of her split mouth burbling with blood. My knees are likely to buckle, and her jaw will not slacken. My grip on the handle of the knife is slick and it fumbles as I drive it into her neck. I wrench it, both hands on the hilt to press it in deep against the violent thrashes of her serpent body—a fish heaving out of land. Heavy breathing, a constant stream of sounds tearing through vocal chords and—two soft, brown hands on mine. The smell of salt water and mangoes as Camelia takes the blade from my hand, hunches her body over it, and drives it down the rest of Dlo's body. It remains wriggling obscenely for a short moment before she slackens. Her jaw remains tight around my thigh as I buckle, and one wide, panicked brown eye looks up at me plaintively. Acrid acidic smell as her insides spill onto the mangrove roots—and Camelia stands over the scene, the knife still between her hands. She stares blankly down at Mama Dlo for several quiet seconds before she turns towards me. Her sobs wrack her frame as she kneels at my side, pulls the hair from my face and strokes my cheek.

"Yuya." Her hands tremble on my face and she smiles, pressing kisses to my face. "Thank you." She moves downwards, pries the jaws open and releases my leg from its clamp. I shout out, hands slapping the earth.

Camelia watches me, face unreadable as her hands trace the tender puncture marks on my thigh. Her brown eyes yellow in the cresting sunlight, and her pupils almost appear diamond-shaped.

"Things are alright now, Yuya," she murmurs, making her way back up to my head. "I love all my children very well. You'll like it here, where the sun is soft. Where we sing all day."

TEA WITH THE
EARL OF TWILIGHT

SONYA TAAFFE

F or the first week, she thought he belonged to the power plant; after
that she knew better. She had read the obituaries.

She saw him first as a silhouette, one more line of the industrial
geometries overhanging the boardwalk of Broad Canal. It had been a
wet, dispiriting winter full of gusts and mists, but with January the water
had finally hardened into a thick pane of cormorant-black ice, chipped
and glossed with refreezing like volcanic glass; it was pond-green at the
edges of the channel where the stubs of older piers stood up like snags,
but the snow lying over the floating dock of the canoe launch could still
pretend to seasonal pallor if the fanned brown branches of the trees
along the old towpath could not. Decades after the coal barges of the
Cambridge Electric Company, she had been vaguely surprised that there
were still girder-framed docks and doors at canal-height, but a sodium
light burned above one recessed portal and the greenish silver of mercury
vapor above the other and someone had put out a wheelie bin on one of
the rust-sketched catwalks, just as if a landfill-bound tugboat might still
chug by. On the other, a slender man in black was smoking. More than
features or expression, she registered the pose: slouched lankily over the
caution-yellow pipes of the handrail as if he had a view of something
better than pilings, pedestrians' feet, the algae-marked and iron-stained

masonry on the other side of the canal. Whatever she saw of his face was pale and pointed, his hair rumpled dustily. He wore no coat in the cold, but she had been caught wrong-footed by climate change herself. He did not glance up at her as she passed, hard-heeled with her hands in the pockets of her pale raincoat; she was not sure afterward why she had thought he should.

If the biscuit-colored blocks and towers of the Kendall Cogeneration Station looked like a space-age set from the '70s, Sid Eilerstein could not help thinking of the frictionless stack of glass cubes that housed her latest temp job as the apocalypse according to Ballard, all aquarium-windowed open-plan just waiting for the waters to rise. At least it left her full name off her ID badge, which spared her having to explain the kind of parents who named their daughter *Siddony* like the second coming of the pre-Raphaelites and got instead a two-time grad-school drop-out with a lavender-gray undercut and tattoos just far enough up her sleeves to pass as an acceptable office drone; she could take the bus on days when the Red Line preferred not to and she walked quickly enough to spend most of her lunch breaks by the Charles, the traffic humming across the metal decking of the disused drawbridge's leaves. Daniel referred to all of her employers interchangeably as Veridian Dynamics. She reminded him that his radical queer game design brought in approximately enough to cover the cost of internet in Spring Hill, even on the third floor of a former Philadelphia-style so haphazardly converted that one of Daniel's boyfriends had not entirely joked about raccoons falling through the ceiling while they fucked. It was better than medical transcription and waiting tables; she tried not to fall into hoping that it would last through the spring. She hurried with the rest of the nine-to-fivers through mornings as gray as salt-streaked concrete, dusks as drowned blue as a harbor's underside, and sometimes she saw the man on the loading dock above the canal, smoking next to the sign that read PRIVATE PROPERTY. He looked more like an art student than a utility worker in his thin black sweater and dark corduroys, his hair ashy in the mercury light; a match-flare lit him from underneath like a storyteller at Halloween. After the third or fourth sighting, she wondered if he was watching people in his own covert way, or merely the motionless water.

In hindsight, she liked to pretend everything would have been different if she had actually gone out with Torrey that weekend night, but they were coughing their way through some kind of post-conference hell-cold and in the end she was just as happy to do nothing more strenuous than make skillet-griddled grilled cheese and curl up to read. *Looks like your industrial sort of thing*, Daniel appended the link with a name she did not recognize in the title; he was only at the other end of the couch, sharing the other half of the amorphous sage-colored throw against the perpetual draft from the windows, but Sid had learned within weeks of their friendship that her housemate would never read a sentence aloud when a swipe and click would do.

Geoffrey Axtell, portraitist of Boston's waterways, dead at 79, read the headline on Universal Hub. The details in the *Globe* obituary were sparing, the accompanying headshot showed a sharp-faced man in salt-and-pepper middle age grinning at the camera, no tormented artist even with a half-finished canvas behind his shoulder. It looked blocky, architectural; all his paintings as she scrolled through a search had the same almost metallic crispness, bright flat pastels or unmixed oils sharpened the one degree past photorealism that made the Brutalist bricks of City Hall Plaza or the tumbling bronze dolphins of the old New England Aquarium seem to scratch their way off the screen. He painted the tideless chop of the Charles like steel-cut scales, the spill of sunset under the Lechmere Viaduct like cranberry glass; sunlight cross-hatched through the rusting trusses of the Northern Avenue Bridge as if it were being rolled and stamped hot. Human figures moved through his city like afterthoughts, brushstrokes for scale—an Esplanade dog-walker, Hull ferry commuters, the smoker by the factory-ripple of a canal.

Slack-jawed as a teen in some stupid found footage, Sid heard herself say, "Oh, shit," so distinctly that Daniel mid-podcast gave her a quizzical frown. Between the hard blue planes of the water and the dirty orange static of sodium light, the figure in loose-jointed lines of black paint leaned on the rail where the reflection of the power station scattered in green and dun and sulfur, not yet shadowed by a boardwalk. The saffron ember of a cigarette smoldered in one hand. She read the title first, *The Earl of Twilight*, and then the date of completion, *1981*, and she closed the profile or interview or gallery archive so fast, the rest of her tabs went with it. Her hands felt as cold as if she had fallen through the canal's ice. For a moment she wanted to scream at Daniel, his ears obliviously stopped with eldritch horrors that could never be worse than fiction, but it passed, like the raw tin taste in her mouth, and after another moment she opened the picture again. It must have been twilight, that lowering ghost-blue air. She knew even then, as with every real haunting, it had always been too late.

Soberly before a close-cropped angle on the Charles River Dam, the locks slanting away from the viewer in stripes of sheared gray and dimpled olivine, Torrey said, "It's not a retro style at all, is the thing. It's exactly the assumed nostalgia of Axtell's neo-Precisionism that gives his work its disjunct charge, like a subliminal double exposure, as if his subjects were trying to project themselves forward into a past they'd already lived—or been built too late for in the first place," and they squeezed Sid's sweating hand.

She had known she would not be able to manage the show at 249 A Street alone, not when she had spent a week avoiding even the trains over the river in case she should glance back and catch, beyond the Strauss-trunnion and counterweight sentinels of the drawbridges that had not been raised since her childhood, the impassable waters of Broad Canal, but she had dreamed of the paintings too often to stay away. Absurdly and reasonably, in person they did not shift behind her back, the black-sweatered smoker flicking from canvas to canvas like stop-motion film, leaving only a spoor of dissipating nicotine behind as each bright-figured scene of Castle Island or Chelsea Creek sank inexorably into shadow like sea-rise, just as the crowd at the opening reception had more than the one snapshot of a face, even if a few of them were of an age to have shared co-op space with Axtell since his move to Boston, she gathered from the short biography on the wall, in 1981. Neither had she had a lover with her in the dreams, their tattooed fingers twined between hers like a grounding wire, improvising with deadpan expertise on a subject she knew for a fact they cared less about than Magic cards—she found it difficult to imagine a plainer declaration of unconditional love

from Torrey Marcial than the willingness to attend a memorial exhibition of dead white cishet dude art, but they looked every inch the
confident patron in their glitter-threaded blazer and peacock-sheen hair,
saying in front of the brown dockworkers' brick of Southie's Our Lady
of Good Voyage, "That so many of his locations are unrecognizable
today—torn down, redeveloped, Boston consuming itself in the sterile
alchemical cycle of an insensate ouroboros—only pulls the work further
into a spectral modernity, the once and never city." She muttered out of
the side of her mouth, "Tell me you're recording this." Round-faced and
razor-sharp, Torrey grinned and addressed themselves to the weathered
oak of the fender piers under the Congress Street Bridge.

After half an hour surrounded by strangers with plastic cups of white
wine and cheese plates, Sid could not quite relax into *Navigating: The
Memory of Geoffrey Axtell,* but she had stopped flinching every time she
stopped before a new painting, some as neatly miniaturized as tilt-shift
photography, others as panoramic as skylines. Any body of water within
city limits seemed to have been fair game for his explorations, from the
marshes of Belle Isle to the still water of Cow Island Pond, but Axtell
had returned most often to Boston's urban waterways, dams and bridges,
vestigial spurs of canals, the Lost Half-Mile. The Charles and the Mystic,
Boston Harbor and the horizon-string of its islands. He had even painted
the co-op itself, the long industrial block of the one-time Regal Litho-
graph Company cutting diagonally into view like the prow of an ocean
liner, its burnt rose bricks glowing against a late sky caught over and over
in its tall granite-silled windows, inlays of Bristol blue glass. The date was
2009, right on the cusp of the glass-shelled Seaport boom. She looked
at *Charlestown High Bridge, 1993, Rowes Wharf, 2000.* The factual
titles puzzled her even as some of the compositions approached abstrac-
tion and she drank a cup of wine from the refreshments table, never mind
that anything less tannic than Shiraz always tasted to her like the smell
of old keys. Torrey was still lazily playing cultural studies docent, Dante's
Virgil as distraction, when they stepped around a white-walled partition
and said in their own voice, "Sid, it's here."

She had no idea why she had expected *The Earl of Twilight* to be
life-sized, except that she had seen him and he was; it was about the

dimensions of the lower sash of a window and it soaked all the light in the gallery into itself, vibrating even more deeply blue than she remembered from staring into her screen as if trying to memorize the picture, desensitize herself to it. She could almost hear the sodium buzzing, its seedy light the color of dead bugs and baby aspirin. The wet smell of the canal was stronger than the brassy tang of the wine. Close enough to the canvas to make out the grain of the paint, the smoker's face was still a sallow blur, the struts and grates and cinderblocks that backed him more pristinely rendered, the night-reflections crinkled at his feet.

"He painted that for his brother."

Sid felt Torrey's hand jump in hers. The nightmare recollection of the escaped figure went through her like nausea, but when she turned, the old-school Boston contralto belonged to one of the artists she had seen milling around the official end of the reception—a glam grandmother in a loose white T-shirt and denim cargo pants, short white hair dip-dyed the same brilliant faience blue as her nails and the glass beads of the heavy necklace she wore like a gorget, all tangled silver wire and chips of nacre and the parhelion flash of labradorite. Her glasses were flattened octagons. Torrey said immediately, "You look *spectacular*," and the woman smiled in appreciative return. "Sheila Francis," she introduced herself; her handshake was dry and wiry, her other hand occupied with a bottle of Harpoon IPA. She gestured toward the painting with it, a motion a little like a salute. "You know, I thought of Geoff for years as the one that got away, but I couldn't have told you from or with what. Maybe that was it. You know about his brother?"

Braced for a tidal flood of raconterie, Sid realized the woman was actually waiting for an answer; she must have managed, "No," because Sheila Francis nodded, not judging and not surprised.

"He didn't talk that much about it. I don't know that he'd even have told me, except I'd seen the photographs. He was born in Bradford. In the UK, not in Haverill. You could hear the accent to the end of his life," and Sid thought fleetingly of the difference between a Boston artist and a *Boston* artist, when she had been born like Jonathan Richman by the Fenway and never felt like a native Bostonian at all. "Hilary was maybe eight, ten years younger. They were both artists. Geoff went to the Slade, had his velvet waistcoat paisley period—eminent blackmail material, once the psychedelia wore off. His style was different then, a lot more fells and watercolors, like all he wanted to do was make up for Paul Nash and Eric Ravilious and all the rest of those autochthonous war artists being dead. Hilary dropped out of the Bradford College of Art, got himself a studio in a derelict mill that sounded more like a squat, and started making sculptures out of local scrap. That's what I saw the photos of. Just a couple of Polaroids, I think that was all Geoff had kept. Vivid, angry little things. You couldn't tell if they had screws or bones. Some of them had names, Geoff said, like he was building his own little retinue of demons, but either he didn't remember or didn't want to tell me what they were. I didn't push. His brother was murdered."

She said it flatly, an anti-punch line. *What happened?* Sid knew she was supposed to be asking, but the canal was at her back and twilight outside the windows and the nausea was making the taste of well-thumbed metal worse. She heard Torrey clear their throat and ask, mock lecturer to real audience in another of their seamless, not effortless code-switches.

"Queer-bashed, probably. He was funny and delicate and I don't know if he was gay or not, but Geoff thought so, even if he never met any of his boyfriends. He was found—there isn't a canal through Bradford anymore, Geoff told me, but there's a kind of crossroads where the start of it used to be, a winding hole. He was in it, but he hadn't drowned. Geoff had to identify him. He didn't talk about that at all." Behind the silver angles of her glasses, Sheila Francis did not look ghoulish, just sad, as if she might have liked the chance to know Hilary Axtell, too. "He moved here about a year later. He painted that picture. And then he painted water, everywhere in Boston, until he had the second stroke. It was quick after that." In the silence that was no such thing with the rest of the reception chatting or condoling around them, she drank from her beer as if to both of their memories.

At least she had not been told that Geoffrey Axtell had been dredged out of the remains of the last canal in East Cambridge where he had painted his brother, or his brother's demon, or whatever his art had made of both of them: Sid swallowed the last of the acrid white wine and said, "We didn't know any of that. Thank you."

Sheila Francis shrugged; the track lighting glinted off her ear-cuffs, more silver and pinpricks of blue. An avatar of winter mornings, fragile ice at the top of the world. "Geoff wasn't big on memorabilia. I won't be around forever. There's not much of him left now, just that painting and his sculptures if he ever sold them and a police file in a box somewhere. Somebody should know."

Out on the ice-plated asphalt of A Street, the wind came blasting off the channel like sandpaper below zero, but it was better than standing for another second in the co-op's gallery, trapped between the gaze of something Sid could not trust to stay in indistinct paint and the friendly attention of a woman who had handed her a dead man's memory like a party favor, as if she was not haunted enough. Maybe it was fury twisting her stomach after all, the hot-wired tremor in her hands as she fumbled with her scarf and her mackintosh and finally butted through the door with her coat flapping open, swallowed in the cold like a bloom of molten glass. The sky above the frontages of brick was bluer still than black, its crescent fleck of moon all but lost in the wing of seagulls lifting from the former Necco warehouse like a fountain of blown white paper, wheeling and drifting in the dusk. She heard their cries as distantly as something she had forgotten about. Past hipsters and ghost signs, she made it as far as the overpass with its roof of netted fairy lights—the eye-blurring blue of LEDs—before Torrey caught hold of her, let her gasp out the dry crack of breath that was not a sob on their smaller, stronger shoulder and then kissed her, cold-gloved, warm-lipped, as real as any urbex horror show.

"He fucking *transplanted* him. He must have known. All that water and industry, all that brick and steel, all the things his brother loved until they killed him, it can't have been an accident. I can't be the only one who's seen him. Oh, my God, Sheila, does she know he's there? Is that why she told me the story? Am I supposed to fucking exorcise him now?"

Her voice scraped and caromed off the underside of the bridge, a pigeon's blundering wings; she was shivering in the circle of Torrey's arms, the skunky leather of their back-patched bomber jacket and the white musk and red fruits of one of their antique perfumes. Their face in the mixed light looked as sculpted as Corinthian bronze and she shivered harder, thinking of Hilary Axtell's art. In their rough-brushed, not entirely tenor voice, they were saying, "I don't think you could see him till his brother died. I don't think anyone could. I don't know if you can exorcise him, either, if he was painted that deeply into the city, but I don't think Axtell did it on purpose. It's just that one picture. There'd be more if he'd made a spell of them," as reasonably as if the question were algebra or anniversary restaurants, and Sid laughed suddenly, ribcage compressed with cold and love.

Above their heads, the huff and squeal of brakes meant the 7 bus was taking the same straight shot toward the Summer Street Bridge as Car 393 of the Boston Elevated Railway, more than a drowned hundred of years ago. Ghosts traced over ghosts, gentrification over projects, nineteenth-century fill of gravel and cellar earth under their feet and the sea rising to reclaim its stolen flats and bays. As close as she could get to Torrey's academic voice, Sid asked, "The author has always been dead, but was the artist ever alive?" Someone threw a bottle from the top of the overpass and they ran on up the catwalk stairs, swearing, into the salt-black night.

In the afternoon on Broad Canal, the only smokers in view were a couple of young professionals on different levels of the plaza's granite steps, like a stock photo. Coming around the corner from Main Street with a sixteen-ounce of matcha latte and a pistachio cherry tart, Sid had not really expected anything else, but the vacancy of the scene still struck her without reassurance, sharp as pencil lines under the clarity of winter sun. The water beneath the span of the First Street Bridge shivered with reflection, mantis-green and sandstone-gold. Steam glittered like crumpled foil from the power plant. Her shadow flattening over the old stone blocks of the canal wall was black as absence, a stalker or a faceless conscience matching her pace behind a grill of shadow railing, between the frames of shadow light poles. Carefully as a confidence trick, she watched the pale bricks and the chimneys, the stratospheric blue of the sky. She saw the sodium light still burning, daylit as memory.

Until 1965, the canal had run as far inland as Portland Street, into the nascent heart of Tech Square with its MAC and CCA and IBM, the wave of the silicon future where an older wave of docks and wharves and factories had broken and dragged back—Torrey's once and never city laid down in the littoral of time, and Sid allowed herself a moment between bites of marzipan crust to wonder what year it was where Hilary Axtell gazed out over twilit water, or whether the right question for a dead man in a painting nearly forty years old was how many. She had seen the maps to overlay office parks with ironworks, soap flakes inter-mingled with pharma R&D; it was an easier double vision than trying to keep an eye on both docks at once, like bones of bare stages where a wheelie bin and a frazzle of nylon rope were the props waiting for the one-man show. It still took an extra gulp of matcha to turn her back on them, her heart hammering faster than the green-earth bitterness under the steamed sweet milk. The dull steel railing chilled through her coat's sleeves, her face and her fingers were already stiffening in the ice-clear air. She said aloud, as if she had not practiced the words in nightmares, "Why did he call you that?

"*The Earl of Twilight*. That's the part I keep wondering about. Was it a nickname? An in-joke? One of your pieces to begin with? There's nothing about them online, incidentally. No photos, no descriptions, no mentions even in local retrospectives. I looked," with Torrey in their sleeveless black sleep shirt nestled against her side, double- and triple-checking every possible lead until the search strings spun off into crimes she had never wanted to know were committed in West Yorkshire and even Daniel, disappeared into one of his deadlines so that Sid saw him almost exclusively at late hours when he ran downstairs to pick up his traditional marathon food of chicken tikka pizza, rattled his fingers on the door and stuck his head in, the classic undersunned geek with two or three piercings and a wing of Comet-green hair, to make sure she was all right. "Did your brother destroy them? His friend said he only kept a couple of snapshots. Did something"—she was not sure how paranoid she wanted to sound, even to a haunting—"happen to them? I couldn't even find a picture of you. I can't even be sure you really lived or died." She said it deliberately, offensively, and nothing answered her beyond the turbines and condensers of the Kendall Cogeneration Station, the rumble-strip bump and rush of cars out on the Cambridge Parkway. Staring so hard into the Impressionist mirror of the water that it blurred without wind: "I think you did."

Two days ago she had walked eastward over the Longfellow, not slowing or speeding even when her shoulders hunched like a blow against the slush-colored overcast; she had returned just as steadily, looking nowhere but straight down the track of the bridge where the Red Line racketed back and forth from the earth, and she had reached the turnstiles at Kendall sweat-soaked with the effort of not breaking into a run. *I knew they were chasing me,* she had tried to explain to Torrey afterward, hands wrapped hard around small hot cups of tea while the dan dan noodles she was still too jumpy to eat cooled between them, *just like I knew the sun was setting and any second it would start to snow. I couldn't outrun them, but I knew I had to try. I kept thinking the bridge was shorter, there couldn't be much further to go . . . He didn't even die here, it's stupid,* but he had brought his death with him as surely as Geoffrey Axtell had brought his memory and now none of them could be separated any more than I-93 could be unwoven from the Zakim or Government Center peeled off the scouring of Scollay Square. She dreamed of bricks and machineries overlaid like double exposures, different waters reflecting from the same angle. Sid had always wanted to get to the bottom of her city, but until she woke she could not remember which one. It was all the same to Axtell, both of them: a ghost that might only have been one man's grief with another's face. When the dams failed at last and the tide rolled up the Charles, would he still be there on his dock of weeds and heavy metals, his cigarette glowing under the dusk-blue water like a phantom light? She thought of cubicles of brackish salt, bridges skimming the storm-surge. The beacons of the dead like bioluminescence in the waves. The scratch of the match-strike was so brisk and dry, she almost could not place it; then she smelled the smoke coiling on the sunlit air.

She did not imagine for a second that she was hallucinating, watching Hilary Axtell flick a spent paper match over the rail of the boardwalk as if he had never heard of the EPA. His slouch and his black sweater were indelible, but his brother's brush had never dressed him in that secondhand-looking navy duffel coat, looped a heather-red scarf around his neck and stuffed a black woolen hat in his pocket and left him bare-headed to the wind, his hair the silvering tousle of beech bark; even on clear evenings, she had never been able to look full into that tired, whimsical face. It was younger than hers, dented hungrily around the cheekbones, a glint under his hair that she realized was an earring of silver or steel. He looked pensive and windblown, the tip of his nose reddening prosaically in the cold. She could have drawn every loose-limbed line of him from memory. Close enough to be lapped in his envelope of old nicotine and rosin solder, she watched a man who had never been alive in the city of his death drag on his cigarette, exhale a stream of smoke that might have been warm as breath or merely ashes; she was not surprised, finally, which did not mean she was not terrified, when he rested his hand on the rail and looked over curiously at her.

His eyes were not filled with time, or twilight, or the trapped and restless water of lost canals; they were gray and Sid thought he might have needed glasses if he had lived. She had a sudden flash of his face behind a welding mask, metal-fleshed as any of his creations. *How much of him* are *you?* she wanted to ask. How much more or less if he had grown around an armature of iron instead of a shell of paint? As steadily as she had watched warehouses knocked to bricks and high tide curling through the streets of the Seaport, she made herself hold his dead man's gaze and not think of a bridge half-recalled in snow and sunset, the night colors of a canvas that had made a city into a spell. His eyes narrowed a little, with the wind or astigmatism, but they widened in a surprise as candid as a clown's as she reached over and took the cigarette from his hand.

She wanted to remember afterward if she had expected its paper to smear like turpentine or drowned rust between her fingers, if after everything she had still believed in a canal that could be restored to innocent emptiness like brownfields turned back to neighborhoods or a sea not yet swelled by the Anthropocene or if she had known even as she felt her heart beat faster than panic and keep on beating that all she might free him from was his stasis of paint. Lying awake in Torrey's arms, Sid remembered only the iridescence of ice and oil, the canyon-shadows of old and young brick, the quick crease of laughter lightening a cold-pinched face while the traffic out on the drawbridges hissed like acetylene. She might have heard glass breaking, like a fever. All she had felt between her fingers was ash. She would never quite know, she thought, what she had unbound into her endlessly building, sea-dredged, sinking city, not unless she met him again under the water, in the twilight of the harbor or the river's scrap-silted bed. She imagined him in mirror of his brother's art, constructing the skeletal maps of Boston to come. No matter the innovations it boasted, she would not look for them in the district off Broad Canal. She knew the future had always been too late.

WAIT FOR NIGHT

STEPHEN GRAHAM JONES

I t was just a day-labor gig. Really, the only reason I'd signed on was
because, for insurance reasons, hiring on meant getting fitted for
a brand-new pair of lace-up Red Wing boots. It was new policy that
summer. Some punk from a few months before had come back and sued
the owners for how his right foot had gotten caught up under the tread
of a little ditch witch. He'd argued he was going to have a game foot the
rest of his life, and that would impact future employment, happiness, his
dreams of being a kicker for the Broncos—everything, to the tune of a
few hundred thousand dollars.

Before anyone else could ease what they considered their least
important foot in the way of any of the equipment, it was new boots all
around—composite toes, ankle support—and all you had to do to lace
those boots on was sign papers that, since your feet were now protected,
you and you alone would be legally liable for them.

After this story, I'd asked if there was a similar reason for the helmets
we all had to wear, and the back braces, and the gloves, but instead of an
answer I got a cuff on the shoulder and a push away into the day's work,
which was cleaning out a creek bed.

We were north of Boulder that day, on the slant up to Longmont.
And I have no clue why this creek bed was getting our attention. It felt

like busy work, really. As near as I could tell, every waterway for miles in every direction was clogged with trash from the flood three years before. Maybe the water had been backing up in a way that was threatening to swamp Diagonal Highway, I don't know. It was a job. There were eleven of us clocking in every morning round about lunch, clocking out just before dark.

Three days into it, we'd found a car door, a Styrofoam head we guessed had once held a wig, and a whole waterlogged library. Seriously, like somebody upstream had seen the flood coming and plopped down on their back porch with a pile of books, Frisbeed them out into the water one by one.

We were piling the junk on heavy-duty trash tarps a truck with a crane could lift out later. It wasn't easy work, but it was good work. Good enough.

Forty yards upstream from us was the real crew, using heavy equipment to haul up the heavy sludge, roll up the dead brush, pull down whatever trees had been undercut by the water, were about to fall over, turn the whole area into a swamp.

I was working alongside Burned Dan when I felt his stillness, followed where he was looking: upstream, the big dozer was chained to a monster willow, pulling it down, away from the creek, which wasn't the way it wanted to go. But, by slow degrees, and with a lot of shaking and jerking, it went.

We were all watching by the time it finally whooshed down.

Burned Dan shook his head in wonder, rubbed his bandanna across his face—not a pocket-bandanna or old man's handkerchief, but the bandanna he *wore* like a train robber, since his leathery skin didn't take to the sun so much anymore. Between his long sleeves and wide hat, gloves and bandannas, he was pretty safe from getting burned again, I figured.

"Bet that root pan stinks," the Reverend said to us all.

I don't think he was really a reverend, but it's not like I was the high school football star I'd taken to claiming either. We all gave each other a lot of latitude. That's how it goes with day laboring. You're always your best self, just down on your luck a bit, only here for a week, maybe two, until your real thing comes through.

"Thirty more minutes and quit," Jake boomed out when he saw us admiring the pulled-over willow. He was our crew's ramrod. You could tell from how straight his back was, from the stick up his ass.

We bent to it, dredging and scraping, splashing and coughing, making a path from the creek to the afternoon's blue tarp.

Once a silver flash bulleted past my right Red Wing, but I didn't say "trout" to anyone, kept that fish secret, if it had even been real.

Thirty minutes later, that five o'clock whistle blowing a couple hours late, my uncle's unregistered Buick fell into its usual routine of refusing to start, and I was the only one still parked in the pullout. I sloped back down to the creek to splash my face, consider my life, and all the decisions I'd made to get me to this point.

Burned Dan was standing there with his back to the water. He was looking out across Diagonal Highway. But I didn't think he was really seeing it.

"You good?" I asked him.

He finally checked back into the world, dragged his dark eyes around to me.

"Chessup," he said. It's my last name, what everybody'd taken to calling me, like they were all playing coach to the football player I'd never been.

"Got to get a battery," I explained, nodding downstream to the dozer.

My idea was to haul it over to the Buick, jump it to life, then leave the car idling, get the battery back in place. No harm, no foul.

Burned Dan shrugged like what was stopping me, then.

I trudged on down there. The dozer was still chained to the tree it had felled, the chain long enough that the crown of the tree wouldn't crash down on whoever'd been throttling the dozer up. I touched the chain and it was tight enough it sung, and I imagined jumping up onto it, walking its length like I was still in high school, was never going to fall.

That was ten-years-ago-Chessup, though.

This Chessup, he crawled awkwardly up onto the dozer, looking for the battery tray, then cussed and spit when he needed a wrench to loosen the strap across the battery's middle. It's usually just a wing nut, easy to crank off with your fingers, but maybe equipment left overnight gets looted.

When there were no tools on the tractor, I walked the length of the chain down to the tree, where one of the little runabouts was parked. Digging through its clatter of tools, though, I started to feel . . . I guess you could call it "not alone"?

I turned slow, expected Burned Dan to be watching me from the tree's gnarled root pan. For all I knew he slept rough out here, was saving money that way. He smelled like he was living outdoors, anyway. Either that or a cemetery.

It wasn't Burned Dan watching me, but I was right about the dead: there was a pale white skull locked in the tangle of roots and dirt that hadn't seen sunlight for . . . since this tree was a baby, right?

I fell back, pushed farther away with my heels.

The skull just stared, kept staring, its jaw loose below it, just connected on one side.

Once my eyes adjusted and my heart fluttered down some, I made out the rest of the skeleton, woven in and out of the wood.

"Hey there," I said to the dead man, or woman, or whatever.

It stared back at me, its mouth locked in a decades-long scream.

I sat up higher, looking for Burned Dan.

When he was nowhere, I approached the root pan. It was taller than me by half. This tree had been standing for . . . a hundred years? At least. Meaning this skeleton was older than that by a little bit.

A dollar sign ka-chinged distantly in my head, and when I centered on it, the slot machine of my hopes opened, clattering possibility down into my throat.

What would someone pay for an old-ass skeleton like this, right? From the Wild West, the Roaring Twenties, the Great Depression, whenever? Sure, I could tell Jake, and he could call in the state, the university, the historians. But, more to the point I could feel myself coming to, what would a pawnbroker in *Denver* pay a scrub like me for this skeleton? Three hundred? More?

I forgot about the battery.

Forty minutes later, using a denim jacket that had been covering the torn seat in the dozer, I'd bagged up probably eighty percent of the skeleton, having to work each bone out from the wood that had claimed it. There were some finger bones lost, some toes, and I can't imagine I got much of the wrist, but it's not like pawnbrokers have anatomy books under the counter for these kinds of transactions. Anyway, it was the skull that would really matter. Touching it had made me aware of the bone beneath the skin of my own cheek.

I was just tying the sun-bleached sleeves of the jacket over the bundle when a shadow fell across me.

"What you got there?" Burned Dan asked, stepping past me to inspect the dark raw dirt in this root pan.

"Rocks," I told him, tying the jacket tighter, kind of trying to hide it with my shadow. "My uncle's new wife—she wants like a border for their tomatoes, I don't know."

"Rocks," Burned Dan repeated, rubbing his hand over the crumbling dirt of the root pan he was right up against now, then turning, to see the creek from this angle. Moving his head slow, he panned over to where the dozer was parked. "The water used to run over there," he said like a fact, then nodded to himself, added, "Bet it did, I mean."

I looked with him, shrugged.

"Sure, why not," I said, standing with my winning lotto ticket, my rattly paycheck.

"Battery in there?" Burning Dan asked, meaning pretty much he knew it wasn't, and, like I had to, I imagined slinging the jacket forward, its weight knocking him senseless. But the next thing after that would be me holding his head underwater, then burying him upstream, where we'd already cleaned everything out.

I didn't try to swing the bundle.

"I'll split it with you," I offered.

He eased over and I held the sleeves of the jacket apart so he could see the bones.

He didn't touch, just looked. Then, curiously, he looked past me, to the mountains, like seeing an old, jumbled skeleton made him suddenly have to get an exact read on his position.

"Almost dark," he said.

"Little bit more," I said about the part of the sun still showing.

"Soon enough," he told me, still clocking the postcard foothills over Boulder.

I shrugged, didn't need to get involved in an argument this stupid.

"Bad luck to steal from the dead," he said, finally coming back to me.

"This isn't 'from,'" I explained. "This *is* the dead."

He chuckled, could appreciate that.

"Trade," he said. "My next check for them." For the bones.

I looked down to them.

We'd been working the same hours, so I knew he was talking about two hundred dollars tomorrow. Or, two hundred if he actually showed up to sign the check over.

"They're all broken up anyway," he said about my stolen bones.

"How do I know you show up tomorrow?" I said back.

"And this too," he said, unhitching his belt and whipping it out from its loops. He worked the buckle off. It was turquoise set in dull silver. "Fifty dollars there," he said. "Easy."

I turned the buckle over, imagining all the backsplash pee I was probably touching.

"How'd you get all . . . ?" I said, motioning to the up and down of him, his scars, his burns.

"That's not for trade," he said, his voice a register more serious.

When I shrugged like you do when negotiating, still fake-looking at the buckle like I was some buckle expert, he said, like it was no big deal, "Or I just take them, leave you with nothing."

I kept looking at the buckle, my heart beating in my throat now. My temples.

Burned Dan was at least thirty years older than me, a kind of rode hard, put-away-smoking thirty years.

Could he still take me?

"Let's not get all . . ." I said, dropping the bag between us. "What, you some amateur archaeologist or something?"

"Something," he said back.

"And I'll help get your car started," he added, throwing his chin over my shoulder, to the dead Buick. "Can't say no to that."

He was right.

"Deal," I told him, telling myself this was good, that my uncle would kick my ass if I took his car to Denver anyway.

Burned Dan knew how to peel the strap off the dozer's battery without a wrench—all it took was fingers as strong as his—and, after working the clamps off the terminals, no wrench again, he hefted the battery out like it was nothing, carried it by his leg up to my Buick.

It had just turned over and caught when gravel crunched behind us. Beside me, Burned Dan's eyes crinkled up in frustration.

"Hands, hands," the highway patrolman now behind us said— *ordered*.

We kept our hands in sight.

"We need to take this second battery off," I said, as clearly as possible. "This alternator's jinky, can't push charge to two at once."

"Back away, back away," the officer said, stepping between us and the engine's ungainly, soon-to-overheat lope.

We let him have his room, saw that his pistol was out, kind of ramping the three of us up into a completely different space. The pistol was pointed down, sure, but it was ready to flick up the instant either of our heels caught on a rock.

"Shit," Burned Dan said.

"I need to see your face," the officer said to him.

"No you don't," Burned Dan said. "Trust me."

"*Now!*" the officer said, the pistol coming up.

"We're not stealing the battery," I heard myself saying. "We're just—we're borrowing it. We were going to return it, honest."

Adding "honest" is the way to convince people, yeah.

Day-laborer Chessup reporting for duty.

Moving slow and reluctant, Burned Dan peeled the blue bandanna down from his face, his eyes holding the officer's for the whole reveal.

I felt bad about it, like I was peeping through a window of a hospital, but I sort of wanted to see, too.

Burned Dan's face was . . . it was destroyed. Burned, yeah, but worse than just burned. I wasn't sure what had happened to his mouth, but it looked to have involved the butt end of a two-by-four, and Dan not being able to protect his face with his hands anymore. For, like, ten minutes of that two-by-four coming down.

"Shit," the officer said.

"Like he said," Burned Dan said, nodding to the Buick, "we're trying to get this coupé started."

The officer squinted his eyes about "coupé"—me too—then looked slow from the battery to us, and finally to the equipment in deep shadow now, down at the creek.

"He with y'all?" he said.

Burned Dan's eyes narrowed and his left hand shot out to my chest, like keeping me there. I looked past him down the slope, thought at first it was the Reverend, come back for the gross thermos he could never keep track of. But this wasn't a man at all.

The skeleton was walking like . . . it was like Claymation, which made it all worse, since Claymation's supposed to be stop-motion, fake. But the motion now, it wasn't stopping. With each ungainly step, the skeleton was gaining flesh somehow.

"The shade," Burned Dan hissed through his bandanna. "It's already night down there, isn't it?"

"Sir, sir!" the officer said to the coming-together skeleton, his pistol angled down onto it now, his head shaking no about what his eyes were seeing.

"He can't hear you," Burned Dan said. "Ears are about the last to form, when you've been down that long."

"'He'?" I had to say.

"Julian," Burned Dan said, like that was the least important part of what was happening here. "He's this old . . . forget it, kid."

The officer's pistol boomed right beside us, a stab of flame lurching out into the gathering darkness, and I actually felt the pressure from the sound wave. It left me in my own quiet, slow-motion place.

First, the shot hit the skeleton, "Julian," in the left shoulder, and blew right through, not slowing his approach even a little.

Second, Burned Dan's hand whipped up for the pistol, took it away from this cop, tossed it behind the Buick easy as anything. His other hand slashed forward, took the cop by the front of his uniform shirt, and threw him headfirst into his own windshield.

Third, Burned Dan looked to me, pulling the bandanna off his face so my deaf self could read his over-enunciating lips: *Run.*

I made the word out because I was watching so close, yeah, but it was because I was watching so close that I saw his teeth sharpening, lengthening, the enamel thrusting up from his gums more yellowy, like ivory. It made my stomach go queasy, my face cold, my thoughts kind of flattening down into an unbroken line. My body knew what to do, though: I fell back into the hood of the cop car alongside the bloody cop, and when I looked up again, Burned Dan was gone, so instead of running I cast around for where he could have got off to.

Julian too, I guess. Down the slope, he stopped and set his bone feet, waiting, his claw hands opening and closing, the new tendons there flexing for the first time. And then the flurry of motion way off to the left became Burned Dan, rushing through the brush for a sneak attack. Except Julian was watching him the whole way. Burned Dan gathered speed all the same, running faster than I would have given him credit for, and when he barreled into Julian, driving him back, where they came down was in the shallows of the creek.

Burned Dan drew his hand back to come at Julian's face, and it wasn't a fist anymore, like I'd been expecting. His hand wasn't closed but open, because he had claws at the end of his fingers now.

If Julian had more flesh, those claws might have done some actual damage. *Julian's* claws did what they were supposed to, though. After Burned Dan's slashing drove Julian's face down hard enough to have broken a horse's neck, Julian snapped his head back up, the one eye that was formed nearly glittering with joy, it looked like.

His right hand came up into Burned Dan's gut, then splashed out his back, fingers extended in what I took to be the most extreme pleasure.

It didn't stop there, either. He kept going up, and up, his unholy, barely-there thigh muscles launching both of them from the water. When they came down on the bank, Burned Dan slamming into it with all of his back, I felt that impact twenty yards away, through the thick soles of my new Red Wings.

"Shit," I said.

It was the only word I could muster.

The cop groaning behind me pulled me away from the fight. He was extracting himself from the windshield bit by cut bit. When he was free enough, he fell forward beside me and managed to stay standing.

"Wh-wh—" he said, about what was going on down on the bank: Julian slinging Burned Dan around by the jaw, trying to drive his face into a tree, or maybe just get that jaw loose.

"You tell me," I said.

The cop took a stumbling step ahead—I guess this is what duty looks like?—pawing at his holster for the pistol he must not remember having lost.

"Hey, hey," I said, reaching for him.

He was past taking advice.

I shook my head, already hating having to do this, but I lunged in right behind him, hooked my right arm around his throat in a sleeper hold. I'd never actually tried it on anybody, had only seen it on TV, but after about forty seconds, he slumped down, must have come up watching the same shows I did.

I lowered down to the ground with him, didn't want him any more hurt than he already was, charges being charges and all. Which is to say: I was still considering the future, yeah. That we both might be getting some of that action.

I blew the cop's thick, nonregulation hair from my lips and looked over his head down to the creek.

Burned Dan, whatever he was, should have been able to knock a skeleton down, I was pretty sure, but that wasn't what was happening. *He* was down now, half in, half out of the shallows. Julian stood over him, leaned back and scream-roared. I'd never heard anything like it—he'd been saving it for decades, trapped under that tree.

Too, I guess he didn't have a tongue yet, so couldn't really pull off any sound *but* a scream.

Not that he needed words for what he was doing to Burned Dan now.

He was squatted over him, had his knees in the mud to either side of Burned Dan's ribs. It was so he could take either side of Burned Dan's head in his hands and slam it back into a rock harder and harder, never mind Burned Dan's hands around Julian's wrist, trying to keep this from happening.

"No, no," I said, standing.

I was supposed to be running, should be a mile away in the ditch by now, screw the Buick. But I couldn't shake the feel of Burned Dan's hand on my chest, keeping me safe. Keeping me out of this.

The cop moaned, rolled over, threw up.

"Stay," I said down to him, stepping over him, shaking my head about how stupid what I was about to do was. But it's not like I'd ever done anything actually smart, right? And it's not like I could really and truly outrun whatever Julian was, either. If I was going down, it wasn't going to be running away.

I yanked the dozer's big battery up from my fender where Burned Dan had balanced it—it was even heavier than I'd thought it would be—and worked my way down to the killing thing that was happening, kind of slinging the battery ahead with my hip, my arms burning from the weight.

Julian never heard me. Ears are the last to form, right?

I raised the battery over my head, which was really a matter of swinging it as high as I could and then ducking fast under it, my arms as straight as I could get them, so my legs could do the lifting. I was still wearing my safety belt, yeah.

"Look out," I said to Burned Dan, even though he was way past hearing anything, and then I brought that battery down into the back of Julian's nearly naked skull.

The blunt plastic corner went satisfyingly deep, and the weight slammed Julian down into the mud right by Burned Dan, and then, like I hadn't even thought to hope for, the battery acid cooked out, sizzling into Julian's head, sending up little threads of sick smoke.

If he could come back from just being a skeleton, though, then . . . well.

No way would this last.

"Dan?" I said. "*Dan?*"

Nothing.

I clenched my jaw because this was stupid—*now* was the time to run, these were exactly the kinds of decisions keeping me where I was. But . . . you can't always do the right thing, can you?

It's an excuse, yeah, but it's the only one I've got.

I came around Julian, lowered myself to my knees beside Burned Dan, and held my wrist over his mouth like in the movies, tried to claw it open with my dull fingernails. It was the only thing I could think of, and the only thing I had, really.

But then—nothing. Just scratches, no blood dripping down. Not because the fishbelly part of my wrist was thick or calloused, but because my nails had been worn down to dirty nubs from all the shovel work, all the bucket carrying, all the rocks I'd had to pry out of the mud with my fingers.

And now Julian was writhing, was coming back.

I looked around for a rock, a sharp piece of metal, a shovel or pole one of us had strategically left behind, to collect later. Any other time, there would have been fifty sharp things within spitting distance to open my wrist on accidentally, but right then, everything around me was dull, useless, leaving me only one option: I stuck my tongue out and slammed the heel of my hand up into my chin.

The blood came instantly, in a hot gush, filling my mouth, nearly frothing it was so eager to spurt out.

I leaned over Burned Dan, drained as much of me into his mouth as I could.

Almost instantly, his eyes opened, and then his hand clamped onto the back of my head, pulled me down into a bloody kiss, his wrecked mouth drinking, sucking, until I had to pull away, tongue last. It was that or become a human raisin.

Burned Dan sat up panting, licking my blood from his lips, his eyes flashing with danger, with hunger.

"What are you?" I said with a really distinct, spattery lisp.

"Pissed," he said, and looked over to Julian, Julian's hand reaching up for the battery crashed into his skull but his fingers finding no easy grip, his new skin sizzling away in the battery juice.

Burned Dan stood in his broken way, not all his joints working right, too many of his bones broken, and drove the heel of his boot down into the battery, forcing it all the way through Julian's skull, the leading edge probably in the back of Julian's throat, prompting a gag reflex if one had even formed yet.

"Five minutes," he said about Julian, and cased the place, grimacing about the work yet to come.

One minute later, using a battery he'd had to work up from the backhoe, the dozer fired up with a column of black smoke that tasted exactly like victory.

Two minutes later, the dozer's thick shiny blade was positioned over Julian.

The next three minutes were a monster getting slammed and cut into pieces by heavy equipment, then mashed with the treads, then mashed again, until it was hard to tell where the ground stopped and he started.

Burned Dan killed the engine, came down to inspect the damage.

I held my hand away from my mouth where I'd had it cupped, let the pooled blood drip away. He tracked that waste down into the dirt and watched me wipe my hand on the leg of my pants, then was watching my pants in a way that made the raw nerves on the exposed part of my tongue try to crawl back into my tongue.

"That'll keep him down?" I asked, leaning over to spit red.

"I wish," he said, and scooped Julian up in his arms, having to hold him close to keep his pieces and parts from spilling through. I followed them down to the part of the creek we'd already cleaned up, where nobody would be going again for . . . I wasn't sure. For forever? Burned Dan swished back into the tall grass, past where high water might carve a new cutbank, and stopped by a tree, nodded up to it. "Get a switch," he said to me. "That one."

I worked a thick green branch off from the main branch. It snapped off at the base, like the bulge there was made especially for me to break it.

Thirty feet back from the creek, Burned Dan used his hands to scratch a makeshift grave, not even a foot deep.

"Want me to get a shovel?" I said to him, talking still painful.

"It's enough," he said back about the hole that was hardly a hole at all. Still, he laid Julian down into it. He was already coming back together, his arms and legs and torso writhing into place.

"How can he—?" I asked, stopping when my mouth filled with more blood.

I caught it in my hand, went to sling it away, but Burned Dan was suddenly there stopping me. He brought my palm to his mouth. His tongue was rough like cat's, and his eyes closed when he swallowed.

"Don't worry about what he can do," Burned Dan said, and held his hand out for the switch. "He's about to be beyond all that again."

I handed him the snapped-off branch, didn't understand.

"Willow grows like this," he said, "from cuttings, not from seeds," and then jammed the butt of the branch down through what was left of Julian's chest, into the loamy earth under his back.

Instantly, Julian's writhing stopped, all his limbs going slack.

"A wooden stake . . ." I said in wonder.

Burned Dan chuckled, stood, kicked dirt over Julian.

I got down on my knees, scooped dirt onto him as well, packing it down and in.

"Not too tight," Burned Dan said. "Roots need to breathe."

I patted softer, turned it more into smoothing.

"Reverend were here, he could say a couple words," I said, each syllable a stab in my mouth.

"I got a couple for him," Burned Dan said.

I stood, lost my footing, and he caught me by the arm, hauled me up, his grip like iron, like I couldn't fall if I wanted to. He wouldn't let me.

We inspected Julian's make-do grave.

"Second time's charm," Burned Dan said.

"Think that's third time," I told him.

"You want to do this again?" he said.

"Second time's charm," I repeated.

The sapling—that's what it was now—stood up maybe three feet, its few leaves catching the breeze.

"This'll keep him for sure?" I asked.

"Until some idiot forgets where he's buried," Burned Dan said with another halfway grin, "lets some work crew pull this tree down."

"In a hundred years," I added.

Burned Dan clamped his big hand on my shoulder and turned me away from all this.

"Your coupé's still running up there," he said. "How much gas you got in the tank?"

"Enough," I said. Maybe that was true. "And, nobody says 'coupé' anymore, you know that, right?"

"Sedan?" Burned Dan tried.

"P.O.S.," I said, hitting each front letter of *Piece of Shit* for him. "Join this century, man."

"This century," Burned Dan said, dismissing the idea as too fleeting to be of any actual substance.

"You still coming in tomorrow?" I asked.

"Owe somebody a check," he said with a shrug that made a dull pop in his shoulder. He grimaced from it, rubbed it in with his hand, and then dropped his right hand fast to hold his jeans up, his belt being who knew where.

"We can talk about whose check it is and isn't," I told him, "I mean, it's not like—"

I felt the hole expanding in and through my chest before I actually heard the sound, filling my head to bursting.

The cop was standing in his official police stance, a curl of smoke twisting up from the barrel of his pistol, his face glittering with windshield glass.

I looked down to my chest, already pumping blood.

"You—" I heard Burned Dan say, and before I even fell, I'm pretty sure, the cop was down, and then Burned Dan was over me, his destroyed face trying to see all of mine at once.

"Kid, kid," he was saying from the other end of a forever tunnel.

"You're a—you're a . . ." I said up to him, reaching for the sharp teeth he'd done such a good job of keeping hidden all these weeks.

"Yeah, yeah," he said back, his big hand behind my head. "You've got to—if you want me to, if you want to live and not die, you've got to ask. Can you hear me?"

"Thought that was . . . thought that was houses," I said. "Homes."

"*This* is your house," he said, tapping my collarbone, my body.

"Does it hurt?" I asked.

"Every fucking day," he said, and he was right, Burned Dan wouldn't lie to me, wouldn't *have* lied to me, which is why, decades later, Boulder finally tall enough to hide the foothills from this same creek, I finally lay Dan to rest where I first met him.

The tree I get the switch from is maybe thirty feet tall now.

I kneel to lace my right boot up tight and take a slow reading of the dips and swells of the grassland all around, promise myself to never forget this place.

It's a lie, but so is everything, right?

I switch knees for the other boot.

One of the old ad campaigns said a Red Wing will last forever, if you let it.

I'll see about that.

WHERE THE OLD NEIGHBORS GO

THOMAS HA

The man standing on the porch that night seemed like an ordinary gentrifier at first glance: young and tall and artfully unshaven. His jeans were tattered, but strangely crisp, and his shirt was loose and tight in all the wrong places. He had the appearance of someone vaguely famous, like his face could have been in a magazine ad or on the side of a bus. And to anyone other than Mary Walker, he would have successfully passed for a human.

Mary widened the opening of her front door, knowing she could no longer avoid him. She clutched the edges of her stained bathrobe and stared up at the man through the tangle of her gray and white hair.

He smiled, and there was something off, as if his features were meant to be stationary, not stretched in that way. "I thought I should finally introduce myself," he said. "I'm the new neighbor."

The man gestured over his shoulder toward the house across the street. It was an ashen block of concrete and glass, with sharp and modern angles, sitting on a pristine lot with a newly paved driveway. Every time Mary looked at it, she felt nauseous.

"I was wondering what you'd be like," she said.

"And?"

"I don't see any horns," Mary replied.

He laughed, and it, like his smile, seemed out of place. "I was wondering if we could talk, get to know one another. Unless this is a bad time?"

Mary pushed her hair from her eyes and looked out at the dark street. No dog-walkers or joggers in sight. "Why don't you come in?" she said, standing aside.

The man was already through the entryway before she had finished her sentence, peering at Mary's walls and looking around the corner into the den. "What a lovely home," he said monotonously.

Mary tightened the frayed belt of her robe and walked behind him, watching as he ran his fingers along one of her sideboards and around the rim of a decorative vase. He paused at the sectional sofa in the center of the living room, then looked to Mary, as if inviting her to sit.

Mary needed no invitation in her own home. She went to an orange armchair in the corner and dropped into it comfortably, then pointed a bony finger at the sofa. The man sat at her direction, a glimmer of annoyance in his eyes.

"So," Mary began. "You're the one who bought Frank Abra's home."

He nodded. "I met him very briefly after the closing. Nice guy."

"Hm." Mary rested a weathered cheek on her hand. "A lot of people on the hill have been selling lately. But Frank? Didn't strike me as the type."

"Truth be told, I don't know much about him," he shrugged. "I think the house was getting to be too much to maintain." The man glanced at other rooms that were visible from where he sat. "You live alone too, don't you?"

Mary ignored the question. "Frank was getting on in years," she said, scratching at a mole next to her eye with her index finger. "Still, I was surprised—not so much as a for-sale sign, let alone a goodbye. First time I knew what happened was when you got rid of the house."

She vividly remembered the day Frank's place had been demolished last spring.

It had started with a rumbling that made her get out of bed and look out the front window. Mary had watched as a slow-moving caravan of construction vehicles proceeded down the road, then encircled the small, Craftsman bungalow across the street.

She had emerged from her home in her bathrobe and marched over the low bushes in her front yard, waving a hand at one of the drivers.

"Hey!" she yelled. "What're you doing?"

"What's it look like?"

"Where's Frank?" She shaded her eyes with one hand and looked up.

"Ma'am, I don't know who Frank is, but he isn't here. You better back up!"

The construction vehicles roared to life, and the ground began to vibrate as they inched across the lawn.

One of the bulldozers began by tearing through the planks of the front deck. It was an uncovered porch that Frank had built with his wife, Callie, in the Sixties. He hadn't had the strength to repair it in over a decade, so the wood splintered and folded like toothpicks as the bulldozer's blade rippled through with no resistance.

An excavator then approached the side of the house and raised its boom, reminding Mary of an animal rearing to strike. The bucket came down and clawed open a hole in one of the walls, bricks raining down onto the dirt. Mary could see into the home through the wound, the lilac-patterned wallpaper in one of Frank's bedrooms shredded. Several minutes later, the wall next to it, adjacent to Frank's chimney, came apart like cardboard.

Mary covered her nose and mouth with her hand, watching as the sections of Frank's house came undone. Even after the machines left, she lingered on the street and walked through the lot where Frank's home had been, a pile of dirt and rubble that was peppered with pieces of what used to hold the house together.

Mary returned her attention to the young man now sitting on her sofa, trying her best to push the image of the ruined Abra home from her mind.

"Did Frank mention where he was headed?" she asked.

"You know," the man furrowed his brow, "I don't think he did. But I'm sure I have his agent's number somewhere if you'd like to get in touch."

"That's nice of you to offer." Mary leaned on the other side of the armchair. "But enough about Frank. What about you? What brings you to the hill?"

The young man stretched his arms over the back of the sofa, making it a point to show how comfortable he was. "I just really like the neighborhood," he said. "Quiet and removed. There's a good energy about it. And the people seem nice."

"Do they?"

"Relaxed, I guess."

"Relaxed," Mary repeated. "I suppose that's one way to put it."

Mary would have described her neighbors as oblivious.

Not one of them had seemed concerned about Frank when he disappeared. For days after his house was demolished, Mary had gone door to door to see if anyone had heard where Frank was, or even that he was planning to leave.

None of the neighbors had answers, let alone cared.

Of course, it might have had something to do with who was asking. Several of them slammed their doors in Mary's face at the sight of her. Others simply pretended they weren't home. Mary could feel their eyes trailing her from their windows, and a few of them who had known Mary from better days, before she had become this way, had a certain look on their faces that she absolutely could not stand, as if they pitied her.

"Are you . . . taking care of yourself, Mary?" One of the older neighbors looked down at her bathrobe with concern.

"What's to take care of?" Mary scoffed. "It's not like I'm having company anytime soon, am I?" She pushed the tangled strands of her hair out of her face. "I'm just comfortable as I am, thank you very much. But about Frank—"

"I'm sorry, but I really don't know," they said. "You please take care, though, okay, Mary?" The door shut slowly, and Mary muttered to herself as she moved on. She made doubly sure to meet every gaze as she marched down the street, before they each turned away, one by one.

One of the neighbors she did manage to catch at the door, a middle-aged man who lived a few houses down the block, listened to her just long enough to hear her mention Frank's name before interrupting.

"If I tell you what I know," he said, "will you stop calling parking enforcement and asking them to tow my goddamn car?"

Mary was used to these confrontations, and she knew that if she wasn't firm about the way things ought to be, the others would walk all over her. Still, she preferred the honesty of this over the feigned sympathy she got from the others.

"If it doesn't have a permit on the dash, I have to call," she replied. "Could belong to some prowler."

"It's *my* car! You *know* that!"

"I really don't like to assume, you know? Anyway, listen, about Frank—"

This door, like all the others, shut on her.

Mary grimaced to herself as she remembered but paid it no mind. In her several decades of living on the hill, her neighbors had never understood how her watchful eye kept danger away from their homes. But she didn't need their approval to keep things in order.

The young man on the sofa cleared his throat, trying to draw her back into the conversation. "If it's not too much trouble, could I maybe get something to drink?"

"Ah." Mary sat up straight and then pulled herself out of the armchair. "Of course. I've already forgotten basic hospitality. What would you like?"

"Water would be fine."

"Coffee," she said to herself. "It's late, but I think I'll need it for a chat like this. Would you like a cup?"

"Well, actually I said—" the man shifted, seemingly unsure if she was hard of hearing. "Sure. Coffee is fine."

Mary shuffled to the other side of the den, leading the young man, who followed close behind her, through a dining room and into a kitchen in the northwest corner of the house. It was brightly lit, with soothing blue walls and shining tile that Mary scrubbed daily. She pointed absentmindedly to a breakfast nook in the corner, and the young man went over and sat in a chair.

Mary let her fingers run across the marble countertop as she moved around the kitchen in a practiced manner. She took two cups from her favorite, but rarely used, china set, gently placing each one next to the sink before producing a pour-over glass coffee maker from another cupboard and eyeing the curved, transparent body under the light just to make sure that there were no unsightly water marks. She brought out a tin filled with ground coffee she'd harvested from the cherries in the backyard, the earthy, gritty smell soothing her while she continued to assemble what she needed.

As she gathered the accoutrements, her mind began to drift, recalling other times when she used to make things in the kitchen for more than just herself, when the thudding of little feet and high-pitched giggling echoed through the halls, joining the sounds of the sink-water rushing and glasses clattering as she stood at the countertop.

But then Mary remembered where she was again, and more importantly, whom she was with, and the pleasantness vanished.

"Hospitality is important, you know," Mary said, more to herself than the man sitting at the nook, as she focused herself again and removed a coffee filter from the bottom of a small box. "Across all cultures, the code between guest and host is paramount. The Greeks had a special word for it . . ."

"*Xenia*," the young man replied.

"*Xenia*," Mary nodded, pouring the ground coffee on top of a filter and setting a kettle to boil. "That's right. So you're familiar. You have to be at your best, because you never know who, or what, could be visiting you."

"I like that." The young man leaned back, watching Mary carefully as she stood at the kettle.

"In the old stories, some of the worst monsters were the ones who broke that code. Innkeepers that preyed on guests. Bandits who took advantage of generous hosts. It takes something particularly nasty to do that in a home. Homes are sacred."

The water came to a boil.

Mary grabbed the kettle and poured the water over the coffee pot, and the hot liquid dripped down into the glass body, filling it gradually. "Milk? Sugar?"

"Black is fine."

"Black it is." She poured the two cups and brought them over.

The man took the steaming cup and raised it to his lips, blowing gently and about to drink, when he noticed that Mary was watching him. Something about the coffee smelled unusual and caused him to stop.

He laughed, but in a way that seemed genuine for the first time that night—an angry cackle mixed with shock.

Mary drank from her cup and looked back at him. "What is it?"

She knew he had detected it.

Mary always mixed small pieces of aspen bark into her coffee, so that its flavor would seep into the drink. Its effect on ordinary people was negligible, but on things like Mary's visitor, it could have irreparable consequences.

"So much for *xenia*," he said, staring intently at the dark, rippling fluid in the cup in front of him.

"Had to try," Mary shrugged.

In truth, she knew this visit had been coming for some time. She had lived too long, and too cautiously, to ignore the warning signs.

After she couldn't turn up any information on Frank, she had gone, as she often did, to her other sources.

Mary set out early one morning up a dirt path behind her house toward the peak of the hill that overlooked the neighborhood. There was a wooded area, filled with blackened trees that had been caught in a brushfire long ago, yet never managed to die or sprout new growth. She followed the path for a few minutes before turning off from it, keeping track of small knife marks she had left in certain trunks.

Finally, at the heart of the woods, she found the carob tree, gray and knotted. She came within ten feet of it and stopped.

"I need to talk," she said.

The leaves rustled, and there was grunting from some unseen space within the branches. The shaking subsided, and there was a silence before something emerged.

Yellow Eyes peeked his head out, appearing in the form of a large, black crow with greasy feathers.

"Whatever it is, I didn't do it," he said. "Haven't been near any of the folks, just like we agreed." The bird shuffled along the branch and turned its head, the ring of one of its eyes focused on her.

Mary watched Yellow Eyes closely. There were times when he would start a conversation, then pounce on her without warning. The last time he had done that, he had been wearing the body of a copperhead, and she could not feel her hand for over a year after.

"Spoken like an innocent," Mary said. "But no. Someone new is moving to the neighborhood and seems like your type."

"My type?" Yellow Eyes said. "You'll have to be more specific. Charming? Good conversationalist?"

Mary turned around and began to walk away.

"Wait." Yellow Eyes fluttered down from the branch and to the ground in front of the woman. "I'll tell you anything you want, if you just, you know . . ."

The bird gestured with his head toward the circle of pale, purple petals around the carob tree, sprouting up from under the grass and weeds on the forest floor, ever-blooming and just as vibrant as they had been when Mary planted them years ago.

Mary had learned at a young age that creatures like Yellow Eyes could never be confronted directly. Instead, there were other ways, mostly forgotten but still passed down in some families, or buried in books, which Mary made some effort to collect over the years. With the right tools and enough time, she knew she could hold her own against them.

In the case of Yellow Eyes, it took patience, but Mary had meticulously tracked him to his nest after he'd first chosen the crow body. She waited until he was away to seed the circle of vervain, then waited months more as the circle strengthened beneath him and bloomed.

This particular seal, the traveler's knot, was one of the better ones she had crafted in her time on the hill. The living pattern of vervain connected him, not just to the mortal form of the bird he had chosen, but to the tree he had made his home. If anything happened to either the crow or the carob, Yellow Eyes would feel every bit of it, and if the damage was great enough, there were no new bodies that could save him from death. It was a terrifying prospect for a creature who was supposed to live forever.

"Tell me what you know, and I'll decide if it's worth your release," Mary said.

Yellow Eyes crept closer, cocking his head one way and then the other. He drew his beak wide and exposed a row of round, human-like teeth, grinning. "I might have heard about someone who's headed this way. But this one, if it is who I think it is, is definitely not my 'type'."

"Meaning what?"

"Meaning, you know me," Yellow Eyes said. "I'm old-fashioned. I like tricks and deals, the art of a good bargain. But these new things that are coming up now—they're emptier and hungrier, no patience for the craft. They don't get any enjoyment out of the chase the way some of us do."

"Then what do they want?"

"What does any monstrous little toddler want? They want to take everything you have, just as soon as they can swallow it."

Yellow Eyes drew closer to Mary. He puffed his chest and spread his clawed feet on the ground, exposing another set of long, dark fingers between his thin crow toes that curled into the dirt.

His tongue flopped out of his mouth as he salivated, growing over-excited.

Mary could see that Yellow Eyes was beginning to forget himself. She moved slowly to the trunk of the carob tree and reached a hand to the lowest branch, thin enough that she could bend it, but substantial enough that it would work for her.

She snapped it.

Yellow Eyes shrieked as the traveler's knot connected him to the sensation of the branch breaking. He dropped to the ground and twisted in pain as if one of his bones had cracked.

"Settle down," Mary said sharply.

Yellow Eyes shrank and gave the closest thing a bird could to a grimace as he breathed through the pain. "Listen," he heaved, "A couple of little Mary Walker tricks aren't going to cut it with this one. He'll break you in half before you can get anything past him."

"Hm," Mary replied, wondering what she would do if that were true. She knew she would have to think this through carefully in advance.

"So?" Yellow Eyes turned his head, wincing. "You asked; I answered. That clears our ledger, I think."

"Does it?" Mary stared down at the creature. "All I learned was that this stranger is tougher than you are, which," she waved at the vervain flowers, "doesn't tell me much at all."

"Oh, come on." Yellow Eyes flapped his wings. "I played nice, and you can't keep me under the power of this seal forever."

"If I survive, I'll give it some thought." Mary headed back toward the dirt path.

"Mary. Are you serious?"

She waved and kept walking.

"This is why no one likes you," Yellow Eyes screeched. "Mary!"

His cawing carried over the hill, and she heard him for most of the walk back through the woods.

But it turned out, in the end, that Yellow Eyes had been right about Mary's visitor.

The young man didn't seem interested in engaging with, outwitting, or deceiving her. He looked down at the cup of coffee in front of him, dosed with aspen, and his resting expression shifted, almost imperceptibly.

His eyes moved very deliberately from the cup in his hands, up to meet Mary's face.

"I prefer it this way," he said. "Really."

Mary began to retort as she stood up from the nook, but the man interrupted her.

"*Sit*," he said quietly.

The old woman felt her body fold into the seat, like a hand had gripped the back of her neck and pushed her firmly into place, forcing her to stare at the man across from her.

"A little bird told me you were going to be trouble," he said.

Mary's brow creased at the mention of Yellow Eyes, but she did her best to keep her expression neutral. It seemed Mary's visitor had more information about her than she anticipated and, like her, had prepared himself in advance of this night.

The young man pushed his cup across the table. "You know, the thing I enjoy most about a fresh brew is the aroma, flavor ... and heat. *Pick it up.*"

Mary's hand moved of its own accord, taking his cup and bringing it closer.

"*Pour it on your hand. Slowly.*"

It had been a long time since Mary had met someone with a silver tongue as strong as his. There were ways to fight this kind of persuasion, with enough preparation and the right tonics, but she knew that it was futile now to try.

She tipped the cup and watched as the steaming liquid spilled onto the back of her other hand, which was firmly pressed on the surface of the table. Little splatters of coffee bounced off of her skin as her hand grew patchy, red and white blisters beginning to form. Mary did her best not to react, but her breathing grew faster and shallower as her eyes watered. She bit deep into her bottom lip as she felt the pain searing up through her arm.

Rivers of coffee joined around her hand and cascaded off the edge of the table, splashing to the tile below.

"Does it hurt?" the young man asked. "It's hard to tell with you."

Even though she could not stop it, Mary wasn't powerless. There were methods she had learned, still taught by older members of certain monasteries who were wary of creatures like this, that were used to slow the connection from the nerves to the mind, even if only for a few seconds.

Mary breathed steadily and concentrated on the sharp, vibrant smell of the coffee, recalling the way it often drifted up the stairs and along the corridors of the house, up to the bedroom on the second floor, and how, when it did, she could pick up its bitter fragrance, even when she was wrapped in layers of her thick, down blankets early in the morning. She was transported to those chilly hours after sunrise when someone else was brewing a pot, and she could hear the whistling of the kettle as she kept her eyes closed, still fading in and out of consciousness. She recalled her daughter's footsteps, her tiny hands pressing Mary's cheeks and poking her nose while Mary pretended to sleep for a little bit longer.

Mama?

Mary trembled until the last drop of coffee had run out, but she did not make a sound.

When she opened her eyes, the young man seemed to be watching her intently, masking just a hint of frustration. His gaze turned to the second cup of coffee, still steaming, but before he could speak, Mary knocked the cup with the back of her red, blistered hand. It flew off the table and shattered on the kitchen floor with a burst that soaked the floor.

The man crossed his arms. "Now why would you do that? I could just make you refill your cup from the pot, you know."

Mary gripped her burned hand and stared silently.

The man moved over in his chair to a spot at the table that wasn't dripping with coffee. He rested his elbows on its surface and put his chin on his clasped hands. "Go on," he said softly. "Cool that hand. And while you're at it, clean this up."

Mary went to the sink and ran her hand under the cold water. She grabbed a wet cloth from a rack and wrapped her fingers, then took another rag to wipe up the coffee.

"I really meant it earlier, you know," the young man said as he watched her clean the floor. "This is a lovely home. Nicer than I would have expected from the way you keep yourself."

"Thanks," Mary replied dryly, throwing the fragments of the cup in the trash and wringing the rag out in the sink.

"It's obvious you have a real reverence for all these *things*," he waved at the furniture and the decorations surrounding him. "You've practically built a museum here, of fonder times perhaps?" The man gave a knowing half-smile and picked up the other cup on the table, holding it to the light and peering at the sides and the bottom. "But no matter how much meaning and memory you imbue these things with, they'll eventually fall apart. Just like you."

He let the cup drop from his hand and crash to the tile floor below, its pieces scattering in every direction.

"Prick," Mary muttered, getting back on the floor.

"What was that?"

She huffed as she stood, then wiped the table in the breakfast nook before throwing the last few shards away. "You heard it."

"You know." He sat forward. "I could burn this place to the ground, with you still in it. And I wouldn't even have to blink."

"Not likely," Mary replied.

"What?"

"Not likely," she repeated. "If that were true, you'd have done it. You wouldn't waste your time with this coffee and small talk," Mary said. "It's clear you want something from me, or I'd be dead."

His eyes darkened. "Maybe this is it. Maybe I want you to suffer."

"Not likely."

"Stop saying that."

"You would have picked a budding young woman to torture or a family to harass. But an old lady like me has no value, and no value, no entertainment."

The young man tapped the table with his fingers.

"We both want this over with, don't we?" she asked. "What's the point in dragging it out now?"

The man appeared loath to admit it, but Mary could tell that he was growing impatient. After a minute of silence, he reached into his jeans pocket and pulled out a piece of paper, unfolded it and put it down for Mary to see.

She picked it up and read it over as she sat down across from him again. "A quitclaim?" she muttered. Mary studied the language of the document a second time. It was a run-of-the-mill human deed for her property, as far as she could tell. Mary had seen a lot of gambits by his kind, but never anything so pedestrian.

"What could someone like you want with my land?" she asked.

"Doesn't matter." The young man's face went purposefully blank. "But the fact that this also gets you out of this neighborhood now strikes me as a bonus."

Mary ignored the insult and read the document again, trying to guess at what the man was leaving unsaid. She assumed that if he could have forced her to sign, he would have already, but something prevented it. He could try to charm, frighten, or bully her, but, in the end, he wanted this transfer to be voluntary for some reason.

"What about the formalities?" Mary asked. "Price, notarization, things like that?"

"The price is whatever you tell me it is. The rest I can make happen tonight, once you sign. It's just paper, after all."

"And is this the deal you made with Frank Abra?" she asked.

The young man stared back without answering.

Of course, Mary already knew what had happened to Frank without the man saying anything. Weeks after the Abra house was demolished, Mary had visited the lot across the street after sundown, when the construction workers were gone.

She had seen that most of the rubble had been dumped, and a giant pit was ready to be filled with concrete for the house's foundation. Mary brought an old metal detector she had gotten at a garage sale years earlier, barely used except for clearing out rusty nails and other debris in her garden. She paced across the Abra lot, waving the detector around, mostly finding coins and scrap, until she eventually came across a piece of jewelry a few feet from where the new house was to be built.

She reached down and pulled a window locket from the soil.

Mary wiped it with the sleeve of her bathrobe and inspected it. She remembered seeing Callie Abra wear the locket every day as she stood out on the lawn and watered their garden, and, after she passed away, Mary saw Frank put it around his neck too, never once putting it aside or taking it off, always grasping it like it was the most important thing on earth. The fact that it was here, and he wasn't, told her everything she needed to know.

Mary slid it into the pocket of her bathrobe and looked around at the lot one more time.

The truth was that she and the Abras had never really been that close. On the best days, she was polite with them, and on the worst, the whole street could hear their screaming matches.

And yet, Mary realized, as she knelt in the dirt, that the neighborhood felt quieter and lonelier without them.

Her fingers crept to the ground, and she touched the soil, feeling its dampness.

Mary remembered the soil as she stared at the young man in her kitchen, thinking of what best to say.

"What will happen to the neighborhood?" she asked him.

"What?"

"The hill. What will you do to them?"

The man shifted in his seat and squinted at her, as if puzzled by her question. "You know, when I first moved here and asked around, it was funny. I didn't even have to pry. Yours was the name that almost inevitably came up when people talked about this street."

"Guess I'm popular," Mary replied flatly.

"Lady Bathrobe," he said. "The Hag on the Hill. Old Tangle-Hair. The Parking Permit Crusader. The Groaning Crone."

"A couple of those are clever, but the rest are objectively bad."

"'Nobody cares about her,' 'Lives alone for a reason,' they told me." The young man watched Mary sink visibly in her chair. "'Why doesn't she do everyone a favor and just die?'"

Mary squeezed her burned hand.

"They don't even want to look at you. Just the sight of your filthy robe and ratty hair puts them on edge. Most of them wish you would just disappear and never come back." He shook his head. "I know I'm not telling you anything you don't already know."

"So what?" she said softly.

"So, why do you care what happens to this place after you leave?" The man pushed the deed closer to Mary. "You don't need this hill, and if I've learned anything, it's that the hill certainly doesn't need you."

Mary lowered her chin and reached into the pocket of her bathrobe. She felt for the Abras' locket, which she kept there now out of habit, and she touched its smooth, metal edges. For the first time, she didn't have a pithy response for the young man, and he seemed pleased.

"How about, instead of pouring your energy into this house and this hill, maybe you take care of yourself, for once, and enjoy those golden years?" He pinched the sleeve of her tattered bathrobe and smirked. "Because whatever it is you're trying to preserve, it's gone, lady. You've got to see that."

The young man seemed like he was finished speaking and sat back down. Nothing about what the man said changed what Mary was going to do next; in truth, she had made that decision some time ago. But still, when it was quiet again, Mary realized she felt a chill, one that usually visited her when she couldn't fall asleep, and it touched her more deeply than anything else that had happened that night.

After a few seconds, Mary stood and began to walk from the kitchen. The young man followed her, through the study and dining room, and back to the den. Mary approached one of the windows at the front of the house and moved back a heavy curtain, so that she could see across the street clearly.

"There." She pointed at his home, the block of concrete and glass, its modern architecture and chic exterior, like a blight on the hill.

"What about it?"

"You want me to sign? Then I want something first. Whether I leave or not, I can't stand the idea of that shitbox sitting there instead of Frank's place. Makes me sick." Mary gestured over her shoulder. "So let's see if you were telling the truth. Burn it to the ground without blinking, or whatever it was you said."

The young man raised an eyebrow and looked out the window. He was strangely hesitant, and Mary could see that it was her turn to press him.

"That's what I thought," she laughed.

"What?"

"Acting smug and lecturing me about the meaning of 'things'. But I can see it, you're just as attached as I am. Bet you picked the design of that place because you saw it in some magazine. Maybe that's how you picked your face too. All you ugly little fiends just want to be pretty deep down, after all."

"Don't be ridiculous," he scoffed, seeming to grow more self-conscious by the second, as if even the vaguest accusation that he shared anything in common with Mary were perverse.

"Go on," Mary grinned. "It doesn't matter to you, does it? You'll still have the land. Just burn that monstrosity on top of it, and I'll believe you're serious about your offer. I'll sign the deed, just like you want, and we can call it a night and stop wasting everyone's time. What do you say?"

Now it was his turn to go quiet.

"Unless . . ." Mary looked out the window. "Your whole scheme was to build a suburb of shitboxes, because you love playing house so much? Maybe that's the problem?"

The man eyed Mary, trying to understand why she was being so insistent, but his expression began to change, his pride and his eagerness to finish things winning out. Before he had uttered a word, she knew that she had him.

The young man looked back out the window and nodded his head.

The flames across the street erupted suddenly, from no single source.

In seconds, the entire concrete and glass house was surrounded by a growing fire. The stone did not burn, but the supports and framing inside began to split and crack as the heat spread.

Mary looked over at her visitor, holding her breath.

He began blinking rapidly, and he touched his throat.

Part of the living room of the concrete house tumbled as a support beam crashed to the ground. Some of the glass at the front of the house began to ooze into liquid, pouring onto the lawn, while furniture inside the structure shrank and collapsed.

"Does it hurt?" she asked. "It's hard to tell with you."

The man opened his mouth to respond, but his voice was only a rasp.

The young man staggered out of the den and toward the front door.

Mary watched from the window as he stumbled across the street toward the flaming house, his silhouette twisting and stretching as the fire raged in front of him.

She imagined that as he stepped across the lawn, he finally noticed, hidden among the blades of grass, the pale, purple vervain flowers, just beginning to bloom—the ones she had planted late at night, well before the foundation in that place had been poured, when she had wandered onto the Abra lot, so small and scattered that they probably never caught his eye before.

She still remembered the sensation of the soil, the dampness of it, as she placed the seeds around the property in the right formation, the beginnings of the traveler's knot that would eventually, quietly bind him to that body and to that home.

The young man now turned to look at Mary in the window. There was no time to return to her house and try to compel her to release the bond of the traveler's knot, and even if he could stop the flames, the house was too far gone, the inside of the structure crumbling, much as the insides of his body likely were. The young man knew, just as Mary did, that it was too late now to avoid what was coming.

His face began to collapse, like desiccated dirt, and his true appearance emerged from what remained of his head. Mary always had trouble seeing the real faces of his kind, but he, like all of them, looked like a shifting pool of ink to her, blurred and shapeless.

After a moment of stillness, he looked away and continued forward into the house, moving through a gap where one of the large floor-to-ceiling windows had melted away. Mary could only guess, but as he went further through the flames, she thought he was trying to hide himself, not wanting to give anyone the satisfaction of seeing what was happening to him in his final moments.

He stood with his back toward Mary as everything came apart around him, his tall shape disappearing in the crackling and roaring that filled the concrete block as the fire stretched to the glowing, night sky.

Mary went to her porch and sat on the top step, covering her mouth and nose with the wet rag on her hand. Other neighbors were at their windows, or on their front steps as sirens drew closer to the bottom of the hill.

As she watched the sky darken, a vast cloud of smoke growing above the neighborhood, a crow with greasy feathers landed on the eaves above her.

"I don't understand," Yellow Eyes said. "You had him in a knot. You could have struck a deal, made him grovel, work for you, even. Why?"

Mary did not turn away from the flames. "Maybe he did something to piss me off."

Yellow Eyes watched the fire, as entranced as everyone else.

"Next time you try to play both sides, you'll remember this, though, won't you?" She looked at him coldly.

The crow turned a solid yellow ring of its eye at the old woman, flexed his wings, then took off toward the top of the hill without another word.

By the time the ambulances and fire trucks arrived, a couple of the house's walls were leaning and another had fallen. Everything inside had already been consumed.

There was, in Mary's mind, nothing more to save.

* * *

In the days after that fire, Mary returned to her daily routine. Standing each morning on her lawn with a cup of coffee, she scanned the dashboards of the parked cars on the street for any without a permit, then she walked down the block to see if any recycling or trash bins were put out early or left too late, in violation of the county code.

When she wasn't watching for unusual cars or strangers entering the neighborhood, she found herself staring at the charred walls of what used to be the concrete house across the street, imagining the old Craftsman in its place while she gripped the Abras' locket in her hand.

Frank would have come slowly down the steps on each of those mornings to retrieve his mail, gripping one of the handrails—sometimes nodding at Mary and sometimes not. But instead, there was nothing but an ugly view of gray rock and blackened wood. Even now, no one was asking where Frank went, Mary realized, and it was unlikely that any of them ever would.

No one ever asks where the old neighbors go, she thought.

Despite herself, Mary continued to dwell on what the young man said to her the night of the fire. As she dusted her sideboards and vases, she often lost interest, like everything had become too tiresome to finish. When she felt that way, Mary wandered upstairs, to one of the quiet rooms that usually sat untouched, the bed inside still perfectly made and flowery wallpaper around it covered with soft light that flowed through sheer curtains.

She knelt in front of a trunk, unlatching and lifting it open, and peered down at a cluttered pile of old dolls and wooden toys, all of them associated with some holiday or birthday that came back to her as she brought her fingers lightly over them.

In those instances, Mary sometimes considered, for a brief moment, finally throwing them out. Her daughter was never going to use them, after all—she would never brew a pot of coffee for Mary downstairs, or chatter away with her in the kitchen while sitting at the breakfast nook, or touch Mary's cheek to wake her up.

Things would never be like they were again, she knew.

But still, she couldn't bring her hands to move, to take anything from the trunk, and she sat paralyzed for longer than she expected. She kept imagining the young man, standing in front of the roaring flames, and thought, for some reason, that she too might begin to crumble and collapse inward, to fall apart bit by bit, if she were to alter anything in the house, no matter how small.

So, instead, Mary put everything back, got on her feet, and then closed the door to the room behind her—each time, more intent than before to leave things in their place, exactly as they were.

DEAD BRIGHT STAR (JULY 1987)

CAITLÍN R. KIERNAN

I dislike coming here. But that's no secret. Dr. Knowles is well enough aware exactly how much I dislike coming to see her, or at least she knows as much as I've told her. I've said, "I'd rather be doing almost anything else." I've said, "It was never my idea, starting this. I wouldn't have, not if I'd have had a choice." I've spent entire fifty-minute sessions staring out her office window at the parking lot, counting the cars that come and go instead of talking, noting their make and model and color and the faces of their drivers rather than puking up any more of my soul to this woman. And she sits there in her swivel chair, infuriatingly patient, watching me, watching me as if even when I'm intentionally doing nothing I'm inadvertently doing something, as if saying nothing is saying *everything* she wants to hear. And that makes this seem all the more like a trap. Inaction is action. Someone said that to me a long time ago, but I can no longer remember who. Someone I went to bed with. Someone I fucked because I had nothing better to do, so I forgot his face or her face and got on with my life and didn't look back. Except to not forget that line, *Inaction is action.* In one corner of Dr. Knowles office there's a small Swiss cheese plant in a terra-cotta pot. And I've been staring at it for fifteen minutes now, not talking just staring at that damn plant, but I can tell that she's about to say something. I don't want her to be the first to speak. I'd rather that be me, if anyone has to say anything, I'd rather it be me. So, I say "Did you know that the Latin name for that plant is *Monstera deliciosa?*"

"No," says Dr. Knowles, "I didn't know that." And she doesn't smile or frown or anything. Except she pretends to be interested in what I've asked her. I can always tell when she's only pretending.

"Well, it is," I say.

"How do you know that?" she asks.

Instead of answering the question, I shrug and I tell her that the name means *delicious monster.* Or *monstrous and delicious,* depending what order you translate it in.

"Did you study botany in college?" she wants to know.

"No," I tell her, and that's the truth. I've told Dr. Knowles a lot of lies, just to keep her happy and pass the time, but that isn't one of them. I stare at the strange glossy leaves, and I just say, "My mom had a big one when I was a kid. Lots bigger than that one," and that's enough about the stupid Swiss cheese plant. Dr. Knowles has gotten pretty good at being able to see when I just want to let something drop, and she doesn't push. She doesn't *push,* but she does *prod.*

I'm quiet again for almost five minutes, and then she decides to prod.

"What you told me about the attic," she says, "was that one of the true things?"

Yes, she knows that I lie to her sometimes. She's known that almost from the very beginning, almost from the first time I came here to this tiny office and had to sit in the waiting room and then had to sit on this sofa and watch the clock or the parking lot or the Swiss cheese plant until my time was up and I could leave.

"Mostly," I tell her, and mostly that's not a lie.

"Could we talk about that some more?" she asks. "We still have thirty-five minutes today. We won't if you don't feel like it, but I wanted to ask, just in case."

"We won't what?" I ask her, asking just to be difficult. "We won't what if I don't want to?"

"We won't talk about the attic. If you don't want to."

"It was just a goddamn attic. What's there to talk about?" And I decide to stare out the window at the parking lot for a little while instead of staring at the Swiss cheese plant. There's a white Volkswagen Bug, and I've always wanted one of those, even if they were invented by the Nazis. When I was a little girl, when I was in elementary school, my mom had one. It was the color of rust, because it mostly was rust, and in places the floorboard had rusted out and there were pieces of plywood covering the holes. And that's twice today my mom has come up, but I don't let myself pause to think about that. What could be more fucking cliché than thinking about your mother in a psychiatrist's office? Almost nothing, that's what. Almost nothing.

"Fine," I say. "We can talk about the attic, if that's what you want."

"Okay," says Dr. Knowles. "Can we talk about Mistral, too?"

And now I'm quiet again for a little while, because she's caught me off my guard, though I don't know why. Why did I think she'd want to talk about the attic if not because of Mistral? Otherwise, the attic was just an attic, just a place where people put things that were in their way and that they probably never wanted to see again. Never wanted to *have* to see again. Isn't that what attics are for?

"Mistral is one of the eight winds of the Mediterranean," I say. "It means *masterly* in French." That part's not true. *Mistral* means *masterly* in the Languedoc dialect of Occitan, which isn't the same as French at all. It's a Romance language, but it isn't French. Anyway, like I said already, sometimes I lie to Dr. Knowles. Sometimes I just tell her things I know are not true. "It's one of the eight winds," I say again. "It's cold and dry and blows on sunny, bright days. It almost drove Vincent Van Gogh insane. He had to battle the mistral day after day after day when he was living at his yellow house in Arles."

"But that's not the Mistral I meant," says Dr. Knowles, as if I don't know. As if I don't know that she already knows that I know. "We were going to talk about the attic, because you said that was okay, so when I asked about Mistral–"

"I know what you were asking," I tell her, interrupting and not caring that I'm interrupting her.

"So, can we talk about *that* Mistral, the Mistral from the attic?"

"You really think we've got time left for that?" I ask her, still staring out the window at the white Volkswagen. I always thought if I could have one of my own I would want it to be green, grasshopper green.

"I think so," says Dr. Knowles. "I think we do."

I stare at the parking lot, the blacktop and white lines and yellow lines painted on the blacktop, and I close my eyes and imagine myself behind the wheel of a grasshopper-green Volkswagen Bug. I imagine myself driving far, far, far away from Dr. Knowles and this whole damn city and everything I have ever known and everything I ever have said. But it doesn't last, the pictures I'm making in my mind of the car and my getaway, of highways in places I've never been, because suddenly I'm thinking about the attic, instead. I'm thinking about the first night in the attic. Or the first day. I have trouble being sure, sometimes, maybe all the time, whether it was night or day. I've gone up the stairs again, the stairs leading to the narrow trap door, and I've pulled the bit of rope again, the bit of rope that opens the door. And then there's the smell of dust and mold and spiders and moths and all the stuff that people put in attics and to forget.

"Are you okay?" Dr. Knowles asks me, and I smile. I didn't mean to smile, I don't think, but I do smile, and I open my eyes.

"I'm fine," I tell her. "Why wouldn't I be fine."

"I was only asking," she replies.

"I'm fine," I say again.

"We don't have to talk about her today, not if you aren't feeling up to it."

"I said I was fine, didn't I?"

Dr. Knowles is quiet for a moment, and then she nods and says yes, yes, that's what I'd said, what I'd told her, that I was fine.

"I wouldn't have said it if it weren't true."

"I know," says Dr. Knowles, pretending she believes what she's saying, and I listen and pretend I believe it, too.

Dry, cold air that smells like the act of forgetting, the desire to forget. The need.

I stop turn my head away from the window and the parking lot, deciding it's better if I look at Dr. Knowles and the Swiss Cheese plant and the clock and the office. There's no grasshopper-green Volkswagen waiting for me down there or anywhere else. It's cruel to think how maybe there could be. It's masochistic.

"I go up the stairs and I open the door. I open the little white door and I climb up into the attic of my mother's house."

"Have you noticed that you always say that it was your mother's house? Wasn't it your house, too? You lived there."

"No," I reply. "I mean yes, I lived there, but it was my mother's house, and she never let me forget it. Not after I was out of high school. Do you want to talk about my mother or do you want me to talk about Mistral?"

"Well," says Dr. Knowles, "I want you to talk about what you need to talk about."

Liar, I think. *You are a filthy liar, even if I don't know why, even if I can't figure out what you have to gain from telling me lies, and you just want to hear the things I don't want to tell you.*

I stand in the attic, and now there's a rectangular hole in the floor at my feet. It would be easy to step into that hole by accident and fall and break my neck. My damn fool neck, my mother would say, but I don't tell Dr. Knowles that's what she'd say. I stand there looking at the hole in the floor, and I reach for the light cord. It's just a frayed length of kitchen twine, the light cord, leading up to a socket and a bare bulb. Nothing fancy in this old house. I find the cord, and when I pull it nothing happens. The bulb's blown out. It might have been blown a long time, because no one ever comes up into the attic. There's nothing up here that anyone wants, only things no wants anymore, only things that were put here so no one would ever have to think about them again.

"The light was burned out," I tell Dr. Knowles.

"I remember," she says.

"We didn't go up there. Mom didn't like for us to go up there. She always said she didn't like the sound of footsteps in the attic, so we didn't go up there very much, my dad and me. Not that there was any reason to."

I don't just pull the cord once. I probably pull it two or three times, and then I think how I should go back down the stairs and get a new bulb out of the drawer in the pantry where we keep light bulbs. I don't do that, though. I can't say why, but I don't do that. I stand there with my hand on the length of twine, peering into the darkness. There's a little bit of light getting in from the tiny window all the way down at the other end of the attic. If I'm up there in the daytime, than it's sunlight sifting through dust and the heavy curtains hung over the window. If it's night, it's the streetlight on the corner, cold white light and not warm yellow light.

"Why did you go up there that day?" asks Dr. Knowles. "I don't think you've ever told me why."

"It was so long ago, I don't think I remember why anymore," I tell her, though that isn't true. But sometimes I have to hold a few scraps of the truth back for myself, even when I'm trying hard not to lie.

Liar. You are a filthy liar, even if I don't know why, even if I can't figure out what you have to gain . . .

"My mother wasn't home," I say. "She'd gone to the market for something. I don't remember what, but she'd gone out to the market, so—whyever I'd gone into the attic, whatever I was up there looking for—that was a good time, because she wouldn't hear my footsteps on the ceiling."

Standing there beside the hole in the floor and the steps leading back down from the attic, squinting into the gloom, I am surrounded by all those forgotten, castoff things, by cardboard boxes taped shut for decades, by stacks of newspapers from before I was born, by ratty furniture and things that were mine when I was a little kid, things that mattered a lot to me back then, but which I have not thought about in ages. Those things, they're nearest the attic door. Board games and broken toys, a rocking horse that my grandfather made, a tall can of Lincoln logs. Children's books in crooked stacks, and I think how they've probably been eaten at by silverfish and roaches and mice and whatever else lives in attics and feasts on children's books.

"You didn't see her right away," says Dr. Knowles, not *asking* but *telling* me, and I think how a lawyer or a judge on a TV show might say that's leading the witness, something like that. "I mean, that's what you've said before," she adds, so I think it must have also occurred to her that there was something untoward about *telling* me what I saw and when I saw it.

DEAD BRIGHT STAR (JULY 1987)

"No," I reply. "I was too busy wanting to go back downstairs. Or I was too busy looking around at all the junk up there. Or both maybe. So no, I didn't see her right away." I say these things to answer her question, but I'm still thinking how sitting on the sofa in Dr. Knowles' office isn't so very different than being in court, up on the witness stand, replying to the prosecution and the defense and the judge—but especially to the prosecution. I'm thinking how maybe the difference between lawyers and psychiatrists isn't as great as most people probably assume it to be (though, if I am to be honest, I can't claim to understand all that much about how anyone but me sees the world or anyone else but themselves).

I look out at the parking lot again, fringed in leafy-green mimosa and magnolia and whatever else, but even with the shade from the trees the day's gonna be so hot the asphalt will be soft long before sunset. And that makes me think about the La Brea tar pits and mammoths and ground sloths and whatever else getting mired in the tar and dragged down to their deaths. And that makes me think about Mistral. No, I mean *really* think about her for the first time since coming into Dr. Knowles' office today. I rub my eyes and turn away from the window again.

"Did I ever tell you about the time I saw the La Brea tar pits?" I ask her, and she looks confused and leans back in her chair and almost (but only almost) frowns at me.

"No," she says, apparently deciding to weather without compliant my so suddenly changing the subject like that. "No, you never did."

"I was ten years old. My dad moved to LA after the divorce, but you know that. He took me to see the tar pits and the museum next to the tar pits with all the bones they'd pulled out of them over the decades. I had nightmares about them for a while afterwards, about what it would be like to get stuck in the tar and slowly pulled down, strangling, suffocating. You know. It must be an awful way for anything to die, even if you are only a dire wolf or only a coyote."

Dr. Knowles nods her head, and I can see now that she gets the connection, that I hadn't actually changed the subject after all. She stops almost frowning and her expression goes all non-judgmentally neutral again.

"The first thing I remember in the attic," I tell her, "the first thing out of the ordinary, was a smell like the tar pits had smelled that day, the sticky, pungent melted tar smell. And the second thing I noticed that was out of the ordinary, or maybe it wasn't but it seemed that way to me, there was this tidy little pile of dead mice right next to the attic door. Like someone had stacked them there a long time ago. They were just husks, little mouse mummies, as if they'd been there so long they'd desiccated."

Or as if something had come along and sucked them all dry.

And maybe that's just what happens to evil little fucking mice that snack on old children's books.

"It was summer, right?" asks Dr. Knowles.

"Yeah, it was July. Like now. And that was the third strange thing," I say. "It should have been hot as blue blazes up there in the attic, but it wasn't. It was cold, like there was an air conditioner running full blast. We didn't even have AC downstairs, just box fans. But I swear, it was like a meat locker up there. I realized that I could see my breath fog."

And across all these years and everything that's happened since, I'm standing in the dark with the rectangle of light at my feet, and there's the tidy pile of mouse husks, and the tar smell burns my nostrils, and I really can see my breath fogging. *Don't you run,* I think. *Don't you dare fucking run. You'll just have to come back later on and spend all the time between now and then feeling foolish and dreading it.* And then I think, *Yeah, but I could come back with a fresh goddamn light bulb.*

"And that's when you realized you weren't alone?" asks Dr. Knowles.

I nod my head, and then I answer, "Yeah, that's when I saw her. She was sitting in an old armchair at the other end of the attic, sort of curled up in it, the way you do in armchairs, just sitting there watching me."

If it's nighttime, it's the streetlight on the corner, cold white light and not warm yellow light.

"How did that make you feel?"

"How do you *think* it made me feel?" And the words are out before I can think better of them or the annoyed tone in my voice, but Jesus, what a dumb goddamn question. I imagine Dr. Knowles, fifteen years younger sitting through some college lecture, learning how to ask perfectly idiotic questions once she got her own practice.

DEAD BRIGHT STAR (JULY 1987)

"I'm sorry," she says, a little too quickly. "I shouldn't have—"

But I interrupt her for the second time this session. "Like being stabbed in the gut with an icicle," I say, wondering if it actually did feel anything like that, what it would feel like to be stabbed in the belly with an icicle, if I'd feel the cold before I felt the pain or if I'd feel both right about the same time or what. "It should have scared the shit out me, especially since I was already jumpy and all. It didn't though. There was just this sharp coldness in my guts, and I stood there staring back at her. She had bright blue eyes. I could tell even from my end of the dark attic, how bright and blue her eyes were, and it's not like they were glowing or anything hokey like that, not like something from a monster movie."

And I can see Dr. Knowles wanting to ask me, *And then what happened? What happened next? And how did that make you feel?* Even though she's heard this all once or twice before and has it all written down somewhere. Or maybe it's just that she sees so many crazy women that she can't keep us straight or she forgets shit. I don't know. I'm not even sure if I'm telling this story exactly the same way that I've told it to her before, but that's okay. Dr. Knowles would probably be the first to tell me that any deviations are significant, that what did or did not actually happen that day or night is entirely irrelevant. It's what I remember, on this particular day, and how, on this particular day, it makes me feel. That's what's important. Or maybe I'm just being an asshole. I am my mother's daughter, after all, and I never rule out that possibility.

"Her eyes were bright and blue," I say again. "Like blue ice, the way ice is blue inside a glacier. That cold blue, like all that freezing air pressing in around me. And I just stood there staring at her, and she just sat there, curled into that old armchair watching me. I wanted to say something, but I couldn't, and I remember wondering if possibly my jaws and tongue had frozen solid. And then she smiled."

Dr. Knowles is chewing at her lower lip, and I wonder if she's aware that she's doing it. I wonder if she's aware that I've noticed.

"Her smile wasn't as bright as her eyes," I go on, "but it almost was, and I realized then I wasn't so much seeing a woman down there at the other end of my mother's attic. No, I was seeing nothing at all, a hole in reality, and maybe it was *shaped* like a woman, and maybe it actually had *been* a woman once, a long, long, long time ago, like how a long time ago all those bones from the tar pits had been parts of living animals. That's what I was seeing, this hole punched in the world, and only those bright blue eyes and that white smile was any more solid than nothingness."

And what happened next? Do you remember what happened next? Is that when she told you that her name was Mistral?

No, that's when she stood up . . .

That's when she came apart.

And what do you think you really saw?

I glance at the clock and am relieved that there's only fifteen minutes to go. Then I rub my eyes and remember that scene in *Ferris Bueller's Day Off* when the clock starts running backwards. At least, I think it was in *Ferris Bueller's Day Off*; it might have been in some other movie, that scene.

"She wasn't real," I say.

"What do you mean by that?" asks Dr. Knowles, and she stops chewing at her lip, and I think she's probably stopped just a second or two before drawing blood.

"I mean it was dark, and I don't know what I really saw."

. . . the most beautiful woman that I ever saw, ever, the most beautiful thing, the most awful thing, the most broken thing, the most utterly irredeemable thing, and she told me that her name was Mistral, and she had a French accent. Or I think it was a French accent. It might have been Occitan, lenga d'òc, *like the word* mistral, *which is a cold, dry wind blowing through the attic of my mother's house.*

"I mean," I tell Dr. Knowles, "that I might have been imagining things. When I was a kid, my mother said I was bad about imagining things. Or just making things up to get attention, so maybe that's all I'm doing now."

Imagining that I saw a hole in the world that called itself Mistral and spoke with a voice like winter. Or lying and inventing her because I'm sick of my life and sick of how one day just keeps coming after another and sick of sitting on this sofa and telling you things I would rather keep to myself.

"I don't think you're making it up," Dr. Knowles says, in that phony way that's meant to be comforting, that's meant to assure me that she trusts me and believe every syllable that crosses my lips is gospel.

"But you don't *know* that I'm not, do you?"

"Are you a ghost?" I heard myself say, and the hole in the world with bright blue eyes and that guillotine smile replied, "No, dear. I'm not a ghost. I remember dying. In fact, I remember dying twice, but I'm not a ghost. Still, if it's easier that way, simpler for you to understand, I don't mind if you think of me as a ghost. Not if that makes it easier on you. I'm not here to cause you any pain."

"No," Dr. Knowles admits to me. "I can't ever be sure that you're telling me the truth. But I do think that what you're telling me means something, even if you're making it all up. Fiction takes the shape it does because there's something we need to get out, something we need to say, and that's as important as whatever might have actually happened. I think I told you that once before, when we were talking about your cousin."

And I almost tell her I think she's full of shit. But only almost.

I can stand another few minutes, so long as the clock hasn't started running backwards on me.

"I mean to tell the truth," I say, but that might just be the worst lie I've ever told.

"I know," says Dr. Knowles, as if she possibly could ever know a thing like that.

"I do mean to."

"I understand," she says, and then reaches for her day planner, and I breathe a sigh of relief. "Maybe this would be a good place to stop for the day. We can come back to it next time. Or we can talk about something else. Whatever you need."

A grasshopper-green Volkswagen Bug, that's all I need. All I need in the world.

"Okay," I tell her, and I reach for my purse on the table, and Dr. Knowles smiles and scribbles in her book.

AND THIS IS HOW
TO STAY ALIVE

SHINGAI NJERI KAGUNDA

Baraka

Kabi finds my body swinging. I watch my sister press her back against the wall and slide to the ground.

My mother shouts, "Kabi! Nyokabi!"

No response.

"Why are you not answering? Can you bring that brother of yours!"

My sister is paralyzed, she cannot speak, she cannot move, except for the shivers that take hold of her spine and reverberate through the rest of her without permission. She is thinking No, no, no, no, no.

But the word is not passing her lips which only open and close soundlessly. Mum is coming down the stairs.

Pata–pata-pata.

Slippers hitting the wooden floorboards in regular succession. In this space between life and after, everything is somehow felt more viscerally. Mum is not quiet like Kabi. Mum screams, "My child . . . Woiiiii woiii woiiiiiiiiiiiiiii! Mwana wakwa. What have you done?"

She tugs, unties the knot, and wails as I fall limp to the ground. She puts her ear on my heart. "Kabi. Call an ambulance! Kab–I hear his life; it is not gone, quick, Kabi quick."

Kabi does not move; cannot move. She is telling herself to stand, telling her feet to work but there is miscommunication between her mind and the rest of her.

Mum screams at her to no avail. Mum does not want to leave my body. She feels if she is not touching me, the life will finish, and the cold will seep in. Death is always cold. She wraps me in a shuka. It does not make sense, but she drags my body down the hall to the table where she left her phone. "Ngai Mwathani, save my child." She begs, "You are here; save my child."

She calls an ambulance. They are coming—telling her to remain calm. She screams at them, "Is it your child hovering between life and death? Do not; do not tell me to stay calm!"

She calls my father. When she hears his voice she is incoherent but he understands he must come.

The hospital walls are stark white. There are pictures hanging on one wall, taken over sixty years ago, before our country's independence. White missionary nurses smiling into the lens, holding little black children; some with their ribs sticking out. This is what fascinates Kabi—she cannot stop staring at the black and white photos. The doctor comes to the waiting room area and Kabi looks away. She knows it in her spirit; she cannot feel me.

It is not until my mother begins to wail that the absence beats the breath out of her. Kabi feels dizzy. The ground comes up to meet her and Dad is holding Mum so he does not catch Kabi in time. The doctor keeps saying, "I am sorry. I am sorry. I am so sorry."

For Kabi, the sounds fade but just before they do, somewhere in her subconscious she thinks she will find me in the darkness. Yes, she is coming to look for me.

But I am not there.

Funerals are for the living, not the dead. Grief captures lovers and beloved in waves; constricting lungs, restricting airflow, and then when and only when it is willing to go does it go. Kabi tries to hold back tears—to be
responsible

oldest
daughter.

Visitors stream in and out. She serves them tea; microwaves the samosas and mandazis that aunty made then transitions into polite hostess.

"Yes, God's timing is best.

No, as you can imagine we are not okay but we will be.

Yes, we are so grateful you have come to show your support.

No, Mum is not able to come downstairs. She is feeling a bit low but I am sure she will be fine.

Yes, I will make sure to feed her the bone marrow soup. I know it is good for strength.

No, we have not lost faith."

But sometimes; sometimes she is in the middle of a handshake, or a hug, or a sentence when grief takes her captive;
binding her sound,
squeezing her lungs,
drawing her breath.

She holds herself. She runs to the bathroom or her room or anywhere there are no eyes
and she screams silently without letting the words out . . .
her own private little world out.

Nyokabi

"Wasted tears." The lady, one of Mum's cousins: second? Or third? Clicks and shakes her head. How long has she been standing there?

I open my mouth, shut. Open again, silence; can only lick my wounds and move away. There is really nothing to say after that dismissal. I shift, angling my body away from her, lifting my half open silver notebook off the bathroom counter. The bathroom door, slightly ajar, is calling me to the space between its bark and the wall. I will not beg for sympathy. The pen drops and I swear I see a spark as it hits the ground. Can you see sound?

"Shit." The word slips out before I realize who I am in the room with. I pick up the pen and attempt to squeeze past her body which is covering the space I saw as my escape route.

A sucking in of teeth. "Kabi, wait!"

I turn my head slightly back. She asks, "What does *gone* mean for you?"

I am confused by the question; have no time for old woman foolishery. Already there is Tata Shi shouting my name in the kitchen. "Yes?" I answer because I must be

Responsible

      Oldest

         Daughter

Always in that order. No time for my grief, no time for Mama's cousin, second? Or third? To sit with and dismiss my grief. The first *yes* was not heard so I shout again, hearing my voice transverse rooms. "Yes Tata?"

And the response: "Chai inaisha, kuna maziwa mahali?"

How to leave politely, because respect; to mumble under my breath something about going to make tea for the guests.

"You have not answered my question."

I sigh, in a hurry to leave, "What was the question?"

"*Gone*, child—these terms that talk circles around death: *gone*, no longer with us, passed away, passed on—what do you think they mean?

"NYOKABI?" Tata is sounding irritated now, she is trying not to, but you can always tell when she is.

"COMING!" I scream back, and to the woman in front of me, "*Gone* is . . . not here."

"Aha, you see but *not here* does not mean *not anywhere*."

This woman is talking madness now. I mumble, "Nimeitwa na Tata Shi, I have to attend to the guests now."

She smiles. "I know you are trying to dismiss me Kairetu but here, take this."

She slips a little bottle into my hand just as I widen the door to leave. She says, "a little remedy for sleep. There are dark circles around your eyes."

I slip the bottle into the pocket of my skirt and run to the kitchen, no time to look or to ask, no time to wonder or to wander, no time to be anywhere or to be anything but the
Responsible
        Oldest . . . only?
        Daughter.

Baraka

This is how to not think about dying when you are alive: look at colors, every color, attach them to memory. The sky in July is blue into gray like the Bahari on certain days. Remember the time the whole family took a trip to Mombasa, and Kabi and you swam in the ocean until even the waves were tired. Kabi insisted that you could not go to Mombasa and not eat authentic coast-erean food, so even though everyone else was lazy and Dad had paid for full-board at White Sands Hotel, the whole family packed themselves into his blue Toyota and drove to the closest, tiny, dusty Swahili restaurant you could find. It smelled like incense, Viazi Karai, and Biryani. Are these the smells of authentic coast-erean food?

This is how to not think about dying when you are alive: take note of smell, like the first time you burned your skin and smelled it. The charring flesh did not feel like death; in fact it reminded you of Mum's burned pilau; attach feeling to memory.

"Tutafanya nini na mtoto yako?" Dad never shouted, but he didn't need to.

"What do you mean? Did I make him by myself? He is your son as well." Mum was chopping vegetables for Kachumbari.

"Yes, but you allowed him to be too soft." Her hand, still holding the knife, stopped mid-air, its descent interrupted, and she turned around to face him, her eyes watery and red from the sting of the onions.

"Too soft? Ken? Too soft? Did you see him? Have you seen your son? The fight he was involved in today . . . he can barely see through one eye. How is that softness?" Baba looked away, Mum's loudness overcompensating for his soft-spoken articulation.

"Lakini Mama Kabi, why was he wearing that thing to school?"

She dropped the knife. "Have you asked him? When was the last time you even talked to him Ken? Ehe? "

Quick breaths. "We went to the church meeting for fathers and sons. I spend time with him."

"Ken, you talk to everyone else about him and you talk at him, but you never talk to him. Maybe if you were here more . . ."

"Don't tell me what I do and do not do in my own house Mama Nyokabi. Do I not take care of the needs of this house? Nani analipa school fees hapa? You will not make so it looks like I do not take my responsibilities seriously. If there is a problem with that boy it is not because of me!"

Smoke started rising from the sufuria. You reacted, pushing yourself from behind the door, forgetting you were not supposed to be in such close vicinity to this conversation. "Mum, chakula chinaungua!"

She rushed to the stove, turned off the gas, and then realized you were in the room, looked down, ashamed that they were caught gossiping. The smell of burned pilau.

This is how to not think of dying when you are alive. Move your body; like the first time you punched Ian in the face.

Whoosh!

Fist moving in slow motion, blood rushing through your veins, knuckles-connecting-to-jaw-line, adrenaline taking over: alive, alive, alive, alive, alive. This is how to be alive. This is how to not think about dying when you're alive.

Of-course this was right after Ian had called you shoga for wearing eyeliner to school and then said, "Ama huelewi? Do you want me to say it in English so you understand F-A—"

"Go fuck yourself!" you screamed and punched simultaneously. And of-course this singular punch was right before Ian punched you back and did not stop punching you back over and over and over but God-knows you kicked and you moved and you were alive.

Nyokabi

On the night before the funeral,

I am exhausted but I cannot sleep. There is shouting upstairs. I close my eyes as if that will block my ears from hearing the sound. A door is banged. I hear footsteps shuffling down the stairway.

I should go and check if everything is okay, but I do not want to. I cover my head with my pillow and count one to ten times a hundred, but I still cannot sleep.

I switch on my phone: so many missed calls, and "are you okay?" texts. I see past them, my mind stuck on a thought. Could I have known?

Google
How to know when someone is suicidal
Offered list by WebMD:

- Excessive sadness or moodiness
- Hopelessness
- Sleep problems
- Withdrawal . . .

Things I have now, things everyone has at some point. I can hear them whispering in the hallway. The main lights are off so they do not know I am in his room. Mum has been looking for every opportunity to pick a fight with anyone and everyone since Baraka...

I switch on the bedside lamp, look around the room, and feel the need to clean, to purge, to burn, everything reminds me of him. I notice the skirt I left on the dark brown carpet, tufts fraying in the corner of the fabric, a bottle peeking out—bluish with dark liquid and I remember the old lady; Mum's cousin, twice removed, or thrice? What have I to lose? I pick at the skirt, unfolding its fabric until I get to the bottle stuck in the pocket. It is a strange little thing, heavier than it should be. I try and decipher the inscrutable handwriting on the white label. One teaspoon? I think it says but can't be too sure. I open the lid, sniff it, and wrinkle my nose. The scent is thick, bitter; touching the sense that is in-between taste and smell. All I can think is I am so very exhausted and I do not want to wake up tomorrow. Can I skip time? I throw my head back, taking down a gulp. Its consistency is thick like honey but it burns like pili-pili.

At first, nothing. I close the lid and drop the bottle. I should have known, probably nothing more than a crazy lady's herbs. Could I have known? I should have known. I should have bloody known. I punch the pillow and fall into it, exhausted.

Time

And this is how it went. On this day that Baraka came home from school with a dark eye and a face that told a thousand different versions of the same story, on this day that mama Kabi burned pilau on the stove, on this day I begin again.

They wake up on different sides of the same house with different versions of time past. Kabi, with her head a little heavy, feeling somewhat detached from her body, hears singing in the shower and thinks she is imagining it. Her bed, her covers, her furniture. "Who moved me to my room?"

Smells wafting from the kitchen and mum is shouting, "Baraka! You're going to be late for school, get out of the shower!"

Has she finally gone mad? Hearing voices . . . a coping mechanism? Two minutes later the door is pushed in and there he is with a towel around his waist, hair wet, and the boyish lanky frame barely dried off.

"Sheesh Kabi, you look like you've seen a ghost! It's just eyeliner, what do you think?"

She cannot move and she thinks this is familiar, searching her mind for memory, and then she thinks this is a dream. Closing her eyes she whispers, "not real, not real, not real, not real,"

"Kabi, you're freaking me out. Are you okay? Kabi?"

He smells like cocoa butter. A scent she would recognize a kilometer away, attached to him like water to plants on early mornings. She opens her eyes, and he is still there, an orange hue finding its way through the windowsill, refracting off his skin where the sun made a love pact with melanin, beautiful light dancing, and she makes a noise that is somewhere between a gasp and a scream.

"Muuuuuuummmmmmmmmmm! Kabi is acting weird!"

"Baraka stop disturbing your sister and get ready for school, if the bus leaves you ni shauri yako. I am not going to interrupt my morning to drop you!"

He walks towards the mirror in Kabi's room and poses, "Sis, don't make this a big deal okay. I know you said not to touch your stuff but I don't know, I've been feeling kinda weird lately, like low, you know? I just thought trying something different with my look today would make me feel better."

She croaks, "Baraka?"

He looks at her, eyes big and brown, outlined by the black kohl, more precious than anything she has ever encountered and she wants to run to him but she is scared she will reach for him and grab air, scared that he is not really there. So instead she stays still and says, "I love you." Hoping the words will become tangible things that will keep this moment in continuum.

He laughs. Their "I love you's" are present but more unsaid than said. "I guess the new look does make me more likeable."

"BARAKA, if I have to call you one more time!"

"Yoh, gotta go, Mum's about to break something, or someone." When he reaches the doorway he turns around, "But just so you know nakupenda pia." and then he is gone.

Okay, she thinks, looks at her phone, notices I am different from what she expected. The thoughts running through her mind, okay, she thinks, hopes? Maybe Baraka dying was just a nightmare? And this is what's real but no, too many days went by.

She collects herself and moves, taking the steps down two by two; she almost trips, steadies herself on the railing and reaches the last step just in time to catch the conversation taking place in the kitchen.

"Not in my house!"

"Ayii Mum, it's not that big a deal!"

Mama Kabi, never one to consider her words before they come

out says, "What will you be wearing next? Ehh? Lipstick? Dresses? If God wanted me to have another girl he would not have put that soldier hanging between your legs."

Baraka is mortified, "Muuum!"

"What? It is the truth." She sees her daughter lurking. "Nyokabi, can you talk to this brother of yours. I do not understand what behavior he is trying."

—And how small this detail is in the scheme of everything. Does she know he was dead?! Will be dead? But how can she know?—

"Sometimes I swear God gave me children to punish me. Mwathani, what did I do wrong?! Eeh?! Why do you want my blood pressure to finish?"

Baraka did not expect her reaction to be positive, but he expected . . . well, he does not know what he expected, just not this, not the overwhelming despair this reaction brings up inside of him; if he had just slipped by unnoticed—but he didn't slip by unnoticed and they are here now and he knows with his mother it is a battle of the will so he tries to reflect strong will on his face but his eyes are glistening.

"Wipe it off."

"But . . ."

"Now!"

Nyokabi takes the chance to intervene. "Mum maybe . . ."

"Stay out of this, Nyokabi!"

Kabi works her jaw, measuring her words. "So you only want me to speak when I am on your side."

Their mother gives her a look and she goes silent.

When he is gone, the black liner sufficiently cleared off his face, another tube stubbornly and comfortably tucked into his pocket, saved for the bathrooms at school, the unfinished conversation hangs in the air between the glances traded back and forth.

"Usiniangalia hivo, I do it for his own good." Mama Kabi looks at her daughter about to add something but changes her mind, busies herself with clearing dishes, signaling she is done with the conversation.

Kabi thinks of the words to tell her, to explain what is happening, but they do not come. How to say—your son will die by his own hand

and I know this because I found his body hanging from the ceiling in the future—

Something clicks. "Mum there is a lady; your second or third cousin, I can't remember her name, but she has long dreadlocks and big arms."

She is distracted. "What are you talking about? Kwanza don't you also need to go to work Kabi?"

"Mum, LISTEN! This is important!"

Mama Nyokabi looks at her daughter hard. "Nyokabi, you may be an adult but you do not shout at me under my roof, ehh?! Remember I still carried you for nine months. Umenisikia?"

Nyokabi restrains herself from throwing something, anything. Deep breaths. "Okay, I just need to know how to find the lady?

Mum?

She's your cousin, the one who always carries cowrie shells."

Mama goes back to cleaning the counter, silent for a moment and then, "Are you talking about mad-ma-Nyasi?"

"Who?"

"Mad-ma-Nyasi. Well, she is named Njeri, after our Maitu; we started calling her ma-Nyasi because after her daughter died she left the city for up country, went to live in the grass, and started calling herself a prophetess of God."

For a moment Kabi's mother is lost in thought. Does she know? And then she remembers she is in the middle of conversation, "Anyway, why do you want to know about her?"

"I just, I just do. Can I get in touch with her?"

"Ha! Does that woman look like she is reachable? I'm even surprised you remember her. She only comes when she wants to be seen but that is probably for the best. She carries a bad omen, that one. Anacheza na uchawi."

The dishes cleared, she wipes her hands and moves away. "Anyway I have a chamaa to go to and I suggest if your plan is still to save enough money to leave this house eventually, that you get to work on time."

And when the house is empty, Kabi texts in that she is sick, and sits in front of her computer, researching,

AND THIS IS HOW TO STAY ALIVE

Google
Potions to go back in time?
Can you change the past?
Skips Articles offered by:

Medium
How To Change The Past Without a Time Machine: The Power Is Real
Psychology Today
How You Can Alter Your Past Or Your Future–
And Change Your Present Life
The Philosopher's Magazine
Sorry, Time Travelers: You Can't Change the Past

Over and over again, unhelpful papers, essays, conspiracy theorists
until she stumbles on,
Time in Traditional African Thought

> *I take as my point of departure for this paper the thesis of*
> *Professor John Mbiti that in African traditional thought a*
> *prominent feature of time is the virtual absence of any idea*
> *of the future . . . Time is not an ontological entity in its own*
> *right but is composed of actual events which are experienced.*
> *Such events may have occurred (past), may be in the process*
> *of being experienced (present), or may be certain to occur in*
> *the rhythm of nature. The latter are not properly future; they*
> *are "inevitable or potential time" (3). Consequently time in*
> *African traditional thought is "two dimensional," having a*
> *"long past, a present, and virtually no future." Actual time*
> *is "what is present and what is past and moves 'backward'*
> *rather than 'forward'". . .*

—John Parratt

And more and more she reads until she thinks she knows what she
must do, and then she starts to feel tired, so so tired and she rests her
head, closing her eyes, thinking, it is possible, not tomorrow, not after,

only yesterday and now. But I dare say "what if" cannot always exist in the same realm as the "what is."

And somewhere on a different side of the city the "what is" is a boy, is a blessing, a blessing moving and breathing and feeling and loving and punching and suffocating and choosing and chasing after what it means to stay alive.

Baraka

This is how I felt it: for a moment during the night Kabi was not here and I was not fully here either—wherever here is for those who exist after life but before forever—and I cannot remember how or where but we were together. Me in death and her in life met somewhere in the middle of time where the division had not taken place. And maybe this is why on this morning before my body is to be lowered into a casket, she sleeps with a half-smile on her face. Baba finds her in my room and gently taps her; there are dark shadows on his face and under his eyes but I do not feel guilt or pain for him. "Kabi, sweetie, we cannot be late. Wake up."

Half still in sleep, she asks, "Late for what?"

"Today is the burial."

She yawns and stretches. "What? Which one?"

He clears his throat and repeats himself, "The funeral, mpenzi. We need to get ready to leave."

The expression on her face shifts, she shakes her head, "No, no burial, he is alive."

Baba is terrified; does not know what to do when his strong collected daughter loses her reason. "It's okay baby, we all, uhh, we all wish he was still alive, uhm, but today," he places his palm at the back of his head, rubbing his neck compulsively, "Today let us give him a proper send-off, ehen?"

"No Baba, he is alive. I saw him. He was alive."

He holds her, rubbing her back, "Hush,

Tsi

      tsi

            tsi,

Hush.

It was a dream, mpenzi. Be strong now, you have to be strong also for your mother."

Nyokabi's face turns bitter. "That woman can be strong for herself!"

"Ayii yawah, daughter, don't say things like that. I know things have been hard but she is grieving."

"No, she is the reason Baraka was so unhappy. She always looks for a reason to be angry, disappointed."

"As much as I wish I could blame anyone more than myself Nyokabi, that is just not true. Your mother's responses always have a valid justification."

"That is just her trying to get into your mind. She is always blaming everyone else but herself . . ."

"Nyokabi, enough."

"And do not think I did not hear her shouting at you. Aren't you also allowed to be in mourning?! You are a grown man! No one, least of all you, should be taking her shit."

"I said enough, Nyokabi!" his voice barely raised but firm, "You will not speak of my wife that way in my house okay? I know you are angry but today is, today is a day for us to come together. Not to fall apart."

Kabi's jaw hardens. "You want to talk about coming together but even you, you were a problem. You and Mum both." She shifts her body up, not making eye contact. "You never let him just be himself, everything that made him him, you had a problem with. You were afraid he would be one of those boys you and the other fathers gossip about, the ones that bring shame—" her voice cracks, "and now somewhere inside of you there is a sense of relief because you never have to find out."

Whoosh!

Rushing of air, palm-on-cheek.

Baba has never touched Kabi before today. How dare he? She holds her face where it is hot and he gasps at what he has done, "Kabi baby.

I'm sorry." He moves to hold her tighter, but she pulls away. "You just," He lifts his hands in exasperation, "You're saying that I wished my son dead. Do you think any parent wishes this for their child? ehh?"

Kabi does not look at him.

"I would do anything to bring him back, Kabi, believe me—any and every version of him. I didn't understand him but . . . but God knows I loved him."

"Just," she whispers, head down, "he was alive." Her eyes well up. "I could have saved him, but I didn't."

Baba stands up. "Darling, we all could have saved him, but none of us knew how." He walks toward the door. "Get dressed, I expect you ready in thirty minutes." He sighs. "I know it doesn't feel like it right now, mpenzi, but we will get through this. Somehow, we will get through this."

When he is no longer in the room, Kabi drops to the floor, on her hands and knees, frantically searching until she finds it.

As she tips her head back, her hand stops midway and she rethinks her decision. Bringing the bottle back down, she dresses in her black trousers and cotton shirt and places the bottle discreetly in the corner of her pocket. She fiddles with it all the way to the service.

Nyokabi: Eulogy

"Baraka used to say that one of the reasons we are here is for here and now. He advocated for fully living in the present moment and I . . ."

Can't finish. The tears closing my throat come out in a sob on stage in front of this collection of friends and strangers. I've been better about holding my tears, keeping them for when I am alone but,

"I just, I just can't talk about the here and now without talking about yesterday." There is mucus running from my nose and I feel the weight of this grief will bring me to the ground. It is not pretty. I look at mum and she does not look at me. Her eyes are hidden behind dark shades and even though I can't see them, I feel her gaze elsewhere. My hands are shaking almost as much as my voice. I can't talk. *"I can't talk*

about the here and now without talking about the absence that exists in tomorrow."

Yesterday tomorrow, yesterday tomorrow, yesterday tomorrow. I close my eyes and he is there behind my lids in the darkness, I see him, and I curse him and I want to say, "How dare you make me write your eulogy?"

But instead I say pretty words, "*God's timing and Baraka means blessing and I—*"

Can't finish. And suddenly there are arms around me and I think it is him but I open my eyes and it is Baba and I fall into him and I stop pretending that I have the energy to be strong and I wail into his shirt and he takes the half open silver notebook in my hand and reads on my behalf and I am led to a chair to sit and I close my eyes and I count to ten times one hundred, fiddling with the bottle in my pocket, and I remind myself how to breathe and I open my eyes and wish I didn't have to so I draw it up to my lips and swallow. It is more than halfway gone; let me go with it. This time I can save him, I know I can. This time he will stay alive.

Baraka

This is how to not think about being alive when you are dead. Do not watch the living. Do not attach memory to feeling. Do not attach memory to feeling but of the things that reminded you what it means to be alive:

Music. Sound and rhythm interrupting silence taught you how to move; you learned, even the most basic beat,

ta tadata ta-ta

ta tarata ta-ta,

ta-tarata-ta-da

Do not attach memory to feeling but remember the time Kabi surprised you with your first Blankets and Wine concert tickets and on that day in the middle of April when the clouds threatened to interrupt every outdoor plan, you prayed.

And you didn't pray to be different and you didn't pray to be better and you didn't pray to be other and all you prayed is that it wouldn't rain and all you prayed is that you would get to listen to Sauti Sol play. And sometimes prayers are like music, and sometimes someone listens and is moved, and this time the sun unpredicted teased its way out of hiding and this time the grass was greener on this side and this time you stood with Kabi out under the still partly cloudy sky and sang "Lazizi" word for word at the top of your lungs and this time you let the music carry you and you took Kabi by the hand and she said, just this once, and you laughed, and you danced until even the ground was tired of holding you up.

Do not attach memory to feeling, do not watch the living but as you watch her swallow the liquid that burns her tongue, you think, *she is coming to find me, somewhere between life and after, in the middle of time, she is coming to find me.*

Time

And this is how it went. On this day when Kabi first became paralyzed with a grief she had never thought possible, on this day when Mama Nyokabi screamed at a paramedic on the phone and screamed at God for more of me, on this day when Baraka decided to die, I begin again.

They both wake up with different memories of time passing. The clock: a tool *tick-tock*ing its way into later vibrates and Kabi opens her eyes. He is singing in the shower and now she knows she is not imagining.

"Baraka!"

LACUNAE

V. H. LESLIE

Be not afeard; the isle is full of noises, sounds and sweet airs.
—*THE TEMPEST*

Malcolm heard Mendelssohn as the island came into view. It was hard not to think of his Hebridean overture amid the rocking of the waves, the dark hollow of the cave in the distance. It was not quite Fingal's; the rocky façade lacked the distinctive neat, angular arrangement, though it too had been formed by a volcanic deluge many millions of years ago. His daughter, Miranda sat at the prow, dwarfed in her bright orange lifejacket, glancing back at her parents as the boat sliced through the water, salt-sprayed and smiling. Dinah shouted something out to her, something cautionary Malcolm supposed, but the sound was taken by the wind and silenced by the churn of the engine. Just along from the cave, Malcolm viewed the white stone house and he let the coin he held drop into the water, just as he had always done when crossing the strait, in payment to the Blue Men—the kelpies

With the engine chugging to a stop, the sounds of the sea took precedence, the pounding of the waves against the hull, the screech of gulls overhead. Malcolm had rolled up his trouser-legs in preparation for stepping from the boat into the surf, but as he did so, a wave broke and he felt the shock of cold, an involuntary re-baptism, as the water seeped through his clothes. He waved away Dinah's attempts to steady him and she turned her attention instead to instructing the ferrymen about their luggage. Malcolm didn't offer to help; it was a job for younger men. Miranda was already up ahead, running excited lengths along the beach, stopping occasionally to examine driftage, or to collect something from the shore that had caught her eye. She greeted her father as he stepped out of the sea with palms outstretched, full of limpet and mussel shells, the coiled remains of periwinkles.

"Look."

But Malcolm was looking past her towards the cave. It could well have featured in the legends of Ossian, the supposed fragments of ancient balladry James Macpherson had discovered and translated in the Romantic era, before he was discredited as a forger. Whether the stories of Fingal and his exploits had come from a third century Highland bard as Macpherson had professed or from Macpherson himself, had never mattered to Malcolm. He saw the landscape of his youth, the crags and gullies where he played through Ossian's lens, charged with heroic energy. But he had been away from home for a long time; like so many of his forbears, he had settled across the Atlantic, not driven out as they had been in those bygone times by the greed of landowners, but lured by bright lights, whilst the brave old world had persisted and endured. Now the songs of home would occupy his twilight years. No mere tone poem like Mendelssohn's would suffice, but a song cycle, a fittingly epic undertaking in homage to Ossian. It would be his *magnum opus*.

Miranda hadn't waited for a reply and was busy jumping the waves, so he made his way past her, up the beach beyond the machair, toward the steps of the stone house. It was just as he remembered it, sand on the flagstones, the embroidery sampler on the wall. He made his way through the warren of rooms, nooks providing vistas out toward the gray Atlantic, until he found himself on a familiar threshold. It was simply furnished, as it had always been, the desk arranged against the window, overlooking the expanse of beach, the rocky foreshore at the entrance of the cave just visible. He had composed here every summer for nine years—the duration of his first marriage—where, some would say, he had produced his best work.

He wondered if it was true, that the last four decades had amounted to nothing more than playacting the role of composer. The *Edinburgh Review* critic had certainly thought so, fancifully comparing him to a "shipwrecked Prospero," exiled from the operatic vanguard, because— in words he now knew by rote—". . . he had bartered his baton for a magic wand, invoking the Disneyfication of his early oeuvre." He remembered pushing the paper across the kitchen table for Dinah to read, the words too potent to be said out loud. The article ended with the assertion that he had produced nothing of value since *The Silence of Amaterasu*. She had ripped out the page, screwing it into a ball.

"Well, *fuck him!*"

He watched Dinah now, helping the ferrymen carry their bags through the shallows, battling the swell and spray, while Miranda orbited their belongings on the beach, piled high like a haul of treasure, or the mound of a bonfire.

He'd expected to be instantly inspired, the music welling up from a long dormant place inside, just by virtue of being back on the island, but he could hear only the words of the Edinburgh Review critic, on a loop like a steady incantation. It struck him as ironic that words he had never voiced could become so resounding in his head. He'd had bad reviews before, especially at the start of his career, when his work was regarded as experimental, but he'd never really paid them much heed. Dinah had said that the Scots were just bitter that he'd been co-opted by the Americans, that they'd lost a national icon. He didn't see it like that; he'd retained his dual citizenship and heeded the siren-call of home, his feet now firmly set on bleached sand, but he did wonder if he was in fact, lost. Not in the sense Dinah supposed, of being cloven between two nation states but lost to a different time and place, akin to the misty void where Fingal and his warrior-ghosts lingered.

He stared at the blank page, trying to summon a melody but fixated instead on the sounds of the house, the animated laughter of cartoons from Miranda's tablet, Dinah clanging in the kitchen, putting away their groceries. When the house settled into silence, he found himself gravitating towards the interior, seeking sound. He found Dinah in the bedroom unpacking their bags.

"Looking for this," she asked, handing him a gray dressing gown, threadbare in parts, his charm against writer's block.

"I didn't think I'd need it," he said, though he put it on anyway.

An oft-repeated dinner party story, before the *Edinburgh Review* critic had styled him a modern-day sorcerer, centered on Miranda's childish confusion between the words musician and magician and her steadfast conviction that her father only made music with the aid of potions and spells. He did, after all, conduct himself in secret, working from his locked study, and he donned a magician's cape, albeit a rather old and gray flannel robe. Dinah had found it too endearing to correct and they kept the pretense going well into Miranda's first few years of kindergarten, where the family pictures she drew all featured Malcolm shrouded in gray, the messy crayon marks making him appear more animal than human. As her drawing became more controlled, she would add symbols to his cloak, stars, a moon, sometimes even adding a magician's hat to the ensemble, so there could be no doubt of his profession. The dinner party guests would laugh imagining the kindergarten teacher's disappointment when Malcolm declined the offer of putting on a magic show for the class.

"Such a cliché," Dinah said, taking in his appearance, "the creatives in bathrobes while the rest of us have to wear real clothes."

He smiled back, rubbed her shoulders, "What do you think of the house?"

"Quaint. Drafty."

The theme-tune of one of Miranda's cartoons started up again and Dinah sighed. Miranda had clearly exhausted her allocation of screen-time for the day.

"Why don't you have an explore with her?" "I'm here to work."

She began to fold the garment in front of her with slow, careful creases. Malcolm noted the tightness of her lips, the silence that would ensue.

"Okay, okay."

"And we need to talk about Ayoko," she said as he left the room, though he pretended not to hear.

Miranda skirted the rock pools along the shoreline, testing their depths with a shard of driftwood. She'd beckon to Malcolm to follow but as soon as he caught up, her attention would be diverted elsewhere, and he found himself trailing behind her again. This new world under her feet absorbed her to such an extent that she missed the seals further out in the bay who had come to observe the new arrivals. They seemed to nod at Malcolm but by the time he pointed them out to Miranda they had swum away.

The waves were pitching steadily higher and Malcolm was glad they had arrived in the calm of the morning. He thought of the journeys made in Ossian's time, if Ossian had ever existed. Heroes were meant to undertake epic voyages and crossing rougher seas made for better stories.

Miranda had migrated up the shoreline and Malcolm found her crouched in the marram grass, a small shell pressed to her ear, as if it were a conch.

"Shhh!"

Malcolm stopped moving in obedience, trying to minimize the crunch of his footfall as he repositioned his body weight.

"It's singing."

She held out the shell to him. It was small and speckled, coiled at its peak; a whelk of some description. The habit of listening to seashells had always struck him as strange practice; that the hollowed interior could emit the rushing of the waves was hardly surprising when the shell's cavity amplified the noise of its surroundings. Far more impressive were the shells that created sound, like the Japanese *horagai*, large conch shells of the right shape and composition, that with the addition of a mouthpiece appended to their spired tips could even be played to produce different notes. Miranda's diminutive find could hardly compete with such titans, but he placed it to his ear anyway.

"Can you hear it?"

Her voice was so different to his; she'd been raised an American, her accent clear and unequivocal, lacking the melodic lilt of the islands. He sometimes felt they spoke different languages.

He nodded noncommittally, hoping it would suffice as an answer and though she pocketed the shell, he couldn't tell if she believed him or not.

The rocks were more abundant as they approached the cave. Craggy pillars guarded the entrance, sharpened from where the sea tormented the shore. He remembered that the cave flooded on a spring tide, the surface underfoot rendered smooth and slippery with bladderwrack. As they moved from the light and further into the dark interior, Malcolm was reminded of what an impressive space it was, not unlike a concert hall, the banding on the gneiss reminiscent of the levels of tiered seating. He felt underdressed in his gray dressing gown.

Miranda climbed deeper into the cave and he gravitated towards a rocky obtrusion in the center, its surface eroded smooth like a crude lectern. The silence swelled as if signaling the commencement of a piece of music.

The wind makes strange noises on the islands, whistling through the ravines and crofts, percussing on the corrugated roofs, strumming the rigging of the boats harnessed at the quayside. But the sound Malcolm heard in the depths of the cave was not devised by the elements, for it was one he recognized all too well. It was raw and unpolished but unmistakably the first few notes of *Amaterasu's Silence*, the aria he had written for his eponymous lead, a divine sun goddess who sought sanctuary in a cave to escape torment from her malevolent brother. "Silence" was a misnomer of sorts, for Amaterasu's sojourn in the cave constituted her most vocal moments in the opera, the cave amplifying her long-dormant song, her internment in stone giving liberty to her voice.

The sound swelled, pitching towards the familiar melody.

"Miranda?"

Was it here where he'd first heard the legend of Amaterasu? It must have been; the island was so saturated with Amaterasu it was hard to unravel any prior memories. It was certainly here that he'd decided to compose, in alto tones, the world beyond Amaterasu's grotto as a place of chaos and dissonance, informed by his habit of listening to the wind

LACUNAE

and rain from within the cave. And perhaps it had been here that he'd decided Amaterasu should not sing until she was safely ensconced in the cave, the lack of her mezzo soprano voice extending for the entire first half of the opera, rendering her song, when it finally came, all the more precious.

As well as this, he'd written a series of lacunae—arranged silences—to disrupt the flow of music and signal changes in Amaterasu's emotional state, increasing in length with every tribulation and ordeal suffered, the longest of which marked the moment the boulder was rolled across the entrance of the cave, shutting out a world now plunged into silence and darkness, a total eclipse of Amaterasu's divine light.

The melody in the cave scaled higher but just as suddenly faded into the sound of the surf. Miranda reappeared, making her way across the rocky terrain, playing stepping stones.

"Miranda, were you singing?"

She didn't seem to hear him, concentrating on balancing across the rocks. But just before she bounded back into the light, he heard her whistling the familiar refrain.

Dinah was at the threshold when they arrived back, the door ajar to the island dusk, like a good fisherman's wife waiting for her husband's return.

"The museum have been in touch," she said after helping Miranda out of her coat.

He waved away the comment, busied himself with pouring a whisky, trying to ignore the paperwork and laptop spread out on the kitchen counter, regretful that the island's remoteness was now marred with internet access.

"They're becoming impatient, we need to commit to dates."

He had been so flattered at first meeting Dinah, when this attractive woman had approached him at a gala dinner, tongue-tied as she tried to put forward her proposal, coyly admitting she was a little star-struck. She wanted to curate a retrospective of his work to mark the thirtieth anniversary of *The Silence of Amaterasu*. The museum she worked for was on board, especially since *Amaterasu's Silence* had featured in a film, a box-office hit, making his work fleetingly popular with a whole new, younger, audience. She'd given him her business card, adding her personal number and underlining her name, Dinah, twice, though the angle made the lines appear more like a caesura //—the pause between music. He had agreed to her suggestion solely to get to know her better, and hardly cared when the project was deferred because of their work schedules and later due to their marriage and Miranda's birth. Now approaching the anniversary of the fortieth year, Malcolm couldn't help feeling that this was Dinah's last-ditch effort to get the show on the road, quite literally, because leaving it any longer would mean him sinking further into inconsequence.

"We never talk about Ayoko," she said, watching him drain his drink.

He used to dream about coming back to the island, the music calling him back across the water. But he hadn't imagined bringing a new wife back with him, or a child. He became conscious of Miranda in the background, sorting shells on the kitchen table. Children were such adept listeners.

"Why would we talk of her?" Malcolm replied, "it's ancient history."

"She's important, to the retrospective."

"It was such a small part of my life—"

"—when you produced your greatest work."

He had taken off his dressing gown when he'd returned from the shore, but now he put it on again, feeling the chill of the house.

"*One* of your greatest works," she corrected, placing her hand on his arm, a condolent gesture.

This was the problem with the retrospective, it implied that everything of worth was in the past, that there was nothing left to come. He knew that in Dinah's eyes he was already washed-up, that it was better to salvage and polish what he had already produced before it was tarnished further by the critics, like treasure salt-worn by the sea.

He watched Miranda move her shells, like counters in a game of her own invention. He thought about the voice in the cave and how unlike Miranda's it was.

"I'd rather not talk about it," he said, and pouring himself another whisky, he withdrew to his study.

* * *

It was louder than he remembered living at the sea's edge. The wind blew unrestrained here, rattling through the old house, blustering papers when the windows were opened, bringing gifts of seagrass and kelp to the door like a loyal pet. It was more deafening on the shore; here you could confide anything to the sea, the words swept away almost immediately by the wind. Malcolm had nothing to confess so he pushed on up the beach, keen to prove Dinah and the rest of them wrong, that he was still capable of making music, needing the peace of the cave to hear his own thoughts.

As he entered, he was again struck by the feeling of walking across a cavernous stage, at the head of an orchestra or playacting a character: *Old man in gray bathrobe, enters stage left*. He leant against the rocky lectern, relieved for the silence. Caves were important in the legends of Ossian too and Malcolm had decided to focus on the moment where Fingal's son, slain heroically in battle, appeared as a ghost above the cave where his body is interred, calling for revenge. The ghosts of dead warriors inhabited so much of Ossian's verse, the departed never happy until a bard sings of their exploits.

"Excuse me?"

Malcolm turned, shocked at hearing a voice in such proximity, though it was faint, no louder than a whisper. The cave appeared empty. He walked further from the light.

"Hello?" he called tentatively, scanning the darkness.

"Excuse me?" the voice rejoined.

He was reminded of the voice the previous day, how unlike Miranda's it had sounded. Cave systems were known to distort and amplify sound, the acoustics of Fingal's Cave for instance harmonized the ebb and flow of the waves as if contriving a lullaby. Though this voice was different still, the sound had to come from somewhere. Malcolm explored the recesses and hollows, unable to discern anyone hiding in the shadows. He moved deeper into the cave, felt the damp surface of the chamber wall, having reached its furthest limits.

"Excuse me," the voice spoke again, "can I have your autograph?"

He had answered many such requests over the years, some not

always graciously, but the words and timbre of voice suddenly summoned its bearer into startling clarity in his mind. It was years ago, after a performance of *Amaterasu*. He'd invited her back to the hotel bar and listened to her congratulate him on his success, his singular talent. She'd mentioned something about an audition, whether he could pull some strings. He couldn't even recall her name.

"Excuse me?" the voice persisted, and Malcolm gazed back into the darkness. He tried to move from the sound, but it seemed to follow him, growing more insistent.

"Excuse me!"

It had been just after his divorce when he was seeing a lot of different women. He remembered buying her too many drinks, before leading her into an elevator bound for his hotel suite, making some vague promise of putting in a word with the producer, a quick grope in the confined space the requisite exchange. He hadn't thought of her since.

The voice had lost its civil cadence and Malcolm realized that it wasn't coming from the cave but from his person. He patted himself down, unsure what he was looking for, feeling inside his pocket a small, chitinous surface. He held it in his palm, one of Miranda's shells, helix shaped, barely significant.

"Excuse me!" the voice said once more, as she had done all those years ago, and he was struck by the memory of her disentangling herself from his embrace as the elevator bell announced its arrival.

The shell dropped to the ground and Malcolm endured the silence of the cave, just as he had done in the elevator cubicle in that interminable moment after his breathing had steadied and the sound of her footsteps had disappeared down the hall.

"This is all a bit staged isn't it?" Malcolm said upon his return, taking in the spectacle of Dinah photographing his study. The room was under siege, books he had never read piled high on his desk, music-stands arranged artfully in shot.

"The museum want me to document the composer's lair, I hope you don't mind."

He did mind, but with the study lacking a lock, he could hardly keep the world out. He thought about issuing a warning, like the one pinned to Miranda's bedroom door back home, *Diva Den: KEEP OUT*, though for Dinah, such a prohibition would only serve more as an invite. It hardly mattered anyway, the study was and always had been an empty shell, it was the cave where all the music came from.

"I was wondering when you were going to return."

He had walked agitated lengths along the beach for hours, trying to make sense of what he heard in the cave. He couldn't go back there, but he didn't want to be in the house either, the memory too disquieting to bring indoors, where his family dwelt. When he had tired, he sat close to water, watching the seals in the bay, until the spindrift pimpled his skin.

"Something on your mind?"

"Just music," he replied, realizing that his lonely meandering would have been plain to see from the study window.

Dinah beckoned him into the room, and he stepped awkwardly over her photography equipment.

"Can you sit in the chair?" she asked from behind her tripod.

He removed his dressing gown and folded it, peeled a red vein of seaweed from the fabric. She instructed him to fold his legs, place his hands together.

"Don't look at me," she said, "pretend I'm not here."

He stared through the series of flashes, shifting under the scrutiny.

"Can you stare out the window and try to look wistful," she smiled, "divinely inspired." His frown became more set and she smiled again before kneeling beside the camera, twisting the dials.

"A quick filmed interview and we're done."

Malcolm shook his head, "Dinah, not now, I don't have the time."

"Well, you've been evading my questions ever since we arrived. I have a job to do too. Besides, it's why we came here."

He wanted to object; he hadn't come here to revisit his past but to write his *magnum opus*.

"I can edit out anything you don't want left in," she assured, "please?"

He looked out of the window, this time without her instruction, saw the waves crest higher, the seals long gone. It was easier to acquiesce.

"So, this is the room where you composed *The Silence of Amaterasu*? Can you talk to me about the process?"

"Well . . ."

"Did you have a routine?"

"I, I typically walked in the mornings and came back in the afternoons and evenings to write down what I heard."

"What you heard?"

"The music in my head, it helps being in such a remote place, without traffic and people, where you can hear yourself think."

"And how important was your first wife, Ayoko to that process?"

He fought the urge to look out of the window and glanced toward Dinah instead where she gestured him to continue.

"She was musical too. She could sing."

"Yes, she sang parts of the early overture—there's that beautiful recording. Why didn't she pursue her singing professionally?"

"She wouldn't have made it on the world stage, her voice wasn't quite . . . right. Besides, my career was just starting up, it was a busy time and we needed someone at home."

He watched Dinah fold her arms. "Things were different then," he added.

Dinah pursed her lips but when she spoke again her voice was steady, professional, "Can you describe your time on the island?"

"When we first came, things were good, we were newlyweds."

"And how did you spend your days?"

"We would walk, have picnics on the beach, sometimes take a small boat out. And in the evenings, we would tell each other stories."

"Stories from your respective homes?"

"Yes, fables and legends, there wasn't a lot to do on the island, especially after dark. We had to come up with our own entertainment. When it stormed, we would head to the cave, listen to the strange sounds it made."

"Go on?"

"We liked to explore the coves and crags. Ayoko used to hum this melody, which eventually became Amaterasu's aria."

Dinah looked up from her notebook. "So, Ayoko came up with the melody?"

"Well, yes," Malcolm replied, "but it's such a small part of the com-position."

"And the story, she gave you the story?"

"She *told* me the story, yes."

"So, she co-wrote it?"

"I don't think I would put it like that."

"But the idea was hers?" Dinah pressed. She stopped the recording, lent forward in her chair.

"What else was hers?"

"What do you mean?"

"The silence, the idea for the silence, was that hers too?"

Before he could say anything, Dinah held out her hand to signal an end to the conversation, a gesture normally reserved to reprimand Miranda, and gathering up her paperwork, she quietly left the room.

Malcolm scanned the horizon, sipping coffee, the morning gray and wet. The house had settled into an uneasy silence since the previous evening, interrupted only by Dinah reading Miranda her usual bedtime story, extracts of which he knew by rote: *The little mermaid sang more sweetly than them all. The whole court applauded her with hands and tails; and for a moment her heart felt quite gay, for she knew she had the love-liest voice of any on earth or in the sea.* Malcolm was relieved for the quiet, for an end to all the questions and talk of the retrospective. But with Dinah's equipment still cluttering his study he was relegated to the corners of the old house, waiting for the rain to relent so he could walk along the beach.

Miranda nursed a bowl of cereal and played with her shells. She was accustomed to the quiet, having been raised by nannies and babysitters, taught that time spent with her parents was to be expended in contem-plative pursuits. The beach had allowed her a level of freedom she had never experienced back home, where she could run with the tides and explore the rock pools, her parents blissfully ignorant of her actions or whereabouts. Like Malcolm she gazed out of the window longingly, willing the rain to stop.

"What are you up to, sweetheart?" Dinah asked entering the room, heading for the coffee pot, her voice unusually buoyant, compensating for the strained atmosphere of the night before.

Malcolm made to reply but saw her gaze directed at Miranda.

"Just sorting my shells."

"So, there's a system?"

Malcolm doubted it. The groupings appeared entirely arbitrary, without any consistency in size or shape or color. Limpet shells and tellins, periwinkles, dog whelks, and cockles all crowded the kitchen table. A cursory glance confirmed that this was a taxonomy devised by a child's mind.

"These ones are my pretty shells," Miranda said, handing Dinah a few speckled examples, "and these ones feel nice."

"They do feel nice," Dinah said running her finger along a pearly veneer.

"And these ones," she said, circling a cluster together very delicately, "sing."

"Singing indeed? Malcolm, do you hear this?"

Malcolm had turned his attention back out the window, observing a glimmer of sun streaking between the clouds.

"Well, they don't all sing," she corrected, "some just speak sweetly."

"And how do you find a singing shell?"

Miranda edged closer to her mother, her response almost a whisper.

"You have to listen very hard."

Dinah's phone vibrated from its place on the table, the shells clattering against the surface.

"Sorry sweetheart," she said, scrolling through her messages.

"Did you know that hermit crabs don't have shells of their own, that they find empty shells to live in, like periwinkles and whelks?"

"No, I didn't know that," Dinah replied, looking at her screen. "Malcolm are you listening?" He mumbled a reply, not seeing why he should listen when she was only pretending to.

"The male hermit crabs terrorize the females into vacating their shells," Miranda continued, using two shells to demonstrate their skirmish, "that's called the *molt*, when the crabs lose their shells. When they are between shells, they mate."

Though the shells of the hermit crabs had been cast aside in her underwater scenario, she placed the shells on top of each other in simulation of intercourse, grating the husks against one another.

"Miranda!" Dinah looked up from her phone, "that's not appropriate conversation for the table," and ushering her out of her chair and towards the door, she added, "I think it's time you got out of your bedclothes and brushed your teeth."

The ringtone of Dinah's phone accompanied them down the hall and Malcolm heard Dinah's phone voice as she answered, the conversation diminishing as she moved toward the sitting room to get better reception. He cast a glance over Miranda's shells, picking up a conical specimen, something distinctly sexual about the ventral cavity. He heard the ring of an elevator bell in his mind before *Amaterasu's Silence* began to play softly.

"I put one of the singing shells in your pocket," Miranda said from the doorway, startling him into nearly dropping the one he held, "did you hear it?"

As if pre-empting Dinah's summons, she returned the way she had come, just as Dinah's voice filled the house, calling her back.

A storm was brewing. Malcolm recognized the stillness of the water, a heaviness in the air, the unusual quiet at the sea's edge. Miranda seemed unaware, her eyes cast down, trawling through knots of seaweed. Malcolm followed her closely, watching how she moved back and forth like the tide, harvesting the shore. What was it that she could see and hear that he couldn't? She had found a small red bucket washed up at the strandline—its companion spade still lost at sea—and requisitioned it for her beachcombing, collecting fragments of pottery and sea-glass, redundant egg cases—mermaid's purses—which along with her shells formed a veritable catch.

Watching Miranda at play, listening to her shells, he remembered what she'd said about her collection, that some didn't sing, they spoke sweetly. The woman in the elevator had certainly spoken sweetly, perhaps that was why he remembered her so easily, before the memory had soured. Miranda held one of the shells higher as if to catch a better frequency before casting it aside, whether due to a lack of sound or because it emitted a sound she disliked, he hardly knew. You would have to speak sweetly, he supposed, to gain the ear of a child.

Though the wind was low, he felt a shift in the air, saw Miranda stand as if summoned.

"Listen," she called.

A low plaintive moan filled the air and they both moved towards it, Miranda breaking into a run, her bucket clattering and spilling. Malcolm thought of the ghost of Fingal's son, stationed at the summit of the cave where his body lay entombed, issuing his ardent battle-cry, calling men to action. And at the same time, he wondered if the voices he'd heard in the cave could carry this far, reminded of *Amaterasu's Silence* rising up from the pit.

Miranda came to a stop, took a cautious step back, and when Malcolm edged closer, he saw why. A group of seals had set up camp at the entrance of the cave, basking on beds of kelp, calling to one another in doleful, drawn-out notes, their song sweetly sorrowful when echoed within the hollowed chamber.

He'd seen a lot of different set designs for Amaterasu's grotto over the years. There were always conceptual treatments, the auditorium itself imagined as the interior of the cave, the stage pared down, either minimalist in principle or economy. Then there were those that drew on a Japanese aesthetic; one popular production imagined the space as a concave white screen onto which shadow puppets—the actors of the outside world—danced, while the haloed-boulder obstructing the cave's entrance filled the backdrop like a full moon.

But Malcolm's favorite by far had seen Amaterasu's story transposed to a frozen tundra, the cave appearing to be made of crystal, the imitation stalagmites not unlike the hexagonal columns of Fingal's cave. It reminded him of the Fortress of Solitude in the Superman comics, a place fit for a hero's retreat. He thought of the chitinous surface of Miranda's shells and of the mineral parity of shell and rock; how the pearlized interiors of clams and oysters, their offspring pearls formed by layers of nacre, could rival the lucent beauty of crystal.

Though Dinah's questions had ceased for the time being, the study was still littered with the remnants of the retrospective. He rummaged through Dinah's files, looking at photographs and concert programmes, newspaper cuttings of reviews and articles. Then he replayed the interview on Dinah's camera, listening to his voice and Dinah's in concert, discordant and off-key. Surrounded by the artifacts of his prolific career, it was plain that nothing had really mattered since *Amaterasu*. It was his *magnum opus*, he was the only one who refused to see it, to think so obstinately that there was still more music to make. Maybe it was time for him to take his bow and let Dinah sing his requiem.

"Who are you talking to?" Dinah said, before realizing the camera was in playback mode. She let it run and joined him in leafing through the contents of his life. Though Ayoko hardly featured, Dinah paused on a photograph of Malcolm rehearsing with the orchestra. A younger man then, he was hunched over the score, making notes, whilst in the background, barely noticeable stood a slight figure, her eyes closed, her arms raised as if conducting the music.

Veins of light flickered on the horizon, followed a few moments later by the grumble of thunder, the din of the sudden downpour.

"Will you come with me to the cave?" Malcolm asked.

He knew it was asking a lot, to relive traditions that weren't her own, to walk in the wake of his first wife.

She looked out at the rain then back at the photograph. "No Malcolm."

She had always loved him for *Amaterasu*, just as others had before, but since the interview he'd seen the doubt in her eyes, the dawning suspicion that he was not the sole author. How could he explain that the island had devised an arrangement for two voices, voices that harmonized so well that it was hard to separate their respective parts, though one had always soared slightly higher than the other. But their duet could not continue forever and as those summers had passed, the world outside had become more clamorous, disturbing their peace until they had to arrange silence just to hear their song. It was Ayoko's idea to add lacunae to the score, to make space for Amaterasu's voice. But her own voice wasn't right to carry Amaterasu out of the cave and onto the stage, not at that time; it wasn't white and male, the qualification needed to head an orchestra, to conduct their *opus*, so she was left to command and inhabit the silence instead.

He was soaked to the bone by the time he made it to the cave, his dressing gown sleek like seal fur. He'd thought only of Ayoko as he hurried through the rain, of the times holed-up in the cave, listening to the tempest outside, her voice rising above the dissonance. He made his way to the stone plinth and upended his pockets, arranging Miranda's shells into a loose circle. He'd brought her entire collection, unsure which of her finds was responsible for the voice he heard on that first visit to the cave. Whether he believed in the magic of Miranda's singing shells or not, the hope of hearing Ayoko's voice again outweighed any feelings of irrationality.

It was an impressive collection. In the flashes of light, he recognized the hinged shells of mussels and cockles, delicate cowries and he opened them up in the absurd hope it might encourage them to sing. And there were whelks and periwinkles, their coiled peaks like the tails of mermaids turned in on themselves. Maybe this was all that remained of those fabled creatures, their imprint echoing in the waves and spirals of nature's pattern, and he was reminded of the little mermaid from Miranda's story, willing to give up her voice in exchange for something greater.

Malcolm heard only the storm for a long time but gradually as his ears become more accustomed to the stillness of the cave, it gave way to a different cacophony. There *were* voices in the shells, voices he recognized for the most part, women that he had hurt or overlooked, loved and spurned. Some spoke, others sang, and some shouted their words vehemently, spitting out their pain in plosive notes, all competing to be heard, their voices, consigned to silence, now liberated within the sanctuary of the cave. Rising above it all was Ayoko's voice, his not-so-silent partner, singing *Amaterasu's Silence* in doleful tones, not just the first few bars this time, but the entire melody, her voice soaring above the din, curating all the pain into a beautiful harmony.

"Malcolm! Malcolm!" he heard his name far off in the distance, was conscious of the reek of seaweed, his cheek wet.

"Malcolm!" came the voice again, calling him from outside the cave. He rose slightly, seeing that he had lain in the pit of the cave, interred overnight, the light streaking through the rock, along with the lapping of the tide restoring him to life.

"My god, are you okay?" He saw Dinah and Miranda run towards him, Dinah kneeling at his side, placing her hand against his head.

"Yes, fine, fine," he replied. She tried to lift him to his feet, but he remained rooted to the spot.

"Let's get you back to the house."

"No. I want to stay here."

Dinah stood over him.

"That's preposterous! You'll catch your death."

"I'm fine," he repeated, leaning against the plinth. "Miranda, fetch me some more of those singing shells," he said and before Dinah could object, she had run back out to the shore to do his bidding. Children were much better listeners than adults, able to perceive possibilities and frequencies adults couldn't even fathom. Untold songs lay undiscovered out there, stoppered like messages in bottles, cast out into a seemingly silent world, just waiting to be found. Malcolm cast a glance about the cave; it was a molt of sorts, an absence in-between, those silenced voices just needed the temptation of a bigger shell to entice them out.

"Malcolm?" Dinah pressed, "we have to leave."

He thought of Amaterasu in her cave, wanting to be left alone, barring the door to the shadows dancing outside.

"I can't," he said, "I have to listen to the music."

"What music?"

He glanced toward the rocky ledge; his chorus of shell already assembled. They all had stories to tell, silences to speak, their pain rendered more beautiful in the depths of the cave. Like Macpherson and his songs of old, he would weave together fragments of forgotten voices and compose a piece of epic proportions, a haunting polyphony, of silence lost and found.

"Malcolm?"

"Wait, they're just warming up. Listen . . ."

Dinah laughed and the sound reverberated through the cave.

"Malcolm," she entreated, after the laughter had faded and she saw he was in earnest, "please."

But he wasn't listening to her. Instead, he could just make out the shell voices in muted concert, muffled whispers, faint glissandos scaling higher. It didn't matter if Dinah was angry with him because eventually her anger would subside to silence and then there was every chance it would find itself lodged in shell, washed up on the beach for him to find. Then he would add her voice to his choir, where the sound would be so much sweeter.

In the distance he heard footsteps through water, Dinah's voice urgent on her mobile, *I think he's had a fall*, calling for action, but diminishing as she made her way up the shore seeking better reception. He wanted to tell her to get her camera, to come back and document the composer's lair but the music was getting louder, calling for his complete attention. He had a lot of listening to do, to atone for all the silence he had imposed on others, while his music had been free to rise above the cave and into the world. He closed his eyes and inhaled the salt air, pulling the damp fur of his gown about him tighter, listening to the song of salvaged voices, as the seals in the bay wailed at the loss of their pups drowned in the tempest.

THE GIRLFRIEND'S GUIDE TO GODS

MARIA DAHVANA HEADLEY

This is the first myth: that your boyfriend from when you were fifteen will come and get you out of hell. He might come, but he won't get you. You will never have an interesting conversation with him, though his haircut will suggest that he should be interesting. He'll buy you a book of poetry called *Love is a Dog from Hell,* and this will convince you temporarily that he understands your transgressive nature. Later, you'll parse that title. You'll wait for him to become what he is destined to become, which means you'll sit around for a year on couches in basements, watching his band get stoned. He will know two chords, then three. He will know nothing about laundry, nor birth control. All his songs will be about the girl before you, who'll wear leather pants and also turn out to be his babysitter.

He will learn how to drive, and you'll find yourself sitting in the backseat while his best friend rides shotgun. He will ferry you to a field to watch the Fourth of July. You'll be on your back on a blanket. There will be a rattlesnake. It will smile at you, and you'll think, *Shit. I'm a goner*.

You'll be gone awhile.

You will eventually find yourself standing on a long dark staircase, dress wet, underwear in your purse, your boyfriend walking in front of you. He will step out into the sun, breaking the rules as he does, turning around to turn you into salt. You will protest that you're not Lot's wife, but Orpheus's girlfriend, that your name, in case he's forgotten it, is Eurydice.

"Everything's always drama with you," your boyfriend will say.

You will be the cold French fry left in the basket as everyone else in your group leaves to find someone to buy them beer.

Here's the reality, girl, girlfriend, goddess, goddamn goner: You're gonna have to get out of hell all by yourself.

This is the second myth: that your boyfriend from freshman year of college will teach you how to fly. The only way to learn to fly anything, you'll know by now, is by getting on it. Magic carpet. Pegasus. Dragon of darkness. It's all the same old shit.

You're still trying to get out of hell, and it's a long climb. You'll think flight may be the answer, but you don't learn to skateboard by watching boys on the half-pipe, and you don't learn to fly by watching boys jump off cliffs, shirtless, skinny, while you hold the car keys.

You'll ignore what you know, and get it on with Icarus in an extra-long single dorm bed. When he rolls off, there will not be any room for you on the mattress, so you'll sleep on the floor. He'll be super sweet though. When you wake up, he'll give you half a protein bar and take you to the free screening of *Satyricon*.

You'll meet his father. He'll have a lot of money. You'll sit at dinner saying nothing while they talk about pilot's licenses and charter planes. None of the boys you date will ever have mothers, but they will all have mother issues.

"He takes after me," your boyfriend's father will say. "I used to date girls like you."

Then, to his son, "I get it, man, I feel you."

You will find yourself standing on a rocky beach, while Icarus and his dad are up in the sky, barely visible. You'll aim the camera at them, taking footage for the documentary your boyfriend will have already managed, through paternal connections, to get accepted into Sundance.

Icarus will be dead by the time the film screens.

You'll flunk out of college due to spending a season in the dark, cutting the footage into a documentary that will win an Oscar. You'll edit Icarus into a generous genius. The moments involving hot wax and feathers? The one where he gave you chlamydia, for sure, despite denying it? You will delete those moments from the footage, as well as the moment when your boyfriend on purpose collided with the sun.

At the funeral, his father will embrace you, grab your ass, and lift you off the ground. This is not the same as flying.

Your name will appear in the credits under *Special Thanks*.

This is the third myth: that the man you marry in your twenties will let you rule alongside him. You'll walk up the long staircase out of hell in a white dress, and then you'll walk down an aisle. You'll get a ring forged at Tiffany. When you fuck him, it'll be thunder and lightning.

You'll think that marrying Zeus will fix your problems, but shocker, spoiler alert, hello woe, it won't.

He'll be newly divorced from a wife who has a long history of turning his girlfriends into cows. You'll live in fear of horns, but she won't turn you into anything. This will be your punishment. You'll remain uncomfortably human.

You'll vow fidelity, and you'll sit on top of your mountain, looking down at the green, cloud-dappled world. You will be missing some information.

Your husband will have an office with a door that locks. He'll sit in there, talking to oracles on FaceTime all day long, but the door will be soundproofed, so you'll only hear mumbles.

When you mention that maybe you'd like to go down the mountain and grab a drink with a friend, he will bring you a bottle of wine, and tell you it's made of grapes from the vine of life, and then he will say "nbd," in the way that someone a few thousand years old would try to use the language of the kids.

When you mention you might like to go out for dinner, he'll take you to a molecular gastronomy restaurant where there's a dish called Haruspicy. It will be gold-leafed guts inside of balloons spun of bird's eye chilies. Your husband will explain the pun to you. You will, by this point, have a classics degree, which, hey, is an attempt at getting yourself stealth to therapy. There will be a specialist sommelier who'll come out and read your fate before you take the first bite.

This will not go well.

Zeus will ignore the fact that you're a vegetarian. "You just haven't had the right meat," he'll say, and offer you a slice of something that is part goat, part fish. "That's pescatarian," he'll say, pointing at the tail.

He will have a closet in which hundreds of sex toys are alphabetized, mounted on pegboard and outlined in black Sharpie, as though they are tools in a home carpentry workshop. You will, the day you open it, see a silhouette of a Zeus-sized swan suit, complete with beak, but the suit itself will be missing.

Your husband will travel without you. He'll take flights that leave when it's still dark out. You'll take his kids to school. There will be an unlikely number of babies, showing up at the door, in baskets, in shoeboxes, in giant eggs. When you ask your husband where they came from, he'll shrug, and say "Women, lol."

"No one says that anymore," you'll tell him.

Zeus will still have an AOL account.

You'll drive all the kids around in a minivan with a trailer attached. You'll bring a salad of canned mandarin oranges, shredded coconut, and marshmallows to potlucks and call it ambrosia.

You'll run into his ex-wife on the stairs from soccer to Olympus and beg her to make you into something, anything, better than this. A bird. A star. A tree, even, just a basic little tree?

"Who are you again?" Hera will ask. "Oh, right. The nympho."

"Nymph," you'll say, but she'll already be two flights above you, her gown billowing, her pedicure perfect.

A few years in, your husband will have an affair with someone younger than you. She'll be made of sunlight, and all the sex toys in his closet will start to glow so brightly under the door you will not be able to avoid knowing all about it.

You will step backward down the staircase. You'll taste salt.

* * *

This is the fourth myth, unwritten in the larger canon, but it goes like this: You will be the woman who finally walks back into the place everyone else calls hell, and you'll stay there.

You will wander the darkness until you know every inch of it. You will be unexpectedly good at winter. You will not be lonely alone.

You'll bed down in an abandoned underworld, gutting fish from Styx and cooking them over the fire you make of the books bad boyfriends bought you. You'll blaze the Bukowski, and fling the Fellini into Phlegethon. You'll melt down your old wedding ring and forge it into a claw.

You will not just be gone, but *goner*. Everyone you ever knew will wonder what the hell became of you, and you will not feel like being in touch.

You'll write your own books. You'll make your own films. You'll paint your own portrait. You'll be the leader of your own band.

You'll fall in love again. You'll fall out. You will not await anyone else's version of salvation.

This myth will not be recorded, but it will be yours. You will not shrink until your body is invisible. You will not become a whisper, a breath, a beast. You will not be the tears that salt the earth.

You will not, in the end, be broken by this history of hell, these hurts, these old boyfriends and husbands and rapists and forget-me-nots.

You'll forget those fuckers, those fucks, those fields other than Elysian.

You will be on your back on a picnic blanket in your own kingdom, with Echo between your thighs, and your phone will rattle, and a smiley face will appear on the screen. You'll throw the thing into Lethe, get up, and walk.

This is the fifth myth, the one they name after you, and you alone, the one that gets written down in blood and scratched into cave walls, the one that women see when they look up at the sky and consider trying to live through this and make it to their futures.

You stand at the mouth of your own cave, looking out over your own kingdom. You step off the cliff when you feel like it, and you spread your wings and soar.

How many times can you be shattered in the toasting, a champagne flute lifted and listing? How many times will you survive, a woman made of her own history, and more than it? How many times can you put your heart back together?

As many times as you need to. You can make it through this.

That's what you'll whisper when they pray to you, asking for ways to leave their own disasters, asking for methods, begging for the lineage of the living.

You will be wounded, you'll tell them, those who ask for clarity, those who want to know how to keep themselves out of hell, *but your wounds will not kill what you were. You will be injured, but your injuries, even if they are fatal, will not erase you. You will make yourself again out of the ashes, and*

you will be loved
you will love
you will be loved
you will love
you will be loved
you will love.

Now you're the one who pours it out and fills it up, and now you're the one who knows what love is worth, who knows what it costs.

They didn't give you this knowledge. You gave it to yourself. You made your own heart, and you made your own mind. You are the divine result of crumpled receipts and pretzel salt, of expired condoms and forgotten phone numbers, of lipstick and longing, of hands opened and spread out, of dogs running and of trucks on the highway, of cheap champagne and of diner coffee, of address books thrown out the window, of paperbacks and of pregnancies, of crow's feet and of silver streaks in the dark night of your hair.

You are made of rolling over to make love at four in the morning and you are made of walking barefoot through the kitchen, heating croissants for the one you've left sleeping. You are made of wild strawberries too small to see until you step on them, of roses smashed at the end of a bodega day, of funerals where you wore your wedding ring and of weddings where you knew that one day, one of you would die first. You are made of road trips and radios, of reading aloud, of hotel rooms in cities neither of you have been to before, of permission, of oysters on platters full of ice made of water from the beginning of the world, of cowboy boots and belt buckles, of blood on thighs, of words written in ink and spit and wine.

You are the one who receives the tributes, the love letters and the text messages from strangers who've fallen for their biggest dreams, the dick pics and the tits and the toasts at all the ceremonies.

You're the one who watches over those who wish for companions, and the ones who are lonely, and the ones who are holding hands right now, fingers laced to those of their beloveds. You are made of deserts and of phone calls, of emojis shaped like things that look like love to no one but you and them.

You are the one who listens. You are the one who climbed up here, skirt torn and rumpled, legs covered in scars from thorns and barbed wire, skinned knees, toenails polished, and you are the one who's on this mountain now, looking down at everyone living. You are still trying to learn how to give it up in the entirety, and you're doing it with the rest of everyone, because hello heart, hello hope, this is how motherfucking goddesses of love get made. Out of smashed things and blasted things and things burnt and blistered, out of old bad knowledge and out of making your way through the holy impossible.

You'll open your hands and from them will fall hotel keys and kissed papers, first dances and worn out high heels, flowers and honey and bees drunk on desire, snakes looking for throats, your boyfriend from when you were fifteen, and all the songs he played you when you were both so young you didn't know how to get old.

They used to call you by another name, but now they'll call you Aphrodite. The job of love goddess is a rotating one. You get it when you get there. You used to be the girl in the dark, but now there's light. That's how the story goes; that's how morning happens.

MONSTER

NAOMI KRITZER

No one at the Guiyang airport speaks English. I have the UTranslator app on my phone, and before I left my colleague Jeanine said that it had worked fine for her. But she'd also said she'd never had trouble finding an English speaker in China. And her trips were to Shanghai and Beijing.

"I'm going to the Guizhou province," I'd said.

"Where?" she said, pulling out her phone to look up a map.

"Like the Oklahoma of China," I said. Southern-ish, rural, inland, poor. Not where the foreign tourists usually go.

At the baggage claim, there's a yellow lab sniffing bags, trotting happily back and forth along the conveyor belt as it snakes into the airport. The dog looks deeply pleased with his work, and I am startled to see him sit down on the belt next to a suitcase, which is the standard signal dogs give when they're flagging something. I look around, wondering if I'm about to see an arrest. No one seems perturbed. Also, no one claims the bag; a short time later it winds past me and I see that its wheels are wrapped and it has no handle. The suitcase is a decoy, riding the belt endlessly to give the dog something to react to on days with no would-be smugglers. I wonder what they put inside it.

My suitcase elicits no response from the dog. I'm irrationally relieved.

In Guiyang, the responses from the UTranslator app get me a lot of very confused looks unless I keep it to single-word requests. "Bathroom?" gets me pointed in the right direction. "Newspaper?" gets me to a newsstand. Of course, all the papers for sale are in Chinese and I can't tell which are going to be filled with news from Beijing and Shanghai and which might have local stories. I buy two papers anyway.

"Where can I hire a car to take me to Danzhai?" is not a successful sort of query but "taxi?" eventually gets me to the right spot. It takes time to make it clear that I really do want to go all the way to Danzhai (it's two-and-a-half hours away), but we finally set off.

I didn't sleep well on the plane, and I very much want to sleep in the car, but I'm too keyed up. I stare out at the wide smooth highway that tunnels straight through the hills and bridges the valleys, trying to catch glimpses of China beyond the guardrails, barely absorbing anything.

All I want from the newspapers is the answer to one question: have there been any more bodies? I hover my phone over the characters, slowly parsing out headlines about trade agreements, a train accident, a pair of extremely old identical twins who are celebrating their birthday.

"Why are you going to Guizhou?" Jeanine had asked.

"Because no one I know has ever been there," I said. This was a lie. I'm here to find Andrew.

I met Andrew my sophomore year of high school.

I was a nerd, which back in the 1980s was the actual opposite of cool (as opposed to now, when it's simply another variety of it). I spent middle school being bullied for my preference for books over people and sweatpants over jeans. Any time I stopped for a drink from the water fountain, my classmates would yank my pants down; the school administrators all insisted that if I just ignored them instead of crying, this would stop. When I started high school, I caved and started wearing blue jeans, even though I hated the way the waistband dug into my sides when I sat.

Freshman year of high school, I spent my lunch periods eating with a few girls I called my friends, who'd more-or-less tolerated me in middle school. Sometimes we hung out on weekends at the mall, where the other girls would coo over "adorable" clothing and I'd self-consciously stroke the scratchy fabric and pretend I wished my mother would give me a clothing allowance instead of just buying me the same L.L.Bean turtlenecks again and again because she knew they had soft tags and I'd wear them.

Andrew was in both my chemistry class and my precalculus class, and he noticed that I spent a big part of the day reading books under my desk. He started asking me each morning what I'd brought to read. Initially I wasn't sure whether his curious tone was the fake-curious voice other kids sometimes used right before they turned into complete assholes. After multiple classes passed and he *didn't* snatch my books away to wipe a booger on them or anything like that, I started feeling a bit less wary. My books were all science fiction, and all came from my neighborhood library, which mostly meant Isaac Asimov, Piers Anthony, and all the older Anne McCaffrey.

"You should read this," Andrew said one day, and handed me a paperback. "It's mine. Don't crack the spine. You'll like it."

It was a copy of *Neuromancer* by William Gibson. The next day, I sat with him at lunch.

Danzhai Wanda Tourist Village is possibly the strangest place I've ever been.

Everything around me looks quaint and old, but in fact it was built from scratch just a few years ago to showcase local ethnic cultures and attract tourists to the area. Local people are employed to wear traditional costumes, walk the street playing traditional instruments, make and sell traditional crafts. It reminds me of a Renaissance festival.

Many of the women in traditional clothing are wearing silver hats with delicately formed butterflies on the top and a jingly fringe right above their eyes. Other women wear their long hair scraped up high into something almost like a bouffant, but with silver ornaments and oversized flowers pinned in. They wear beautifully embroidered jackets and skirts, and silver belts, and large silver necklaces that look like someone cut a circle and hammered the silver out into a crescent. Everything jingles as they move. I wonder if the metal jewelry is heavy, if the clothing is uncomfortable, how much is prescribed, and how much is left up to them.

The men and women minding the shops are mostly wearing more ordinary clothes, although a few have the hairstyle with a smaller ornament pinned in. I can't tell whether the tourists shopping in the stores are from other parts of China, or just other parts of Guizhou.

UTranslate doesn't work any better here than at the airport. Fortunately, the hotel has a sign in English over the door telling me it's a hotel, and "Room?" is easy enough to understand.

I know I'm not going to find Andrew today. It's going to take time. Today my job is to check into the hotel, *not* nap, and adjust to the time change. This would all be easier if I'd arrived in early evening rather than midmorning. I resolutely leave my suitcase on the bed instead of lying down myself and go back outside.

At the end of the street there's a public square, and three young women have set up a table with carved drinking horns and little bowls of what I'm pretty sure is a potent alcoholic beverage. Two have the silver hats; the third has the hair ornaments. They are beckoning visitors over and feeding people the drink out of the horns. I am quickly jostled up to the front, where one of the women smiles and sings a song as she pours the drink into my mouth.

You could poison a lot of people this way I think as I swallow obediently and then wonder what sort of person I am to even think such a thing. The alcohol is strong, and I hope it's not rude if I stop drinking. The ladies don't stop smiling when I pull my head back, so if I'm being rude, they're too polite to mention it.

I like meeting new people, one of the affirmations they made me repeat back when I went to therapy years ago, pops into my head. "Xie xie," I say, the one word of Chinese I know: thank you.

"Thank you," I said to Andrew when I gave him back the book. "It was great." I'd brought along one of my own paperbacks to lend him, one I'd bought on my own rather than checking it out from the library— *Startide Rising*.

"If you used a bookmark instead of putting your books facedown they'd last longer," he told me when he finished it.

"Sometimes I dog-ear the pages," I said.

"You do realize that makes you an actual *monster*."

"It's my book! I can fold down corners if I want!" Sometimes I'd fold down corners just so I could easily get back to a particular page to reread it. I didn't tell Andrew that I occasionally even did that with *library books*. Just the older library books I checked out again and again, though—especially the story collections from the bottom shelf. Not the new books.

Andrew had a girlfriend, a goth girl named Nadine who went to the other school, and she had a whole cluster of nerdy friends. Suddenly on the weekends I had something to *do*, and when *Star Trek IV* came out I had people to *see it with*. Since none of us had much money, we spent most of our weekend afternoons haunting local parks or the family rooms of the kids with more absent parents. Having an entire *group* of friends was a shocking novelty to me. The friends I'd had before were willing to put up with how weird I was. Never before had I had friends who were weird *with* me.

Andrew was my closest friend in the group: he loaned me books and comics, made movie recommendations. I rented *Alien* on video because he'd recommended it so highly. Also *Blade Runner*. He was brilliant but lazy, sliding by with adequate grades because he didn't want to do the work. "High school is pointless," he said. "I already know everything they're telling us. There will actually be things for me to learn once I get to college."

There were a lot of on-again off-again romances in the group—two kids would get together, spend a couple of weekends holding hands (or making out while the rest of us yelled "get a room!"), amicably break up.

When Andrew and Nadine broke up, Nadine disappeared from the group.

Months later, I ran into Nadine waiting tables at a diner near the U. I was by myself, with a stack of books and homework and ten dollars for bottomless coffee and a big plate of fries. "Nadine!" I said, delighted, when she came to my table. "I haven't seen you in forever!"

"Oh, hi," she said, giving me a faint smile. "Yeah, guess it's been a while."

"How are you? I've missed you."

MONSTER

"You have? Huh, okay." She took out her pad. "I'm actually working, so . . . do you know what you want?"

I gave her my order and let her take my menu and tried to shake off my hurt feelings. She was busy; I was a customer; I didn't want to be a pest. I spread out my Spanish vocabulary cards and worked on them as I dipped fries into ketchup one by one and ate them, flipping them around so I didn't double-dip even though I was the only one at the table. She came around twice to refill my coffee and water, not making eye contact, and finally stopped, my mug still in her hand, and said, "Are you still hanging out with Andrew?"

"Yeah," I said, a little hesitant. He had a new girlfriend. Was she jealous? Was that what this was about? *I* wasn't the one dating him. I wasn't into him that way.

"You know he has a dead rabbit in his freezer? Or did. He was going to dissect it."

Nadine clearly expected a response, but my main question was, was she saying he *killed* the rabbit or did he just find a dead one, because . . . I mean, we cut up animals in advanced biology. They were from a supply house, of course, not picked up off the street, but . . . I didn't know how disturbed to be about the whole idea.

"He wanted me to *watch*," Nadine added.

"Ugh," I said, sympathetically.

"He talked about wanting to know what everything looks like on the inside. *Everything*. Just . . . I don't know, Cecily. Be careful, I guess."

"Is that why you disappeared?" I asked.

She gave me a look that I couldn't identify. Pity? Exasperation? "Yeah, Cecily," she said, flatly. "That's why I disappeared. Do you need anything else or should I bring you the check?"

I had been planning to get a slice of pie, but there was something about Nadine's glare that made me antsy. I decided to just go. "Check," I said. "Thanks."

She took my money up to the register and brought me the change. "Keep it," I said.

"Thanks," she said, and put the change in her apron. And then stood there, chewing on her lip and staring at me. "Don't be alone with him," she blurted out, finally, as I started to gather up my books.

"Why?" I asked.

"You just don't want to be alone with him. Trust me."

I'd been alone with him dozens of times, and nothing bad had ever happened to me. "Okay," I said, not arguing. "Thanks."

I didn't tell Andrew I'd run into Nadine. The next time I wanted to get French fries and coffee and a booth to do homework while I was near the U, I chose a different diner.

To order in the Danzhai restaurants, I point at things other people are eating. I have a whole roast fish, still on the bone, in a rich sauce; I have eggplant with ground pork in a sauce that runs red with chilies and oil; I have plates of some sort of green vegetable that looks vaguely like turnip greens but with florets.

Dozens of vegetables came from the same wild herb, *Brassica oleracea*; we selected for flowers to get broccoli, buds to get brussels sprouts, leaves to get cabbage, roots to get kohlrabi. If this is Chinese broccoli, which seems likely, that's yet another cultivar of the same plant. I wonder how long it takes to go from *B. oleracea* to ornamental kale through old-fashioned trait selection. I eat it with chopsticks, thinking about what steps I'd go through to get from ornamental kale to cauliflower in a day, using gene editing. Leaves, flowers, color, roots . . . I wonder how much I'd forget to do, what the results would be. I can't think of any new *B. oleracea* cultivars that gene editing has brought us—maybe because we already had every variation that seemed like a good idea to anyone, developed the old-fashioned way.

We've always done this, some shadow in my mind whispers. I shake off the thought.

When I eat at the hotel, I get the same waitress again and again, not because she speaks English but because she's a little less easily frustrated by a customer who doesn't speak any Chinese. "You should just bring me something you think I'll like," I tell her. "I'm not fussy." UTranslate balks at this, so I try the word "anything," and then "you choose for me," with an expansive gesture.

She brings me out a soup, with fish chunks bobbing in it and slices of tomato in a rich red broth. "Perfect," I say, and she smiles back, clearly pleased with my reaction. A little while later she brings out a glass of black tea. The tea farm is somewhere near here, and I can see the leaves unfurling in the water like those children's toys that go from a tiny little capsule to a full-sized giraffe-shaped sponge when you drop them in water.

There is a theater in the tourist village that hosts a daily performance reenacting the legend of the Golden Pheasant Girl. This is apparently a well-known local legend. There's a statue outside of a woman mid-transformation, and on a hill nearby there's a metal statue of a golden bird. Actual male golden pheasants are very showy, with feathers shading yellow to gold to red. The females are the dull brown of most girl birds.

I buy a ticket to the show. They gesture for me to wait and spend five minutes digging out an English-language program that includes a summary of what I'm about to watch.

The buildings here are mostly unheated, and the theater is as cold as everywhere else. There's a handy little plastic clapper on each armrest, though, so I can use that to applaud while keeping my gloves on.

The stage itself has video screens built into the sides and along the back, which they use for some of the theatrical magic. There's a lot of dance and song, puppetry, smoke effects. In the story, the people flee the losing side of a war, crossing a giant river, and resettle somewhere that they are safe but have no food. There's a beautiful wedding sequence and then both the man and the women leave to seek out a magical tree that gives the seeds of every known plant.

In the staging, the tree is silver and resembles the hats the women here wear; I'm not sure if those hats are supposed to symbolize the tree or vice versa because the program doesn't tell me. Both the man and the woman reach the tree and are told that one of them will be given the gift of the seeds but the other will be demanded as a sacrifice.

Both try to be the sacrifice; the man is pushed back as the woman's sacrifice is accepted. She ascends to the back center of the backdrop and then raises her arms to be transformed into wings; lights, video, and flying wires are used to change her into the golden pheasant for the performance, although she looks rather more like a phoenix. The man, temporarily forgotten, regains the spotlight as she flies away and he's blown back by the wind from her wings. Weeping, he takes the seeds back to his people.

I find myself thinking about how you would transform a human woman into a golden pheasant with gene editing and wrench my thoughts away from that particular abyss. Instead, the ballet over, I find a shop in Danzhai that has newspapers and buy another stack, then take them back to my room and spread them out on my bed to hunt through for stories about bodies. This time I find one, but it's a domestic murder-suicide in Xi'an and nothing about it sounds particularly mysterious. I wonder how much I'm missing just from UTranslate's obstinacy.

Combing through newspapers fills me with tension because it's simultaneously passive and time-consuming. The whole trip is like that: passive and time-consuming, and I'm on edge, and don't know what to do. They were so confident that Andrew would seek me out, if I came. I am less and less sure that they were right.

When I check my e-mail one last time before I go to bed, I have an e-mail from a mysterious address that says, *Just like the story, sometimes sacrifice is required, Cecily, if everyone else is to survive.*

I reply immediately: "Where are you?"

"Andrew? Andrew!"

We were at Andrew's house, in the family room, watching a James Bond movie. I remember it was a James Bond movie, but not which movie. His mother stormed in and furiously shut off the TV. "A C?" she snapped. "A C *minus*?"

"I guess my report card came," he said, staring out the window and not looking at either his mother or at me.

"If you would just *do the homework and turn it in—*"

"I already know everything that's on the homework. They want me to do the same problem forty times in a row until I die from tedium."

"I'm sorry your schoolwork does not hold your interest," his mother snapped, "but my *job* is not *one hundred percent* intellectually stimulating, either, and if I decided to just never go to boring meetings *I would be fired.*"

Andrew's family was Chinese, but Chinese American for a number of generations. He liked to describe his mother as a grades-obsessed dragon lady. Even though I was generally on Andrew's side, I knew this wasn't fair. When it came to grades, his mother was basically exactly like my mother. My mom threw a fit when I let my grades slip in middle school. (I was trying to fit in. It didn't work.)

"What is it going to take to get you to work up to your potential?" his mom demanded. "Or at least in the *near vicinity* of your potential? The same *metropolitan area* as your potential?"

"Maybe classes that weren't so boring," Andrew mumbled. "I need to walk Cecily home, I'll be back in a few." I finished gathering up my coat and Andrew slipped out the door after me.

"Sorry," I said, uselessly, as we walked back to my house, six blocks away.

"Not your thing to be sorry for," he said. "My mom is my mom. I'll never be the kid she wanted."

I thought about that as we walked, whether I was the kid my parents had wanted. The summer I was ten, my father tried to get me to learn to play tennis. He took me to the tennis court on the weekends and he signed me up for classes. I went to the classes and swung my racket and practiced with my father and remained absolutely terrible at tennis. At the end of the summer he let me quit. Would he have preferred a kid who was good at tennis? Probably, actually. But he didn't yell at me about it. He gave away my racket and never brought it up again.

Possibly my mother would have liked a girl who liked wearing uncomfortable pretty clothing. When I was little she would buy me dresses made from stiff, crunchy fabrics with lace on them. I remembered one enormous fight when I was eight: she'd wanted me to dress up for a family wedding. Her promises of wedding cake and a Shirley Temple children's cocktail got me as far as the car; when I started crying and asking to turn around because the seams itched, she swore that if I just ignored the itching, it would go away. This was a lie, just like with teasing. When we got to the church, I sat down sobbing on the big stone steps leading to the front door and refused to go inside. My father wound up taking me home.

There was a park about halfway between my house and Andrew's house, a weird little former quarry with a stone formation called a "council ring" that looked like a good place to hold a very outdoorsy meeting, or possibly sacrifice a goat since there was a big stone in the middle. We sat down on the low stone wall of the ring. Andrew smoked a clove cigarette, which his mother would have been even more furious about than his grades.

"Sorry we didn't get to finish the movie."

"I can kind of guess how it went."

"Sure, but we missed some good action sequences."

I shrugged. "It's not that big a deal. Are you going to be okay when you get home?"

"There'll be a lot more yelling, but it'll stop once I tell her I'll work harder in school, which of course I won't, but she won't know that."

I laughed. Andrew always made me laugh.

"I think you're the only person who understands me," he said.

"I feel the same way," I said. "I mean, that you're the only person who understands *me*, not that I'm the only person who understands you."

"I knew what you meant."

"Well, that stands to reason, right?"

I was angry at his mother, and a little bit at him—would it *actually kill him* to do his homework?—and I felt awkward and embarrassed at having seen the fight, but the conversation at the council ring felt like a grace note in the day, anyway.

"Say, do you think you could let me copy the precalculus homework?" Andrew asked. "In the mornings, before we go to class? Just to get my *mother* off my back. *I* don't care about my grades."

"Sure," I said. "No problem."

In the morning, my e-mail has an e-mail from a friend back in the US asking if I'm going to see the Great Wall of China while I'm here. I send back a note offering probably-too-much explanation of Chinese geography: I am currently as far from the Great Wall of China as she is from the Grand Canyon. She lives in Portland, Oregon. If someone came to visit her in Portland, would she suggest they hit the Grand Canyon while they were there? China, like the US, is very big. I look at my block of text, delete it, and say, "it would be about a seventeen-hour drive from where I am. So, no."

There's nothing from Andrew. I go downstairs for breakfast and load up my plate with two fried eggs and four of the Chinese-style steamed rolls, baozi. I spot a fellow westerner across the room; he's the first white person I've seen since I arrived in Danzhai. He looks either jet lagged or extremely hungover. Possibly both.

After I've finished breakfast I check my e-mail again and debate whether to send another message to the mystery address. I decide it's a little too soon and go out to walk around Danzhai again.

I brought Chinese currency with me—a stack of pink bills with Mao smiling benignly on them. Mao is a lot less popular in China than he once was, but he's still on the money. I suppose this is also true of George Washington in the US. Anyway, having brought money, it seems reasonable to spend some.

I like the long, quilted coats that the clothing stores are selling, and the fabric is soft, but they're all sewn for smaller women with narrower shoulders than I have. Even the vests don't fit me properly. I admire a jointed silver fish at a jewelry store, embroidered purses, handmade bird cages that are lovely and interesting but would be very difficult to get home. They do batik here, all dyed in a blue dye that's almost the same shade as denim, and I buy a batik tablecloth.

At that night's dinner at the hotel, the other westerner is looking less hungover and catches my eye. "Join me?" he invites, in British-accented English. I pull up a chair across from him. "I'm Tom Lewis."

"Cecily," I say, and we shake hands.

"What brings you to Danzhai?"

"I could ask you the same question. I wanted to go somewhere unusual, somewhere no one I knew had ever been."

"You picked well, then. I'm a travel writer. Not sure if I'm going to write up this place or not; it's a bit of a bore."

I bristle instinctively, even though I haven't found what I'm looking for. "What do you find interesting?"

He rattles off a dozen cities I've never been to and tells me about the night life in Kuala Lumpur. I think he's trying to impress me. I wonder if he tries to impress everyone he meets, or just women, or just white women? He snaps his fingers at the waitress, and I cringe, worried that the waitress is going to think that we're *together*. He orders something in Chinese and says to me, "what are you having?"

I tell him I'd like the whole fish, and he translates that into Chinese for me.

"Why doesn't UTranslate work here?" I ask.

"The makers are having some sort of fight with China's Great Firewall," he says. "You should've come last week, the problem it's having is new."

"Is there another app that will work?"

"The official Chinese app is having some sort of dispute with the keepers of the app store, so no. What is it you're planning to do tomorrow? Perhaps I can be of assistance."

What I want to say is, *I'd rather get by with a Chinese-English paper dictionary from the 1980s than drag along someone who snaps his fingers at waitstaff*, but I never actually have the guts to be quite that confrontational, so I just laugh awkwardly and say nothing.

"Have you gone to see the prison?" he asks.

"The what?" I say, not entirely certain I've heard correctly.

"There's a former mercury mine about a half hour from here. It's been used as a movie set a few times. There's an abandoned town to one side, an abandoned prison to the other. Hire a driver and you can give yourself a tour. I mean, you'll have to get out once you're there. The roads are all overgrown. It's picturesque, if you like that sort of thing. My friend Percival Abbot—you might know of him?—did a photography exhibition on it a few months back."

Our food arrives and we have an awkward meal together. I have not heard of Percival Abbot, although a quick Internet search when Tom steps away from the table confirms he is, in fact, a photographer whose website telegraphs that I really *should* have heard of him.

"Are you thinking of going to soak in the spa later?" Tom asks as we're finishing dinner.

"No," I say, even though I immediately think, *Spa?* I don't really want Tom's uninvited company.

* * *

"Don't touch me," I said to Marc, the boy who'd just gotten in the lunch line behind me.

"As I'd want to, Fartknocker." My last name was Grantz; how this got turned into "Fartknocker" by my tormenters was a mystery to me.

I felt his hand on my ass as I raised my tray so the lunch server could put my food on it. I flushed hot with fury. "I told you not to touch me," I said.

"I didn't. Maybe your clothes want to flee your foul body, Fartknocker."

I had pulled the tray down and was holding it in front of me; at that, I whirled, turned it sideways, and hurled French fries, hamburger, and the tray into his sneering face.

My mother came to pick me up from the principal's office, looking harried and frustrated. "I don't want to hear it," she said as I followed her down the stairs and out to the car. "You need to stop letting people get your goat. He just wanted a reaction from you and he got one, didn't he?"

Also grease and ketchup all over his shirt, and maybe that would discourage him from tormenting me where ignoring him hadn't? I burst into tears, because that was what I always did when I got angry enough, and said, "I wish I'd kicked him in the balls."

"Don't do that either," Mom said. "Your grades are really good, Cecily, but if you've got a serious disciplinary record it's going to be hard for you to get into college."

Andrew came over after school, since Mom had said I was grounded but hadn't said I wasn't allowed to have visitors. "Boys are the worst," I said.

"Football players are the worst," he corrected.

"Does Marc play football?" I never knew who played what. It just wasn't interesting enough to keep track of.

"Probably."

"I hope he gets hit by a bus."

"Yeah, about that. We've got to talk about your *technique*, Cecily. Throwing a tray is very showy and all but it wasn't going to do any real *damage*. You have to hit people like that where it *hurts*."

"Do you think I should have kicked him in the nuts, instead?"

"Testicles are actually a smaller target than most people think. No, revenge is a dish best served cold."

We talked for hours about things we could do to Marc: laxatives in his food, stink bombs in his locker or slipped into the pocket of his letterman's jacket, infect him with head lice. None of these ideas were particularly practical: we didn't have access to his food, we didn't know of anyone with an active case of head lice, he'd certainly *notice* if either of us slipped a stink bomb into his pocket. That was fine, though. Revenge, for me, was a dish best imagined and never served up at all. If I was going to do anything, it would be a hurled tray in a moment of anger, not a carefully crafted boutique-quality revenge plot.

Andrew got roughed up, a few weeks later, supposedly for looking at another boy in the locker room for a few seconds too long when they were changing after gym class. It was Marc with one of his teammates.

"The frustrating thing," he confided, "is that even if I can get laxatives into his food, he won't know why he's being punished. He'll just think he's eaten something that disagreed with him. I wish I could hit him back hard enough in the moment to make him sorry he'd messed with me."

"You could learn a martial art, maybe." Thanks to the success of the *Karate Kid* movie there were about eight million karate schools in our town alone.

"Unlike in the movies," Andrew said, "you have to take classes for years before you're actually any good. Also, I'm pretty sure if you beat someone up at school they'll kick you out, even if they *richly* deserved it."

"Also, if you've got a serious disciplinary record it could keep you out of college," I said, like my mother had.

Andrew sighed. "All I want is to make the people who deserve to suffer, suffer," he said. "Is that *really* so much to ask?"

Two weeks after that, Marc's car, sitting in the student parking lot, went up in flames. No one seemed to know what had caused it. I asked Andrew if it was him, and he raised his eyebrows and said, "Whatever would make you think that?" instead of answering. And he was right: if it *was* him, Marc had no idea why he'd been punished.

* * *

The spa, it turns out, is in a separate building from the hotel, and I have to go out into the street to get there. Once I'm there, the attendant checks my room key, then shows me a locker room with complimentary slippers that are barely half the size of my feet. I change into my bathing suit and venture out the far door.

There are two pools, steam rising from the water. The website mentioned a hot spring. I wonder if this is actually spring water, or if they heat it somewhere and pipe it in? I'm a little shocked by just how hot the water is; initially it's too hot to immerse myself in, so I stick just my feet in the water and then ease the rest of myself in as I adjust to it.

There's a button you can press to turn the soaking pool into a whirlpool, and I try it. The bubbles are nice but the noise is a little like sitting next to a blender. I decide to just soak.

Somewhere out there is Andrew. He knows I'm here. He knows I want to find him. I imagine him striding into the spa, right now, as unlikely as that is. What would I say to him?

How did I ever believe that I knew you?

Instead, it's Tom who strolls in. "Oh, hello," he says. "I heard you changed your mind! Isn't the water nice?"

I sigh and make a noncommittal, non-conversational sort of noise, hoping he'll take the hint and settle into the other pool. He climbs into mine, of course, and sits down next to me.

"What do you mean that you *heard* I changed my mind?" I ask, since apparently conversation is inevitable.

"I asked at the front desk where the other westerner had headed. You're rather conspicuous, my dear."

"You don't say."

He prattles on for a while about some beach in Thailand that's so popular with British tourists there are more white people there than Thai people, and then moves on to the question of *authenticity* and whether that's something you should even be trying to seek out. I smile and nod, which is all he seems to particularly want from me.

At least, it's all he wants from me until he scoots in closer and suggests we go out for a drink. I rocket out of the pool like the water has suddenly turned to acid, and retreat to my hotel room, with its locked door.

It's not until I get there that I wonder if he's *not* a travel writer. If he's actually here for the same reason I am. If he's looking for Andrew.

The summer after my sophomore year of college, I had a research fellowship to work with a biochemistry professor there. I'd gone to a small, highly competitive, intensely nerdy college. It felt like I'd spent my whole life up to that point as a fish out of water, leaping from jar to cup to puddle in a desperate bid to stay alive, and suddenly I'd found my way to the ocean. To water, to other fish, to the place I'd always belonged but never had been able to find. That was college, for me.

Not so much for Andrew. He'd applied to that same college, but he hadn't gotten in. He hadn't initially gotten into the flagship state university, either; his grades were too low. He'd enrolled at the local community college, then transferred to the state university after a year. He was doing okay, but he had big classes, few friends, professors who were unimpressed by his estimation of himself.

I visited home for just two weeks at the end of the summer. Andrew and I met up at a local park and he told me stories about his summer working at the local pool. He'd gotten lifeguard certification but, he told me cheerfully, he was probably the world's worst lifeguard, using his dark sunglasses to conceal naps.

"What if someone actually gets into trouble?" I said.

"They'd better yell loud enough to wake me up, then," Andrew said in a cheerful tone.

People who are drowning can't yell. They have water in their lungs; that's literally what drowning means. I didn't want to scold him. Surely no one had actually died on his watch, or I'd have heard. Also, I was never certain when he was joking. I forced a laugh, told myself this was definitely a joke, and described the research fellowship a bit. We were doing DNA sequencing, using one of the first automated machines for that purpose; I was studying the genome of a bacteria that mostly just lives harmlessly on human skin but can on occasion cause raging infections of various kinds, or food poisoning. I found the fact that it could be harmless or deadly really fascinating. It took me longer than it probably should have to realize that Andrew was a lot less interested than I was.

"You really are a nerd," he said, finally. I wasn't sure I was right that I was hearing contempt in his voice—I mean, this was Andrew. My best friend. My best friend from high school, anyway. I'd told him earlier about Beth, my best friend in college, who grew up in Arkansas and liked to crochet mathematical forms. I'd brought along a yarn stellated rhombic dodecahedron she'd made me for my birthday. I wondered if I should show that to Andrew, like I'd planned, or if that would make him angrier. More contemptuous.

What's wrong with me, I thought, and then I thought, *there's nothing wrong with me. The problem here is him. He's acting like an asshole.*

I made some excuses and left.

We didn't talk for twenty years.

Genetics became my life's work. Sequencing, first, through my undergraduate years and the beginning of graduate school. Genetic engineering, starting midway through graduate school and continuing through my postdoctoral work and my years at the university. CRISPR, when CRISPR became available, was just one more tool, but a particularly fascinating one. My focus was genetic diseases in humans.

There are basically two approaches to genetic diseases. The first is to test people—this has gotten cheaper and easier every year—and discourage carriers from having genetic children with other carriers. If one parent carries the gene for cystic fibrosis, but the other doesn't, none of their children will have the disease. The problem with this approach is that because carriers will continue to have children with noncarriers, the genes themselves stay in the population and at least a few babies with genetic diseases are more or less inevitable. (Please note, I'm not talking about eliminating neurodiversity from the population, or anything that could possibly be a reasonable human variation. I'm talking about diseases that cause years of misery and an inevitable early death, like cystic fibrosis, or diseases that just kill any child unlucky enough to have them, like Tay-Sachs.) The second approach is to step into the genome with the tools we have and simply fix it. If we use something like CRISPR to edit an embryo's genome, we can not only ensure that the child born from that embryo will not have Tay-Sachs or cystic fibrosis, we can ensure that they will also not grow up to pass along that particular gene.

Using techniques like this on humans beyond the embryo stage is years away. Or at least, I assumed it was years away.

Andrew got back in touch through Facebook. When I friended him back, he sent me a private message—CECILY, *wow, when I found out your family had moved out of town I thought I'd never catch up with you again. What are you up to these days?*

I'm a professor at Johns Hopkins, and Andrew was a lot more enthusiastic about my work now than the last time we talked, which was reassuring; he'd matured, clearly. And we'd both grown up; I was no longer the angry, insecure girl I'd been at that point in my life. I'd found my place in the world a long time ago.

We started chatting regularly again. Andrew told me about his job at a biotech start-up. It had taken him a lot longer to get through college and it didn't sound like he'd gotten through a doctoral program, but skills count for more outside of academia and he'd always had an abundance of intelligence and creativity. He'd signed a nondisclosure agreement, he said. As head researcher at a university lab, I had not.

"I would give *anything* to see that paper you're working on," he said one day, after I'd told him about the research I was doing into whether gene-editing technology—not CRISPR, but I'd started with CRISPR—could be used beyond the embryonic stage.

I sent it to him.

When the FBI agent came to my lab, I assumed she was looking for my colleague Jeanine, who developed a process for recovering DNA from centuries-old bones. She was not. "Dr. Cecily Grantz?" she asked. "Do you have a few minutes?"

I looked at the clock on my desk and said, "I have a class to teach later today, but not until 2:00 p.m. How can I help you?"

She closed my door, and pulled up a chair, like a student looking for help with a confusing assignment. "I'm Agent Locke," she said. "I'm here to ask you a few questions about someone I think you know."

What's Andrew done? I thought.

On some level, I must have known all along.

Agent Locke showed me photos: Andrew's one-person lab, with a tidy row of molecular printers directly adjacent to a hospital bed with restraint straps dangling down. The home freezer where he kept genetic samples for his record-keeping. And the bodies. The bodies that had torn themselves apart as his serum had wreaked its horrifying havoc. There were many bodies. He'd run test, after test, after test.

He'd lured in homeless teenagers. *Do you need a place to stay?* read an e-mail message he'd sent to two dozen separate runaways. *I'm here for you.*

There was a video interview with a girl who'd survived, barely. "I was an A-student," she said in thick speech with a tongue that no longer wanted to cooperate. "My ex-boyfriend was stalking me. I had no way to protect myself. I wanted to be strong. He promised me this would make me strong."

He'd used *my research* for this. Then adjusted the serum. Improved it. Changed his approach. Found more test subjects.

Left their bodies in shallow graves.

Agent Locke wanted to see what I'd sent to Andrew. I gave her everything I had.

I never knew him, I thought. *Not really.*

He was confident in the serum, Agent Locke told me before she left. In the end, he'd used it on himself. It had given him inhuman speed, reflexes, and strength. He'd used them to escape the armed officers who'd come to arrest him. "He broke their necks," she said, matter-of-factly, "with his bare hands."

The morning is cold and windy, and I put on extra layers before finding a car to take me to the abandoned mining town.

The town isn't entirely abandoned, nor are the residents actually a secret: a clothesline runs across the former town square, with four T-shirts and two pairs of pants drying in the morning air. As I hike up a narrow trail past a four-story apartment building, a dog waits calmly in the doorway of the apartments, not approaching, his tail slowly waving back and forth.

I think I can guess which buildings have inhabitants just based on where the satellite dishes are and where the glass windows are intact. I follow a trail up the hill. My socks and leggings get covered in tiny burrs; I also spot four patches that have been cleared of weeds and planted with something that might be that *B. oleracea* cultivar I've eaten every night at dinner.

Back down the hill, near the river, I look over at the rusted wreckage of a very ruined car and step inside what appears to have once been an auditorium.

If Andrew is here, he's given no sign.

The driver takes me through a mine shaft cut straight through the mountain and to the disused prison on the other side. This prison was abandoned in the 1970s, along with the mine; as with the town, there are nonetheless people living here. They grudgingly open up the gates when the driver bangs on the door and yells at them.

They are using the prison as a chicken farm. The doors to the empty cells all stand empty; inside, they reek of chicken droppings. When I step inside one, a chicken gabbles at me nervously and flaps her way to the other side of the cell, leaving a feather drifting in the air.

Most of the buildings in this part of China are unheated. Certainly a prison would have been no exception, and the visceral unpleasantness overwhelms me for a moment. I wonder if the prisoners here were criminals or political prisoners, victims of the Cultural Revolution, who they were.

I briefly imagine Andrew here.

It's what he deserves battles with *no one deserves this*. I don't even know what justice would look like after what he's done.

Anyway, he's not here. The longer I stand here the more certain I am that he would never hide in a prison. I can go.

When I arrive back at Danzhai Village, I can see a crowd gathering on the square outside the performance space: there's music and dancing. They're wearing traditional clothes but the music sounds more modern. I walk up for a closer look and get pulled into the dance by a smiling lady with a silver hat. There are choreographed steps that the locals are all following, although tourists who join in are all given enthusiastic encouragement. I feel foreign, heavy-footed, and stupid, but let them egg me on for a few minutes. "Good try!" one of them says in sympathetic English.

The statue of the Golden Pheasant Girl looms over all of us, lit by little spotlights as the sky grows dark.

When your people are starving, and the gods or dragons or magical tree demands a sacrifice, you might volunteer yourself; you might race to be the first to volunteer yourself, to spare someone you love.

I leave the square, walk down to the edge of the river, and think about monsters.

Nadine tried to tell me. Andrew himself tried to tell me. Did I turn away from these warnings because on some level it felt like being the one person the monster would never harm made me special?

How sure are you that this will work? Jeanine asked when I told her a little about the plan, when she agreed to keep an eye on my lab when I left for the two-week winter break. *What if they're wrong about whether he values you?*

That's not why I've been dreading finding him. I'm confident he won't hurt me. I've been dreading finding him because I'm here to turn on him. To betray him.

Because *that* is what you do when your friend is a monster. Truly a monster—not a part-time monster like a werewolf who can be contained with proper precautions, not a misunderstood monster like the Beast from the fairy tale, but a *monster*. You don't defend them. You don't deny it. You do what you have to do.

That doesn't mean you *want* to do it.

Back in my room, I pull up my social media and post some pictures I've taken: the chickens at the prison, the big empty room in the ghost town that used to be an auditorium. There were some Chinese characters painted in red on the crumbling wall, and now that I'm at my computer I plug that photo into a translation program and find out that the words say "NO SMOKING."

Maybe, I think, I've looked hard enough. Maybe I can just go home. Tell them I couldn't find him.

Then I see the picture I took of the clothesline strung across the village square. There's a pair of pants hung neatly by the ankles, but for the first time I take a closer look at the shirts. There are six: two work shirts, four T-shirts. The T-shirts have printing on them.

There's one with a TARDIS; one with a dragon; one with a math joke.

He was there. He was *there*. I just didn't recognize the signal.

I lie awake that night for hours, still drawn by that thought I had earlier: I don't have to go through with this. I could spend another day walking around Danzhai and go home pretending I tried my best. I fall into fitful sleep about halfway through the night, then wake at some very early hour because of a commotion in the hallway outside.

I put on my glasses, open my door, and step out to see what's going on.

A few doors down from mine, a room is open, light spilling out, hotel staff crowding frantically around. One of the women sees me, and she gestures for me to come. She pulls out her phone and speaks into it: it translates her words into flat, British-accented English. "You speak English. Please tell this man that we have called for a doctor."

My door shuts behind me, and my heart pounds as I follow her down the hall.

In his hotel room, Tom is lying on the floor, writhing in pain. Around him are things the hotel staff have brought to try to help—a kettle of hot water, a bowl of ice, towels, a bottle of pills, a bottle of alcohol. He's barely conscious. I can see the veins in his forehead bulging out like swollen twigs, the blood inside black and thick. It's the serum—the unfinished, fatal version. I wonder how Andrew got it into him. I can guess why: I was right. Tom isn't a "travel writer," he came here to find Andrew.

The staff backs off and lets me speak to him. I'm not sure he's conscious. "They've called an ambulance," I say. "They told me to tell you that a doctor is coming."

Tom opens his eyes a sliver, looks at me. "It's not going to help, is it? It's not." His tongue isn't cooperating; his throat is thick and his voice is raspy.

There have been some survivors. I don't think he's going to be one of them. I don't want to tell him that, so I ask, "Do you want me to tell anyone where you are?"

He tries to gesture toward his nightstand. His arm flops to the side. "My wallet."

I take it down and open it. It's a thin, impersonal wallet—no pictures of children, no coffee shop or grocery store loyalty cards. Just a UK driver's license, two credit cards, and a wad of cash. Plus a single handwritten index card saying "if found . . ." on it, with an e-mail address and a phone number. "There," he whispers.

"Who's this going to reach?" I ask.

He tries to speak, and for a moment can't. I think I see his lips forming "MI6," but what comes out, in the end is just, "They're no threat to you." His eyes close and a moment later he starts gasping, the air catching on the edges like burrs on clothing as his throat swells. If he could control his hands he'd be grasping desperately at his throat. I stand up and back away, putting the wallet down on his bed.

"Where is the doctor?" I ask the staff, not sure if anyone can understand me. "He needs a doctor right now or he's going to die."

The ambulance has arrived outside and the Chinese EMTs—or whatever they're called here—run to Tom's hotel room. I clear out, give them space to work, and am standing back in my own hotel room as they bring him out a few minutes later. Silent, and covered by a sheet.

The staff member who frantically brought me to Tom's side knocks on my door a few minutes later. She has a tray with tea, and sliced melon, and the steamed buns they serve at breakfast. Also a newspaper, because she's seen me buying newspapers, and I flinch a little at the sight of it. I certainly don't need that today.

Her face is tearstained and filled with guilt and shame. I want to reassure her that this catastrophe in her hotel was not her fault, but I don't want to dig myself into a hole I won't be able to get out of if anyone comes asking questions, so I say *xie xie* and let her go.

Today, the clothesline is empty. I go to the entrance of the building that has the satellite dishes, hand the dog a treat I've brought along to increase the chances of friendship, and make my way down the hallway.

This building is inhabited, but it's filthy. There are doors that are closed; other doors are open, with trash spilling out. I can smell peppers and rice cooking, overlaying the smells of mildew and dry rot. Somewhere in the building, there's a TV on. I know it's a TV just from the buoyant tone of the voices. TV Announcer Voice is one of those weird cultural constants.

When I reach door 28, I knock on it. Twenty-eight was my favorite number when I was a kid. (It's a perfect number. That means that if you break it down into its factors, and add those numbers together, you get the number again. 1+ 2 + 4 + 7 + 14 = 28. Andrew didn't much care about perfect numbers, but he listened to me talk about them.)

He answers the door.

I'm not entirely sure what to expect, but I'm surprised to see that he's shaved and clean, so "unshaven" was apparently what I was expecting. His hair is a lot grayer than in the pictures he had on his social media. "Cecily," he says, and his voice sounds exactly like I remember, which is also, in its own way, a surprise. "Come in." He steps back from the door and I follow him into the apartment.

There's a table, two rickety chairs, a large cask of water, a small gas burner. He puts water on to boil, and silently makes tea for both of us. I watch the leaves unfurl, not speaking.

"You came all this way," he says. "I'm sorry I can't offer you nicer surroundings."

Unbidden, the image of the bed with the straps rises up in my mind and I bow my head over my tea and pretend to drink it. He watches me, and I look up in time to see his face shift. He thought I'd come to help him. Or to warn him. Or just to see him. But he knows, now.

"How soon are they coming?" he asks.

"I don't know," I say.

He looks up at the ceiling, blinks back tears.

"Why not just kill me?" he asks. "Why betray me?"

"I seriously considered that option," I say. "But I was going to have to pass through Chinese customs. Also, I'm really not a violent person. Imagine me coming at you with a gun, even if I could get it through Chinese security. Or a knife."

Tears spill down his cheeks. "I've seen you throw a tray full of food into someone's face."

He doesn't flinch away from my hand as I reach out, wipe his tears away with my thumb. "Yeah, and remember how ineffective that was? I got a trip to the principal's office out of it, that was it." I wipe his tears off on the side of my pants. "Why did you do it, Andrew?"

"I told you years ago. I wanted to be strong."

"But to sacrifice all those people. You didn't go seeking out the football players who were sexually harassing girls in the cafeteria line and assaulting boys in the locker room."

"No. I looked for people who needed to be *strong*. I looked for the people I wanted to *help*."

It's strange how easy it is to talk to him. Still. Here. My tea is growing cold on the table by my hand. "Why did you come here?"

"I had to get out of the US before the bulletin went out. I speak Mandarin Chinese and around here, I thought maybe I could pass myself off as being from some other part of China. This region is where my grandfather came from, the one who immigrated to the US. It's quiet. I thought I could hide here, and maybe no one would come after me."

"They'd have followed you to the ends of the earth, Andrew."

He hears a hint in my voice, even though I didn't mean to put one there.

"Do they want my formula?"

I don't answer, which is answer enough. He laughs. A little bitterly, a little triumphantly.

"Well," he says. "I guess I have a bargaining chip after all."

"Didn't you assume that from the beginning?"

"You never know," he says. "People have been known to waste what's right in front of them."

It's true. They have.

He picks up his tea, and his teacup slips out of his sweat-slicked, unsteady hand, crashing to the floor. He stares after it, at his hands, which are shaking. He touches his face, feeling the sweat on his cheeks, and he looks at me. I stand up, realizing that staying as long as I did may have been a mistake.

"They're not coming," he says. "You're the only one. Why—what did you do to me—what's happening?"

I step away, and he reaches out and grabs my wrists. I can feel his inhuman strength, and I wonder if I'm about to find out just how wrong I was that he wouldn't turn it against me.

"The FBI came first. They told me what you'd done. The CIA came second. And they wanted me to make you an offer—to tell you that if you gave me your formula to bring back to the US, and it was useful to them, you could come home. There'd be no charges. They knew you were here, but they thought I'd be able to approach you."

"But instead," he says, "You decided to kill me."

"I demanded your notes. I said I needed whatever they had so that I could tell—or at least guess—before leaving China whether you were giving me fake information. They gave me what they had. I designed a bacterium that's harmless to most humans. Harmless, in fact, to any human who hasn't had the serum. It's fatal to you. It undoes, but only partially, what your serum did for you."

"I don't need to kill you," he whispers. "*They'll* kill you."

"Maybe," I say. "I'm going to tell them that your serum wasn't as good as you thought. That you died from its effects. Hopefully that'll discourage them from further research."

"What if it doesn't? What if they just start with the notes I left behind? You don't think the US Military will kill thousands to get this serum?"

"No," I say, honestly. "Not because they aren't evil. But because in the end, even the strongest, fastest, smartest human is still a human, and still the weakest link in the chain."

Overcome with dizziness, Andrew lurches to the side, grabbing his table for support; he tries to lower himself back to his chair, but misses, and lands hard on the floor. His window to kill me has probably closed.

He covers his face with his hands, and then says, "You're a terrible liar. You're the worst liar I've ever met. You barely fooled me for five minutes and I don't think you'll be able to fool the people who sent you."

"Maybe not," I say. "But if your serum dies with you, it'll still be worth it."

He laughs, very faintly, and waves toward a corner. "My laptop," he says. "Password is your name."

His clothes are soaked with his sweat, and now he's starting to cough, as his lungs fill with fluid released from their own cells. He gasps for air, like Tom did. Unlike Tom, his eyes are open. Open, and fixed on me. I watch as the whites of his eyes turn red, then black, as the blood vessels in them hemorrhage.

One summer day when we were sixteen or seventeen, we went to a park and climbed up onto the roof of the picnic shelter and watched the sunset, and watched the sky grow dark, and then lay on the warm roof and looked up at the sky and watched for falling stars. It was the night of a meteor shower and my parents weren't willing to let me stay out all night to watch it at its height (which was supposed to be 3:00 to 5:00 a.m.) unless I wanted to do that from our backyard, but they were willing to let me stay out until midnight, so that's how late we stayed.

"Are you going to wish on the falling stars?" he asked.

"That seems silly," I said. "I mean, they're not anything magical. They're caused by debris from a comet. They just *look* cool."

"You're so scientific," he said, complaining a little. "I bet you wished on shooting stars when you were little."

"Yeah," I say.

"So what did you wish for when you were little?" he asked, when I didn't elaborate.

"I wished for a friend," I said. "It wasn't just falling stars, either. First star of the night, white horses, whatever. I always wished for a friend."

The story I'm going to tell is that he was dead when I arrived.

Andrew's right that I'm not a very accomplished liar. But this is a simple lie.

They will definitely want his laptop. But he's given me the password—and that means I can ensure that the data is unrecoverable, even if he didn't.

I take gloves out of my pocket, pour out my tea, and return the cup to the cabinet, thinking about the step I'm about to take. Laptops are often very personal. Mine has my work in progress, but it also has notes, journal entries, letters, musings, poetry.

I would very much like to take the time to read all the things on Andrew's laptop that are *not* his research notes for the serum.

But I've already murdered my friend; if I don't destroy his notes, that will have been for *nothing*. So I wake the laptop, unlock it. I format the hard drive, then encrypt the formatted drive, making a fist and tapping the keyboard randomly to create a key for the encryption. Then I close the laptop and slip it into my bag to bring home, and sit down at the table, and wait for the rise and fall of Andrew's chest to stop.

LAST NIGHT AT THE FAIR

M. RICKERT

T he fair still comes to this town; that might give you some idea. The rides haven't changed much, either. The Ferris wheel still spins its circular course, lit at night with colored bulbs. From up there you can see the tent where the 4-H exhibits sport award-winning ribbons, and the building where the baked goods and canning entries are judged. It only lasts four days, four wondrous days if you are young and, for that first day, it is all a person can do not to steal chocolate chip cookies from the display or dip a hand into the case that contains the blueberry pie and pumpkin loaf, though once the flies descend all temptation is lost.

Old now, my favorite time to attend is early in the morning before the fair officially opens. I meander down the midway without the barkers or masses of people, not yet sticky and unsteady with littered popcorn cartons and other garbage, well before the drinking begins and the demolition cars rev their engines. Early in the morning, I walk through time, all the way back to my childhood and, in this way, return to that last summer when I was young.

When we were young, and the grownups told us we would never have more freedom. We thought they were wrong. Look at them, driving wherever they want to go, eating whatever they desire, dictating what words we can say, telling us when to come home and when to go to bed.

It seemed impossible that they were right, but as I walk the early morning midway back in time, I see us running wild with an abandon since lost, not just to the trajectory of age, but to a reality arisen from fetid ground that forever replaced the innocence of childhood with fears we never imagined, shootings, and kidnappings, molestations and the like.

We scared each other with stories of ghosts seen only in mirrors in the dark, zombie hitchhikers, and the lion either escaped or released from some misguided adult's fantasy of exotic pet ownership into the Wisconsin landscape. There were reports of sightings all summer as it made its way across the state, and I remember many a long night turning restlessly in the dark, the mechanical whir of the fan blowing hot air over my skin, itchy with mosquito bites, thinking I might have heard a roar or a cry through my open window, only to pad across the thick shag of carpet and observe the quiet street below, so still it was hard to believe anything exciting could ever happen there as I craned my neck to look up at the sky where the Big Dipper hung.

"See that?" my father told me earlier that summer. "See how it's right above our house? You're lucky to live beneath the Big Dipper. While you sleep it pours all the magic out. Onto you, especially."

"Me?" I asked.

"No matter what happens," he said, "you gotta believe this, Anne Marie. Your life is going to be special."

I did believe him. Why wouldn't I? It had been good for so long. Only now do I understand what I did not know then, that he had already gotten the diagnosis; the cry that sometimes woke me probably came from my mother, and the roar from him, or maybe it was the other way around.

That night, I looked up at the Big Dipper dripping all the magic over our little house, leaning my ear close to the screen, then walked across the room to unplug the fan which emitted a faint blue spark I didn't have the sense to find alarming. And, in that silence, I heard it again. I returned to the window, and listened, not to a lion's roar, or the rumbling engine of the hitchhiker's ride, certainly not the whispers of a mirror-trapped ghost, but the fair music still playing hours after I'd watched from our screen porch beside my father, fallen asleep on that hot night wrapped in a blanket, the drunken passage of the last revelers passing our house until my mother found me and said, "What are you doing still up? Go to bed now, Anne Marie. The fair is over."

But it wasn't! I heard the music through the distant dark and wondered what the fair was like after everyone went home. Did the Tall Man pluck stars from the sky? Did the Ferris wheel unleash itself from the brackets it resided in? Did the woman who made funnel cakes keep dipping them in powdered sugar to pass out to anyone who dared explore the midway? Did the man who ran the ringtoss win at his own game and pick out the giant stuffed bear for his prize, and did the horses turn their heads as they pranced free from their carousel as they had in *Mary Poppins*?

I had to find out and, as soon as I decided I would, the music grew louder. Not so loud as to wake the snoring grownups but loud enough that any minuscule residue of doubt was dispelled. I changed and tiptoed down the stairs past the blue glow of stovetop light and out the back door, pausing for a moment to inhale the perfume of August night air, sweet with the scent of early apples mingled with cut grass and something else, something just on the edge of going sour, fall's approach, I suppose. I wasn't even surprised to discover my husband standing in the front yard, staring at the house. Of course, I didn't know he would be my husband then. His name was Stanko, given to him for obscure reasons by an eccentric grandfather, but we all called him Stinko and, as evidence of his good nature, he never seemed to mind.

"Hey, Stinko," I whispered. "What're you looking at?" He turned in surprise, his eyes wide. "Anne Marie," he said, as if it were the most ordinary thing, as if it were the middle of the day. "Did you ever notice how the Big Dipper hangs right over your house?"

"What are you doing out here in the middle of the night?"

"Why, I don't know exactly," he said. "I heard music. What are *you* doing?"

"What do you think? Come on!" I took off running, and he followed. If you are wondering how things worked out between us, I can tell you we were married fifty-six years before he died, and he never stopped following me wherever I went.

So we ran through the night streets of Oakdale, past all the houses closed up tight, past massive hydrangea borders, and lilies with blossoms hanging shut from drooping stems. We ran through the silver halos of streetlights right back into the dark again, and when I see us there, from all this distance, I think we look like little ghosts.

We ran all the way without stopping until we stood across the street from the fair, enchanted by the lights, the bright sounds, the scent of popcorn and burnt sugar.

"What now?" Stinko asked.

I shrugged as if I knew better. "What do you think?"

"I don't know, Anne Marie. Doesn't it seem strange? Maybe we should go back."

I looked at him with his brow furrowed beneath his yellow hair, cut so short it stuck out a bit, and shook my head, acting braver than I felt as I proceeded through the gate.

"Welcome! Welcome! So glad you decided to come," the Tall Man greeted us, smiling down from his great height, surrounded by stars.

"Thanks," Stinko said, then turned to me and whispered, "Anne Marie, I just realized. I don't got any money."

"What's that? What's that you're saying?" the Tall Man asked. "Speak up so I can hear you, pardon the pun."

"We don't have any money," I shouted. No money and no way to get any, either. I'd spent my allowance and all I'd saved of it throughout that summer in the first three days of the fair, which left me broke on the last when I had glumly pretended interest in the cows and sad rabbits.

"Money? Money? Who said anything about money?"

"I did."

"You don't need money on this night," the Tall Man said. "Don't they teach you anything these days? Welcome! Welcome!"

I turned around, stunned to discover kids lining up behind us. It was unusual to see children I didn't know in Oakdale, and I wondered where they'd come from, but then Stinko took my hand in his and I was confused by how that felt. His skin was warm, his grasp neither too tight, nor too loose.

"Come on, Anne Marie! What are you waiting for?"

We rode all the rides and got dizzy but never sick. We spun in circles until the floor fell out, and we were held up only by air. We rode carousel horses that maintained their stance but did whinny and breathe beneath us. We rode the Ferris wheel and saw, from its highest point, the small dots of joy careening about, the 4-H tent, the baking hall, and the empty buildings where the farm animals had been kept.

"It makes sense when you think about it," I said. "I mean, they belong to people who took them home."

"Yea," Stinko said, "but Anne Marie, what is this, anyway?"

Rather than admit my own ignorance, I laughed. "Come on," I said. "Aren't you hungry?"

We ate funnel cakes and hot dogs, drank all the soda we wanted, dipped French fries into ketchup and licked the salt from our fingertips. We played ringtoss and darts, winning at both, and more than once almost forgot our stuffed bears on a bench when we went on a ride. We did everything, and we did it again, over and over, until we returned to the Ferris wheel. When it stopped for a while, leaving us at the top, we were too tired to feel alarm.

"Anne Marie, look." Stinko pointed straight ahead at the sky striped with dawn.

"I think it's time to go home," I said. "Before they wake up, and worry."

"But look," Stinko said. "Do you see it?"

"See what?"

"Look."

I squinted and leaned forward, far enough that the cab rocked, and Stinko rested his hand over mine, initiating that feeling again, the one I was too young to identify.

"Do you see it now?"

"It's all so tiny," I said. "Like it could disappear."

"There," he pointed, thrusting his skinny arm out. "Right down the middle of the road. Look."

In spite of the fantastical night we'd just spent together, my mind could not accept what I saw. Initially, I sorted it out as an enormous house cat, but of course no domestic creature would be so large.

"The lion."

Together we watched it make its passage right through the center of town, even as the occasional light appeared in a window, signaling the homes of early risers. I held my breath and, years later, my husband told me he did, too, as we watched the majestic creature first pass his house, and then mine. Just as the Ferris wheel creaked forward, the lion leapt from the road into the Maylers' cornfield, so thoroughly disappeared it was easy to wonder if it had ever been there at all. We arrived back on Earth to the sound of the engine shutting down with a clunk. The music stopped, too, and, like candles blown out, the lights blinked off.

I can guess what you are thinking. If it hadn't happened to me, I probably would think it, too. I have no proof to offer. Even the stuffed animals we'd won that night were forgotten and left behind. We were halfway home before we realized we'd abandoned them on the bench by the Ferris wheel. We couldn't go back, we agreed. It was already morning, and we worried that our parents might discover us missing. We couldn't imagine how terrible our punishment might be.

Even though I pretended it didn't matter, and made fun of Stinko for doing so, he walked right past his house to make sure I made it safely to mine and, when we got there, leaned over and kissed my cheek, then took off, running back down the street as though he was worried the lion would return. I thought for sure I would be in trouble, especially when I opened the door and smelled the coffee. My mom was in the kitchen, standing by the stove, but she didn't even turn to look at me. "My goodness, Anne Marie. What got you up so early?"

I opened my mouth to answer but, for some reason, let it close without a word. I guess you might say that was the morning I left the entanglements of a child and stepped into a separate world all my own. I walked across the kitchen and surprised my mother with a hug, wrapping my arms tight around her waist, as if afraid she might disappear.

"Oh, Anne Marie," she said. "Who told you?"

"Dad told me," I said.

"He did? When did he? I thought we agreed to tell you together."

"I'll never forget it, either," I said.

"What's that, dear?" she asked as she rubbed my back.

I pulled away to look up at her. "You know," I said. "About the Big Dipper hanging right over our house, dripping all that magic on us."

"Oh. Is that what he said?"

I nodded with a smile I recall as beatific, wiser than anyone was how I felt when I left my mother standing in the kitchen in her old bathrobe, staring at me, her secrets intact. I walked upstairs to my little bedroom where I plugged the fan in, kicked off my shoes, and fell into bed. You might say you have found evidence that this memory is of a dream, but you would be wrong.

Everything that has happened since then is the dream. That's how it feels, sitting on this bench, watching the lion meander in my tracks down the midway toward me. The closer it gets, the more my heart burns, and breath falters. I close my eyes against the inevitable suffering. It was such an ordinary life, but it was so wonderful! I wait, and wait, but nothing happens. When I open my eyes, the lion is gone; the boy I once knew standing in its place. "Anne Marie," he says. "I have been looking for you." He reaches for my hand, his fingers clasp around mine, and we are running together with the lights and the music and everything good dripping over us as though there has been no time at all between the first and last night at the fair.

OTHER RECOMMENDATIONS FROM 2020

I n previous volumes, I usually didn't offer a recommended reads/honorable mentions list. Last year, with a new start with a new publisher I did include such a list. Because writers and readers expressed an appreciation of this, I've included one again this year.

These two hundred novellas and stories (and the thirty stories making up the contents) are a fraction of the *hundreds* of stories I read each year. I'm sure I invariably forget to include some good stories. Some stories slip through the cracks. Maybe my notes are inadequate. And, of course, I can't read everything published. (Or even know it exists.) Please recognize these probable faults as you consider this list. One other warning: these are dark enough for me, but others may quibble they are not "dark enough." Feh. It is my list.

Those with an asterisk (*) are highly recommended.

Novellas
Eugen Bacon, *Ivory's Story* *
Yaroslav Barsukov, *Tower of Mud and Straw*
Aliette de Bodard, *Of Dragons, Feasts and Murders*
Georgina Bruce, *Honeybones*
Nino Cipri, *Finna*

P. Djèlí Clark, *Ring Shout**
Jeffrey Ford, *Out of Body*
Lisa L. Hannett, "By Touch and by Glance" (*Songs for Dark Seasons*)
Stephen Graham Jones, *Night of the Mannequins*
Kathe Koja, "The Marble Lily" (*Velocities: Stories*)*
—, "Pas de Deux," (*Velocities: Stories*)*
Sarah Langan, "You Have the Perfect Mask"(*Lady Churchill's Rosebud Wristlet #42*)*
Seanan McGuire, Come Tumbling Down
Oghenechovwe Donald Ekpeki, "Ife-Iyoku, Tale of Imadeyunuagbon" (*Dominion*, eds. Ekpeki & Knight)
Tochi Onyebuchi, Riot Baby*
K. J. Parker, Prosper's Demon
Caitlin Starling, *Yellow Jessamine*
Nghi Vo, *The Empress of Salt and Fortune**
—, *When the Tiger Came Down from the Mountain**

Stories
Marc Abbott, "The Foreclosure" (*Nightlight 309*)
Nadia Afifi, "The Bahrain Underground Bazaar" (*F&SF* 11-12/20)
G. V. Anderson, "Hearts in the Hard Ground" (*Tor.com* 09/09/20)
Laura Diaz de Arce, "Frijoles" (*Latinx Screams*, eds. Castro & Pelayo)
Simon Avery, "The Black Paintings" (*Black Static #75*)
Laird Barron, "Ode to Joad the Toad" (*Miscreations*, eds. Murano & Bailey)
M. Bennardo, "The Ordeal" (*Beneath Ceaseless Skies #297*)
Zabe Bent, "Sela, Thief" (*Breathe Fiyah*)
Sue Bentley, "Old God" (*The Third Corona Book of Horror Stories*, ed. Williams)
Simon Bestwick, "We All Come Home" (*After Sundown*, ed. Morris)
Lindy Biller, "The Banquet" (*Apparition Literary Magazine* 09/24/20)
Aliette de Bodard, "The Inaccessibility of Heaven" (*Uncanny #35*)
—, "In the Lands of the Spill" (*Avatars Inc*, ed. VanderMeer)
Brooke Bolander, "Where the River Turns to Concrete" (*The Book of Dragons*, ed. Strahan)

Gregory Norman Bossert, "The Night Soil Salvagers" (*Tor.com* 06/24/20)

K.C. Mead Brewer, "The Angel Finger" (*Craft* 10/16/20)

Samantha Bryant, "His Destroyer" (*Slay: Tales of the Vampire Noire*, ed. Kurtz)

C. Buchanan, "The Wasp-Keeper's Mother" (*Kaleidotrope* Summer 2020)

Nadia Bulkin, "Operations Other Than War" (*Miscreations*, eds. Murano & Bailey)

Christopher Caldwell, "If Salt Lose Its Savor" (*Uncanny* #33)

Isabel Cañas, "Silver As the Devil's Necklace" (*PseudoPod* 723)

Rebecca Campbell, "Child of Shower and Gleam" (*Shadows & Tall Trees 8*, ed. Kelly)

—, "Thank You For Your Patience" (*Reckoning #4)**

Rae Carson, "Badass Moms in the Zombie Apocalypse" (*Uncanny #32)**

L Chan, "Carving You Out of Memory" (*Black Telephone Magazine #1*)

Vajra Chandrasekera, "The Translator, at Low Tide" (*Clarkesworld #164*)

Kay Chronister, "Too Lonely, Too Wild" (*Shadows & Tall Trees 8*, ed. Kelly)

—, "White Throat Holler" (*Thin Places*)

Nino Cipri, "Velvet" (*Baffling #1*)

L. Clark, "Forgive Me, My Love, for the Ice and the Sea" (*Beneath Ceaseless Skies #296*)

ZZ Claybourne, "The Air in My House Tastes Like Sugar" (*GigaNotoSaurus* 03/01/20)

Ray Cluley, "In the Wake of My Father" (Black Static #74)

Albert E. Cowdrey, "Falling Angel" (*F&SF* 01-02/20)

—, "The Tale of Two Witches" (*F&SF* 11-12/20)

Leah Cypess, "Stepsister" (*F&SF* 05-06/20)

Gillian Daniels, "Bobbie and Her Father" (*The Dark* #63)

Kristi DeMeester, "Sleeping in Metal and Bone" (*The Dark #60*)

Anya Johanna DeNiro, "A Voyage to Queensthroat" (*Strange Horizons* 08/10/20)

W. C. Dunlap, "The Front Line" (*Breathe Fiyah*)

Malon Edwards, "All the Horrors, and the Hope You'll Make Them Right" (*Eyedolon* 10/01/20)

Erin Eisenhour, "The Black-Eyed Goddess of Apple Trees and Farmer's Wives" (*Beneath Ceaseless Skies* 07/16/20)*

Meg Elison, "Familiar Face" (*Nightmare* #88)

—, "The Pill" (*Big Girl*)

Corey Farrenkopf, "What Friends Don't Tell Friends About Basements" (*Bourbon Penn* #22)

Casilda Ferrante, "My Brother's Keeper"(*Unsung Stories* 07/10/20)

Paul Finch, "Branch Line" (*After Sundown*, ed. Morris)

Gemma Files, "Cut Frame" (*Final Cuts*, ed. Datlow)

—, "Come Closer" (*In That Endlessness, Our End*)

Geneve Flynn, "Little Worm" (*Black Cranes*, eds. Murray & Flynn)

Vanessa Fogg, "The Breaking" *(Mithila Review 15)**

Ephiny Gale, "The Candle Queen" (*Beneath Ceaseless Skies* #295)

Ozzie M. Gartrell, "The Transition of Osoosi" (*Fiyah* #13)

John Gaskin, "The Gathering" (*Strange Tales: Tartarus Press at 30*, ed. Parker)

Richard Gavin, "Scold's Bridle: A Cruelty" (*Grotesquerie*)

Craig Laurance Gidney, "Myth and Moor" (*Evil in Technicolor*, ed. McDermott)

Elana Gomel, "Mine Seven" (*After Sundown*, ed. Morris)

Sergio Gomez, "Come, Play" (*Latinx Screams*, eds. Castro & Pelayo)

J.T. Greathouse, "The Gwyddien and the Raven Fiend" (*Beneath Ceaseless Skies* #316)

Dicey Grenor, "Diary of a Mad Black Vampire" (*SLAY: Tales of the Vampire Noire*, ed. Kurtz)

Orrin Grey, "The All-Night Horror Show" (*The Dark* #58)

Thomas Ha, "Balloon Season" (*Fusion Fragment* #3)

John Haas, "The Debt" (*The Third Corona Book of Horror Stories*, ed. Williams)

Lisa L. Hannett, "Deep in the Drift, Spinning" (*Beneath Ceaseless Skies* #312)

—, "A Grand Old Life" (*Songs for Dark Seasons*)

Lucie McKnight Hardy, "Resting Bitch Face" (*Black Static* #76)

Nin Harris "When Hope Is Lost, Touch Remains" (*Podcastle 620*)*

V. G. Harrison, "Message in a Vessel" (*SLAY: Tales of the Vampire Noire*, ed. Kurtz)

Alix E. Harrow, "The Ransom of Miss Coraline Connelly" (*Fireside 7/20*)

Maria Haskins, "Cleaver, Meat, and Block" (*Black Static #73*)*

Grady Hendrix, "Murder Board" (*After Sundown*, ed. Morris)

Katherine L. Hester, "Bunting" (*Bracken #7*)

Karen Heuler, "The Constant Lover" (*Conjunctions:74*)

Crystal Lynn Hilbert, "To Inherit Hunger"(*Bourbon Penn 21*)

Millie Ho, "The Fenghuang" (*Lightspeed #120*)

—, "A Moonlit Savagery" (*Nightmare #9*)

Brian Hodge, "Insanity Among Penguins" (*Final Cuts*, ed. Datlow)

Liam Hogan, "Amy's Game" (*34 Orchard #2*)

Amanda Hollander, "A Feast of Butterflies" (*F&SF* 03-04/20)

Kat Howard, "The Lachrymist" (*Lightspeed #126*)

Claire Humphrey, "We Are the Flower"(*Podcastle #627*)

Andrew Michael Hurley, "Hunger" (*Strange Tales: Tartarus Press at 30*, ed. Parker)

Alledria Hurt, "Ujim" (*Slay: Tales of the Vampire Noire*, ed. Kurtz)

Kathleen Jennings. "The Present Only Toucheth Thee" (*Strange Horizons* 06/08/20)

Stephen Graham Jones, "Lords of the Matinee (*Final Cuts*, ed. Datlow)

Eygló Karlsdóttir, "Footprints in the Snow" (*The Alchemy Press Book of Horrors, Vol. 2*, eds. Coleborn & Edwards)

James Patrick Kelly, "The Man I Love"(*F&SF* 03-04/20)*

Michael Kelly, "The Other Side" (*Unsung Stories* 07/24/20)

Christopher Kenworthy, "Shattering" (*Black Static #74*)

Justin C. Key, "One Hand in the Coffin" (*Strange Horizons* 01/20/20)

Cassandra Khaw, "Hungry Girls" (*Final Cuts*, ed. Datlow)

Caitlín Kiernan, "Seven Dreams," (*Sirenia Digest #167*)

—, "L'hommes et la femme terribles" (*Sirenia Digest #176*)

T. Kingfisher, "Metal Like Blood in the Dark" (*Uncanny #36*)

Nicole Kornher-Stace, "Getaway" (*Uncanny #33*)

John Langan, "Alice's Rebellion" (*After Sundown*, ed. Morris)

Gabriela Lee, "Rites of Passage" (*Black Cranes*, eds. Murray & Flynn)

Stina Leicht, "Forgiveness Is Warm Like A Tear On The Cheek" (*Evil in Technicolor*, ed. McDermott)

Jennifer Lewis, "Holy Communion" (*Entropy Magazine* 03/05/20)

Darcie Little Badger, "Unlike Most Tides" (*Drabblecast* #425)

Allison Littlewood, "Hungry Ghosts" (*Shadows & Tall Trees 8*, ed. Kelly)

K. R. S. McEntire, Encounters (*SLAY: Tales of the Vampire Noire*, ed. Kurtz)

Dafydd McKimm, "Gingerbread" (*Flash Fiction Online* 03/20)

Clara Madrigano, "Driving With Ghosts" (*The Dark* #60)

—, "Mother Love" (*The Dark* #56)

—, "Lost in Darkness and Distance" (*Clarkesworld* #170)*

Emma Maguire, "Under the Corn" (*Verity La* 06/01/20)

Lyndsie Manusos "How to Burn Down the Hinterlands" (*F&SF* 11-12/20)

Melissa Marr, "Of Roses and Kings"(*Tor.com* 04/27/20)

Arkady Martine, "A Being Together Amongst Strangers" (*Uncanny* #34)

Rosemary Melchior, "Salt" (*Luna Station Quarterly 041*)

Rati Mehrotra, "The Witch Speaks" (*Lightspeed Magazine* #119)

Samantha Mills, "The Limits of Magic" (*Apparition Literary Magazine* #11)

Michael Milne, "The Bone Gifts" (Glitter and Ashes, ed. Ring)

Lee Murray, "Phoenix Claws" (*Black Cranes*, eds. Murray & Flynn)

Ray Nayler, Eyes of the Forest (*F&SF* 05-06/20)*

—, "Outside of Omaha" (*Nightmare* #96)

David Erik Nelson, "All Hail the Pizza King and Bless His Reign Eternal" (*F&SF* 07-08/20)

Mari Ness, "The Ruby of the Summer King" (*Uncanny* #35)*

Dimitra Nikolaidou, "The Honey of the World and the Queen of Crows" (*Beneath Ceaseless Skies* #304)

Thana Niveau, "Bokeh" (*After Sundown*, ed. Morris)

—, "The Hate Whisperer" (*The Alchemy Press Book of Horrors, Vol. 2*, eds. Coleborn & Edwards)

Christi Nogle, "Resilience" (*Pseudopod 704*)*

Errick Nunnally, "Uniform" (*Fiyah* #14)

Aimee Ogden, "Buttercream and Broken Wings" (*Beneath Ceaseless Skies #307*)

—, "More Than Simple Steel" (*Escape Pod 751*)

L'Erin Ogle, "Memories Written in Scars" (*Consumed: Tales Inspired by the Wendigo*, eds. Snider & Snider)

Reggie Oliver, "Collectable" (*Strange Tales: Tartarus Press at 30*, ed. Parker)

Nancy O'Toole, "Gretel" (*Luna Station Quarterly 018*)

Suzan Palumbo, "Tara's Mother's Skin" (*PseudoPod 718*)

Sarah Pinsker, "Two Truths and a Lie" (*Tor.com 06/17/20*)

Rhonda Pressley, "Fatal Memory" (*Black Static #76*)

Laura Purcell, "Creeping Ivy" (*After Sundown*, ed. Morris)

Chen Qiufan, "Debtless," trans. Blake Stone-Banks (*Clarkesworld #163*)

Jenny Rae Rappaport, "Girls with Needles and Frost" (*Beneath Ceaseless Skies #315*)

Nicasio Andres Reed, "Body, Remember" (*Fireside 10/20*)

Endria Isa Richardson, "The Black Menagerie" (*Fiyah #15*)

Ranylt Richildis, "The Stitch Beneath the Ice" (*Strange Horizons 07/20/20*)

M. Rickert, "The Little Witch" (*Tor.com 10/28/20*)*

Karlo Yeager Rodriguez, "As the Shore to the Tides, So Blood Calls to Blood" (*Beneath Ceaseless Skies #301*)

Josh Rountree, "February Moon" (*Beneath Ceaseless Skies #303*)

Carlie St. George, "Monsters Never Leave You" (*Strange Horizons 06/29/20*)

—, "Spider Season, Fire Season" (*Nightmare #94*)

Shannon Sanders, "Company" (*Strange Horizons 02/10/20*)

Jason Sanford, "Where the World Ends Without Us" (*Beneath Ceaseless Skies #299*)

Yah Yah Scholfield, "All That the Storm Took" (*Fiyah #13*)

Nibedita Sen, "Mandragora" (*Fireside 03/20*)*

Angela Slatter, "The Heart is a Mirror for Sinners" (*The Heart is a Mirror for Sinners & Other Stories*)

"New Wine" (*Cursed*, eds. Marie O'Regan & Paul Kane)

"The Three Burdens of Nest Wynne" (*Strange Tales: Tartarus Press at*

30, ed. Rosalie Parker)

Michael Marshall Smith, "It Doesn't Feel Right" (*After Sundown*, ed. Morris)*

David Tallerman, "Not Us" (*Nightmare #97*)

Steve Rasnic Tem, "Sleepwalking with Angels" (*Shadows & Tall Trees*)

"The Walls Are Trembling" (*Apostles of the Weird*, ed. Joshi)

Natalia Theodoridou, "Georgie in the Sun" (*Uncanny #33*)

Sheree Renée Thomas, "Head Static" (*Nine Bar Blues*)*

—, "Madame and the Map: A Journey in Five Movements" (*Nine Bar Blues*)*

—, "The Parts That Make Us Monsters" (*Strange Horizons: Fund Drive Issue*)

Vincent Tirado, "Your Name Is Oblivia" (*Fiyah #15*)

E. Catherine Tobler, "Blue Hole, Red Sea" (*Evil in Technicolor*, ed. McDermott)*

—, "True In His Fashion" (*Three-Lobed Burning Eye #31*)

Eugenia Triantafyllou, "My Country Is a Ghost" (*Uncanny #32)*

Tlotlo Tsamaase, "The River of Night" (*The Dark #66*)

L. Tu, "If You Want to Erase Us, You Must Be Thorough" (*Uncanny #33*)

J. Tudor, "Final Course" (*Subterranean: Tales of Dark Fantasy 3*)

Christine Tyler, "My Sister's Wings Are Red" (*Beneath Ceaseless Skies #298*)

Stephen Volk, "Agog" (*The Dark #62*)

—, "The Naughty Step" (*After Sundown*, ed. Morris)

Tim Waggoner, "The White Road" (*The Horror Zine's Book of Ghost Stories*, eds. Rector & Wild)

Wendy N. Wagner, "The Smell of Night In the Basement" (*PseudoPod 730*)

Damien Angelica Walters, "A Perfect Hunger, a Certain Rage" (*Eyedolon 01/31/20*)

Catriona Ward, "A Hotel in Germany" (*After Sundown*, ed. Morris)*

Karron Warren, "Three Rooms, with Heliotrope" (*Tales of the Lost II*, eds. Johnson & Dillon)

Michael Wehunt, "A Heart Arrhythmia Creeping Into a Dark Room"

(*Miscreations*, eds. Murano & Bailey)

Martha Wells, "The Salt Witch" (*Uncanny #37*)*

Neil Williamson, "Down to the Roots" (*Shadows & Tall Trees 8*, ed. Kelly)

A. C. Wise, "Exhalation #10 (Final Cuts, ed. Datlow)*

"Teeth Long and Sharp as Blades" (*PseudoPod #728*)

"A Thousand Faces Minus One" (*Evil in Technicolor*, ed. McDermott)

Merc Fenn Wolfmoor, "Bring the Bones That Sing" (*Diabolical Plots #65B*)

Claire Wrenwood, "Dead Girls Have No Names" (*Nightmare #95*)

ABOUT THE AUTHORS

KELLEY ARMSTRONG is the #1 *New York Times* bestselling author of the Otherworld series, as well as the *New York Times* bestselling young adult trilogy Darkest Powers, the Darkness Rising trilogy, and the Nadia Stafford series. Her latest series, the Rockton novels, are mysteries. She lives in rural Ontario, Canada, with her husband and three children.

DALE BAILEY is the author of eight books, including *In the Night Wood*, *The End of the End of Everything*, and *The Subterranean Season*. His story "Death and Suffrage" was adapted for Showtime's *Masters of Horror* television series. His short fiction has been frequently reprinted in best-of-the-year anthologies. Bailey has won the Shirley Jackson Award and the International Horror Guild Award, and has been a finalist for the World Fantasy, Nebula, Locus, and Bram Stoker awards. He lives in North Carolina with his family.

ELIZABETH BEAR is the Hugo, Sturgeon, Locus, and Astounding Award winning author of dozens of novels; over a hundred short stories; and a number of essays, nonfiction, and opinion pieces for markets as diverse as *Popular Mechanics* and the *Washington Post*. Her most recent novels are *The Origin of Storms* (Lotus Kingdoms 3) and *Machine*

(White Space 2). She lives in the Pioneer Valley of Massachusetts with her spouse, writer Scott Lynch.

ZEN CHO is the author of the Sorcerer to the Crown novels, *Black Water Sister*; *The Order of the Pure Moon*, a novella; and various works of shorter fiction some of which are collected in *Spirits Abroad*. Her most recent novel is contemporary fantasy *Black Water Sister*. She is a Hugo, Crawford, and British Fantasy Award winner as well as a finalist for the Locus and Astounding Awards. She was born and raised in Malaysia and resides in the UK.

WENMIMAREBA KLOBAH COLLINS is a Black queer writer based in San Juan, Puerto Rico. She holds a BA in Fine Arts and Literature and is currently pursuing an MFA in Creative Writing and Critical Visual Studies. Her work is in *The Dark*, *Samovar*, and in Akashic Books' Duppy Thursday series of Caribbean stories.

ELAINE CUYEGKENG is a Chinese-Filipino writer. She grew up in Manila, where there are many, many creaky old houses with ghosts inside them. She writes about eldritch creatures, monsters with human faces and the old, old story of art and revolution. She now lives in Melbourne with her partner. Cuyegkeng's work has been published in *Pseudopod*, *Strange Horizons*, *Lackington's*, *The Dark*, and *Rocket Kapre*.

BRIAN EVENSON is the author of scores of works of short fiction and many books of fiction, most recently the story collection *The Glassy, Burning Floor of Hell*. His novel *Windeye* and collection *Immobility* were both finalists for the Shirley Jackson Award. His novel *Last Days* won the American Library Association's award for Best Horror Novel. Evenson's novel *The Open Curtain* was a finalist for an Edgar Award and an International Horror Guild Award. He is the recipient of three O. Henry Prizes as well as an NEA fellowship. He lives in Los Angeles and teaches in the Critical Studies Program at CalArts.

JAMES EVERINGTON's most recent collection is *Trying To Be So Quiet & Other Hauntings* and he has co-edited (with Dan Howarth) three anthologies, the most recent of which is *Pareidolia*. He has also authored the novel *Paupers Graves* as well as more than thirty works of shorter fiction. He lives in Nottingham, England, and, if you are buying drinks, he'll take a Guinness.

CRAIG LAURANCE GIDNEY is the author of the collections *Sea, Swallow Me* and *Skin Deep Magic*; the novels *Bereft* and *A Spectral Hue*; and numerous short stories. Both his collections and *A Spectral Hue* were finalists for the Lambda Literary Award and *Bereft* won both the Bronze Moonbeam and Silver IPPY Awards. In 2020, *A Spectral Hue* was a Carl Brandon Parallax Award Honoree. *Hairsbreadth*, a fairy tale novel, is serialized on *Broken Eye Books*. Gidney is a lifelong resident of Washington, DC.

THOMAS HA is a former attorney turned stay-at-home father who enjoys writing speculative fiction during the rare moments when both of his children happen to be asleep at the same time. He lives with his family in Los Angeles.

ELIZABETH HAND is the bestselling author of fourteen genre-spanning novels and five collections of short fiction and essays. Her work has received multiple Shirley Jackson, World Fantasy, and Nebula Awards, among other honors, and several of her books have been *New York Times* and *Washington Post* Notable Books. Her sixth collection, *The Best of Elizabeth Hand*, was published earlier this year. She lives in a small town on the coast of Maine and sometimes in Camden Town, London.

ALIX E. HARROW is an ex-historian with lots of opinions and excessive library fines, currently living in Kentucky with her husband and their semi-feral children. She won a Hugo for her short fiction and debut novel, *The Ten Thousand Doors of January*, was a nominated for the Hugo, Nebula, Locus, World Fantasy, and Goodreads Choice Awards.

Her second novel, *The Once and Future Witches*, was named as one of the Best Books of the Year by NPR Books.

MARIA DAHVANA HEADLEY is the *New York Times*-bestselling and World Fantasy Award-winning author of eight books, most recently *Beowulf: A New Translation. The Mere Wife*, a contemporary adaptation of Beowulf, was named by the *Washington Post* as one of its Notable Works of Fiction. Headley's short fiction has been shortlisted for the Nebula and Shirley Jackson Awards, and for the 2020 Joyce Carol Oates Prize. She grew up in the high desert of Idaho on a survivalist sled dog ranch, where she spent summers plucking the winter coat from her father's wolf.

STEPHEN GRAHAM JONES is the *New York Times*-bestselling author of twenty-five or so novels and collections, and there's some novellas and comic books in there as well. Stephen's been an NEA recipient, has won the Texas Institute of Letters Award for Fiction, the Independent Publishers Award for Multicultural Fiction, Bram Stoker Award, four This is Horror Awards, and been a finalist for the Shirley Jackson Award and the World Fantasy Award. He's also made Bloody Disgusting's Top Ten Horror Novels. His most recent novel, *My Heart is a Chainsaw*, was released earlier this year. Jones lives in Boulder, Colorado.

SHINGAI NJERI KAGUNDA is an Afrofuturist freedom dreamer, Swahili sea lover, and femme storyteller hailing from Nairobi, Kenya. She is currently pursuing a Literary Arts MFA at Brown University. Kagunda work hs been longlisted for the Nommo Award and shortlisted for the Fractured Lit Prize. Her work has also been published in *Fantasy* and *Kh ré* magazines. She is also the co-founder of Voodoonauts: an Afrofuturist workshop for black writers.

CAITLÍN R. KIERNAN is the author of fifteen science fiction and dark fantasy novels, many comic books, and more than two hundred published short stories, novellas, and vignettes. They are also the author of scientific papers in the field of paleontology and is a research associate and fossil preparator at the McWane Science Center in Birmingham, Alabama. Kiernan's most recent novel is *Tindalos Effect*; *Comes a Pale Rider* is their seventeenth collection. They are a four-time winner of the International Horror Guild Award, a two-time winner of the Bram Stoker Award, and have been honored with the World Fantasy Award twice. Kiernan is also the recipient of the Barnes & Noble Maiden Voyage Award, the James Tiptree Jr. Award, and the Locus Award.

SOLEIL KNOWLES is a Bahamian writer currently working on her BA in English and Creative Writing. In her free time, she can be found eating plantain chips and watching reruns of *Avatar: The Last Airbender*. She lives with her plants and books.

NAOMI KRITZER is a writer and blogger who has published a number of short stories and novels for adults, including the Eliana's Song duology and the Dead Rivers trilogy. Her short story "Cat Pictures Please" won the Hugo Award, Locus Award, and was a finalist for the Nebula. Her first YA novel, *Catfishing on CatNet* won the Minnesota Book Award and the Edgar Allan Poe Award. Its sequel, *Chaos on Catnet*, was published earlier this year. Naomi lives in St. Paul, Minnesota, with her family and cats. She also writes about politics (mainly elections) in Minneapolis and Saint Paul.

VICTOR LAVALLE is the author of the short story collection *Slapboxing with Jesus*, four novels (*The Ecstatic, Big Machine, The Devil in Silver*, and *The Changeling*), and two novellas, *Lucretia and the Kroons* and *The Ballad of Black Tom*. He is also the creator and writer of a comic book: *Victor LaValle's Destroyer*. He has been the recipient of numerous awards including the World Fantasy Award, British Fantasy Award, Bram Stoker Award, Whiting Writers' Award, a Guggenheim Fellowship, Shirley Jackson Award, American Book Award, and the key to Southeast Queens. Raised in Queens, New York, LaValle now lives in Washington Heights with his wife and children. He teaches at Columbia University.

V. H. LESLIE is the author of a short story collection, *Skein and Bone*, and novel *Bodies of Water*. Her short stories have appeared in a range of journals and anthologies. Leslie has been nominated for the World Fantasy, British Fantasy, and Shirley Jackson Awards and she won the Lightship International Prize. She has been awarded fellowships for her writing at Hawthornden in Scotland and the Saari Institute in Finland, and her non-fiction has appeared in *History Today*, *The Victorianist* and *Gramarye*.

H. PUEYO is an Argentine-Brazilian writer of speculative fiction and comics. Her work has appeared before in *The Magazine of Fantasy & Science Fiction*, *Fireside*, and *The Dark*, among others

DANNY RHODES is the author of three contemporary novels, *Asboville*, *Soldier Boy*, and most recently *FAN*. His short fiction has appeared in numerous publications including *The Horror Library*, *Black Static*, *Cemetery Dance*, and *Best New Horror*. His essay on the ghost stories of L. T. C. Rolt appears in *Horror Literature from Gothic to Post-Modern*. He is a lecturer in Creative and Professional Writing at Canterbury Christ Church University.

Before earning her MFA from Vermont College of Fine Arts, **MARY RICKERT** worked as a kindergarten teacher, coffee shop barista, Disneyland balloon vendor, and personnel assistant in Sequoia National Park. She is the winner of the Locus Award, Crawford Award, World Fantasy Award, and Shirley Jackson Award. Her novel, *The Shipbuilder of Bellfairie* was published earlier this year. Her novella *Lucky Girl, How I Became a Horror Writer: A Krampus Story* will be published in the fall of 2022.

SONYA TAAFFE reads dead languages and tells living stories. Her short fiction and poetry have been collected most recently in the Lambda-nominated *Forget the Sleepless Shores* and previously in *Singing Innocence and Experience*, *Postcards from the Province of Hyphens*, *A Mayse-Bikhl*, and *Ghost Signs*. She lives with one of her husbands and both of her cats in Somerville, Massachusetts, where she writes about film for *Patreon* and remains proud of naming a Kuiper belt object.

STEVE RASNIC TEM, a past winner of the Bram Stoker, World Fantasy, and British Fantasy Awards, has published 470+ short stories. *Figures Unseen* gathers some of his best. Other collections include *The Night Doctor & Other Tales*, *The Harvest Child and Other Fantasies*, and the forthcoming *Thanatrauma*. His novel *Ubo* is a dark science fictional tale about violence and its origins. *Yours to Tell: Dialogues on the Art & Practice of Writing*, written with his late wife Melanie, is now available. A transplanted Southerner from Lee County Virginia, Tem is a long-time resident of Colorado.

SHEREE RENÉE THOMAS is an award-winning fiction writer, poet, and editor. Her work is inspired by myth and folklore, natural science, and Mississippi Delta conjure. *Nine Bar Blues: Stories from an Ancient Future* is her first all prose collection. She is also the author of two multigenre/hybrid collections and edited the World Fantasy-winning groundbreaking black speculative fiction *Dark Matter* anthologies. She is the associate editor of the historic Black arts literary journal *Obsidian: Literature & the Arts in the African Diaspora* and editor of *The Magazine of Fantasy & Science Fiction*. Thomas also writes for Marvel. She lives in her hometown of Memphis, Tennessee near a mighty river and a pyramid.

CATHERYNNE M. VALENTE is the *New York Times-* and *USA Today*-bestselling author of over forty books of fiction, poetry, and criticism, including the Fairyland series, *Space Opera*, *Deathless*, and *The Orphan's Tales*. Her most recent novels are *The Past is Red* and *Comfort Me with Apples*. She is the winner of the Hugo, Nebula, Otherwise, Lambda, Sturgeon, and Locus Awards, among others. She lives on a small island off the coast of Maine with her partner, son, and extremely judgmental cat.

A. C. WISE's work has appeared in publications such as *Uncanny*, *Tor.com*, *Shimmer*, and *Clarkesworld*. Her work has won the Sunburst

ABOUT THE AUTHORS

Award for Excellence in Canadian Literature of the Fantastic and she has twice been a finalist for both the Nebula Award and the Lambda Literary Award. She has published two collections and a novella. Her debut novel, *Wendy, Darling,* and a new short story collection, *The Ghost Sequences,* were published earlier this year. In addition to her fiction, she contributes review columns to *The Book Smugglers* and *Apex.*

JOHN WISWELL is a disabled writer who lives where New York keeps all its trees. His work has appeared in venues including *Uncanny, Nightmare, Nature Futures, Diabolical Plots, Fireside, Daily Science Fiction, Flash Fiction Online, Pseudopod, Cast of Wonders,* and *PodCastle.* He is a Locus Award Finalist and Nebula Award Finalist. He wishes every family a home that loves them.

ACKNOWLEDGMENTS

S pecial thanks to all the editors responsible for the initial publication of these stories. Also to my editor Rene Sears, publisher Jarred Weisfeld, and cover designer Jennifer Do. All stories are reprinted with permission of the author.

"Recognition" © 2020 Victor LaValle. First publication: *The New York Times Decameron Project*

"Odette" © 2020 Zen Cho. First publication: *Shoreline of Infinity 18*

"Das Gesicht" © 2020 Dale Bailey. First publication: *Final Cuts: New Tales of Hollywood Horror and Other Spectacles*, ed. Ellen Datlow

"The Sycamore and the Sybil" © 2020 Alix E. Harrow. First publication: *Uncanny #33*

"The Stonemason" © 2020 Danny Rhodes. First publication: *Black Static #75*

"Desiccant" © 2020 Craig Laurance Gidney. First publication: *Slay: Stories of the Vampire Noire*, ed. Nicole Givens Kurtz

"Open House on Haunted Hill" © 2020 John Wiswell. First publication: *Diabolical Plots #54A*

"The Genetic Alchemist's Daughter" © 2020 Elaine Cuyegkeng. First publication: *Black Cranes: Tales of Unquiet Women*, eds. Lee Murray and Geneve Flynn

ACKNOWLEDGMENTS

"Swanskin" © 2020 Alison Littlewood. First publication: *After Sundown*, ed. Mark Morris

"The Dead Outside My Door" © 2020 Steve Rasnic Tem. First publication: *Black Static #77*

"Lusca" © 2020 Soleil Knowles. First publication: *Fiyah #13*

"To Sail the Black" © 2020 A. C. Wise. First publication: *Clarkesworld #170*

"Nobody Lives Here" © 2020 H. Pueyo. First publication: *The Dark #66*

"On Safari in R'lyeh and Carcosa with Gun and Camera" © 2020 Elizabeth Bear. First publication: *Tor.com* 11/18/20

"The Thickening," © Brian Evenson. First publication: *Conjunctions 74*

"The Owl Count" © 2020 Elizabeth Hand. First publication: *Conjunctions 74*

"Color, Heat, and the Wreck of the Argo" © 2020 Catherynne M. Valente. First publication: *Strange Horizons* 09/07/20

"Ancestries" © 2020 Sheree Renée Thomas. First publication: *Nine Bar Blues: Stories from an Ancient Future*

"The Sound of the Sea, Too Close" © 2020 James Everington. First publication: *Shadows & Tall Trees, Vol. 8*, ed. Michael Kelly

"Drunk Physics" © 2020 Kelley Armstrong. First publication: *Final Cuts: New Tales of Hollywood Horror and Other Spectacles*, ed. Ellen Datlow

"Call Them Children" © 2020 Wenmimareba Klobah Collins. First publication: *The Dark #64*

"Tea with the Earl of Twilight" © 2020 Sonya Taaffe. First publication: *Nightmare #96*

"Wait for Night" © 2020 Stephen Graham Jones. First publication: *Tor.com* 09/02/20

"Where the Old Neighbors Go" © 2020 Thomas Ha. First publication: *Metaphorosis* 09/20/20

"Dead Bright Star" © 2020 Caitlín R. Kiernan. First publication: *Sirenia Digest #171*

"And This is How to Stay Alive" © 2020 Shingai Njeri Kagunda. First publication: *Fantasy #61*

ABOUT THE EDITOR

Paula Guran is an editor and reviewer. In an earlier life she produced the weekly email newsletter *DarkEcho* (winning two Stokers, an IHG Award, and a World Fantasy Award nomination), edited *Horror Garage* magazine (earning another IHG and a second World Fantasy nomination), and has contributed reviews, interviews, and articles to numerous professional publications. She's been reviewing for *Locus Magazine* on a regular basis for the last five years.

This is, if she's counted correctly, the forty-ninth anthology Guran has edited. She's also edited scores of novels and some collections. After more than a dozen years of full-time editing, she is now freelancing.

Guran has five fabulous grandchildren she would be happy to tell you about.

She lives in Akron, Ohio, with her faithful cat Nala.